Michael Holman was brought up in Zimbabwe and now live~ London. He was Africa editor of the London *Financial Times* from 1984 until 2002; and between 1977 and 1984 was the *Financial Times*'s Africa correspondent, based in Lusaka, Zambia.

Praise for *Last Orders at Harrods*

'It is not easy to write a novel which combines humour with an understanding of the serious issues facing contemporary Africa. In this delightful novel, Michael Holman, a writer who has for many years commented on African affairs to a world-wide readership, has produced a book which is not only an entertaining and amusing read but also a profound comment on the political and economic landscape of Africa. The style is engaging, the characters lively, and the end result is a superb novel born of years of engagement with Africa'

Alexander McCall Smith, author of
The No. 1 Ladies' Detective Agency series

'Some devastatingly hilarious moments . . . a satire that should be required bedtime reading at Gleneagles'

Scotsman

'This wickedly satirical novel is also a serious critique of Africa's troubled state'

Guardian

'A corrupt dictator, menacing secret police, a bumbling British journalist and the big-hearted bishop's widow who runs the

Harrods International Bar (and Nightspot) on the edge of "East Africa's biggest slum". These are the spicy ingredients in this sharply written novel set in the fictional country of Kuwisha, lent a wolfish satire by its overtones of Evelyn Waugh's African romp *Scoop* . . . Jolly good fun'

Daily Mail

'Gently satirical fable centring on the owner of a buzzy East African nightspot, the Harrods International Bar. When London's famous store threatens legal action over its name, street urchins and aid workers rally'

Mail on Sunday, Summer Reading Recommendation

'Gripping, informative, satirical . . . a road map through the social, economic and political landscape'

Sunday Standard, Nairobi

'Rather like Evelyn Waugh on acid meeting Alexander McCall Smith, veteran Africa journalist Michael Holman's book *Last Orders at Harrods* is an explosion of pure reading joy . . . For the sheer joy and vitality of this book *Last Orders at Harrods* gets my vote as book of the year thus far'

Cape Times, South Africa

'An immensely important book that fearlessly slaughters sacred cows, cuts through the rubbish and tells it as it is. The plot is educated farce, in the way that Tom Sharpe's novels are, but the message is deadly serious'

Geographical magazine

Last Orders at Harrods

An African Tale

MICHAEL HOLMAN

(ABACUS)

ABACUS

First published in Great Britain in 2005 by Polygon,
an imprint of Birlinn Ltd
This paperback edition published in 2007 by Abacus
Reprinted 2007 (twice)

A CIP catalogue record for this book
is available from the British Library.

ISBN 978-0-349-12009-6

Papers used by Abacus are natural, recyclable products made from
wood grown in sustainable forests and certified in accordance with
the rules of the Forest Stewardship Council.

Typeset in Baskerville by M Rules
Printed and bound in Great Britain by
Clays Ltd, St Ives plc
Paper supplied by Hellefoss AS, Norway

Abacus
An imprint of
Little, Brown Book Group
Brettenham House
Lancaster Place
London WC2E 7EN

A Member of the Hachette Livre Group of Companies

www.littlebrown.co.uk

To Michela Wrong:
my turn . . .

Acknowledgements

This novel would never have been started, let alone finished, but for Professor Andrew Lees in London, and Professors Pierre Pollak and Louis-Alim Benabid and their team, at the University Hospital, Grenoble, who gave me a new lease of life; the loving care of Gabrielle Stubbs; and the persistence of Patti Waldmeir, who put me on the road to Grenoble. I am indebted to Sandy McCall Smith for his generous advice and support. I am grateful for the warm hospitality provided by John Goldson, Simon Mungai and colleagues at Crater Lake Camp, Naivasha, Kenya, where the writing of *Harrods* began; and for the encouragement of Ann Grant, and the kindness of her staff at the Residences, Pretoria and Cape Town, where the writing continued. Without Julian Harty's patient help, it might well have ended there, for my computer problems would have overwhelmed me. My heartfelt thanks to Neville Moir at Polygon for his support from the start, and to Caroline Oakley. Andrew Gowers, editor of the *Financial Times,* has generously allowed me to draw on articles originally published in the *FT*. And I greatly appreciated the expertise of Rye Barcott and Salim Mohamed, president and manager respectively of the Nairobi street children's association, Carolina for Kibera, Inc. (cfk@unc.edu).

The land of Kuwisha and all the characters in this novel are figments of my imagination. Nearly everything else is true.

The proverbs at the head of each chapter have been collected over the years by the author. They reflect an African country's time-honoured wisdom. Most should strike an immediate chord with the reader. Some may nevertheless seem obscure, so an explanation and interpretation are offered in an appendix.

Prologue

"'Dawson urged the ageing Dakota lower over the mangrove swamp . . .'"

The security officer in charge of the final departure checkpoint at Kuwisha's international airport had almost finished going through Cecil Pearson's green canvas holdall. Wearing the dark glasses that are the ubiquitous uniform of his profession in Africa, the man was now reading aloud from the last of the half dozen notebooks he had set aside for closer inspection, frowning as he did so. He read the sentence a second time, louder and slower, in a tone of scorn and mounting incredulity:

"'Dawson urged the ageing Dakota lower over the mangrove swamp . . .'"

The official looked up at Pearson, his expression of calculated indifference changing to outright hostility, and returned to his scrutiny of the offending notebook. He looked up again at the anxious journalist, who was perspiring slightly in his outfit of crumpled linen jacket and freshly ironed jeans, and read on:

"'An ancient hunger stirred in the young pilot's loins . . .'"

Nose wrinkled in exaggerated distaste, the man grimaced.

'Not very good, Mr Pearson, not good at all.'

The contents of Cecil's intestines had turned to what seemed like ice water in nervous anticipation of the scrutiny that he was certain he would have to undergo on his departure from Kuwisha. He must have been mad to have teamed up with that malodorous, glue-sniffing street urchin, crazy to have embarked on a hare-brained scheme to scupper President Nduka's re-election chances.

Before leaving for the airport that evening Pearson had gone through his notebooks thoroughly, expunging names and telephone numbers, just in case they fell into the hands of Kuwisha's Central Intelligence Organisation. Perhaps he should have posted everything to London. But he could not possibly have anticipated this public examination, the sheer humiliation of having the opening lines from the draft of his novel subjected to the appraisal of the intelligence agency's duty airport officer.

The official, in his mid-forties, wore a nondescript black jacket with the flaming torch insignia of Kuwisha's ruling party in its lapel, and a shiny green nylon tie. What set him apart, what conveyed a sinister authority, were those wrap-around dark glasses. Slowly, carefully, deliberately, he took them off, and replaced them with a pair of reading spectacles, which he pushed firmly onto the bridge of his nose. It was as if, thought Pearson, the man had removed a badge of office, and adopted the role of literary critic. He seemed almost vulnerable without the opaque shades, a tortoise without its shell. His right eye had a white crescent encroaching on the pupil, the product of years of exposure to the African dust and the continent's harsh sun.

He glanced quizzically at the fair-haired passenger in his mid-thirties who was standing before him, and returned to his examination of the grubby notebook, battered by travel, creased by constant referral and stained by the juice that had leaked from a clutch of mangoes packed for the journey to London.

Pearson took a quick look over his shoulder. He was dismayed to see that the queue for the security check was lengthening, and the nearest passengers could hear every word of the exchange. As he sought to explain the lines he had jotted down in the notebooks, his sense of intellectual discomfort grew.

'It's the opening sentence of a novel I'm trying to write,' he said defensively.

'In fact, it is not even my own introduction. It's a sort of in-joke, by a friend of mine, another journalist. He works for the New York Times . . .'

It was quite true. The two of them had been bandying around the sentence for years, and Pearson thought it would be fun to use it as the start of a book. But as he began his explanation, he realised that it seemed juvenile and implausible, and his voice tailed off. The officer looked at him contemptuously.

'Don't lie to me, Mr Pearson. Be a man! A total man! Never lie! A writer must take responsibility for his own work. This is no damn good, no bloody good at all.'

On a continent where bad language was rare, the mild expletives shocked Pearson. The officer snapped the notebook shut, and placed it back in the holdall.

'No bloody good at all,' he repeated, raising his voice and replacing the round-rimmed reading spectacles with his sinister dark glasses. He beckoned the next passenger who was grinning broadly, enjoying Cecil's discomfiture. The official irritably motioned in the direction of the stairs leading to the airport apron, where the British Airways 747 was waiting to take Pearson and other passengers flying to London from the East African state of Kuwisha.

'Go!' he ordered, 'Go!'

Cecil was about to protest and then thought the better of it. Picking up his holdall, he walked on and handed over his boarding card at the departure lounge desk.

'Hi there,' said the stewardess, inspecting the ticket. Pearson winced at the studied and spurious informality. Thank goodness only his surname was on the ticket. The day was coming when the use of initials would be a thing of the past. First names would be registered in a computer, and both would then be printed on the boarding card.

'Hi there,' was bad enough. 'Hi there, Cecil' would be the last straw.

Such an exchange brought out the Young Fogey in him. He traced this conservative bent to an early age, when endless teasing about his first name – his father had been a great admirer of Cecil John Rhodes – had encouraged him to grow a thick skin. Yet for all his irritation, his overwhelming emotion was one of growing relief as he walked the last carpeted yards to safety. Pearson knew he had been foolish, but it had been in a good cause. And he was, thank God, getting away with it. He turned left as he boarded the plane, and headed for the business class section.

Before he sat down, he removed the cassette from his jacket pocket, and took the tiny tape recorder and earphones out of his holdall.

If the contents were as revealing as he suspected, his career was about to get a huge boost. It could well be the splash, the paper's top story. He toyed with possible headlines: 'Kuwisha's leader forced to pull out of poll.' It would surely put him in the running for the foreign correspondent of the year. He played with the magic words: 'award winning journalist.' Perhaps there was a book in it.

But first he had to check that the tape was audible.

He took the cassette, inserted it in the recorder, and pressed the playback button.

Now came the test. Pearson closed his eyes, gulped down the glass of fresh orange juice brought by a cabin steward, and waited for the reassuring sound of the aircraft door thudding shut. What he was about to listen to could, he felt certain, help shape Kuwisha's future . . .

It had been a tough couple of days. His head, bandaged where the rioter's stone had left a deep cut and a painful bump, was starting to throb again. The words of the security officer seemed to reverberate in his ears:

'No damn good, Mr Pearson, no bloody good at all.'

1

'He who follows the warthog's trail risks
meeting the lion'

Dawn was breaking over Kuwisha.

Not even the damage wrought by the torrential rains, especially heavy overnight, was enough to distract Charity Mupanga from her ritual, or to spoil the pleasure she took in this time of the day.

The owner and manager of Harrods International Bar (and Nightspot) stood under its blue and white striped awning, next to the blackboard menu topped with its proud promise, 'Good Food, Best Prices', and looked out over Kireba, East Africa's biggest slum. Charity yawned, stretched, yawned again, chewed vigorously on the short stick that served as a toothbrush, and smoothed down her green apron. She gave a grunt of irritation as her hand encountered the slip of paper she had thrust into her pocket the night before. A registered letter from England awaited collection. Almost certainly it was from those cheeky London lawyers.

She thrust out her bosom, and prepared to meet another day.

Business had been brisk the night before. Customers had lingered, waiting for a break in the unnaturally heavy rains before heading home. Charity had decided not to risk the muddy, unlit track to the modest two-room brick house that was Kireba's only clinic and which she shared with cousin

Mercy, its senior nurse. Instead she had spent the night on a mattress kept behind the bar for that purpose, pestered by persistent mosquitoes.

A whiff of wood smoke from the first fire drifted past, as fragrant and evocative as the fresh-ground coffee for which Kuwisha was famous. Soon it would be replaced by more fundamental smells. Early morning greetings carried across the valley in the clear air, accompanied by the clinks from the tinsmiths as they hammered discarded cans into buckets, saucepans, mugs and paraffin lamps. The bells of the bread-sellers rang out, mixing with the cries of the vegetable hawkers, as they headed into the city, carts piled high with lettuce, cabbage, maize cobs, slim green beans, and clusters of scrubbed red carrots, as shiny as the faces of children after their morning wash. From the middle distance came the growing growl of traffic and the blare of hooters.

They were all comforting, familiar sounds. And when the sun shone and the air was warm, and the people of Kireba were allowed to go about their business, unmolested by the police and without the harassment of politicians or greedy landlords, the clamour of the slum was to Charity's ears like the buzz of busy bees.

But on that morning, any laughter had been drowned by the heavy rain, and Charity detected the beginnings of a sullen, discordant murmur. Water, water, everywhere: and if you lived in Kireba there was not a drop to drink without risking some debilitating, potentially fatal, intestinal infection.

Residents were well used to fending for themselves. But few could recall such a combination of natural disaster and government indifference. There was even talk of a protest march to State House, which was within their sight – or would have been, but for protective rows of eucalyptus trees behind a high security wall and an electrified fence.

The floods were not the only reason for the unsettled mood

6

in Kireba. The slum was alive; indeed, if the growing number of people living there was a yardstick, it was thriving. Yet the city around it, on which Kireba residents depended for work, seemed to be dying. Banks and supermarkets, cinemas and big companies were moving out of the city centre to the suburbs. Once fine hotels were looking seedy. Restaurants were closing down. At night only security guards and street children were left behind, in charge of barren canyons of drab buildings and potholed roads.

But none of these worries could be allowed to interfere with Charity Mupanga's daily commune with her Maker. She gave her head a quick, sharp shake, like a boxer ending the break between rounds.

'Keep your thumb up,' she muttered, and breathed deeply. She began to count her blessings. And the first of these blessings was the glorious daily dawn that Kuwisha shared with the rest of Africa, the period when the colours of the land were bathed in translucent light, when the chirruping and cooing of birds carried softly through the morning air, and the continent was at ease. The jagged outlines of the shanty town's tin shelters were still in soft focus, and the handful of cooking fires that had been lit by the early risers twinkled benignly. Reality had yet to emerge.

It was the time when she felt most strongly the soothing presence of her late husband, David Shikuku Mupanga, Anglican bishop of central Kuwisha, who had died in a car crash five years earlier. It seemed entirely proper to her that she used this special time of the day to share with David her feelings for Edward Furniver, manager of Kireba's savings society, and to seek the advice of her dear companion. The feelings were becoming stronger and deeper, although she found it hard to express them. But for the first time since David's death the prospect of a new, permanent relationship did not make her feel disloyal to his dear memory.

As Kireba awoke, so the sound of people stirring punctuated the silence. And as they prepared for a new day, Charity soaked in the music she never tired of: the music of laughter, of whistling, of singing, each with its own scales and melodies. The singing in particular lifted her heart, and put her worries into perspective, and for a few precious minutes the intrusive London lawyers were put aside: joy and tragedy alike seemed to provoke an instinctive all-embracing response, and the peoples of Kireba, of Kuwisha and beyond opened their hearts with unselfconscious grace.

Africa sang like other parts of the world breathed.

2

'Do not trust a jackal that fails to howl at the moon'

It was said that if you sat at Harrods International Bar (and Nightspot) for long enough, most of Kireba's movers and shakers would eventually put in an appearance, such was its popularity.

The bar stood at the point where the slum's muddy track, dubbed 'Uhuru Avenue' by the locals, was crossed by the railway line. The location could hardly have been better. The railway was the dividing line between the city and Kireba, and *Harrods* provided a meeting place for two worlds. Charity had selected the site wisely.

She had also been resourceful in her choice of materials. A steel container, once used on freight ships between Africa and Europe, served as the kitchen, where Charity did the cooking on gas stoves and charcoal braziers. It also housed the all-important fridge, run off an extended electricity cable, which was plugged in at cousin Mercy's clinic. A second container, attached to the first to form the letter L, was the indoor eating area, popular on cold days, and where smoking was banned, a decision that had created a stir among the regulars. The area between the arms of the L had been covered in concrete, finished off with a red polish, and shaded by a striped blue and red canvas awning, courtesy of an international soft drinks company. Under the awning were a couple of dozen wooden tables and chairs, and a wooden trellis, covered with purple bougainvillea, which provided additional shade.

It was not long before the bar became renowned for its ice cold Tusker beer, freshly prepared passion fruit juice and mango juice, cashew nuts fried in chicken fat, salted peanuts, baked in their shells, and crunchy roasted potato peelings. This enticing array of 'bitings' was but the start. On a blackboard outside the bar, written in chalk and changed each day, was a nourishing menu, tailor-made for the pockets as well as the palates of a varied clientele.

For those with a little extra cash, there were pigs' trotters, sometimes boiled but more often baked, giving them a crisp outer skin, encasing succulent meat. For patrons on a tight budget, Charity's spicy chicken necks, the cheapest in town, were a bargain. Cobs of tender green maize, the ears turning yellow-brown after a few minutes on the brazier, under the watchful eyes of one of the township gang called Mboya Boys, and tangy avocado soup with a hint of lemon, were popular seasonal dishes. A year-round staple was the tasty maize and pumpkin soup, made to a recipe provided by the late Bishop Mupanga himself, and which had been passed on to him by his mother. And for those with only a few ngwee to spare, there was always maize-meal and groundnut relish, rather like thick gravy, mopped up with hunks of cornbread.

Across the top of one of the containers, in one-foot-high letters, in the olive green Charity had insisted on, a local sign-writer had emblazoned the words 'Harrods International Bar'. Unfortunately he had miscalculated the space available, and after getting as far as 'International', had to continue around the corner. It had been the sign-writer's idea to fill the extra room by adding the last two words, 'and Nightspot', and putting them within brackets. And while it seemed a trifle odd to new patrons, habitués accepted the display without a second glance.

Charity was pleased with her work. Every time she looked at

10

the sign, she was reminded of her father, and felt proud. Since the letters from London had begun arriving, she also felt anger and defiance.

She could not remember just how old she had been when she first heard how her father got what he called his 'European name'. His telling of the story had become a family tradition, recounting it every Christmas, when they gave thanks for their good fortune.

After lunch, when all were replete with sweet potatoes and goat meat, one of the children would pipe up: 'Tell us the story . . .'

The request was taken up like a refrain: 'Yes, tell us the story . . .'

Her father would call for silence, and to the accompaniment of good-humoured heckling he would begin:

'I have been asked to tell you the story of how I got my European name . . .'

Those in the audience who had heard it before would sit back, and make themselves comfortable. Each year, however, there were at least a couple of youngsters to whom the story was new and exciting, and they fastened on every word.

Telling the story could take nearly an hour, for there were many diversions from the main theme. But in its shortest form, it went something like this:

'I was a young and arrogant man, new to the city and its ways, when I applied for the job of gardener at the Residence of the British High Commissioner.'

This was the signal for audience participation, taking the forms of 'oohs' and 'aahs' of mock wonderment, and paving the way for a single interjection which always raised a laugh:

'British' – though it sounded more like 'Breeteeshi' – was delivered amidst much shaking of heads and in a tone that combined resignation and irritation and affection, like a reference to a favourite uncle who has eloped with a notorious bar girl.

11

'At the time, my wise kinsman, who is no longer with us, was the night *askari* at the Residence. I was nervous, so I arrived early for the job interview, which was to be with the wife of the high commissioner.

'It also gave me time to talk with my kinsman. We shared a Star cigarette while we discussed the health of the cattle back at home, the state of the rains, the beauty of our young women, and the merits of the men who sought their favours. And we also spoke about the job, and what allowances it offered.

'It was when we were discussing the latest outbreak of fever among the cattle, and the wisdom of treating them with the healing green water from Crater Lake, as it is now called,' said her father, 'that my kinsman asked a very strange question. He asked me: "What is your name?"

'I was shocked. Was he losing his memory? Did he not know me? Had he not fed me my first cob of roasted corn? Had he really forgotten my name? Nothing that had been said during our talk suggested that my kinsman's memory was uncertain.

'So I told him what I thought he knew well: some friends call me Muputukwana, and my nickname at mission school was Ndabaningi, but mostly people call me plain old Mwai Gichuru Tangwenya.

'Then my kinsman really worried me, for he said: "Don't be a fool, boy. How long have you been in the city?"

'I had been warned by my grandfather that living in big towns turned even good people a bit mad, so I was not unprepared for this rudeness.

'"Nearly a week," I said.

'"Have you worked for a white man before?"

'"Never," I replied.

'My kinsman's voice got softer. "Let me tell you something that you might find very strange, young Mwai Gichuru Tangwenya."

12

'I realised that his memory was as good as ever. Then he said to me: "What I now tell you is even stranger than the fact that the Mopani people are not circumcised."'

Hoots of laughter followed.

' "Some white men are good, some are bad. But I must tell you that nearly every white man, good or bad, has a problem with our languages, and with our names."'

The audience nodded in agreement. It was sad, but true.

'My kinsman, who was wrapped in a blanket that smelled of wood fire, just like the smoke from our village, and whose carved pipe was from Arusha, in Tanzania, shook his head.

'"They just cannot speak our languages, not even one. And they cannot pronounce our proper names. Many, many of our young men fail their job interview for this reason."

'I had to ask him to explain.

'"It is very simple," he replied. "When the Europeans have to choose between a man with a name they cannot pronounce, that is, an African name, and a man with a name that is familiar to them, that is, a European name such as Sixpence or Shilling, who do you think they choose?"

'Phauw! I was very, very worried. My interview was due soon. Finding a new name, even a European name, is no small matter. One can easily look foolish. It should not be rushed.'

Solemn nods of agreement from the audience followed. Even in modern Kuwisha this held true.

'My main rival for the job was a young man from my district – a loafer, but clever. He called himself Willard, like the potato crisps made here, in Kuwisha. It was a good name, easy for white people to remember, easy to say. A very good name. My heart fell.

'My kinsman saw that I was troubled, and asked me to help him with sweeping. In return he said he would give me a shilling, which in those days was enough for the bus fare home.

13

So I picked up a broom, and sang the song about leaving the village where I was born.

'And although I thought about it, still I had no European name.'

'Shame! Shame!' responded the audience.

'Then, just before the interview, a wonderful thing happened. I was about to empty the leaves into a bin outside the kitchen door. I first looked inside the bin, checking for snakes. And then I saw it.'

Youngsters in the audience took this as an opportunity to hiss, and frighten the toddlers.

'No, it was not a snake. I saw a plastic bag, that was green, a very good, strong bag which I have always wished I had taken. On that bag was written the name: "Harrods of London". In big gold letters! I learnt later that the bag had been brought back to Kuwisha, after home leave in England, by the high commissioner's wife.

'I knew then what my European name would be. I took the name Harrods. Even Willard agreed that it was a fine name. And the wife of the high commissioner – who was a very good madam – awarded me the job. That is the story of how I got my name, and a very good name it has proved to be. It has served me well,' concluded Mwai Gichuru Tangwenya, otherwise known as Harrods.

Each year he sat down to whistles of approval from the youngsters, mature applause from the adults, and a loving hug from Charity.

No-one in Kireba had been surprised when Charity honoured her father by naming her establishment after him. Indeed, any other name was unthinkable. Many residents still remembered the gentle and distinguished old man who had been the proud but shy guest of honour at the opening ceremony. Just weeks later he had died in his sleep, on the family *shamba*; and while Charity grieved, she took comfort in the fact that his life had been good and his end had been dignified and painless.

Acting on her instruction, Furniver had passed on a summary of this story to the London lawyers.

Surely, Charity had argued, even these London people would understand why she could not change the name of Harrods International Bar (and Nightspot)? Perhaps the registered letter awaiting collection was a formal acknowledgement of their mistake? Somehow Charity doubted this . . . and she braced herself for bad news.

3

'Beware the leopard that limps when the lion roars'

The special time of day was ending, and the working day was beginning.

Charity yawned once more, rubbed her eyes, and scratched her arm vigorously. Those high-pitched curses of the night that made sleep well nigh impossible, malaria-carrying mosquitoes, had retreated after their assaults on her body. Their daytime counterparts, noisome flies, were taking their place.

A few hundred yards away, a pair of skinny teenage boys peeked out cautiously from the abandoned water pipe that had become their home, and surveyed the sodden landscape of mud, debris and plastic-sheeted huts before emerging. Like rats out of a drain, thought Charity affectionately, two little rats called Titus Ntoto and Cyrus Rutere.

'Too late for breakfast,' she teasingly called out as they got nearer, and the boys broke into a trot.

Somewhere about their persons would be a tube or bottle of glue. Charity did not need to see the glue to know that it was being used – the evidence was in the enlarged pupils of their eyes, in their runny noses, and in their twitchy movements.

She waved at a fellow worker, a charcoal burner, who returned the greeting, and whistled at his thin brown mongrel, ribs protruding, ordering it to heel.

'You look like a chicken that has been caught in the rain,' said Charity, and they both laughed.

Suddenly she was distracted by an outraged cackle from an angry cockerel, which was being stalked by Ntoto and Rutere. They had just missed capturing it, and the bird scuttled away, crowing in triumph and relief.

'Good morning, Mama,' said Ntoto and Rutere in unison, as they approached.

'Any breakfast' – it was pronounced as two words, 'break fast', and as they said it, their right hands conveyed invisible food to their mouths – 'Any break fast for us this morning?' asked Rutere.

'Break fast, Mama,' echoed Ntoto.

The two fourteen-year-olds had an unusual friendship, one which triumphed over the fact that they came from different parts of Kuwisha. Ntoto, tall for his age and painfully skinny, was a member of the country's largest tribe. Rutere, the runt in the family litter, was from a small clan, part of an alliance of minorities that had been led by President Josiah Nduka since before the boys were born. Decades after independence, where you came from, your first language, whether you were circumcised, these still were the factors that dominated relationships and allegiances. But for Ntoto and Rutere, their friendship transcended differences of tongue and the politics of the foreskin: it was a bond that had been forged in adversity, and tested by hunger and deprivation.

Charity looked sternly at the grubby pair. The arrangement was that the boys would carry out various chores, ranging from washing dishes at *Harrods* to collecting mail, in return for meals, and generous doses of affection and discipline.

'Wash first,' said Charity. 'Food is in the kitchen. When you have finished, you must go to the post with this piece of paper, for something very important.'

Since the post office in the city centre was not due to open for an hour, there was time for the boys to linger over their plates of maize meal, and scraps of meat, left over from the night before, and covered with peanut gravy. They accompanied the meal with mugs of hot, sweet cocoa, giving small sounds of satisfaction, eating with the single-minded concentration of those who knew what it was like to go hungry, and not talking until they had cleared every morsel.

Then they again carefully washed their hands in one of the plastic bowls of water set out between the tables, dried them on the towel provided, and helped Charity with the first chores of the day.

The first wave of customers called in for tea and hunks of bread, which they dunked in the same peanut relish enjoyed by the boys, but which had been warmed up on the gas stove. The tea came with two generous spoons of sugar; for those with a sweet tooth and prepared to part with a couple of extra ngwee, she would add a dollop of condensed milk.

By the time the boys had finished sweeping the premises, washing dishes from the night before, and restocking the fridge with Tusker beer and soft drinks and fruit juices, it was well after seven.

'Go! Even if it is early, you can be first in the queue. So go.'

She flapped her apron at them as they trotted off. Charity looked at her watch and then at the sun, as if checking the timepiece's accuracy against the more reliable indicator provided by Nature. It would soon be time to begin the preparations for lunch. First there were the table tops to be wiped clean, plastic chairs to be unstacked. Then she set to work in the kitchen, and soon the aroma of roasting groundnuts and corn ears drifted across from the oven.

A busy day lay ahead.

Edward Furniver, Charity's neighbour, financial adviser and close friend who had helped her find the money to set up *Harrods*, was particularly fond of 'bitings'. He now dropped in almost every day, much to her quiet pleasure, in what had become a gentle and genteel courtship.

Less welcome were the foreign journalists and aid workers, who were also to be seen more and more frequently in Kireba. It had become fashionable to visit the slum. Charity had lost count of the number of visitors who ended their tour of Kireba with a drink at the bar. Their behaviour reminded her of the one and only time she had visited a game park in Kuwisha, and at sundown she had sat on a game-viewing platform, overlooking a watering hole.

'These people who come to Kireba, they are like the tourists in the game parks,' she had told Furniver. 'They sit in their buses, or on their verandas, safe, and watch the animals as they come to drink water. These people who come to *Harrods*, they are the same, looking, looking at the animals of Kireba.'

She snorted derisively.

'I hear them, Furniver. I hear them talking.'

Charity was a fair mimic.

'I say,' she said, in a passable English accent, 'I've spotted a charcoal burner, just behind that coffin maker. And look! Just over there! An Aids orphan, being looked after by a very kind nurse.'

And then, amused by her own vivid image, she could not help laughing, and Furniver had joined in.

The sun was beginning to creep over the horizon. It was getting late, by Charity's standards. The next wave of customers would soon arrive. It was time she put on the water for tea. Every morning clean water was brought over from the clinic by the duty Mboya Boy, and it took ages to boil.

She contemplated the blackboard menu. Her aid worker friend Lucy had told her that one of the biggest names in the aid business was due to visit Kireba the next day, and might drop in – Hardwick Hardwicke, president of the World Bank. Not that Charity cared very much about his rank or status. Her job was to feed people – good food at fair prices. What bothered

19

her was the fact that nobody could say whether he would want a Tusker beer or a cola, or fresh mango or passion fruit juice. And what would this man like to eat? A bowl of avocado soup, sprinkled with fresh ground pepper, and a plate of fried chicken, rounded off with a couple of sugared dough balls, should be good enough for anyone. She would have to ask. Perhaps young Lucy would be able to tell her. One never knew these days. Europeans had so many strange diets.

Charity ran a cloth over the chairs, wiping off the puddles of overnight rain. It was turning out to be one of those hot and sultry African days when time not so much as stood still, but slowed down. The hotter it got, the lazier the hours. They behaved like sleepy, underpaid Kuwisha secretaries, debilitated by bilharzia, exhausted by the long journey into work, and who moved with painful deliberation, conserving energy, going about their business as if they were walking under water.

Impossible though it seemed, more rain was on its way. Any one could smell it coming, even Edward Furniver, with his beak of a nose that got so red when exposed to the sun. Charity chuckled, a rich, gurgling sound that began in her belly, as she recalled a sharp exchange with him. Perhaps she had been a bit harsh.

'Love the smell of rain,' he had said. 'Rather like a really good cigar.'

The comment had attracted a scornful response from Charity.

'When rain comes, Furniver, you can smell the rain coming. Smells like a cigarette? Poof!'

She had wrinkled her own broad nose, part in distaste, part in derision. As far as Charity was concerned, cigars and cigarettes were interchangeable, a distinction without a difference.

'Cigarette! Cigarette! That is foolish talk. It is the smell of rain, and that is that. In this country we smell the rain, like

20

this . . .' Charity's nostrils flared as she sniffed loudly, defiantly and conclusively:

'Anyway, Furniver, smoking cigarettes is bad for you.'

David Shikuku Mupanga – 'Bishop of the battered, Shepherd of the shattered,' as his flock liked to call him – delivered some memorable sermons in his time. There was one in particular, reprinted by a local newspaper, and which Charity kept in her purse. But this morning she recalled not a sermon, but a family prayer which David had composed for their children, now young adults – David Junior, a talented musician who was currently touring Britain with his band, and his sister, Blessing, who was well on her way to becoming an accountant.

She knew it by heart. Charity recited aloud the prayer's opening couplet:

> *When you rise, each day, at dawn,*
> *Praise the Lord for this fresh morn.*

As David had acknowledged with a chuckle, the rhyme went downhill from there. Nevertheless, when David Junior and Blessing were at home, they made a point of reciting the lines over breakfast. The prayer, written before Aids began to take its toll, reflected both the Bishop's Christian faith, and his concern about the dangerous driving that cost Kuwisha thousands of lives each year. Charity now taught the doggerel to the Mboya Boys she took under her wing, hoping that its commonsense values would help them in their troubled and brutish lives:

> *When you rise, each day, at dawn,*
> *Praise the Lord for this fresh morn.*
> *And keep in mind these lessons few,*
> *This way you will your soul renew:*

21

Look both ways crossing street,
Or else you could your Maker meet:
Don't overtake on corners blind,
Keep sharp lookout for who's behind!
Wear your seatbelt, check your tyres;
Tell the truth, for God shuns liars.
And on the potholed road of life,
Respect the vows of man and wife.
Now clean your teeth, wash your face!
May you stay safe in our Lord's embrace.

For a minute or two Charity closed her eyes. The lines, banal though they were, always made them prick with tears. Whenever she said the prayer, aloud or under her breath, she felt that David was beside her: as her bishop and spiritual adviser, her friend and supporter, and above all, her husband and the abiding love of her life.

She had made the right choice to come and live in Kireba. David would certainly have approved. He had never felt at home in the suburban house that came with his bishopric. Eyebrows had been raised when, after his death, she told the church committee which discussed her future that she planned to open a bar and restaurant in the slum.

'It is not proper,' declared the committee chairman.

Charity had got angry.

'Who will pension me?' she asked. Anyway, she said, she would be satisfied if she could provide wholesome food at fair prices. And unlike her friends Mildred and David Kigali, leading members of their fundamentalist Christian sect, she saw nothing wrong with beer in moderation.

And what better way to help the street children, teaching them hygiene, giving them food in return for working at *Harrods,* and cheering them on from the sidelines in her capacity as deputy president of the Mboya Boys Football Club?

Charity gazed across the valley and noticed, with an impatient 'Tsk', that the track which the residents called Uhuru Avenue, in ironic tribute to the official Uhuru Avenue that ran through the centre of the city, had yet again become a black stream of filth, spreading into homes.

She was sure that the outbreak of diarrhoea in Kireba pointed to cholera. The weak and the vulnerable were being hit first. Babies, toddlers, and old folk were dying. Cousin Mercy's estimate, based in part on the cases reported to the clinic, and partly on the tales recounted around the tables at *Harrods*, was at least thirty fatalities, and rising. The results of the laboratory test were expected that morning.

Appeals for help had been ignored. Worse than that, they had been hushed up by the government, because ministers feared that the tourist trade, Kuwisha's lifeblood, would suffer should word get out.

She watched in horror, nose wrinkled in disgust, as the evil-smelling black tide lapped at the doorways of the shanty homes, sliding past some and embracing others, like a sinuous python engulfing its quarry with effortless power. Snakes! Charity loathed snakes . . .

4

'Rotten bananas make the strongest beer'

'Cholera!' cried Lucy Gomball, East Africa representative of the Oxford-based aid agency WorldFeed, doing a blue-jeaned, barefooted, pink-toed jig of excitement around her kitchen table.

'Cholera!' she cried again, her husky voice rising a pitch.

Lucy's suspicions had been confirmed. The test had proved positive. The specimen had been sent from the Kireba clinic for analysis at a private laboratory. The suggestion had come from Mercy, had been organised by Lucy, and the costs covered by WorldFeed. It had paid off handsomely.

'I knew it! I knew it! Well done, Mercy, oh well done. I'll phone Cecil right away. Yeeesss!'

She punched the air in celebration.

Lucy did another circuit of the table, slim hips swaying to the music of a local radio station as she punched out Cecil Pearson's number on her mobile phone.

From the moment she had awoken that morning and switched on the short-wave radio next to her bed, she had just known it was going to be a good day. In Mogadishu and Mombasa, from Dar es Salaam to Dodoma, from Kisumu to Kampala, correspondents for the BBC's Africa Service were reporting the grim news that lifted her spirits and made her heart beat faster. The unseasonal rain that followed the prolonged drought had turned into a deluge. Dried-up creeks had become rivers. Usually placid rivers had turned into raging torrents, stained ochre by the rich soil of Kuwisha, carried east on the journey to the warm blue waters of the Indian Ocean.

The rain had poured down overnight, drumming on the corrugated iron roof of Lucy's bungalow, keeping her awake until the early hours of the morning. There was no rain elsewhere in the world quite like it. The huge tepid drops, as big as large peas, had hammered the run-down capital. It brought to life the old saw: 'How do you make chaos in Kuwisha? Just add water.'

The drains simply could not cope with the normal rains, let alone with this extraordinary storm. Yesterday the city's traffic jams, bad at the best of times, lasted well beyond the rush hour as drivers inched their way along the flooded streets, fearful that they and their car would all but disappear into potholes as wide as a bathtub and nearly as deep. To make matters worse, vandals had yet again smashed the traffic lights at one of the main intersections.

Telephone lines collapsed, and power cables went down, depriving swathes of the city of electricity. Sewers overflowed, adding to the trials of those who were forced to leave their cars and wade to safety. Roads that were all but impassable at the best of times, unless encountered in one of the many four-wheel-drive vehicles with which Kuwisha was richly blessed, had been washed away, along with the several bridges on the trunk route to the country's main port.

Each year Kuwisha experienced what was tactfully called 'a food deficit'. Each year international donors duly rallied round to ensure that the country, once held up as an African model of economic development, did not go hungry.

This time, everyone agreed, this time it was different. The drought had been bad enough. But the floods that followed had destroyed the sparse crops that had managed to survive the drought. Food would have to be imported on an unprecedented scale, and distributed on a transport system that had all but collapsed. And now, hard on the heels of the floods, like a jackal at a kill, came the scourge of cholera.

Lucy had been long enough in the field to have become as shrewd a judge of what made good copy as any journalist. 'Floods threaten thousands' was not bad. But confirmation that this dreadful disease had taken root in the slum that was home to half a million, in the heart of Kuwisha's capital. Now that really was a decent story! She could just see the headline: 'Cholera hits Kireba.'

'Come on, Cecil, you lazy sod, get up,' she muttered impatiently, pausing in mid-jig to put a band around her long fair hair, and to take a sip of the Kuwisha coffee she had prepared just before Mercy called.

'Answer the phone.'

The knocking seemed to become a hammering, and Cecil Pearson stirred. Shadrack Gachara, his diminutive house steward of uncertain age, gave a final thud on the bedroom door as he brought in the early morning tray of tea.

Two spoons of Kuwisha's best leaves, brewed in a brown china pot, were accompanied by a small jug of milk, covered by a bead-fringed circle of muslin. Placed alongside this was a small bowl of sugar of indeterminate colour, neither white nor brown, and a teacup and saucer. On the side of the cup was the faded coat of arms of the Outspan, the capital's gracious old hotel, now running to seed – but a favourite haunt of Pearson's.

The downpour that had added to misery in Kireba had rattled the tin roof of the 1930s bungalow where the young journalist lived. He had had a restless night. His departure from Kuwisha was imminent, his relationship with Lucy Gomball unresolved, and his obsession with the role of the World Bank in Kuwisha unrelieved. Fiction and reality had merged and blurred in Pearson's dreams as he tossed and

26

turned in his untidy bedroom. He was physically secure in his comfortable picturesque home, protected from intruders by the padlocked steel gates at the top of the wooden staircase that led from the ground floor; emotionally, he was going through a turbulent period.

In his overnight fantasies, the names of Josiah Nduka, Kuwisha's 75-year-old president, and Hardwick Hardwicke, appeared in the headlines of a local financial magazine, which inexplicably had a picture of a pouting Lucy Gomball on the cover. Yet at first sight, the magazine's contents read like an International Monetary Fund report.

But when Pearson, deep in the grips of a nightmare, looked more closely, phrases were confused and jumbled. 'Confidential budgetary irregularities' and estimates of 'donors' exceptional spending' spilled over into the columns setting out the exchange rate of the ngwee, Kuwisha's ever-weakening currency.

Shadrack's knock had come just as he was being asked by Hardwick Hardwicke to explain the relationship between the state subsidy of dairy products, the rate of inflation and the value of the ngwee. Pearson lay bathed in sweat as his steward padded across the room, gnarled and calloused feet clicking on the polished teak tiles, and pulled the curtains to let in the early morning light. It was well after seven, and the rain had paused. The sun blazed in, making Pearson blink as he reached down for the cup. Shadrack flinched slightly as he got a whiff of stale breath. He cleared his throat:

'He who treads in hyena dung will not smell the lion.'

The steward waited expectantly. Cecil groaned. He rued the day he had responded to Shadrack's infuriating habit of offering impenetrable African proverbs on random occasions. Pearson's retaliatory stock of English lore had soon been exhausted, and anyway, 'A stitch in time saves nine' seemed mundane in comparison with the exotic nuggets of the accumulated wisdom of the peasantry of Kuwisha offered by his steward.

Pearson now passed some of the long hours spent in ministers' waiting rooms and in airport lounges making up new proverbs – although he told the sceptical Shadrack that he had gathered them in the course of his travels.

'He who hears the hyena's bark lives in fear of the leopard,' he mumbled.

Shadrack looked at him suspiciously. As Cecil stretched out an arm to switch on the bedside radio, he caught a disbelieving expression on his steward's face. Both men suspected the other of making up the proverbs. Neither was prepared to say so.

'Mr Punabantu left a message last night. He says to ring him about the interview with the president.' Shadrack's tone was one of deep disapproval, which lightened when he continued: 'And Miss Rucy is calling,' as he bent down to gather the clothes Pearson had dropped on the floor the night before.

Like many of the citizens of Kuwisha, Shadrack found it difficult to pronounce words with an L, and tended to transpose an R.

Cecil shot up. The president's press secretary had managed to get hold of him late the night before. The interview was on. But why would Lucy call at this hour, unless it was important. He wrapped a towel around his waist, and went to the phone in the hall, taking the cup of tea with him.

'Cecil? What took you so long? Guess what? Mercy's been able to confirm it. Cholera! Cholera, Cecil! Official.'

'That's splendid, just marvellous,' replied Pearson, genuinely pleased for her. 'How many dead?'

'At least eleven, and absolutely oodles more to come. Might reach thirty.'

He pursed his lip, and shook his head. Fond as he was of Lucy, this was a time for frank talking.

'It's not enough. Not really. Need quite a few more for a

28

decent story. Though cholera is a jolly good start,' he added judiciously. 'But we really need more bodies . . . still not a story for the *Financial News.*'

'Of course there'll be more, Cecil. I promise.' Lucy pouted down the line. 'Promise. Bags more. And you've got a marvellous peg, with Hardwicke due to visit the place . . .'

She was pleading now, at her most flirtatious.

'Just think . . . "Aid agency officials warn that scores will die in cholera outbreak . . . worst toll since independence" . . . as long as you don't quote me by name.'

His silence spoke volumes. She was now close to getting her man. Lucy snorted with delight. He was almost hooked.

'Don't you dare quote me . . . let's meet at *Harrods.* We can pop in to the clinic, arrange a photograph, talk to Mercy. I'll ring her on her mobile, ask her to tell Charity we're coming round.'

Pearson replaced the old-fashioned Bakelite receiver, gulped his tea, and got dressed. He looked around the bungalow that had been his home for the past three years, surrounded by the removal company's tea chests, packed to the brim with his possessions. They were due for collection later that day.

Like Charity Mupanga, he had to decide on an affair of the heart. Should he make clear to Lucy that he wanted her to join him on his next posting? But what would he say if she invited him to join her wherever WorldFeed decided she should go next? What if it were Bujumbura, or Kigali, or one of the other African capitals where WorldFeed had set up an ever-expanding permanent presence? He was fond of Lucy, there was no doubt in his mind about it. But was he that fond?

Pearson decided to brave the floods and call in at his office in the centre of town, on his way to meet Lucy at *Harrods.* He parked his car, a battered Land Rover which he had bought to replace the Subaru stolen soon after his arrival in Kuwisha. He

29

composed the opening lines of a cholera news story as he walked across the red-tiled lobby of Cambridge House, a grey, grubby, squat five-floor building in the city centre. The notice board, which warned 'Danger – Slippery Surface' had been taken out for its daily airing, and a cleaner was making desultory movements with a mop, which he dipped every now and then into a bucket of dirty water.

The Asian proprietor of a general goods shop across the road was observing Pearson closely. He was, Pearson assumed, part of that nervous and vulnerable community's early warning system. Any excitement, any unusual activity among the journalists who used Cambridge House as their headquarters, was carefully noted. Bad news would spread like an African bush fire with the wind behind it, running down Mobutu Sese Seko Street with its Indian-owned curio shops and foreign exchange bureaux and car hire companies. When appropriate, action was taken. Currencies were bought and sold, usually leading to a further weakening in the rate for the ngwee on the city's black market.

Pearson took the lift to the second floor, and turned into the passage leading to the *Financial News* office. As he made his way down the gloomy corridor, he encountered the familiar combination of smells: rancid cooking oil from the canteen, stale cigarettes, the sickly sweet odour of the men's urinal, mixed with the sharp aroma of disinfectant.

The door of the Japan Television News Agency was locked and bolted as usual. No doubt the bureau chief was yet again out of the country, pursuing a story everyone else had forgotten about. It sometimes seemed to Pearson that when the agency's bureau chief arrived on the scene, you could be sure that the story was over. But there was something admirable, even heroic, about the patient, polite, dogged determination with which his colleague pursued the news that was invariably out of date.

A press conference was getting under way in the canteen, before an audience of the building's messengers, the Kuwisha office managers of the dozen or so foreign press bureaux, and the retinue of assorted hangers-on that accompanied the politicians who put in regular appearances.

Apart from the veteran Associated Press correspondent, the only representative of the world's media was a fresh-faced girl in her early twenties who was writing down every word that came from the platform.

Pearson was about to pass by, but paused when he saw who was speaking: Newman Kibwana, the leader of the Official Front for the Restoration of Democracy, the breakaway faction of the Front for the Restoration of Democracy.

Wagging his finger, thumping the table, the dapper young lawyer was getting into his stride:

'I have evidence of plotting and confusions. Dark corner meetings are taking place . . .'

Kibwana mopped his brow with a red silk handkerchief, which he carefully folded and returned to his jacket breast pocket.

'Nduka plans to rig the elections. Nugilu will stand down, as a result of his talking sweet to her. And she will stand down at the last minutes, when it will be too late for any person to take her place.'

It was not the first time Pearson had heard this claim. It had been the main topic of conversation during his visits to *Harrods* over the past couple of weeks. But Kibwana was the first senior politician to go public with the rumour, and this gave Pearson pause for thought.

Anna Nugilu, the presidential election candidate of the main opposition party, the Democratic Alliance, was a brave woman, as Pearson had discovered when he followed her on the campaign trail for the *Financial News*, or *FN* as it was known. She had first encountered the power and prejudice of a conservative male-dominated society when she was at her most vulnerable. She was still mourning the death of her husband, a London-trained dentist, when his will had been challenged by up-country relatives. Her soul had been hardened during the long and bitter dispute that followed, with relatives demanding that the will, in which her husband had named Anna as the sole beneficiary, be declared null and void. She had won in the end, and it was a battle that prepared her well for the brutal cut and thrust of Kuwisha politics.

Her election in 1992 to the city's central constituency was a triumph in itself. The defeated incumbent, the minister for rural roads, had a well-deserved reputation as a political thug in a party with many contenders for that title. She increased her majority four years later, and as the opposition continued in its fragmented attempt to overthrow President Nduka, she was emerging as one of the few politicians capable of leading a credible challenge.

But if what Kibwana was saying was true, the challenge could be stillborn. According to the lawyer, the president was trying to persuade Nugilu to drop out of the contest at the last minute, which would leave the opposition in disarray. In return, she would be given a seat in his cabinet and an unimpeded run at the next poll – by which time Nduka would have retired.

Kibwana, a bright and engaging man with a line in flowery rhetoric, denounced what he called 'clandestine State House bargainings', at which President Nduka was subverting democracy. The politician reached a climax:

'They are to meet this week, before Uhuru Day, I warn the people of Kuwisha. They will plot to steal the erection.'

The audience listened with massive unconcern.

'Mrs Nugilu will step down at the last minute,' he said once again. 'It will be too late to replace her. That is known for a fact,' he declared, as barely a ripple of interest disturbed the listeners.

One of the many office assistants stood up.

'My first question is in four parts,' he began, and Pearson's heart sank. As a rule of thumb, when the question was longer than the likely answer, it was time to go. Nobody else gave any indication of leaving, however. Instead there was a mass shuffling of rumps, and the audience seemed to settle down for a long haul.

Newman Kibwana's denunciation would be reported by the girl, who did occasional pieces for the BBC's *Focus on Africa*. Reuters would consult the Associated Press correspondent, and something might appear on the wires. If Kibwana then turned the publicity to advantage, and played his cards right, he would be invited abroad by the British and American governments as part of their democracy-building programme, and would be on the list to meet the next visiting minister from London or Washington.

He would either be described as 'impressive' and held up by Kuwisha's foreign partners as evidence of President Nduka's decision to liberalise the political climate; or he would be used to show that the president's failure to ease his authoritarian regime had created an angry and frustrated opposition, home to capable but alienated young professionals, who could well lead a revolution onto the streets.

And there were more potential wrinkles to the story. Kibwana's predecessor as party leader had recently stood down. A day later a story appeared in the *Kuwisha Times*, suggesting that his appointment as chairman of Kuwisha's long promised anti-corruption body was imminent. This also was open to two interpretations. The cynics saw it as confirmation that the commission was a toothless bulldog and a source of state patronage that provided jobs for the boys; the optimists were heartened, treating it as evidence that the Old Man, as they liked to call Nduka, wanted to leave behind a cleaner, more honest administration when he eventually retired.

To the best of Pearson's knowledge, no ruling party on the continent had ever managed to reform itself from within. Nor, for that matter, did African politicians resign over matters of principle. Not that they did in Europe. But in Africa, principles were flouted with a frequency and a brazenness that defied belief.

Did a substantial opposition really exist in Kuwisha, Pearson wondered, as he hovered uncertainly in the canteen doorway, or was its main function to milk the funds of gullible donors?

It was entirely possible that Newman Kibwana represented a fresh wave of African democrats, and that one day he would supplant President Nduka. It had happened, after all, in Zambia, where an obscure trade unionist had become president, even if he had then gone on to become a vain autocrat. Pearson paused, pulled both ways.

Was the press conference one of dozens of such inconsequential events? Or could it mark a formative stage in the making of post-colonial Kuwisha? He took a further look at the BBC stringer, and decided it might just be the latter. He slipped in beside her, notebook in hand.

'Could you give me a fill,' he whispered, unable to stop himself looking down her blouse.

He learnt nothing new from her briefing. But the first glimmerings of an idea came to him, an idea that, if successfully implemented, could help shape the future of Kuwisha and bring the corrupt career of President Nduka to an end. At first he had dismissed the scheme as little better than an adolescent prank, something to be joked about with his colleagues as they sat on the veranda of the Outspan, drinking beer and gin and tonics. But the more he thought about it, the more tempting it became.

There would be little risk for Pearson. He was about to

return to London, where he would work on the foreign desk for a few months until his next posting. Most of his possessions were already in tea chests, and would be sent on to London. What remained could be squeezed into his canvas holdall. A few minutes later, having jotted down his London number on the back of his business card and giving it to the young woman, he left the press conference and continued on his journey to *Harrods*.

As he drove, he continued to turn over the idea in his head, and by the time he reached the bar, had convinced himself: it could just work.

5

'The baringa nuts are always green
when hunger strikes'

Cyrus Rutere sucked his prominent and stained front teeth in disapproval, ran an exploratory forefinger around the rim of his nostrils, and looked around nervously.

'*Mungiki*,' he muttered, 'surely, it is *mungiki*.'

Mungiki, the fastest growing political movement in Kuwisha, combined a religious fundamentalism with a political agenda: street boys with attitude, Pearson called them. If the lads from Kireba had an aspiration beyond survival, it was to own a car, and by fair means or foul, to have the money to run it. The *mungiki's* objective, as far as it was known, was to put all cars into communal ownership, if not to abolish them altogether. There were disturbing stories about oathing ceremonies, sinister blood-letting events . . . Titus Ntoto and Cyrus Rutere – Cyrus in particular – loathed *mungiki*.

The morning traffic on the city's main road was far worse than usual. It was barely moving, and the floods were not entirely to blame. Once again the lights at the intersection of Independence Drive and Uhuru Avenue were not working. Somebody was sabotaging the system, smashing the traffic lights – but why? What was the purpose? It seemed to be happening at the start of every week, and the incompetent officials at City Hall were beginning to take notice.

Even the policemen, on what they liked to call 'traffic duty', looked slightly shamefaced as they collected their fines for offences real or imagined.

The post office on Kaunda Street was no more than ten minutes away, and the two boys continued to enjoy a breather in their journey from Kireba.

Squatting on their haunches, at the foot of the lights, Ntoto and Rutere took in the noisy scene. Had Charity been there, she would have recognised the hunger in their eyes. If the foreigners who frequented *Harrods* looked at the residents of Kireba like tourists studying the game at a watering hole, Ntoto and Rutere were two young predators – wild dogs, perhaps, waiting for a kill.

They would never dare take on the 4x4s by themselves, no more than a hyena would attack a healthy buffalo. These vehicles were too big, their passengers too powerful. The youngsters would have to wait until bigger animals got to work, such as sophisticated car thieves from South Africa, part of a network that stretched across the continent. And when the men had done their business, the boys could feed on any carcass they might leave behind, its engine removed, and as immobile as a disembowelled kudu.

With eyes narrowed the boys looked on as the vehicles with a bewildering range of acronyms emblazoned on their frames moved slowly past, hooting their frustration. The names meant little to the boys. All they knew was that they were big and influential: Danida and UNDP, Difid and UNIDO, Noraid and Christian Aid, Oxfam and Save the Children, part of a parade of international concern and compassion, the hieroglyphics of their involvement displayed on door panels that served as escutcheons of the aid business. The organisations they represented pursued every cause – apart from obesity – that involved or afflicted mankind in general and Kuwisha in particular. Female genital mutilation, environmental degradation, child abuse, renewable energy, gender discrimination, intermediate technology, health care for nomads, promotion of the informal sector, the welfare of pastoralists, teaching illiterates: it seemed that not a concern was neglected and not an interest group unrepresented.

Within the air-conditioned interior of their vehicles, usually on the back seats, sat the men and women who did so much to help the frail economy of Kuwisha tick over. They were rich targets for the street vendors, who were making the most of this opportunity.

On a normal day they would be sprinting alongside a customer's car as it gathered pace, handing over the purchase, delving for change, and dodging oncoming traffic. Today the street boys were moving at a leisurely pace, up and down the marooned vehicles, whose occupants had become a captive market. They went from car to car, sidestepping the water-filled potholes, moving back and forth, to and fro, as alert to a flicker of curiosity or interest as an auctioneer on a slow day at market, as assiduous and as persuasive in their patter as life assurance salesmen, as they good-humouredly touted their wares.

Festooned with fake mobile phones from Taiwan and hose pipe attachments from China, calculators made in South Korea and sunglasses from Portugal, foreign magazines from around the world and flashing key rings from Hong Kong, plastic sandals made in Taiwan and shoulder bags claiming to be made in Italy, locks and screwdriver sets from eastern Europe, cartons of fruit juice from South Africa, these determined sellers tirelessly made their pitch . . .

Only the melting popsicles and the packets of peanuts, the hapless chickens dangling by their feet, the cobs of roasted maize, the twists of *bhang*, and the local newspapers were made in Kuwisha. And of course the emeralds, displayed in glass test tubes, green embers glowing in beds of cotton wool, supposedly smuggled into Kuwisha from nearby Tanzania, and sold to gullible tourists, who would eventually discover their true origin.

The barks of the *matatu* boys, those barefoot conductors who clung to the side of their overloaded taxis as they solicited customers, added to the hubbub. They shouted the details of the route, collected fares, abused their rivals, propositioned pretty girls, and now swore in frustration as they thumped the sides of their battered vans, decorated with biblical exhortations.

'God will provide', 'Shun the Devil's work' and 'Blessed are the meek' declared the hand-painted slogans.

Their passengers, packed as tight as rows of corn on a maize cob, sweated patiently. The drivers leant on their horns, and gesticulated angrily. Time was money. The journey from Kireba to the city centre should take twenty-five minutes, perhaps thirty-five minutes on a bad day. At this rate it would take at least an hour, twice the time, which meant half the number of fares.

'Why pay if there is no delivery?' asked one furious driver, and his passengers nodded in agreement. Why hand out bribes to get your *matatu* licence if city hall could not keep the traffic moving? A deal was a deal. This shoddy behaviour gave corruption a bad name.

Ntoto and Rutere, elbows resting on their scabby knees, digested their breakfast and watched this world go slowly by.

'It is surely *mungiki* who have broken the lights,' said Rutere. He loudly cleared his throat and spat into the gutter, as if underlining a statement of the obvious.

Ntoto grunted sceptically, but was distracted for the moment by a pressing task. He was running his fingers through his hair, scratching every now and then, looking fixedly ahead of him as his probing fingers pursued their quarry. Suddenly activity was concentrated on a spot above his left ear.

'Eh-heh!' he exclaimed with satisfaction.

For a couple of minutes, Rutere put his concerns about *mungiki* aside, and looked over his friend's shoulder, like a *matatu* commuter peeking at his fellow passenger's newspaper. He watched engrossed as Ntoto cracked between the nails of his right thumb and index finger whatever creature he had found in his peppercorn curls. Titus examined the result closely, before flicking it away and continuing the conversation.

'It is not sense,' he said to Rutere. 'Why would these *mungiki* break the traffic lights, and then sweep away the glass?'

Rutere shrugged.

'We know the *mungiki* break things, just to break them.'

'Yes,' said Ntoto impatiently. 'Yes, Rutere, but why should they sweep? And why always green that is broken?'

It was all very puzzling. Whoever had smashed the traffic lights seemed to have cleaned up afterwards, leaving only slivers and shards of glass at the foot of the lights.

Rutere found it hard to relax. Shuffling and slithering amongst the vendors were an unusual number of the city cripples, vigorously propelling their wasted and distorted bodies between the cars and the puddles and the *matatus* and the municipal buses. The lucky ones sat atop a device that looked like a tea-tray on wheels, using a stick to pole themselves along the tarmac. The rest made do with bits of carpet or cardboard.

Ntoto and Rutere watched quietly, curiously, as the vendors patrolled the lines of cars, and the cripples solicited for coins. They were joined by elderly bent-backed blind beggars, leaning on knobbled sticks, and towed by small boys, palms outstretched, who added their voices to their masters' pleas for coins, and offered singsong incantations and praises to those who responded.

One of the cripples approached Ntoto.

'Look out! Look out!' Rutere hissed, spotting the boy as he pulled himself towards them, his backside protected from the rough tarmac by a rubber mat made from strips of old car tyres. With each thrust of his powerful arms, the teenager's tattered grey shirt rose, revealing a catapult tucked into the waistband of his khaki shorts. Ntoto did not move; but Rutere remembered his grandmother's warnings, and edged away.

Only the other day the nurse at the Kireba clinic had tried to reassure him that being a cripple was not infectious.

'Don't be foolish, Rutere,' she had admonished. 'Only ignorant people blame the spirits. Polio is the cause of legs that don't work. You are very lucky. Thanks to Charity, you have been vaccinated.'

But Rutere was far from convinced. He remembered that his granny had lectured him, just before his parents' disappearance in the terrible Kireba riots in the late 1990s, about the dangers of bad *muti* and the powers of hostile spirits. He conceded that the nurse might know about vaccinations; but his gran knew about the world, and the mysterious forces that shaped it. He would take no chances.

He looked fixedly at the culvert in front of him, and rearranged a few pebbles.

Ntoto greeted the boy, whose muscular upper torso made his wasted limbs, as thin as the legs of one of the storks that perched on Kireba's rubbish dumps, look especially fragile.

'Business good?'

The cripple glanced sharply at Ntoto, and then shrugged.

'Not bad.'

'People tell me *mungiki* are the ones who are breaking the lights,' said Rutere, not looking at the boy.

The cripple seemed to agree:

'Mungiki are everywhere.'

Rutere gave Ntoto a condescending look:

'See? I told you.'

The lad, about the same age as Rutere, was about to dispute something, but had second thoughts. Instead he asked Ntoto about the Mboya Boys' chances of winning the final of

Kireba's Under-15 football cup. A fellow cripple, watching from a distance, called out, and the boy slid away. As he moved off, he deliberately let his wasted legs trail close to Rutere, who jumped out of the way, cursing and muttering under his breath.

'*Mungiki!*' exclaimed Ntoto, and sniggered.

'Let us go. What are you doing, Rutere?'

'Collecting rocks. In case . . .'

'*Mungiki* are not here. They did not break the lights,' said Ntoto.

'I am sure,' he added, as Rutere looked sceptical.

'So who broke the traffics?'

'Not *mungiki*.'

'How do you know?'

'It was not *mungiki*,' was all Ntoto would say, and for the time being at least, Rutere had to be satisfied with that confident assertion.

Edward Furniver, manager of Kireba's only savings bank and normally a late riser, had begun his day unusually early, woken by persistent knocking on the downstairs door.

Furniver put on his threadbare green and grey striped dressing gown, unbolted the steel grill, and went through the customary exchange of greetings that Kuwisha etiquette demanded. Standing on the doorstep, one hand resting on the saddle of an elaborately decorated bicycle, the other holding a smart brown trilby, was Nellson Githongo, one of the co-operative's first customers.

The middle-aged man was distressed.

'I am in default,' he said, thrusting the bicycle at Furniver. The machine had been bought a few weeks earlier with a loan from the savings bank.

'You must repossess me.'

In vain Furniver tried to point out that there was a discretionary period of grace before any repossession. As a long-standing saver, and with an otherwise unblemished payment record, he would undoubtedly qualify.

Githongo was insistent. For a few moments Furniver had to suppress an urge to laugh aloud. If his former colleagues could see him now, in the heart of Africa, in the middle of a shanty town, standing in the doorway of his 'office' in a shabby dressing gown, discussing the terms of a loan that would hardly buy a decent malt whisky, they would conclude that he had lost his marbles.

Home was a one-bedroom flat above the Kireba Co-operative Bank's offices, one of the handful of brick and mortar buildings in the slum. He had opted to live there against the unanimous advice of Kuwisha's expatriates, who had warned him that it would be a dangerous act of folly. The ladies from this community had, during the first few months of his stay, tried to persuade him to move to the safer 'low density' enclaves of civilisation, and resorted to appeals to the baser appetites of a fifty-something bachelor, making regular gifts of home-made cakes and jams.

Their husbands made clear that they regarded him as mad, a view shared by Kuwisha's remaining white settlers. He had declined all offers of alternative accommodation, and to the general surprise of expatriates and settlers alike, he had come to no harm. His flat had remained unburgled, and he had yet to be mugged. Neither fact was unconnected with the discreet presence and protection of members of the Mboya Boys United Football Club, and in particular members of the Under-15 football team, whose ubiquitous presence Furniver had come to take for granted.

Suddenly the electricity supply, erratic at the best of times, cut off, just at the point that Furniver was about to concede Mr Githongo's request. The stand-by generator automatically took over, and kept the all-important computer running, but it was too modest to cope with the additional demands of the air-conditioning system.

Power cuts were frequent, but Furniver had turned them to an advantage, telling himself that the informal atmosphere of *Harrods* bar was a better place to do business than the office of the society. To see the man from whom you needed a loan sitting at a table, casually dressed, sipping a mango juice and nibbling on a handful of groundnuts, was a far less intimidating prospect for potential clients who would never have dreamt of crossing the threshold of a commercial bank.

Githongo clasped Furniver's right hand in both of his.

'You must take it. I have broken the rules,' he said.

There was little alternative but to store the bike in the ground floor strong room. He handed a receipt to Githongo, who thanked him profusely and hurried off. His parting words, however, added to Furniver's sense of unease: 'Look out for *tsotsis*, sir, look out for *skellums* and loafers.'

Clearly something was not quite right. It did not take much for Furniver to convince himself that he needed to consult with a committee member. And since Charity Mupanga happened to be the nearest, he prepared to set off for *Harrods*, a journey of but a few hundred yards.

If the truth were told, Furniver found it more and more difficult to resist the virtues of Mrs Mupanga. She was, he had come to realise, a most extraordinary woman. Indeed, such was her common-sense approach to life that he wondered whether he should not at least consult her about his embarrassing itch. After all, her cousin Mercy was the nurse in Kireba's clinic. Perhaps Charity could raise the matter with her?

Among Charity's many virtues was thrift – unlike his ex-wife, she was admirably prudent with money, something Furniver knew from first-hand experience. He was, or at least had been, Charity's bank manager, although he preferred the term 'adviser'. He had monitored the society's loan that had enabled Charity to purchase a second-hand fridge when she set up *Harrods* – a loan that had since been repaid ahead of schedule.

And then there was her sheer presence and personality. Who else, Furniver mused, could deal so effectively with those pre-teen thugs in the making, the members of the infamous Mboya Boys United Football Club?

There were several other places in Kireba that sold beer, but these were dark and insalubrious hole-in-the-wall joints, where strange characters lounged, shady business was transacted, and decent residents of Kireba did not tarry. Charity, on the other hand, managed to run *Harrods* as a respectable family eating place, and seemed to have enlisted the boys to her cause. Quite how she had done it, Furniver could only guess, until two occasions had provided a clue. On the first, about two years ago, he had wandered in to the bar unusually early, only to find it deserted. But from the back of *Harrods,* from behind a grass partition that surrounded the area where the food was prepared and cooked over the charcoal braziers that helped give the roasted goat meat its characteristic woody, gamey flavour, came the smack of flesh on flesh alternated with howls. This was followed by a rapid-fire delivery of angry and passionate Swahili, which Furniver, much to his regret, had not at that stage mastered.

From his vantage point – he was concealed by the refrigerator – he watched one of the Mboya Boys scuttle through the bar, his dusty cheeks creased by tears. But he also noted that clutched in one hand (the other was holding his glue bottle) was an oily packet which, Furniver was sure, contained grilled chicken necks, a dish for which *Harrods* was renowned.

The next occasion could not have been more different. It

was a few months later and once again Furniver had come to the bar at a slow point in the office day. The same boy, whom Furniver now recognised as Titus Ntoto, was showing Charity what seemed to be an exercise book. It was the sort used in the local schools, which Ntoto and his friends could not afford to attend. After several minutes of close scrutiny, and animated exchanges, this time mostly in English, Charity patted the boy on his head, a gesture that prompted a rare, embarrassed smile from the lad. Charity delved among the food dishes for a couple of minutes, and re-emerged with an enamelled tin plate carrying a serving of grilled goat meat, which sat atop of an enormous mound of the porridge-type maize-meal which was the country's basic food, swimming in peanut relish. This was then handed over with some ceremony.

After a further one-sided exchange, with the occasional finger wag, the boy trotted off. Furniver had occasionally wondered how it was that many of the Mboya Boys spoke such good English, good even by the standards of a country of natural linguists, where most of its citizens could speak English and at least three local languages. Now he realised that they had been taken under the maternal wing of Charity Mupanga.

Truly, she was an exceptional woman.

If anyone could explain Nellson Githongo's odd behaviour, it was Charity.

"'Look out for *tsotsis*, sir, look out for *skellums*.'" What on earth did the blighter mean, Furniver wondered as he locked the office door behind him, stepped outside, and recoiled at the powerful sun-ripened stench of a flooded Kireba.

Ntoto and Rutere continued on their way to the post office, pausing outside the Bata shoe shop for a knowledgeable discussion about the merits of different brands of trainers. But when the boys passed the stores with electronic devices, televisions, radios and stereo sets, both fell silent as they mentally marked out what they would loot in the happy event of a riot. The *askaris* watched them suspiciously, and the Asian owners waved them away from the shopfronts.

Ntoto muttered angrily, but there was important business to complete. They would not be provoked.

Rutere, still worried about *mungiki*, waited on guard at the main entrance to the post office while Ntoto went inside. He was the first, and so far the only customer. Ntoto, barefooted like all Kireba urchins, rapped impatiently on the wooden counter, with its thick patina of sweat and dust and grime. The lady in charge, head resting in her arms crossed in front of her on a plastic topped table, looked up, irritated to have had her sleep disturbed.

'Who is knocking?'

Ntoto made an elaborate display of looking for someone else in the high ceilinged room, once part of the High Court in the colonial era. But this was as far as he dared tease the lady, for she was not to be trifled with. She was, after all, the Keeper of the Registered Mail, and could withhold a long awaited letter on a whim, or – as was more likely – pending the payment of a larger than usual bribe, or 'service payment' as she called it.

'Am sorry to disturb, Mama. I have been sent by Mrs Charity Mupanga to collect this letter.'

She took the proffered slip and looked at him with sleepy distrust. Polite street boys were a rare phenomenon. She nevertheless imposed no more than her normal tariff – twice the face value of the stamps – and watched curiously as the boy ran towards the exit. When he had got up sufficient momentum, Titus slid across the polished wooden floor for the last few yards, a skateboarder without a skateboard.

Once outside, Ntoto and Rutere closely inspected the sealed

envelope, addressed to Charity but marked for the attention of Edward Furniver.

'Let us open it,' suggested Rutere. 'We can tell Mrs Charity that it was the post office people.'

Ntoto was tempted. But as he examined the letter he had been given, with its red and blue airmail edging, decided against it. There was something intimidating about the envelope, and the sooner he got back, the better. The precision with which the address had been typed, in large crisp black letters, was impressive. This was no ordinary correspondence. It clearly had not come from David Mupanga Junior; nor had it come from the Leeds seminary, where the Bishop had studied, for it had a London postmark.

You could learn a lot from letters, he had soon realised after accepting the job as Chief Postman for *Harrods* – provided Rutere could be his deputy. More than that, he enjoyed the task. It made him feel part of a family; and on his last birthday – an arbitrary date, since he had no idea when he was born – he had been thrilled to receive a card from Charity and Furniver when he collected the post one day.

> *Master Titus Ntoto*
> *Harrods International Bar (and Nightspot)*
> *Kireba*
> *Kuwisha*

The envelope and the card, the first he had ever received, had been left in Charity's keeping, along with other precious documents, including a newspaper cutting about his hero, Mr Tom Mboya.

Rutere, who had given his friend a pineapple that was only slightly overripe, a twist of *bhang*, and a fresh egg, had been unusually quiet. Ntoto had found him later behind *Harrods*, crying to himself, but managed to slip away before Rutere spotted him.

He had told Charity about what he had seen, and she seemed unmoved.

'That Rutere, he is foolish,' was all she would say, although Ntoto noticed that the slice of birthday cake she gave Cyrus was at least as big as his own portion.

Two weeks later, Rutere got his own birthday card. He was all smiles.

'I had forgotten which day was my birthday,' he confessed to Ntoto. 'I thought Mrs Charity also had forgotten . . .'

On most visits to the post office there was something personal for Charity in the mail. Over the past few weeks it had been a postcard, with a picture of Kuwisha's fabled game reserves. Each one came from David Junior.

When the third such card arrived, Ntoto could not restrain his curiosity.

'David is like all young men,' she had told him. So before her son left for London, Charity had given him twelve local postcards, each with a British stamp which she had bought from Cecil Pearson, addressed to Charity Mupanga at *Harrods*. Each postcard had four hand-drawn boxes, alongside carefully-lettered statements:

> *I am well*
> *I am eating*
> *I am behaving*
> *I need money*

The last one had already been ticked.

'Why tick this one yourself?'

Charity's reply was short and to the point:

'Sons always need money. If he has no money, he must come home. He can work on the *shamba*.'

Then there were the monthly newsletters from Leeds, and local post, mainly bills.

This registered letter from London, however, was special – nothing like it had come before.

Rutere watched as Ntoto frowned, and smelt the envelope – a gentle, exploratory sniff the first time, and vigorously the second time. There was a fragrance he could not identify.

'It is a clue,' he told the mystified Rutere. 'I am sure, or nearly sure, that this is a very important letter. Very important,' he added.

'It has been sent to Mrs Charity by a man who is big enough to have a secretary.'

Rutere's eyes widened.

'What *muti* can tell you this?'

Ntoto clucked impatiently.

'Rutere, you only talk of *mungiki* and of your grandmother's *muti*. Where is your brain?'

Rutere shrugged.

'Then tell me about this clue.'

'If you smell this envelope, carefully, it smells like flowers. Men do not smell of flowers – but big men, very big men in London, have secretaries who use perfume.'

Ntoto was not absolutely certain about this. He depended on the little black and white television set at *Harrods* for this insight. And there was an element of wishful thinking. But if the glamorous white ladies whom he watched avidly did not have a delicious fragrance about them he would be astonished.

'So I am sure this is a very, very important letter, sent by a big man . . .'

With that, the two boys parted company outside the post office: Rutere planned to call by the city's central market to rummage for rotten fruit put out the night before by the stall holders in their daily clear-out.

Normally Ntoto would have accompanied him, but they

50

agreed that the sooner the letter was delivered, the better. He trotted most of the journey back to *Harrods*, slowing down with the caution that was second nature to any boy from Kireba as he approached the bar.

Charity was not to be seen. She was almost certainly in the kitchen supervising the cooking. Customers were relaxing, and her friend Edward Furniver was in his usual place in his usual chair, a glass of mango juice to hand, and a bowl of salted groundnuts within easy reach.

Every now and then he moved his bottom from side to side. Ntoto giggled. It had been happening for a few days now: 'Like a dog with worms.'

That journalist from London, Pearson, was also there, with the aid worker from England, Lucy, who used strange words like empowerment, and spoke about ownership and civil society.

Ntoto was not sure what to make of these two, both in their mid-thirties, and both fair-haired. They seemed good people: Pearson paid him and Rutere well for looking after his car when it was parked at the *Financial News* office, and he and Lucy had become frequent visitors to *Harrods*. But Ntoto could not help noticing that Pearson touched Lucy often, too often, as if they were married. And they were not even engaged! Ntoto found this behaviour embarrassing. Charity and Furniver, on the other hand, seldom touched each other. It was all in their eyes, and they spoke with their looks.

Ntoto took a quick sniff from his glue bottle, and tucked it back under his sleeve. He watched the bar for a further minute or two. You could never be sure that off-duty policemen were not at one of the tables. As far as Ntoto was concerned, policemen were never to be trusted, on or off duty.

He focused his attention on Furniver, still sweating after the journey from his office, and then fixed his gaze on the banker's half-open briefcase that was alongside him. Ntoto suspected that the fruit juice Furniver was sipping had been reinforced by a shot of the clear liquid from a small bottle which, he had spotted on several occasions, the banker carried in his case.

There was no time to lose. Dark clouds that had been building up on the horizon were advancing on Kireba. The wind had suddenly dropped. Ntoto looked around for the last time, put aside any feelings of friendship for his targets, and prepared to attack the unsuspecting and defenceless trio.

6

'When the buffalo move south, wise men check their trouser buttons'

❦

The first of the day's planes flew over Kireba, its wheels out and ready for landing. Had Charity or Ntoto looked up, they would have been able to see the rivets on the undercarriage, it was so low. It was the closest most of the passengers would ever get to the slum. Within an hour or so of the aircraft's arrival, a pink tide of newcomers from Europe would spread across Kuwisha, heading for the beaches and game parks, before returning to their overseas homes a fortnight later, wearing tans and multi-pocketed safari suits, clutching wooden giraffes and soapstone chess sets, ebony key tags and stone hippos, Maasai spears and sheepskin rugs. Some of the visitors would return with other deadly, insidious souvenirs, the result of visits to massage parlours, and liaisons at nightclubs.

Many of the passengers had been to Kuwisha before, such was its popularity as a holiday destination. For one very important passenger, however, it was his first official visit to Africa as the recently appointed head of the world's most important development agency.

Bathed in a shaft of early morning sunshine that came in through the cabin porthole, sitting in his business class seat, Hardwick Hardwicke, president of the International Bank for Reconstruction and Development, otherwise known as the World Bank, put away the papers, preparing for landing. A compact, plump man, horn-rimmed glasses on the end of his nose, in his early sixties, whose foul language and short temper was legendary, he had spent much of the overnight journey engrossed in a bundle of files on Kuwisha.

Stretched out in the adjoining seat, mouth agape and snoring softly, was the legendary Jim 'Fingers' Adams, guide, confidante, and chief public relations adviser to Hardwicke. The Bank was facing a testing time in Kuwisha, and Hardwicke was glad to have the services of one of the best jugglers of the code-word vocabulary of the aid and development business.

It was Fingers, he recalled with appreciation, who had used the term 'dysfunctional military activity' to describe a coup attempt in nearby Uganda. And 'budgetary anomalies' had become a much-loved phrase by Bank economists who needed to account for 'unaudited and unauthorised spending' – another Fingers coinage, and one which embraced presidential financial indulgences, from private jets to shopping trips to London.

And in the opinion of Fingers, Hardwicke needed all the help he could get. He had not been long in the job. The former commercial banker had been widely acclaimed as the right man to lead the world's most influential development agency. His boundless enthusiasm for Africa was matched by a belief in what he called 'a new generation of leadership' on the continent. He advocated consultation with these leaders, urging African 'ownership' of the policies they would be expected to implement; and calling for a fresh start in tackling the continent's woes.

His first speech, drafted by Fingers, had struck a provocative note.

'The relationship between the Bank, the donors and most of the African governments is akin to a bad marriage,' he had declared:

'The two parties have known each other intimately, but no longer can the one surprise, inspire, delight or engage the other. Indeed, the relationship is dominated by expectation of failure or disappointment, which in turn helps shape response. The Bank is not a marriage guidance agency. But I believe we can act as an honest broker, and help restore an excitement that has been lost, and help recover some of the magic that all couples need, but which has faded.'

It was all good stuff. But Fingers had his doubts, even though he had written the speech. Who could be against the principles and policies that Hardwicke enunciated with such enthusiasm? African ownership of development blueprints, transparency and good governance, the involvement of civil society, the critical importance of locally trained management, the need to encourage the private sector, the role of the informal sector, all those words and phrases and concepts that were essential to the aid lexicon could be found in every subsequent speech Hardwicke had made, and which Fingers had drafted. But did his boss really understand the reason for this strange, damaging intimacy between the World Bank and its African clients?

Or was he like a victim of Nigeria's financial scams, which had become popular when Fingers was based in the Bank's Lagos office. Known as '419s', they were so called after the legal clause that set out the offence. 'Obtaining money by deception' was the dry, technical description. But it did not do justice to the shrewd con artists who drew on an acute understanding of the victims' psychology, and appealed to an emotion nearly as powerful as the sex drive – greed.

A typical 419 would begin with an offer of easy money.

A letter or email to the victim would claim that a long dormant fund had been discovered, containing millions of dollars of an African dictator's ill-gotten wealth. In return for the use of the victim's bank account for deposits of the money abroad, the perpetrators of the scam would offer a cut of twenty per cent. From the start, the con men turned to advantage Nigeria's dreadful and well-deserved reputation for corruption. If the country was as corrupt as was made out, the potential victims told themselves, then anything was possible.

And if the targets of the scam, mainly businessmen and women in Europe and North America, felt that Africans were a bit dim and naive, and untutored in the ways of the world, the psychological climate for deception was even better. Once sucked in, the victim became the greatest supporter and defender of those who were defrauding him. Perverse though it might seem, the victims would get angry with hapless consular officials in Nigeria who had the temerity to suggest that they were the targets of exceptionally clever con men. And when Fingers, or anyone else for that matter, urged them to cut their losses, and give up on their search for a windfall, few were prepared to do so.

The easy life seemed so close, one tantalising step away. Just one more payment, just one more bribe for the Central Bank official who was holding up the paperwork, just one final 'stamp tax', all costing a few thousand dollars – which of course the victim would be asked to pay – and the vital document would then be released, allowing the transfer of millions of dollars. It never happened, of course. There was always one last hurdle to clear.

In much the same way, claimed some critics, the Bank poured good money after bad, desperately believing that a development bonanza – Africa's recovery – was just around the corner. A few hundred million dollars here, a low interest loan there, coupled with frank talking and appropriate reforms, and that elusive target of self-sustained growth would be reached. But twenty-five years after the Bank had first rung alarm bells, reporting a deepening economic crisis on what was then a war-torn continent, recovery remained a remote prospect.

Hardwicke refused to accept that the Bank's strategy was flawed, despite the growing misgivings among his staff. Dangling a carrot in front of a donkey might get the beast to move in the direction the owner wanted, Fingers cautioned his boss. But what if the animal was a carnivore? Big carrot, small stick, was bad enough – but the man who dangled a carrot in front of a lion was likely to get eaten.

On the corners of the potholed streets of Kuwisha's capital, the newspaper and stationery vendors had set out their wares. The papers and magazines, envelopes and rubber stamps, staplers and punches, bottles of glue and cartons of paper clips, were neatly laid out on the cracked and uneven pavement. Usually they were gritty with the dust of the land, but today they were damp from the endless rain.

The newspaper headlines were dominated by lurid reports of a dreadful crash in which a bus and a local taxi, or *matatu*, racing to be first to a narrow bridge, had both tumbled into a ravine. There was also outrage over a road improvement fund that had gone missing. Some stories implied that the chairman of the fund, a senior member of the ruling party, was responsible. Two of Kuwisha's dailies managed to squeeze a reference to the 'critical visit' of World Bank president Hardwick Hardwicke on the front page, but for the third, it barely merited a mention, and the item was buried on an inside page.

Kuwisha had been here before, had seen it all. Its officials had become adept at humouring the international donors and the charities and the institutional aid givers, responding to each development fashion and theory, as if living in a social laboratory where the rest of the world searched for an answer to the problems of the continent.

It was not that the donors made no impact, or were unappreciated. The city thrived on aid. Restaurants and supermarkets catered for aid workers, garages did a roaring trade maintaining their vehicles, the property market flourished, airlines were kept in operation, all thanks to the custom of the workers at the United Nations agencies and the staff of the NGOs – the non-government organisations – whose numbers increased as Kuwisha's problems deepened.

But munificent a donor as the World Bank had become, most citizens of Kuwisha, however, were indifferent to Hardwicke's arrival. The forthcoming talks on fresh aid were seen as just another step in the ritual dance involving donors and the government. It was a dance as familiar as that of the tall, lean Maasai, bouncing up and down, up again and down again, seeming to hover at the peak of their lift-off for a split second longer than any other member of the human race can manage, as they bounce, bounce, bounce for the tourist cameras.

7

'Beware the wildebeest that sleeps with the hare'

Ntoto circled warily, well aware of the devastation that he could unleash during his metamorphosis into an airplane. He was not one of those fat, innocuous things from Europe that daily flew over Kireba, bringing hundreds of thousands of tourists to Kuwisha each year. Those planes had no appeal for him, slow and cumbersome as they were. Indeed, he positively disliked them. One of them had killed an Mboya Boy called Justus. The twelve-year-old had stowed away in the compartment above the wheels, and Ntoto had been amongst a group of friends who had cheered from their vantage point at the airfield perimeter fence as the plane took off. According to customers at *Harrods*, who had read newspaper accounts of the tragedy, the frozen body of Justus had tumbled out as the plane approached Heathrow.

No, Ntoto had become one of those jet fighters, the sort that flew so dangerously low, just above the city, in tight formation, on Uhuru Day. He knew that it was as close as he would come to fulfilling his secret ambition to be a pilot.

The Ntoto jet was small and fast and compact, with a devastating sting, delivered through the weapons slung under its wings. Once he had worked out his plan, he moved fast. Clutching the letter in his left hand, he made a high pitched whine to simulate the noise of the plane's engine as it thrust in response to the revving motion of his right hand. Then, with both arms outstretched, he launched his attack. He had the advantage of surprise as he came in, and the rising sun was behind him. With a graceful swoop and pinpoint accuracy, he dropped the bomb, which looked remarkably like the just-collected letter, into Furniver's briefcase, a split second before jumping nimbly over the foot that Pearson had suddenly thrust out in an effort to trip him.

'Ack-ack-ack,' cried Pearson.

An outraged Ntoto immediately made an emergency landing, and began to hover, like the helicopter from England that he had once seen on the outskirts of the city during a recent joint military exercise with Britain. He confronted the journalist.

Pearson's action was entirely in the spirit of the game – provided the journalist had kept to the rules. Ntoto was in no doubt. Pearson had broken them. What was more, it was not the first time this had happened.

'You did not ack-ack-ack in time,' Titus said furiously.

According to the rules, anyone who was seated and who came under attack was entitled to try and trip an approaching aircraft – provided they simulated the sound of anti-aircraft fire, and did so before extending their leg, crying out as they did so: 'Ack-ack-ack.'

'I bloody well did,' said Pearson, looking to Lucy for support.

'No, you jolly well didn't,' said Lucy. 'Only after you tried to trip him. So childish, Cecil. Keep to the rules. After all, you helped draw them up. Childish! Ntoto wins a dough ball.'

'You did not ack-ack-ack in time. Miss Lucy says so,' declared Ntoto with satisfaction, jogging on the spot to indicate that he was now a police helicopter, which he had seen on the black and white TV set at *Harrods* that Charity had installed for her customers. The set usually worked – except when it was raining.

Charity emerged from the kitchen, and coming up on him from behind, flicked Pearson's ear with her forefinger.

'Ouch! That damn well hurt,' said Pearson, grabbing his ear and massaging away the pain.

'You swore. I will have no swearing, of any kind. And you cheated,' said Charity calmly. 'You did not ack-ack-ack properly. You were late. I was watching.'

Furniver chipped in.

'Pearson, you're a cheat. Get lost, Ntoto. Get your dough ball.'

Ntoto stopped jogging. He shot a contemptuous glare at Pearson, dropped into a half crouch with his hands flapping, and radioed the control tower that he was preparing to fly off. Then with right wrist revving close to full throttle, he disappeared into the *Harrods* kitchen to collect his dough ball.

Not before a final salvo in Pearson's direction:

'Cheat! Cheat!'

'Scram, Ntoto,' said Furniver, exasperated.

'We've got business to discuss,' he said, taking the letter out of his briefcase. He was about to open it, when Charity interrupted.

'Later, Furniver, later. Private. It is private.'

She held out her hand, and took the envelope Ntoto had just delivered. She examined it briefly before tucking it into her apron pocket. She had little doubt it was from the London lawyers. It took great resolve not to read it, then and there. But Furniver had to realise that while she appreciated his help and advice, *Harrods* was her responsibility; and this was certainly not a matter she wished to discuss while customers were around.

Furniver gathered his case, gulped the last mouthful of his glass of mango juice, and was about to set off. Then he remembered the encounter with Nellson Githongo.

As Charity listened to the story about Githongo and the bicycle, her frown deepened.

'I'm stumped,' concluded Furniver. 'Technically, he is right. He is in default. But I really don't understand . . .'

Charity interrupted.

'Nellson Githongo is very clever. He must expect trouble.'

'I don't get it. Why the bicycle business?' asked Furniver.

She looked at him pityingly.

'Have you not seen that there are more scoundrels here in Kireba, always more troublemakers when people just want to vote at elections? You must have noticed, Furniver.' Sometimes she wondered if he saw anything around him.

'So . . .?'

'If there is trouble in Kireba, his bike could be stolen. He wants it to be safe. So he leaves it where it cannot be stolen, safe in the bank, with you. Of course he could pay his loan if he wanted to. He has money. Last night, even, he had three Tuskers. Three!'

Charity allowed herself a chuckle.

'That Githongo, he is clever, very clever . . . and we must look out, Furniver. Trouble can come quickly to Kireba, with all this election nonsense.'

Furniver could not help feeling rather foolish. It seemed that Githongo was no fool. Then he looked at his watch, and cursed. He was now certain to be late for the shareholders' meeting.

'About the *shamba* . . .'

His voice trailed off.

He remembered the last time they had visited the plot, and he thought he had made his feelings for her clear.

Charity had been roasting cobs of maize over a charcoal fire, and she offered one to Furniver. With strong broad hands and elegant fingers, she had gripped her own cob, and he had looked on fascinated as her splendid white teeth tore into the corn, raking the ears line by line, and giving the odd murmur of satisfaction.

She had caught him watching, and admiring.

Charity cocked her head, and gave him a quizzical look.

'Why are you not eating? Do you want more beer? What are you looking at, English?'

He could not help blushing. He had got used to the fact that for Charity it was a demonstration of friendship to address him by his family name. But when she called him English there was an intimacy which made his heart beat faster.

He stammered his reply:

'Your, er, teeth, Charity. Jolly, um, jolly good, er, teeth. Yes, absolutely. Strong. Teeth.'

Charity had returned to the maize cob. She seemed not to have got the message. Next time he would be even more explicit . . .

'About the *shamba*,' said Furniver.

'I'd um, love to, er, stay.'

Charity eyed him suspiciously.

'You agree? No sort of nonsense at all? None. No hanky-hanky.'

'Hanky-panky, hanky-*panky*,' he corrected her, and wondered if he could ask her to keep her voice down.

'Of course not! For goodness sake, Charity. It's not my, er, style, whatever.'

She frowned.

'I know you men, Furniver. And I do not care whether you call it hanky-hanky, or hanky-panky,' she said firmly. 'It is for marriage only. Especially now days.'

Suddenly she was shaking with laughter, and slapped a somewhat bemused Lucy on the back.

'When will you get married, Lucy?' she asked, and dug Pearson in the ribs at the same time.

Furniver made his excuses and left. In this mood Charity was positively dangerous.

'Back after lunch, my dear.'

He gave her a kiss on the cheek, and there was a distinct spring in his step as he made the muddy journey to the nearest road, where he could flag down a *matatu*.

The trio that remained continued their discussion.

It had begun an hour earlier, when Lucy and Pearson had turned up at *Harrods* after first calling in at the clinic to interview Mercy and arrange for a photographer to take pictures of the patients queuing for treatment. The visit had sparked an idea from Lucy: why not launch a fund-raising appeal that would allow WorldFeed to revive a scheme to provide clean water for Kireba? she suggested.

They picked up where they had left off.

'Tell me, Lucy . . .'

Lucy winced. Whenever Charity opened with these words, she knew she would be asked questions that would be hard to answer.

'These non-government people, are they trained?'

'Not as such.'

'Are they paid? Is it true that they get more money than locals . . . Why are they so young? Why are there so many of these people?'

Lucy struggled to answer. Yet she was as qualified to reply as anyone in the aid business. Indeed, she could serve as a role model in the aid generation: graduate of Sussex, a post-graduate diploma in development studies from London's School of Oriental and African Studies, and possessed of a keen mind and a compassionate heart, concealed beneath a skin of carefully cultivated cynicism.

Thousands upon thousands of non-government organisations, or NGOs, had been founded during the last twenty or so years, providing launching pads for the careers of countless young aid workers. And as the West withdrew from Africa, Lucy explained, reducing its number of diplomats and missions, so the NGO movement expanded to fill the vacuum left behind.

Cecil couldn't resist butting in.

'The hacks' most important contacts used to be dips. Not any more. Today it's the NGOs. They provide the info, seat on the charter, transport when we arrive, place to stay. It's called BB&B – Bed, bonk and briefing.'

Charity looked disapproving; and Lucy ignored him.

Water had become her priority. Passionate, articulate, persuasive, she now mounted her soapbox and painted a picture of a decent Kireba. Clean water would not only end cholera and combat other diseases, argued Lucy. It would transform the working day.

As if on cue, a group of women passed *Harrods*, buckets in hand, heading for the nearest standpipe, one of half a dozen that served the slum. One waved at Charity, and said something which prompted peals of laughter.

Lucy begged Charity to translate.

'She asked: Why are we behaving like men? Lounging and talking. Behave like women! Tell that white girl to stop loafing, and help us carry buckets!'

A funeral procession followed, and the table fell silent.

When conversation resumed, much to Lucy's fury Pearson was dismissive about her scheme. Any money raised would be lost to graft, inflated contracts, bribes and kickbacks, he argued. The first step was to end the corruption that was sapping Kuwisha, and that meant getting rid of President Nduka.

'Patronage, corruption, same thing. He runs the country through patronage, and his patronage destroys Kuwisha. Until he and his system are destroyed, WorldFeed is wasting its time and its money,' said Cecil.

Charity tried to cool things down. It was not the first time she had heard the two argue along these lines.

'Decent toilets. We need decent toilets.'

But Lucy wouldn't be put off.

'You've never done anything worthwhile, Cecil,' she said angrily.

'All your editorials, all your columns . . . haven't changed life in Kuwisha a jot, not a bloody jot.'

'And your lot has made a difference?' Cecil hit back. 'Twenty years after you began putting aid into this place, more people are poor, schools are dreadful, the health service is terrible. Things are worse, not better. And you say I'm wasting my time?'

Charity silently intervened, raising her finger to her lips.

'Could this man Hardwicke from the Bank help?' she asked.

Lucy gave Pearson a baleful look, but Charity's suggestion had caught her fancy.

'Absolutely. We really could get the support of Hardwicke,' she said with growing excitement. 'He's due to visit Kireba to inspect that housing scheme. He could be buttonholed then.'

She went on to stress one thing in particular: any initiative should be inspired by the residents of Kireba. Furthermore, they should be consulted regularly; and ultimately the project planners should be answerable to them.

'Ownership! It's all about ownership,' declared Lucy.

Cecil snorted, but decided to keep quiet, not out of deference to Lucy, but out of fear of provoking Charity's wrath. It was not the time to list the history of past efforts to bring water to Kireba. Anyway, Lucy had the bit between her teeth:

'It would need the backing of WorldFeed, but the chances of that are jolly good. After all, we are pressing the right buttons,' continued Lucy, her enthusiasm turning her face pink.

Charity chose to appear baffled.

'Buttons? What are these buttons? I thought we are talking about water. Buttons are the business of the Kireba ladies' sewing circle.'

66

Lucy suspected that her friend was teasing her, but Charity's expression gave nothing away.

'What I mean is that we'd be tackling development issues from the grassroots up, and not imposing our ideas from the top. Obviously, we would be following the main aid and development agenda issues, such as, well, water projects are making a comeback, and health . . .'

Lucy took a deep breath.

'And sustainability is absolutely critical; and if you can show it is a community backed scheme, we're in the pound seats.'

She looked at Charity. She would be the ideal local chairperson . . . her church background, her role in Kireba as a community leader, and of course she was the right gender.

'What about it?'

'What?' said Charity.

'Oh for God's sake, Charity. I've just been banging on about it. Setting up a plan to deliver clean water to Kireba. What do you think?'

'Toilets, first,' said Charity.

'But what about water, clean water? WorldFeed could help raise the money, I'm sure we can, Charity – especially if you are chairperson. You would have to make at least one visit to Oxford, of course . . . to help us explain things, and encourage other donors.'

Lucy took her silence for assent.

'In principle, Charity, would you agree? Please? Part of the money would be used to buy decent toilets, the rest would provide a clean water system for Kireba.'

Charity considered the proposal for a few moments.

She thought of saying 'What about the buttons?' but decided that it would just make Lucy cross.

'That,' she said, 'is good.'

'And will you chair the appeal?'

Charity shook her head.

'No,' she said firmly. 'No. That is a job for loafers.'

Lucy knew when to give up.

'OK fine. But can we at least put you on our board of advisers?'

Charity gave a grudging, ambiguous nod.

Lucy hugged the owner of *Harrods*, and jotted down thoughts and ideas, beginning with a list of names that would give the project credibility and assure potential donors of its integrity. She needed someone to front the project, someone who was young, with a rising profile, up and coming . . .

'What about Newman?' suggested Pearson, seeking to make amends for his earlier comments. He drained his glass of mango juice and scooped up the last of the roast peanuts.

'Of course,' exclaimed Lucy. 'Absolutely perfect!'

Newman Kibwana, the charismatic young lawyer, would be ideal. She had met him on the cocktail circuit, and had been a fellow dinner guest on a couple of occasions. If Pearson had his number, she would ring him then and there. Cecil flicked through his contact book.

'Bless you, Cecil,' said Lucy sweetly, and Pearson knew that she had not forgiven him.

She caught Kibwana in his office, just as he was leaving for court:

'Newman? It's Lucy Gomball, from WorldFeed. We met . . . yes, yes . . . Look, this cholera thing.'

Her fingers curled and uncurled a stray lock of her fair hair as she spoke.

'We're thinking about a water project for Kireba. And we're looking for someone to chair the appeal.'

Five minutes later, it had been settled. Kibwana could hardly have been more enthusiastic, particularly when Lucy asked if he would be free to travel abroad to raise funds.

'We must meet. When can we get together?'

Diaries were consulted, the venue and time agreed.

'Super,' said Lucy, 'see you then.'

Lucy and Cecil headed for Pearson's car. As they carefully picked their way across the muddy wasteland, Cecil broached a delicate subject.

With elaborate casualness, tossing the last of the nuts into his mouth, and with a feigned world-weary air, he disclosed his news:

'Gathered from Punabantu that Nduka wants to see me . . . don't know if I'll take it up.'

Lucy's response dripped scorn.

'He wants to see you? I happen to know, Cecil, that you have been pestering poor Puna for weeks . . .'

Lucy loathed Nduka with a passion that matched Pearson's; but she also was scornful of his belief that journalists could make a difference through what they wrote.

'Why toady up to Nduka? Just report the news. Instead you give yourself airs and graces – all those editorials. They don't count for a row of beans . . .'

He was right. Lucy had not forgiven his scepticism about her water proposal.

Suddenly she stopped, grabbed Cecil's shoulder, and examined the soles of her tennis shoes.

'Oh God! Absolutely yucky! Is it what I think it is, Pearson?'

Pearson, grateful for the respite, curbed the urge to giggle, commiserated, and held her hand while she went to work with a handy stick. A few damp blond tendrils strayed across her neck, and Lucy's ears looked good enough to eat. He could not resist giving her a kiss on her shoulder when she had finished her distasteful task. Her apparent indifference to the gesture cheered him up no end: he had been forgiven.

Concealed behind the pile of old car tyres which his friend the cobbler was turning into sandals, Titus Ntoto looked on. Holding hands, touching again, and kissing, all in public! As the two visitors drove off to the city centre, Ntoto continued on his way to the market, where he hoped to catch up with Rutere. With any luck, they would return that night with fresh supplies of rotting fruit. Mangoes, sweet as toffee below their black skin, juicy chunks from discarded pineapples, over-ripe bananas . . . he smacked his lips in anticipation.

Her visitors gone, Charity took advantage of the mid-morning lull in business, poured herself a Tusker – which she allowed herself on special occasions – pulled up a chair, and sat down. The first deep quaff of ice cold beer tingled all the way down to her belly. It was followed by an explosive belch, and she had a quick look round to check that there was no Mboya Boy in earshot.

No Mboya Boys could be seen, but she had nevertheless been heard.

'You are never alone with a Tusker,' said Eveready Kosgei, the local coffin maker, wiping his brow, and swigging a cola as he emerged from the kitchen. He handed over the price of the drink. Business was booming, and he was a regular at *Harrods*.

'Beg pardon,' said Charity, and they both giggled.

He returned to his open site after a few minutes, and Charity sat alone with her thoughts.

Her decision to confide in Furniver, to tell him about a ghastly recurring nightmare, had taken a load off her mind. It had been the previous Sunday, after a lunch in his flat of chicken and pumpkin and tender green beans. She had not intended to fall asleep, but once settled into the deep, red-cushioned sofa which had pride of place in the flat's whitewashed living room, she could not resist closing her eyes.

Immediately – or so it seemed – the locusts were back in her head.

She awoke to find Furniver anxiously wiping her brow with his handkerchief, and noticed that his fingers, big, like sausages, had the ochre soil of Kuwisha under the nails. He insisted on growing lettuce and carrots in a tiny garden, next to *Harrods*. The sight calmed her.

'I'm having the same dream, Furniver, a dream that one day the orphans will eat us.'

Something new and dreadful was happening, she told him. It was frightening enough that the people who were dying of Aids were mainly young and productive. But values were dying with them, the values attached to families and to age, values that had sustained Kuwisha for generations. That the old people were also dying, did not unduly distress her, for it was part of Life's order. But now there was no-one to take over, no generation to take the place of dying grandparents. They too had died, or were dying, of Aids. This was not the natural order.

'Who will look after the young people?' she asked Furniver. 'Children without grandmothers and grandfathers? Who will teach them about how to behave? Who will tell them about manners, and show them that you should have respect for old people, and to honour tradition? Who will hug them?'

Charity shook her head.

'Who will teach them about the songs of their people, about the tales of their tribes? What will happen to my little rats?'

Furniver could only squeeze her hand.

'In my dream, Furniver, there are many locusts, many, many locusts, but with the heads of young people.'

She shuddered at the recollection.

'They are so many, that the sun is made dark by the swarms, always eating, eating, eating. Eating leaves from trees, eating the grass . . . and then their heads turn into the heads of rats, but still looking like people, still eating – but now eating the maize from our granaries, even eating the seed set aside for the next season planting . . .'

She had looked at Titus Ntoto and Cyrus Rutere. The two youngsters, who had carried fresh vegetables to the flat, had

71

been invited in to finish off the meal, and were now fast asleep, rolled up in a clean blanket, stretched out on the first floor balcony. Her compassion and her love for them was not diminished but enhanced by the horror of her vision.

'So that is why I am fearful. One day, Furniver, one day, the Ntotos and the Ruteres will eat us. We cannot blame them, for they want to live. But surely they will eat us, unless . . .'

'Unless what?'

Charity tried to lighten the mood, which had become as dark and gloomy as the sky over Kuwisha.

'If you have no unless, then you despair. And my David always said that despair was a sin. But do not ask me, Charity Mupanga, to tell you, Edward Furniver, what this unless might be – we all have to look for unless. Clean water is a start, literacy, good toilets, mosquito nets, condoms, discipline, leadership, self-respect . . . all together, they make this thing, which I call unless . . .'

It was time she opened the London letter, addressed to 'Ms Charity Mupanga, The Proprietor, Harrods International Bar (and Nightspot), Uhuru Avenue,' and marked: 'For the urgent attention of Edward Furniver.' She snorted derisively. Ms Charity Mupanga indeed! Charity had no truck with the title 'Ms'. She was Mrs Charity Mupanga, and proud of it.

It was the third she had received from the firm, and she feared it would be the most serious.

The first letter, sent by airmail, had followed hard on the heels of a story Pearson had written for the *Financial News*, setting out Kuwisha's economic difficulties. He had given a photocopy to Charity. Among several local businessmen and women interviewed, Pearson had quoted 'Mrs Charity Mupanga, proprietor and owner of Harrods International Bar (and Nightspot)'.

What was more, in the story he had inadvertently given

72

away her address. He described her looking out over Kireba while bemoaning the impact of low coffee prices on beer sales at *Harrods*, and criticising the government's failure to do anything about the dreadful state of Uhuru Avenue, 'a few steps from Mrs Mupanga's popular bar'.

A reference to *Harrods* in the world's leading international financial newspaper had triggered the attention of a prominent firm of London lawyers, Fanshawe and Fanshawe, Turnagain Lane, London EC4. Their fierce vigilance on behalf of companies that had retained them to monitor the world's press for trademark violations was legendary. The use of the name *Harrods* was a flagrant breach of trademark, and the lawyers were in no doubt: it deserved a forthright statement to that effect.

The first letter had been a standard demand that *Harrods* of Uhuru Avenue, Kuwisha, cease trading under that name. Had it been up to her, Charity might have sought advice. But Furniver had been confidently and cheerfully dismissive.

Then came a second letter, saying the same thing but in a more peremptory fashion. And now this one.

It made no reference to the story of how her father acquired the name *Harrods*, other than the acknowledgement that the letter setting it out had been received. The response was cold and matter of fact, and brought home the nature of her predicament.

'They really do mean it,' said Charity to herself. Once again there was a cold feeling in her stomach, but this time the sensation was not at all pleasant. The sting was in the final paragraph of the letter:

'*Unless you confirm in writing that you will cease trading under the name of Harrods by the end of this month,*' it concluded, '*we will have no alternative but to seek redress in Court. We will of course seek costs, and I must advise you that outlays to date are already substantial.*'

'Outlays ... outlays' she mouthed the word. Why did

people have to use words like *outlays* or *resources* when what they meant was plain money? Doubts about the quality of Furniver's advice were creeping in. And if she did have to pay money, where would it come from?

Charity pushed the Tusker to one side, and rested her head in her hands. For the first time she realised that the future of her bar and nightspot was at stake: its very existence could be in jeopardy, and the name of her dear father could well be dragged through the courts.

8

'If you eat the ugali [maize meal] you must stoke the fire'

The day moved on. The breakfast rush was over, and the takings were safe in the clinic. Charity began the lunchtime preparations, peeling avocados and chopping onions, every now and then attending to an early customer dropping in for a drink.

More water was needed. Charity put two fingers to her mouth, and let out a piercing whistle. Within minutes, an Mboya Boy was setting off to Kireba's only tap, container in each hand – knowing that his reward would be a dough ball.

There was nothing she could do until he got back. Charity seldom dwelt on the past, but today seemed to be different. She felt a need to take stock of her life and its events, the periods of sadness and joy. Her deepest and abiding sorrow had been the loss of David, when she had been in her mid-thirties, and he was six years older. Her greatest and enduring comfort was the fruits of their marriage, David Junior and Blessing. But Charity nevertheless yearned for company.

She had borne her loss and her loneliness after her husband's death bravely and stoically. Indeed, until not so long ago, Charity had not thought of herself as lonely. She certainly was not short of friends of both sexes, including that up-and-coming opposition politician, Anna Nugilu, whom she had first met at a church tea that she had hosted, when David was still

75

alive. But Charity was increasingly preoccupied by a single question: was there, would there ever be, a man who could replace David Mupanga in her heart, and in her bed?

In Kuwisha's past, a suitor for a maiden's hand had to show his worth with an act of bravery. Times had changed, but perhaps this legal business might be Furniver's modern challenge. Could he cope with those clever lawyers in London and protect her father's name?

Charity was starting to have her doubts. He seemed to lack the cunning that the task required. Yet the more she saw of Edward Furniver, and the closer she got to him, the more she liked him. True, he was losing his figure and developing a paunch, his brown hair was thinning, and his clothes sense was so conservative it bordered on the bizarre: identical blue Sea Island cotton shirts, all tailor made, pink socks, and a sand-coloured suit, every day of the week. And there was never any deviation from this pattern.

She was already helping to keep his weight in check by limiting the number of Tuskers he was allowed to drink at *Harrods*. She had her suspicions: could he be a compulsive drinker, for whom alcohol was an essential daily drug? It was also true that he was sometimes morose, and sometimes irascible, yet his sharp tongue was used with equal effect on black and white alike, and only the young and the very old were exempt.

After a slow start, his Swahili had become rather good. And he loved the Kuwisha countryside. The two of them had, over the past few months, taken to chaste expeditions to Charity's modest *shamba*, setting off on Sundays at dawn, attending the early morning church service on arrival, and returning late the same day.

On her one-hectare holding, in the sprawling green hills that were famous for some of Kuwisha's best coffee, Furniver would join her uncle Casper and her numerous nephews, and toil away in the fields, weeding, hoeing and picking the green coffee berries. But before he set to work he insisted on making what he called a 'decent' cup of coffee.

The white man would roast in a thick-bottomed steel pan a handful of beans, picked on the *shamba*, cleaned and dried the season before. Then he would use what looked like a large pepper grinder to reduce the beans to a consistency that was somewhere between sugar and caster sugar, and tip the dark, aromatic grounds into a glass jug, called a cafetière, which he insisted was essential to 'decent' coffee and which he insisted on bringing with him. The final step was to pour in the water, drawn that morning from the *shamba*'s borehole, the very second it started to boil on the old-fashioned but reliable primus stove. There was a slight hiss as the water met the coffee and bubbled to the top of the jug, before Furniver pushed down the plunger which filtered the dark liquid.

He had shocked Charity when he told her how much a cup of coffee would cost in one of the cafes that had become so fashionable in North America and Europe. At first she thought he was joking, but he insisted that it was true: a single cup of coffee bought at one of the popular London cafés cost more than the growers in Kuwisha were paid for a kilo of their best quality beans.

During the Sundays that Furniver worked on the *shamba*, neighbours from miles around would find reason to drop by and watch him at work, stripped to the waist, wearing plimsolls and shorts. It was not a pretty sight, as his pink and perspiring body started to turn lobster-red in the Kuwisha sun. But the spectacle of a sweating white man, getting the rich soil under his fingernails, doing his share of the backbreaking work, was a rare, almost unheard of, event in Kuwisha. It was as remarkable, the neighbours agreed, as the sight of the late Bishop, God rest his soul, doing much the same thing when he had been alive. But a capacity for hard work on the *shamba*, admirable though it was, Charity reflected, was well short of

77

evidence that Furniver could cope with the latest challenge from London . . .

Charity looked around. Where was that Mboya Boy? She was about to whistle again when he returned, and was ordered to wash his hands before helping her shell the peas.

Perhaps she was wrong: perhaps it was not fair to make a final judgment of the man based on his ability to deal with London lawyers. Instead, should he be judged by his work on the *shamba*, and his plan to connect its borehole by a pipe to the two-room house? Or his enthusiasm for solar panels, and for wind power; and his support for a co-op that would buy the best beans:

'We could market them abroad, as organic coffee beans from Kuwisha,' he proposed enthusiastically.

Charity was unsure about the organic business.

'No insecticide, none at all?'

Furniver nodded in confirmation.

She had shaken her head doubtfully.

'I do not like *goggas* [insects]. I don't like flies, I don't like mosquitoes. I believe plants don't like flies; coffee bushes don't like flies.'

She looked at him suspiciously, waiting for his response, but he had learnt it was sometimes best to keep his powder dry. He didn't fool Charity.

'I see you, Furniver,' she said, as her friend's jaw tightened, and his lower lip jutted out.

'I see you and your cheeky lip . . .'

They had both laughed.

The more she thought about it, the less doubt she had. As a matter of principle, she should fight her corner.

It was not right, not fair, that a London duka, however big, should be able to claim exclusive use to the name *Harrods*, even if this far-away company was the first to use it. Those lawyers were clever – a word she pronounced 'clay-vah', in tones rich with contempt. To be called clever was not a compliment. Or at best, it was a backhanded one. The President of Kuwisha was 'clever', meaning full of guile and cunning; and the London lawyers were 'clever', as well as pompous and arrogant. Nellson Githongo was very clever, and also very cheeky. Charity, on the other hand, was too honest and too decent to be called 'clever'.

She had left school at eleven. In a country dominated by men, Charity had been fortunate to have enjoyed five years of primary education. She was determined that Kuwisha's up-and-coming generation of young women would have better opportunities. She urged them to vote for Anna Nugilu, the only politician who made sense to her, in the coming presidential election.

So while Charity Mupanga had none of the learning that came with the university education Furniver had enjoyed, she knew what was fair, what was truthful and what was decent.

Deep in her heart, however, the letters from London frightened her. She could deal with most things, but London lawyers were beyond her ken.

'What is the matter with these people?' Charity muttered. Perhaps she should not have encouraged Furniver in his provocative and disrespectful response. Was it possible that between them, she and Furniver had provoked this latest threatening letter?

Chicken necks!

Charity suddenly remembered. Chicken necks! She had to check that the promised chicken necks were on their way. But chicken necks were not the problem. It was the Worcestershire sauce she needed, essential to the recipe. The dish was Furniver's favourite, and she had promised him that it would be on the menu today. But she was running out of the recipe's vital ingredient, originally recommended by her husband.

David had developed a taste for the sauce during his time at the seminary in Leeds, and on his return to Kuwisha would scour city shops for bottles of the spicy brown liquid, and build up a stockpile.

The sauce was also needed for the famous avocado soup, already chalked on the *Harrods* blackboard as the 'special' for the day. She might have to change her suppliers. Despite all her efforts to explain her special needs, the avocados were coming in too ripe, far too ripe. Charity had long ago discovered that if one wanted the nutty flavour of avocado in the soup, half of them had to be slightly under-ripe when they were sieved. It made for a more laborious task, but it was one happily performed by a team of volunteer urchins, led by Titus Ntoto, their hands thoroughly washed and fingernails clipped under Charity's strict supervision. In return they got a square meal and – should they wish – a place to sleep at night, without fear of molestation.

Where, she fretted, was that Rutere? It was his turn to sweep the bar, and to clean the tables and the chairs, and to light the charcoal oven which cooked the corn bread.

The sky crackled with lightning and thunder rolled. Plump drops of rain started to fall. Furniver might not be able to get back to *Harrods* before the storm broke. Still, tomorrow would do. And anyway, she needed more time to think about the next step in the effort to protect and preserve her father's name.

9

'Marula fruit always tastes sweet to the elephant'

It was at times like this, Furniver thought to himself, that he missed Davina. Not that he regretted their divorce. But the swelling, concealed deep in the cleft of his posterior, was not the sort of thing one could ask anyone who was not an intimate to investigate. It certainly did not seem a suitable subject to raise with Charity.

The rain, still pelting down, had made it all but impossible for Furniver to drop round to *Harrods*. Getting back to his office after the shareholders' meeting had been difficult enough, and he had spent the rest of the working day catching up on administration. It was far too early for bed, and apart from wanting to go through the *Harrods* file kept in the office, he had to finish recording the children's story he had written for his granddaughter.

Putting on his dressing gown over his cotton shirt and khaki slacks, Furniver went into the modest office that adjoined the bedroom, and sat at his untidy desk. For the next ten minutes he made notes on a typewritten sheaf of papers before him. Then he cleared his throat, and began reading aloud into the tiny tape recorder that he carried with him, usually in his briefcase:

'. . . "*My government has watched with growing concern the increase in cat-chasing incidents at post boxes. We are determined to stamp it out . . . two slots in every box will soon be mandatory. One low slot for our feline friends, one higher slot for us. Let me make this solemn promise: the cats of Britain are safe in this government's hands."*

Backbenchers cheered. It really was a splendid speech.

The picture of the Prime Minister shaking Stripey's paw was on the front page of Cat News *the next day, with the caption that said it all:*

"Thanks a Slot, Tony!"'

The last few lines of the penultimate chapter safely on tape, Furniver felt this was as good a place as any to pause for the night. Furniver pressed the Stop button on his recorder, and dropped the machine into his briefcase. There were still a few pages of his story left, but they would have to be dictated later the next day. His granddaughter's birthday was two weeks away. Provided Ntoto took the cassette to the city's central post office in the next twenty-four hours, it should reach her in plenty of time. He shifted uncomfortably in his chair.

He got up and went to the office filing cabinet a few feet away, and extracted a folder marked 'Harrods', scratching and probing, his shoulders moving this way and that as he manoeuvred for position.

This bloody business with the London lawyers! Fond as he was of Charity, he now bitterly regretted getting involved. That was not quite true: what he regretted was the advice he had given to her.

Furniver succumbed to the temptation to have a further scratch. He leafed through the file, and wished he had taken Rupert Fanshawe's original complaint more seriously. From the very start, he now realised, he should have advised Charity to settle, however painful it would be. Instead he had relished the idea that a law firm in London was spending costly time pursuing a shanty bar in an African slum, presumably misled about its status by the imposing address to which they had written – Uhuru Avenue.

In a dry, pro forma text, the first letter had ordered that the bar should 'forthwith' cease trading as *Harrods*, on the grounds that that name had long been registered for the exclusive use of Harrods of Knightsbridge, London.

The second letter in the file had come a fortnight later, and this time the peremptory tone irritated and provoked Furniver. The deliberately pompous response, sent on behalf of Charity but in his name, on notepaper headed Harrods International Bar (and Nightspot), easily run off on the printer attached to his office computer, had now backfired.

Far from treating the exchange as a joke, Charity had taken it increasingly seriously, insisting that she would not settle, not on any terms. He continued to flick impatiently through the *Harrods* file, shivering slightly in the cool of the air-conditioner.

'Got it,' exclaimed Furniver. It had seemed so clever at the time, and he postponed his evening bath for the few minutes it took to re-read it. It purported to have been sent by the local law firm of Furniver, Katanga, and Nkumbula, and was every bit as provocative as he remembered.

Rupert Fanshawe
Fanshawe and Fanshawe
Turnagain Lane
London EC 4
Sir,

I am in receipt of yours of the 18th inst.

I am instructed by my client, Mrs Charity Mupanga, to say that she does not recognise your client's claim to enjoy exclusive world-wide use of the name Harrods; and she states her firm intention to continue trading as Harrods International Bar (and Nightspot).

Attached is Mrs Mupanga's personal account of how her father acquired the name Harrods.

On her instructions I am writing to inform you that she proposes to lodge a counter claim for breach of trademark over the use of the name Harrods, which she understands to be a general store, otherwise known here in Kuwisha as a duka, and which trades in London.

This counter claim will be heard in the high court of Kuwisha.

Mrs Mupanga has, however, indicated that she would be prepared to pursue an out of court settlement if you indicate your reciprocal willingness in the seven days following your receipt of this letter.

Mrs Mupanga regrets that she has to seek the protection of the high court of Kuwisha, but instructs me to tell you that she is determined that justice will prevail.

I await confirmation of your acceptance.

Yours faithfully,
Edward Furniver

Furniver cringed. He had been rather pleased with it at the time. Now the letter read as a pitiful challenge from an incompetent amateur. Those London lawyers meant business. Clearly they were determined to settle the matter on their terms. He and Charity were in a pickle, however you looked at it, and he, Edward Furniver, the trusted and respected banker to the people of Kireba, was to blame.

There was a noise downstairs, at the front door. It was probably his steward, Didymus Kigali, arriving to prepare the evening meal.

Furniver had initially been reluctant to accept Charity's recommendation that he employ Mr Kigali – he could not bring himself to call him Didymus.

'He's almost twice my age, he insists on wearing a uniform that makes him look like an elderly cricketer, and now you tell me that he's an elder in his church, and the husband of your best friend Mildred, who also happens to be a relative of yours.'

'Yes?' said Charity, eyes narrowing, her hands on her hips.

84

'And his duties include ironing my, er, smalls?'

It had been far too early in their relationship for Furniver to refer to his underpants.

'Smalls, I don't care about. But underpants, yes, of course.'

'It's going to be like employing my dad,' said Furniver plaintively.

'Good. Then there will be no panky. A lot of women will chase you. Kigali will watch for panky. And he will be grateful for what is a good job. And you must read his references,' said Charity. 'He is very proud of them. Give him respect. Respect.' And she stalked off . . .

It was indeed Mr Kigali on his doorstep, dressed as usual in spotless whites, his wrinkled brown knees peeping out between his long socks and his even longer shorts. The old man apologised profusely, and unnecessarily, for being late. It was remarkable, thought Furniver, that Mr Kigali had turned up at all, given the dreadful weather. All he fancied, he told his steward, was a soft-boiled egg, toast and Marmite, and a pot of tea.

'After my bath, please,' he added.

He returned upstairs, and peeled off his dressing gown and the rest of his clothes as he made his way to the bathroom, exploring as he did so the inner sanctum of his cleft yet again, resentfully and fearfully.

Not for the first time, Furniver wished he had met Charity's late husband. By all accounts, his death had deprived Kuwisha of a talented son. What, he wondered, would Bishop David Mupanga have advised him to do? Two volumes of the Bishop's works, kept on Furniver's bookshelves, were splendid repositories of good sense and wisdom. But neither *God and Ethnicity: seeking unity in a plural society* (Longfellow, East Africa, 1995), nor *Free at Last: the collected sermons of David Mupanga* (Longfellow, 1998) – both out of print, but circulated around Kuwisha in photocopied editions – could be expected to offer insights into his predicament.

Furniver yearned for a confidante with whom he could share his problem, and from whom he could seek counsel. It was conceivable, he mused, that Bishop Mupanga, who had been renowned for his pragmatism, might well have suggested that Charity's reaction to such an intimate matter would be an excellent acid test of character. What tougher an examination of a prospective partner's suitability could there be? He cautiously felt the swelling, and turned off the hot tap.

Essentially a shy man, Furniver had not yet formally broached the possibility of lifelong partnership with Charity Mupanga. He found the prospect of a Christian wedding, which he was certain she would insist on, somewhat uncomfortable, for he was eclectic in his faiths. But when it came to courtship, he had certain inviolable standards. A request that she inspect his bottom at this stage in their relationship for what might at best be a boil seemed to him presumptuous, even in this liberated day and age. Call me old-fashioned, he thought, but such an experience was certainly no substitute for a proposal over a candle-lit dinner date. And a boil was bad enough. What if the swelling should turn out to be a far more distasteful ailment? The persistent itch made this increasingly likely, and the possibility that he was playing host to a truly horrid tropical affliction, one which he could not bring himself to name, was something that Furniver could barely contemplate.

The discomfort was located in that part of the anatomy that his Maker had decided should be hard to inspect for oneself. Indeed, it would be impossible to see the swelling without a mirror – even if one's body enjoyed the flexibility of youth. But if you were the wrong side of fifty, and your joints were far from supple, and if you were overweight, verging on tubby, an exploration was both difficult and dangerous, even with the help of a mirror. Goodness knows what would happen if you made a stretch too far.

He would make one last effort to investigate it himself, Furniver decided, before admitting defeat, risking embarrassment, and seeking the advice of the doctor recommended by the British high commission, a young woman who looked as if she was barely out of her teens. First he would give his stiffening limbs a fighting chance. He picked up the John D. MacDonald novel he had selected earlier from his bookcase and eased his pink and slightly hairy body into the hot water, laced liberally with bath salts, and immersed himself for a long soak.

On the scale of life's concerns, he reflected, his physical discomfort counted for naught; and despite his earlier grim thoughts, the bath restored his confidence. Surely something could be worked out with the lawyers. And as the Kireba People's Co-operative Bank's chief executive – indeed, its only executive and its only employee – soaked in the green suds of his bath, and followed the fortunes of Travis McGee, John D. MacDonald's ace detective and trouble shooter, he began to believe that he was, with Charity Mupanga's help, within reach of contentment, if not happiness . . .

10

'If the snake hisses, the elephant coughs'

Ntoto looked up at the lowering skies and hurried on to the water pipe that was home to him and Rutere. Halfway to the market he had been forced to turn back, such was the intensity of the storm. Rutere, who had got back before him, must have had a productive journey if the pungent sweet smell of rotting bananas that welcomed him was anything to go by. He pulled aside the grimy plastic curtain that covered the entrance. Together with the odour of unwashed boys, old fruit, industrial glue, and a hint of *bhang*, it made for a well-nigh overpowering combination in the gloomy space.

Ntoto wrinkled his nose appreciatively.

'Well done, Rutere.'

They tucked in. Some of the bananas were so overripe that the boys did not try to peel them. Instead they made a hole with their thumbnails in one blackened end, and enthusiastically sucked out the contents. Those they did not eat were tossed, skin and all, with an occasional handful of sugar which had been 'borrowed' from Charity, into a small steel drum, its bubbling mash heated by a fire made out of scavenged pieces of wood and bits of charcoal. And every few weeks the liquid was filtered through a scrap of cloth and funnelled into a old whisky bottle.

Rutere had already been drinking. Swaying on his feet, he handed the bottle to Ntoto, who took a long swig. The raw liquid burnt its way down his gullet until it reached his stomach, where it nestled like a comforting hot compress.

Outside, the rain hammered down, and the noise was soothing. Ntoto took a final slug, smacked his lips and let sleep embrace him. All things considered, it had been a good day . . .

It was one of life's ironies that the Mboya Boys' bitter enemy, Mayor Willifred Guchu, had been instrumental, albeit indirectly, in providing them with their refuge.

The first, and so far the only, scheme to provide water to Kireba had been launched soon after Guchu had been elected mayor some ten years ago. It had had a promising start. Giant excavators gouged a trench six feet deep and six feet wide out of the rich red soil, and the huge concrete pipes were laid in their wake. Unfortunately for the residents of Kireba, the trench never reached the water reservoir, which was its destination, some five miles away.

The contractors claimed that they had not been paid the second instalment. Auditors called in by the contract managers, the United Nations Development Programme, reported 'serious discrepancies and several major anomalies' in the accounts. Both the UNDP accountant and Mayor Guchu came under suspicion, but there was no hard evidence. Something had to be done, nevertheless. The accountant was posted to Nigeria, a move that left his colleagues divided. Some regarded it as harsh punishment for what they felt was a minor transgression; others saw it as a fitting reward for initiative, and were envious of the rich pickings that awaited him in west Africa. The mayor himself emerged more powerful than ever, keeping the Landcruiser which he insisted had been purchased out of his own funds.

Whatever the reason for the non-payment, Phase One of the UNDP City Water Project was suspended. The trench ended abruptly, just short of the point at which it was intended to divert the foul-smelling Kireba River. Older residents could remember fishing the river and swimming in it. Over the years, however, it had become little more than an open sewer.

For Titus Ntoto and his fellow gang members, the pipes were a haven in which they were safe from the truncheon-wielding policemen and the well-intentioned expatriate ladies who served on the Adopt-a-Street-Boy committee. It took a brave man or woman to face such squalor and to risk being pelted with filth by the urchins, whose throwing arms performed with an accuracy that would be the envy of a professional cricketer.

Ever since Ntoto could remember, there had been a feud between the boys and Authority. On one memorable occasion the street children had been rounded up by the police, and held in the cells before being dumped well beyond the city limits. At least that had been the plan. When the time came to move the children from the police station into waiting trucks, the police recoiled in disgust and disarray: scores of youngsters had covered themselves in their own excrement, and made a break for freedom.

Ntoto had been amongst those who had made good their escape, but there had been a high price to pay. Casual beatings of street children became the order of the day. Ntoto vowed he would take revenge on Mayor Guchu and his bully-boy police – but they were hollow vows and empty threats, made from the safety of the pipes that had become the boys' home, and fuelled by draughts of home-brewed liquor.

Usually these pipes, close to Kireba's main waste dump, were safe from the regular African storms. But the storms that had been breaking over Kuwisha night after night this season were spectacular, and the one that broke that evening was in a class of its own. In the early hours of the morning, the over-flow from the dam that formed part of Kireba's boundary broke through the old earthworks, originally thrown up in preparation for the laying of the pipes. Joined by the existing floodwater, the torrent roared down the pipes, driving all before it, like a giant emetic of Nature.

Before Ntoto and Rutere could rouse themselves from an alcohol-induced stupor, the wall of water was upon them. They were bowled along by a filthy, frothy wave that finally spat Ntoto out on what used to be the banks of the Kireba River, and deposited Rutere even further downstream. The next morning, drenched in the accumulated detritus, Titus Ntoto lay semi-conscious. But not even his terrible hangover could block out the voices that were soon to rouse him.

11

"Fortunate is the bird that nests while it sings'

Furniver was lost to the world, on a Florida houseboat where ace detective Travis McGee was navigating his way through a maze of drugs, corruption, adultery and murder. The office phone gave three rings, and then stopped, which usually indicated that a fax had come in. He swirled the bathwater, made a mental note to check the machine when he had dressed, and prepared for what he feared would be an ordeal.

He eased himself out of the bath, and began towelling himself dry. Still naked, he moved to his bedroom, cautiously fingering the bump, but taking great care not to scratch it. What had been a disturbing possibility was in his mind at least becoming a nasty probability. Furniver recalled the advice he had received from old Africa hands when he first arrived in Kuwisha which he had found puzzling at the time.

Most of it was straightforward: how to tell if your house steward was watering the whisky and stealing the sugar, how many days off to allow for funerals, the importance of references, or the merits of a daily gin and tonic as a malaria prophylactic. But one pearl of settler wisdom, the significance of which he had not fully grasped, stood out. Time and again Furniver was urged, in tones that were deadly serious:

'Make sure your boy irons your underpants.'

At first he dismissed it as an example of settler eccentricity, or an elaborate joke, the point of which he had not yet grasped. Until, that is, he decided one day to seek enlightenment from the Oldest Member at the Thumaiga Club, the institution that was as old as Kuwisha itself.

It had been early in Furniver's stay, before the savings bank had been established, and he was staying at the Club. The OM, widely believed to have played an important and unpleasant part in putting down Kuwisha's pre-independence troubles with the locals, or the 'indigenous' as expatriates now called them, was deep in his usual chair, in front of a log fire and talking, as much to himself as anyone who would listen.

'Back to the future,' the OM was grumbling, 'back to the bloody future.'

'What on earth do you mean?' asked Furniver.

The OM was slightly inebriated, but this alone didn't account for the passion in his voice. With a faraway look in his eyes, and a gin and tonic in his hand, he began to recite: 'Morning at the Murchison, picnic at Pakwach, sandwiches in Sudan.'

Furniver took his courage in both hands. You disagreed with the OM at your peril.

'Sudan? With a war on? No one ever picnics at Pakwach these days, and I thought that the Murchison Falls was knocked off the tourist map by Idi Amin and has never really recovered.'

'Point is,' said the OM, unfazed, 'the journey could be done in the so-called bad old days, before we threw in the towel, and gave these bods independence. Travelling round this part of the world was easy then. And when it gets as good as it was, it will be a darn sight better than it is now. As I say, back to the future.'

He tapped a battered copy of the 1960 edition of the *Year Book and Guide to East Africa*, never far from his hand. Kuwisha had become independent a few years later, but as far as the

93

Oldest Member was concerned, 1960 was the year the rot set in.

Pearson had once asked the OM why he had chosen that date:

'Bloody Lancaster House! Constitutional conference. Gave the buggers self-government. Slippery slope, thin end of the wedge.'

For reasons that Furniver could not fathom, the OM took a benevolent interest in him, possibly because he insisted that the banker must be related to 'Boetie' Furniver, the district commissioner who had ruled his pre-independence patch of Kuwisha with a rod of iron.

The OM turned to an advertisement on page eight, and read the text aloud.

'East African Airways – Linking East Africa with the World . . . Fourteen different airlines provide services to and from Nairobi . . . linked with Bombay, Karachi and Aden by the twice weekly tourist Canadair services of East African Airways. Scheduled services to every part of the Central African Federation, as well as to Mozambique, Beira and Lourenco Marques in Portuguese East Africa, and to Johannesburg and Durban in the Union of South Africa . . . short-haul routes stretching from Entebbe through Jinja, Kisumu, Nairobi, Mombasa, Tanga and Zanzibar.'

'Good Lord,' said Furniver. He beckoned the waiter for a second round of gin and tonic.

'There's more to come,' said the OM, and turned a few pages.

'Here's one of the best bits: "Package tours to Serengeti, two day excursions from Entebbe to Murchison Falls . . . holiday on the Nile . . . at Butiaba the SS *Robert Corydon*, a modern inland marine vessel, is boarded for the journey across Lake Albert to Pakwach, where a river steamer takes the visitor down the Nile to Nimule, through scenery of unqualified grandeur, where game is plentiful."'

The OM had made his point. Forty years ago one could fly to more places from Kuwisha than you can today. What is more, you could drive on safe roads, and be sure of ending the day at a decent hotel with clean sheets.

Furniver broke into the OM's reverie. There was something he had to know.

'About the, er, steward and the, um, underpants, and the ironing business . . .'

He kept his voice down, just above a whisper, in the hope that the OM would follow his example, and do the same.

'Why should you make sure your boy irons your underpants, with a very hot iron?' roared the OM, as he sat upright in his armchair, galvanised by the subject.

'Because it kills the eggs of the bloody *jipu*! Isn't that right, Wheatcliff?'

The head waiter who was passing nodded his head, and threw another log on the fire. Wheatcliff and the OM had grown up together on the same farm. At twelve, the OM had been packed off to boarding school, and the relationship between the two boys had changed fundamentally. But something of the old friendship must have remained. Indeed, it was said in the club that Wheatcliff owed his job to the OM, which some members saw as evidence of a liberal heart – though none dared say as much in his hearing.

Seeing that Furniver was still baffled, the Oldest Member took pity on him and explained, in words of one syllable, one of the grim realities of life in the East African tropics.

By the time he was finished, Furniver was horrified. And now, long after that exchange, Furniver had to face the possibility that his steward had broken this iron rule of hygiene in the tropics. Was this wretched discomfort he was enduring, and the acute embarrassment that he faced, the price he was paying for disregarding settler wisdom – wisdom that was scoffed at by 'liberals', but which had been tried and tested over the years? Was he being punished for indulging his steward, Didymus Kigali? Had he, God forfend, failed to handle his 'boy' in the correct fashion?

Furniver went through the checklist of advice, ironing underpants apart, he had received from the remaining veterans of pre-independence Kuwisha. Had he, in the vernacular of the old white settlers, allowed his steward to become a 'loafer', a man who was lax and lazy? Had he 'spoilt' him by allowing weekends off and introducing eight-hour working days? Had he allowed Kigali, an elder in the Church of the Blessed Redeemer, so much leisure that the boy was in danger of becoming 'cheeky', a frame of mind that encouraged subversion and bred dissidents? Had he encouraged his boy to get ideas above his station, by allowing him to watch the flat's television set? Was he paying him too much, breaking the code that bound expatriates and settlers together as one?

Furniver would have to plead guilty on every count. He had done all this. What is more, he had done it without being prompted. The only request made by Mr Kigali had been for time off on Saturday afternoons, so he could deliver sermons at his church.

There was one question, one question above all, that Furniver had to answer: Would this decent, God-fearing old man commit a heinous, unforgivable offence, and neglect to iron his employer's underpants?

Certainly not, decided Furniver. But the itch seemed to get more insistent by the hour. He thought hard. Suddenly, with a sense of shame, and a shudder of distaste for the consequences, Furniver recalled a morning after the night before. It had been an enthusiastic send-off for the first secretary at the French embassy. Furniver had woken the next day, worse for wear, and running late for an appointment.

Didymus Kigali had, as was his custom, left the newly washed laundry, fresh dried under the sun, in the kitchen,

96

ready for the hot iron. Furniver remembered searching impatiently in his drawers for clean and ironed pants, thus overlooking the pile of neatly ironed underwear on the shelf in the built-in cupboard. So he had rummaged in the kitchen, and pulled on a pair of underpants, which had been washed, *but not ironed*.

Furniver groaned at the recollection, and cursed himself. What a fool he had been! What a price he was paying!

12

'When the elephant spits out its phlegm, don't try to measure its tusks'

The rains that soaked Kuwisha did not disturb the slumbers of Ferdinand Mlambo. The senior kitchen *toto* at State House happily snored away, deep in a sleep induced and enhanced by bedtime puffs of Mtoko Gold, Kuwisha's best *bhang*. He was dreaming of his ambitions, distracted from the cares of the world, safe and warm, under the table in the State House kitchen, a rotund dormouse deep in a nest of blankets and old newspapers.

Mlambo was a young man with prospects. Technically he was a citizen of Kuwisha. But although he had been born in the capital fourteen years ago he felt that he was Zimbabwean, and his friends regarded him as Zimbabwean. His grandparents were from that country, as were his mother and father. To be a Zimbabwean in Kuwisha could be a problem under most circumstances. Jobs were scarce, and there was growing resentment of foreigners who had jobs that could be done by locals. But for Mlambo, the fact that he was treated as a foreigner was a positive advantage.

The boy, who followed the complexities of Kuwisha politics with a shrewdness developed out of a well-honed instinct for survival, knew full well that the presidential elections, due to be held in the next few weeks, could see an upheaval in the country's affairs. President Nduka could quite possibly lose. Were he to go, there would be a massive change in the State House staff, a change that was certain to favour the kinsfolk of the new president. But with any luck, Mlambo would survive, provided he kept his head down. So it was a positive advantage to have no identification with, and no apparent sympathy for, any one of Kuwisha's many indigenous ethnic groups.

To the outsider's eye, to be kitchen *toto* at State House, the official residence and centre of government, might not seem a job of great import. Even if it was pointed out that Ferdinand Mlambo was not simply a kitchen toto, he was the senior kitchen toto, who could – and often did – make life hell for his two subordinates, the job still seemed insignificant.

Yet only an outsider could come to this conclusion. As senior kitchen toto, Mlambo was answerable to Lovemore Mboga, the formidable State House steward, widely believed to be a member of Kuwisha's Central Intelligence Organisation. The boy's duties ranged from shining the silver for State House banquets, to acting as the president's food taster. And more than that, perhaps most important of all, he had become the unofficial supplier of *bhang* to the State House staff.

Thanks to his position at State House, Mlambo ate well. Indeed, his duties ensured that he ate like a prince, a major factor in his rapid growth. Although he had only just turned fourteen, he could pass for a lad several years older. Compared to the ill-nourished street urchins, he looked like a young giant, and had the swaggering confidence of a man of destiny.

His parents, his four sisters, his three brothers, his uncle and aunt who still lived in Zimbabwe, they all knew that if he played his cards right, there was a good chance that Ferdinand Mlambo could rise to the rank of State House steward.

It was a busy life, and Mlambo had little spare time. But the leisure time he had – usually on Sunday afternoons, when the president was inspecting his prize-winning herd of cattle on his country estate, a two-hour drive from State House – was spent with his friends, playing for the Mboya Boys United football team.

As he slept and dreamed, Mlambo's feet twitched. He was reliving the day the Mboya Boys had won the Lardner-Burke cup, named after a philanthropic white settler who had backed the African nationalist cause during the colonial era. By general agreement the cup final was the climax of the football season in Kireba. This year's game between the Mboya Boys, nicknamed the Never Sweats in tribute to their casual style of play, and the Lily Whites, a church team renowned for their thuggish tackles, had attracted a decent crowd.

As many as 500 had gathered around the pitch. A further 100 or so, plastic beer cups in hand – Charity had banned glasses after a particularly nasty brawl – watched from the comfort of *Harrods*.

At 2-2 and with ninety minutes coming up on the referee's watch, extra time seemed inevitable, and the Lily Whites were closing ranks. The sleeping Mlambo's feet were now twitching furiously. The Lily Whites had reckoned without the formidable trio that was at the heart of the Never Sweats. From well inside his own half, Titus Ntoto looked around, and swept the ball to the head of Cyrus Rutere on the left wing. Rutere nodded it down into the path of Mlambo, who from his sweeper position had thundered down the pitch in a do-or-die effort.

He lashed out, the ball ended up in the net, the crowd roared, and the referee blew for full time. The Mboya Boys whooped with delight, and Mlambo led the team's charge as they sprinted the fifty yards or so to the safety of *Harrods*, pursued by angry supporters of the Lily Whites. The team took shelter behind the imposing presence of Charity, who, arms folded across her chest, interposed herself between a baying knot of Lily White supporters and the panting boys.

Mlambo jerked awake, his heart pumping furiously, sweat beading his forehead, and vowed to smoke less *bhang*.

In real life, Charity had shooed the pursuers away, and invited the coach of the losing team to drown his disappointment in Tuskers. In the dream however, there was no such happy ending, and Charity had offered him over to the furious Lily Whites, tugging him by one of his ears, gripped firmly between thumb and forefinger.

Mlambo tumbled out of his nest. Deep down in his superstitious soul, alarm bells were ringing . . .

Edward Furniver had not intended to spend so long in Kuwisha. He had seen himself as no more than a well-intentioned stranger who was passing through.

The son of a British diplomat who had married an English teacher, Furniver had come a long way from the City of London, where he had made a modest fortune over twenty years as an investment banker. He had learnt, baffled and hurt, that Davina was determined to divorce him only when a letter arrived from her lawyer while she was on holiday in the Antibes – with the lawyer, he later learnt. He gave in without a struggle, took early retirement, and decided to travel the world, beginning with Africa.

It was, he acknowledged, a somewhat irrational act of defiance, and a perverse identification with the hapless continent that was synonymous with debt, disease and disaster.

'It's on the bones of its arse,' as a colleague contemptuously put it.

But soon after stepping out of the cocoon of BA's business class comfort into the clammy heat of Lagos' international airport – his first port of call on a journey that would take him to Kuwisha – he experienced what he came to call Africa's 'serendipity factor'.

He had been waiting for his luggage to come through when

he was enthusiastically hailed like an old friend, and his hand pumped.

'Bugger off,' said Furniver firmly and calmly, just as Africa hands had advised him.

'Go away, just bugger off.'

This blunt approach was, all agreed, the only way to deal with the assortment of rogues found at Nigerian airports – ticket touts, currency dealers, and 419 con men.

To Furniver's astonishment, the 'tout' had laughed approvingly, and made a number of derogatory remarks about Nigeria. The penny finally dropped. He realised that the man he was being so firm with was in fact a Lagos-born, London-based mini-cab driver, who had carried Furniver to various destinations. The man had been on the same flight to Lagos, on his annual visit home.

He insisted on seeing Furniver safely to his hotel.

Yet for all the serendipity, Furniver soon came to appreciate that for most of the continent's people, life was fragile, cheap, dangerous and unpredictable. And for an outsider like himself, a close relationship with the continent was like making friends with a feverish wounded giant: you could never be sure whether the blow that might fell you as you tried to bring relief was a reflex response to a spasm of pain, or a clumsy gesture of gratitude.

From Lagos he flew to Cape Town, and worked his way north, until ending up in Kuwisha, where he saw an opportunity to put into effect a plan he had been considering for years. Micro-banking – lending small amounts of money to people too poor to obtain commercial bank credit – was, he felt convinced, part of the elusive answer to Africa's woes. Boredom was the final impetus. Having looked around the continent for somewhere he could put his theory into practice, he decided that Kuwisha was as good a country as any. And Kireba was as good a place as any to start. If the concept could work in a country drained by endemic corruption, sapped by years of mismanagement, demoralised by failure, and let down by its leaders, it could work anywhere.

The Kireba People's Co-operative Bank was a great success. Despite its impressive name, it was no more than a society which lent small amounts of money, drawn from the combined savings of its members, to individual members, who would almost certainly be turned down by any regular commercial bank, on the grounds that they lived in Kireba. Successful loan applicants had to do little more than to satisfy Furniver that they would put the loan to good use, and would, in the judgment of a panel of their peers, repay it. By most standards, the loans were so small as to be small change. But they made a tangible difference to the lives of the recipients.

The intricate scale models of bicycles, lorries and cars made out of wire by street children, for example, needed nothing but skill, imagination and a pair of pliers to construct. Pliers, however, cost the equivalent of a house steward's weekly wage, which was a handsome sum when compared to the pittance earned by a parking boy. A loan sufficient to buy pliers and a bundle of wire could turn an unruly adolescent into a self-sufficient worker who could earn enough to repay the society's low interest loan in a few weeks.

For the past three years, Furniver had been general manager of the co-operative he had founded. Administration was simple and cheap. Put the details into a computer, and push a button every so often, and that was all that was required – plus, of course, the peer pressure. It was something that left Furniver troubled. In theory, it meant that the borrower's friends would express their disapproval should the borrower default. Self-interest played a critical part. They too wanted a loan, or possibly were recipients of a loan themselves. The former would have to wait longer for money to become available; the latter would have to pay a higher rate of interest.

This was what in polite society was meant by peer pressure. In Kireba, as Furniver had belatedly discovered, the term was usually a euphemism for a sound hiding administered by the local vigilantes. It worked very well, he had to admit. The demonstration effect of the beatings – one unfortunate defaulter was never seen again – was so effective that the society's ratio of bad debts to loans outstanding was the envy of his commercial bank colleagues.

From a modest base of 500 members and capital of 500,000 ngwee, provided by an obscure international charity, the society had steadily grown. There were now nearly 3,000 members of whom 500 were borrowers. The results in Kireba were as evident as green shoots in a desert. Shoe-cleaners, watch repairers, tailors, vegetable vendors, coffin makers, hairdressers, corncob hawkers, model makers, curio sellers, all owed their start in commercial life to the bank's modest loan.

It showed, said Furniver, that it was possible to transform a community with a modest amount of capital, spent in ways that were decided by the locals. With a hand-operated pump and a few thousand feet of plastic piping, women could be released from the daily backbreaking burden of carrying water. Provide a loan that was enough for the purchase of a locally made, fuel-efficient stove, and hundreds of trees could be saved.

The moment of truth was approaching. Despite the soak in the hot bath, the bump was devilishly itchy.

A week had elapsed since Furniver had worn those unironed underpants, and this was the generally agreed incubation period. Furniver shuddered. He now had no doubt that he was the unwitting host to a *jipu*. This abomination of Nature must have laid its eggs on his underpants while they were outside drying. Once on Furniver's frame, the eggs flourished in the sweaty warmth of his buttocks, where they burrowed below the surface of the skin. And now at least one of those eggs was turning into a maggot, which would flourish, wriggling and irritating as it prepared to pop out.

Furniver moaned in self-pity.

He took comfort, however, in remembering the other half of the advice given by the Oldest Member.

'Should the worst happen, old boy, sack the native, and then suffocate the blighter,' said the OM. He chuckled grimly. 'That'll teach 'em.'

At the time, Furniver could not help feeling shocked. While he had soon got used to the reactionary views expressed by many of the settlers, the suggestion struck him as a bit extreme, even by their robust standards. With great politeness, and taking his courage into both hands, he indicated his reservations:

While there was certainly a case for drastic measures, said Furniver, on the whole, all things considered, and in this day and age, he would be most reluctant to do away with his steward simply because the fellow had failed to iron his underpants.

The Oldest Member had nodded sympathetically, and regretfully.

'You've got the right attitude, young man, but you've got the wrong end of the stick. I don't blame you. Perfectly reasonable. And you're probably right.'

The OM checked himself.

'Said probably right? Huh! Definitely right. Getting to be a bit of a liberal in my old age.'

He gave a dry chuckle, which became an extended cough as he got carried away by his own joke.

'Just wish more youngsters shared your views. It would only be what the bugger deserved. Might have got away with it in the Old Days.'

His pale blue eyes misted over with happy recollections of pre-independence Kuwisha.

'No, no, old chap, this is what you do: you smear Vaseline on the place where the eggs of the bloody *jipu* have burrowed their way in. Damn maggots then won't be able to breathe. Get 'em when they come out for air. And you sack the native, preferably after giving him a good talking to behind the *kia*.'

The OM beckoned the bar steward.

'Know what I mean?'

Furniver had no idea what the OM meant, although he could guess. A *kia* was the southern African term for the hut at the bottom of Europeans' gardens, which housed their cook and gardener. He knew that much; and he suspected that a 'talking to' might not involve much talking. He decided not to ask. Life was complicated enough.

The Oldest Member took a swig from the gin and tonic that had just been delivered, and patted Furniver on the knee.

'You're sound. Sound chap. Not like some we get here. Bunch of left-wing tossers. Word of advice. Don't go round broadcasting your views. Keep them in the family, so to speak. Let off steam over a G and T with me. Not popular with the local Johnnies. As for the bloody aid workers . . .'

The Oldest Member stood up, shook Furniver warmly by the hand and tottered off, muttering to himself:

'Bloody good idea, nonetheless, damn sensible. Improve their ironing, that's for sure . . .'

Furniver had another scratch. It was time for action.

13

'Only dogs can tell the difference between hyenas and jackals'

Hardwick Hardwicke's initial impressions of Kuwisha were far from favourable. The World Bank president watched the billboards and hoardings slip by on the journey from the first meeting at the central bank back to their city centre hotel.

If the advertisements for patent medicines were any indication, Kuwisha was a nation beset by headaches and malaria, intestinal worms and thin blood, vitamin deficiencies, and an unpleasant variety of liver ailments and kidney problems, while the skins of its citizens were either too dry or too dark. The cures on offer included petroleum jelly and skin lightening creams, pills and potions that would enrich your blood, beers and stouts that would improve your sexual prowess, and soft drinks that would provide access to a world of suave and handsome young men surrounded by attractive women.

Hardwicke nudged Fingers, and pointed out one particularly lurid poster.

'That's your problem, Fingers.' He guffawed. 'That's why you sleep so much. You've got worms!'

He and Fingers had been met at the airport by Marcus Reuttman, the Bank's resident representative in Kuwisha, whose three-year term was coming to an end, and whisked away to the Intercontinental Hotel in a black Mercedes provided by the Ministry of Finance. The meeting with President

Nduka was next, confirmed at the last minute. There was no time to lose.

As they drove Reuttman outlined the programme that had to be crammed into less than forty-eight hours: apart from the meeting with the president, finance ministry officials and sessions with local World Bank staff, there would be a visit to a pilot housing project in Kireba which was intended to be the start of a massive upgrading exercise, final negotiations on a $300m infrastructure loan, and possibly a press conference before departure.

Hardwicke read the draft, prepared by Fingers, now wide awake, of what would be his main speech during the visit.

Kuwisha, Hardwicke believed, provided the opportunity to establish a test case, to create an African precedent. The meeting with President Nduka was expected to be the highlight of his east African tour, and he was confident that it would mark the start of a new, frank and constructive relationship between Kuwisha and the Bank. But he was determined not to come across as an easy touch.

'The Bank is not a bountiful provider; it is not an infinite source of funds; nor does it have a monopoly of ideas,' Hardwicke was due to say.

'If anything, we are a catalyst, a supporter of fresh strategies, drawn up after consultation and debate . . . For many years, Kireba has been seen as a symbol of what is wrong . . . yet it can be seen as an example of hope . . . empowerment of civil society . . . citizens an inspiration of how people who are poor in resources but rich in ideas, can aim for the stars . . .'

Hardwicke paused, his marker pen in hand.

He turned to the man who had again fallen asleep in the adjacent seat in the back of the car, breathing heavily through part-open mouth, and nudged him in the ribs.

'What's this, Fingers: ". . . can aim for the stars"? Sounds like bullshit to me.'

Fingers shifted his position, and opened his eyes.

'Bit of poetry,' said Fingers. 'Take it out if you don't like it.'

Hardwicke turned to the itinerary for his visit.

'Kireba pilot housing project . . . Meet Mboya Boys United football team . . . remind me, will you? Who the hell are the Mboya Boys?'

The Mboya Boys United Football Club was more commonly known with varying degrees of fear, envy and admiration as the Mboya Boys. They had taken their name from a Kenyan politician, Tom Odhiambo Mboya, a young and articulate trade unionist who seemed to represent the best of a new generation of African leaders, but who had been assassinated in 1969, before he reached the age of forty.

No-one seemed sure just how the boys fastened on the name Mboya. Lucy had quizzed Ntoto while the boy was having a mango juice and a fresh bread roll baked by Charity, during a lazy Sunday morning.

'Tell me, Titus, why the name Mboya?'

Her curiosity had irritated Ntoto. He did not like being called Titus for a start. He played dumb, pretending not to have heard.

Lucy appealed to Charity.

'Tell him to talk, to answer me.'

'If he does not want to talk, he will not talk, and I cannot make him talk.'

Ntoto stood silently, and shot Charity a grateful look.

'You can show her.'

Charity disappeared into the back of *Harrods* and emerged with a plastic bag that contained Ntoto and Rutere's most precious possessions, and handed it to Titus.

He returned it.

'You show her,' he said, looking at his feet.

Charity pulled out a creased and grubby local newspaper article, a photo of Nelson Mandela cut out of a magazine, and

109

a black and white photo of a man with a smiling, chubby face. She handed the cutting to Lucy.

On a continent with few heroes, Mandela and Mboya were the boys' role models.

The Mboya Boys Club had been created for one reason – the boys' passion for football.

It had been the initiative of Titus Ntoto, in order to qualify for membership of the Kireba football league, brainchild of a young US marine captain, who spent many of his leisure hours working in the slum during his posting to Kuwisha.

Access to the league cost nothing. Nor could it be bought with ngwee. But – and here was the ingenious feature – teams had to earn a certain number of community service points, starting afresh each year, if they wanted to keep up their membership. The points system had been so designed that unless a team took part in at least one community event, such as clearing rubbish, they would be unable to qualify.

There were now thirty teams, and three leagues, serving the 1000 or so boys and girls who had signed up. Its assets were modest: a dozen footballs, a handful of referees' whistles, and – for use in the league finals only – a goal net and two sets of kit, stored for safety in the clinic run by Charity Mupanga's cousin, Mercy.

When membership of the league was first proposed at a gang meeting, it was a matter that threatened to divide the boys. None of them had any relish for the point-scoring tasks that membership required – such as clearing the rubbish, or digging out sections of the stream that served as a sewer. No-one was more sceptical than Ntoto himself, but nevertheless he decided that the matter would have to be settled by discussion.

A hundred yards or so from the water pipe in which Ntoto, Rutere, and many of the boys had set up home was what, at first sight, looked like a mound of earth, some thirty metres in diameter. It was not so much earth, as layers of rubbish that had settled over the years. In the middle were the rusting hulks of an old bus, its rusted frame like the skeleton of a beached whale. Two cars, stripped of their parts, were more recent adornments, and one of them could not have been there more than two or three years. The bus now served as a rudimentary clubhouse, while the cars helped conceal a small lined pit, dug by the boys, in which they kept their only football, a collection of football boots, not all of them matching pairs, a large plastic bottle which was filled with water for the half-time drinks, a radio-cassette player, and a handful of tapes.

On the day membership of the league had been discussed it had been too hot to sit inside the bus, but the speakers climbed onto its top and from this makeshift podium made their case for or against joining. Initially the majority of the Mboya Boys had held out against applying for membership, but as time wore on, it became clear that the mood was changing. The first season of the scheme, when the boys had looked on enviously from the sidelines, had proved a great success; and as more leagues were formed, and the grand football final approached, the lure of membership overcame any dislike for community chores.

Ten so-called 'community points' were required for full membership, and the Mboya Boys soon qualified, earning six in one weekend when they cleared 100 metres of pathway along the side of the evil-smelling black rivulet that ran through Kireba.

It had been during that initial debate on the merits of membership that Cyrus Rutere first came to Ntoto's attention. The boys had been divided, and Ntoto himself was uncertain. But when Rutere put forward a well reasoned case for joining, he tipped the balance. Ntoto did not hesitate, took his advice, and joined up. From then on, the two boys forged a friendship, and

111

Rutere, shrewd, cautious and pragmatic, though inclined to the superstitious, became the equivalent of consigliere to Ntoto's don.

There was one other item on that day's agenda: how to deal with the newcomer to Kireba, Edward Furniver. The Mboya Boys had nearly split over the issue, almost equally divided between those who wanted to steal the computer the white man foolishly kept in his office, and those who advocated knocking him on the head and snatching his briefcase. Titus Ntoto thought both ideas had merit, but feelings were running so deep among the Mboya Boys that unless he found a third way, a damaging division seemed inevitable.

It was then that Rutere had made the suggestion that may well have saved Furniver's bacon.

'It is my turn to speak,' said Rutere.

'Stand up, stand up,' cried one boy in the audience, a cruel jibe at Rutere's modest height.

'True, I am small, and nothing can change this; you are tall,' replied Rutere with dignity. 'Nothing can change that. But I am clever, and nothing can change this . . .' He paused. 'And you are stupid . . .'

As repartee went it was not sharp, but his infuriated tormentor had to be restrained from punching Rutere.

'Let Rutere speak,' said Titus quietly. The response was immediate, prompting Rutere to wonder whether the stories he had heard about Ntoto were true.

Rutere seized the opportunity.

'We want to play football, yes? If you want to play football you must have a team.'

The boys nodded their agreement.

'And if you play proper football, in a team, you must play other teams. But only Kireba will play Kireba boys, for other places are afraid of us. So we must play in this Kireba league. But if we play proper football, in a proper league, we need uniforms. And we have no money for uniforms, or for boots.'

Rutere warmed to his theme. 'Remember when we last played against ourselves?'

There was a rumble of acknowledgement. Who could forget the fight that had broken out during the game between two pickup sides, when the ref had given a penalty? Who in their heart of hearts could blame him, unable to distinguish a member of one team from the other, dressed as they were in the same tattered rags?

'What is the answer?' Rutere had asked rhetorically.

'We must ask this white man, Furniver, to help us. He must give us a loan, and we can buy twelve white shorts and twelve red T-shirts for the team. And we will pay back with community work.'

His argument won the day. Furniver had responded positively, and repayment terms were generous even by the bank's standards, for Furniver had found a way to reduce the cost of the loan by writing off a third of it as 'Publicity and Public Relations'.

When the Mboya Boys team next took the field in their new kit, across the front of each T-shirt were the initials KPCB, and on the back was the slogan 'Save with the People'.

Rutere not only won the day. He won over his tall tormentor, who just happened to be the striker for the Mboya Boys football team that was to win the league cup that season.

The car carrying Hardwicke and Fingers slowed down.

'Traffic lights on the blink again,' said Reuttman, the Bank's resident representative. 'Probably another power cut. Sooner they sign the loan agreement for the new power plant, the better.'

Within a few yards of the lights, the car had crawled to a halt.

If Fingers thought he could go back to sleep, the briefing completed, he was mistaken. Hardwicke looked up from the file on the meeting to come, and nudged him in the ribs.

'I see that Nduka's overspending on defence again. Time to clamp down,' said Hardwicke.

Fingers decided not to respond immediately. Instead he wriggled the little finger of his right hand in his right ear, frowning slightly as he did so. The intrusion made an almost imperceptible moist noise, concluding with a soft plop as he withdrew the digit.

Hardwicke tried to ignore the provocation.

'What can we call the latest loan?' he asked. 'I gather that the president insists on going through with that arms order. Says it's to put down the rebels. If we give him the benefit of the doubt we need to call it something respectable.'

Fingers wondered whether to tell his boss that the defence order included helicopters with night sights, something the country's air force chief had lusted after ever since seeing the equipment on display at Farnborough air show. This was not the time to upset Hardwicke, he decided. He thought for a few seconds.

'Let's call it "pre-humanitarian assistance".'

The Bank president nodded. Fingers really did have a way with words.

'Now leave your ears alone. Or do it in private. Bloody disgusting, the noise it makes . . .'

Fingers ignored him, and his digit proceeded to explore the recesses of his right ear, while working with his other hand on a news release for the press.

'Have you got that statement ready?' Hardwicke asked.

'Five minutes, Hardwick. Five minutes.'

Balance. As always it was a matter of balance. If Hardwicke were seen to be too tough, he would be accused of being insensitive to the country's plight; if he failed to condemn the government for its failure to introduce economic reforms, he would be accused of going soft.

By the standards of Fingers' profession, it was a reasonable task.

Fingers owed his nickname to his speed and dexterity on the keyboard of his Olivetti Lettera 32 portable typewriter, which he had been forced to leave behind in favour of the ubiquitous laptop computer. But his fame was built on more than digital dexterity: he was a master of the ambiguous word or phrase, a wizard of the weasel-word vocabulary of development. He had achieved renown within Bank circles when, during an earlier visit, he had coped with the sensitivities of Kuwisha officials while overseeing a hard-hitting economic report on the country.

The title – *Kuwisha: Seizing the Moment, Realising the Opportunity* – gave no hint of the bleak contents.

The task that now faced Fingers was equally tricky. Kuwisha remained a loyal ally of Washington, and at the core of Western policy in the region. The country had had military agreements with the US and Britain since independence, provided a reliable base for international aid operations, and several United Nations agencies had their headquarters in the capital. In short, Kuwisha, for all its faults, was useful to the West in general, and to Washington and London in particular. It was most definitely not a country the World Bank wanted to offend, an island of stability in a troubled part of the continent.

The unavoidable main issue to be addressed was corruption. Kuwisha had become – despite its stability – synonymous with sleaze. But this time the Bank was confident that it had leverage. Hardwicke was certain that he – or rather his staff – had finally caught the current administration with its hands in the till.

The most brazen of the various scams involved the president

himself. It was not merely the fact that he had acquired a presidential jet using state funds; he had paid at least $10m over the going rate, most of which, it seemed, had ended up in his own pocket, or in the coffers of companies controlled by his family. The president had also connived in, or was the main beneficiary of, a series of deals in which the owners had been strong-armed into selling their businesses, ranging from oil distribution to vehicle franchises.

The latest example of the president's seemingly insatiable hunger for money was a series of land sales on the country's coast. The ploy was simple. Nduka had first signed an agreement giving a foreign-owned company the right to establish a prawn breeding and processing plant on a stretch of coastline north of the coastal resort of Walindi. But no sooner had this been done, than a series of counter-claims emerged from the land registry office. Had the claims been filed by ordinary, God-fearing citizens, determined to win compensation for loss of property that had been in the family for generations, sympathy would have been abundant. But a cursory investigation revealed that the claimants were, with barely an exception, top officials of the ruling party, officers in Kuwisha's armed forces, and members of President Nduka's family, including his son Albert.

If all this was not enough, the Brits were hinting that they had Nduka on the ropes over some maize deal, which they hoped would be sorted out during Hardwicke's visit.

Just before Hardwicke was about to announce that the five minutes were up, Fingers was ready.

'At a time when Kuwisha is fighting against the terrible impact of the floods that have left tens of thousands of people without homes or food, the World Bank is at your side . . .

'But there is a high price to pay at times like this for weak institutions and inadequate policies . . .

'Reform is vital – however hard it seems . . .'

116

'Our message is strong and unequivocal,' the statement concluded.

'If Kuwisha and its leaders set their development agenda, and take the lead in implementing it, the World Bank will be a full partner in their efforts.'

For anyone familiar with the code word vocabulary of the Bank, the message was clear. No government could emerge unscathed from the climatic battering that Kuwisha had experienced, but the country was also the victim of mismanagement.

'If we work together, as partners, Kuwisha can at last realise its enormous potential.'

He was particularly pleased with the way in which he had managed to slip in the word 'potential'. It was short of the kick in the pants that Kuwisha's critics wanted, but certainly not the endorsement sought by President Nduka.

14

'Foolish is the mujiba [herd boy] who eats the
marula berries'

For David Podmore the visit by Hardwick Hardwicke could
not have been better timed. Over the past few weeks the First
Secretary at the British High Commission had been trying to
get hold of Mayor Guchu to pass on a discreet, unofficial and
heartfelt message of concern about maize shipments, but with
no success.

The mayor had made himself unavailable for good reason.
He suspected, correctly, that the High Commission was
attempting to interfere in what he considered was a private
business matter. Some large orders for maize, Kuwisha's staple
food, had been placed by a commodity company with British
links, and in which the mayor had a substantial financial stake.

There was nothing necessarily wrong with this.

Kuwisha's 'food deficit' had always been filled by maize
imported on commercial terms. But Podmore had not been
able to trace the shipments after they reached Kuwisha's main
port. According to his sources at the docks, the maize had definitely been off-loaded. And a few days later it reached depots
at various points around the country. But in the process, no
customs duty appeared to have been paid. Awkward questions
were now being raised, and the visiting World Bank team was
expected to put the matter on their agenda when they saw
President Nduka.

Podmore had raised the problem at the weekly meeting of senior staff under the chairmanship of the high commissioner.

The high commissioner, a man on his last posting and whose political instincts were sharpened by his determination that he would retire with a knighthood, listened closely as the first secretary set out his concerns.

'If this is the case,' concluded Podmore, 'and I stress if, there are grounds for bringing our concerns to the attention of the president. Through Guchu. Informally of course.'

'How much did you say was the difference?' the high commissioner asked, somewhat nervously, referring to the amount that would be saved by not paying customs duty.

'At least two, maybe three, million dollars,' said Podmore.

The high commissioner chewed his pencil. The amount was not, in the scale of these matters, particularly big. Under what passed for normal circumstances, it would probably not have attracted comment. It was the principle that mattered, and some principles mattered far more than others. Three million dollars just happened to be the amount that Britain's development ministry was donating towards the cost of the food Kuwisha would have to import.

To Podmore's delight, the high commissioner had given the go-ahead for him to make informal contact with Guchu. Since that meeting at the High Commission, the world price of maize had gone up significantly, and Podmore had calculated that the profit on the deal could be as much as $4–5m. Deduct the contributions to the ruling party election funds and payoffs along the line, those responsible would have a net profit, he reckoned, of around a million dollars.

The message Podmore needed to convey to Guchu was delicate but simple: it would be much appreciated if the margin on the deal could be reduced from the outrageous to the acceptable. The mayor's response would no doubt be predictable, though he would never say so in as many words.

An election was weeks away: where else did Mr Podmore think the ruling party's campaign funds would come from?

Approaching Guchu was easier said than done.

How, the diplomat wondered, could he deliver a stern but tactful message that in an informal way conveyed the concern of Her Majesty's Government about the maize deal from which Guchu was making an unacceptably high profit? It had to be a contrived meeting, discreet yet in a public place. Above all, it had to be deniable, for if the message, or warning, call it what you will, went unheeded or was bluntly rejected, HMG needed to have the option of claiming that it had all been a dreadful misunderstanding.

The excitement was too much for him, and he began pacing the room. His posterior seemed to have a life of its own, busy, energetic, distracted. Had it been a dog's tail, it would have been constantly wagging.

Podmore cursed the High Commission's air-conditioning system that made it impossible to open his office window, and blow the smoke from an illegal cigarette into the outside air. He flicked through the local papers, with their reports about the visit by Hardwicke to Kireba.

Suddenly the solution to the Guchu problem struck him.

'Got it!'

Podmore gave an involuntary shudder of satisfaction, in which his hindquarters quivered, rather like those of a neutered cat attempting to spray on the furniture.

'Got it!'

He did another dance around his desk. Panting after his exertion, Podmore pulled in his developing paunch, took a peek into the mirror above his desk, rearranged his thinning fair hair to cover his bald patch, and pulled his shoulders back.

By and large, David Podmore was pleased with what he saw.

*

Pearson made the short journey to Borrowdale, one of the capital's green and leafy suburbs where together with her dog Shango, Lucy Gomball lived. Its quaint English name had survived post-independence attempts to change it to something more in keeping with Africa, as indeed had the suburb itself. It had become a sanctuary both for the settlers who had decided to call themselves white Kuwisha, and for upper class, indigenous Kuwisha who had, unconsciously, become black Brits.

The dog was a Rhodesian ridgeback, but he was not pure bred. At some stage in his canine ancestry, a jackal or a street mongrel had contributed his or her genes to the murky pool that made up the dog. According to the local vet, this accounted for the khaki-coloured animal's low-slung hindquarters, his exceptionally powerful jaws, and above all, his uncertain temper.

Lucy, tall and lean as well as fair, had made her career with WorldFeed since her early twenties. She had been pursued ever since her arrival in Kuwisha nearly three years ago by a succession of admirers – journalists, diplomats and aid workers. But if there was a male who had a claim to Lucy's heart, it was Shango – reason enough for every contender for her hand to loathe the malevolent, yellow-eyed creature, invariably draped around her pink-toenailed feet, growling at whatever man who happened to be her current suitor. Some of Lucy's would-be partners had been driven to desperate measures. It was rumoured that Pearson's predecessor had tried to poison Shango, but the resilient animal had recovered, nursed back to health by a loving Lucy. Since then the cunning beast would accept food from no hand other than hers.

The house which doubled as WorldFeed's East African headquarters was a comparatively safe redoubt in a crime-plagued city, thanks to the twenty-four-hour-a-day presence of security guards at each and every gate, and the live-in domestic staff: gardeners who tended the rolling green lawns, and a house

121

steward who would hand down the job to his son, having first taught him how to water the gin, dilute the whisky, run the kitchen, and continue the long-running feud against the night security guard, who came from Somalia.

The term 'live-in' was not strictly correct, however. The 'domestics', as most expatriates called them, never stayed in the main house. They lived near, or adjacent to, the homes of their employers, often in a single room, at the end of the garden, tucked discreetly behind a short row of banana trees. The more fortunate ones had a toilet and shower attached, but most domestics had to make do with an outside tap.

Pearson parked on the gravel frontage, and greeted the gardener, who had snapped to attention and thrown a mock salute. The journalist was a familiar visitor, and the object of much ribald gossip among the staff, along the lines of did-he-or-didn't-he succeed in pressing his case.

'Not a chance,' sniffed the head steward, and he was right. Lucy Gomball felt much the same way about her many suitors and their sexual demands as President Nduka felt about the International Monetary Fund and the World Bank, and the reforms they tried to impose on Kuwisha: they were regarded as unwelcome intrusions on sovereignty, and invariably a messy business.

Both Lucy and the president realised they probably had to comply in the end, but had decided that it was best to hold out as long as possible. Even then, they were reluctant to complete the process. More often than not, they defaulted before the conclusion, only to start again after a decent interval, which allowed both sides to recover lost face.

Cecil Pearson sighed. Mug of coffee in hand and lust in his heart, he was sitting at the kitchen table in Lucy's home. He had as much success with Lucy as the IMF and the Bank were having with Kuwisha. And he was no nearer to resolving their relationship: neither he nor Lucy was sure whether they wanted it to survive his imminent departure from the country.

Perhaps there would be a chance for a heart-to-heart exchange later in the day. He took a sip of coffee, and ran a professional eye over the press release she had prepared.

'The people of Kireba are at serious and immediate risk from cholera following the unprecedented and unseasonal floods that have hit the region. At least 30 – mainly children – have died. Not only Kireba residents are threatened. Their neighbours in the city itself are vulnerable. Without a prompt and generous response from the international community the situation will deteriorate rapidly.'

It was dramatic, but not too specific. 'At risk' and 'vulnerable' could mean anything. For Cecil, however, attuned to the needs of the *Financial News*, the plight of Kireba was marginal. He had to concede that cholera gave the story an edge that had previously been lacking. But the real news, as far as he and his paper were concerned, was the visit of Hardwick Hardwicke and the World Bank team.

It was still too early for Lucy to start ringing around the foreign press corps, and she listened tolerantly to Cecil's explanations of the budgetary fiddles and irregularities the Bank would have to investigate. The subject seemed to give him the intellectual equivalent of an erection, but left her cold and indifferent.

Cecil tried to explain his excitement.

'It's really important, Luce . . .'

It was not a good start. Lucy disliked any abbreviation of her name, and she had told Cecil so. But time was short, and she let it pass.

'If I'm right about the overspending, they'll miss the first quarter target by at least ten per cent. But the agreement with the IMF makes it quite clear: the deficit has to be reduced to at least three per cent of GDP . . .'

In this mood the man was unstoppable. Mounted on his favourite hobbyhorse, he could ride it indefinitely. There was only one thing for it, decided Lucy. She got up from her desk and sat alongside him on the couch, the emergency appeal in one hand, pen in the other.

'What do you think of the changes I made,' she asked.

Lucy leant forward, as desirable as she was deferential, maximising her cleavage beneath the soft cotton fabric of her WorldFeed T-shirt:

'Is there anything you'd like to insert?'

The combination of Lucy's breasts and Kuwisha's budget anomalies was too much for Cecil. He stifled a groan as his flesh began to succumb, and his mind struggled to engage with Kuwisha's impending financial crisis.

Just as he was about to make an advance, there was the sound of gravel crunching as a car drew up outside the front door.

'The hacks are here,' Lucy said brightly, getting up from the couch.

'Be a sweetheart, and make more coffee.'

WorldFeed's exciting news had spread through Kuwisha's foreign press corps as quickly as diarrhoea in a refugee camp. Journalists began drifting in. Some left as soon as they got the press release; some lounged around, gossiping; others needed a fill, which Lucy provided.

Pearson looked on with admiration as he watched an old hand in the aid business go to work. She really was wonderfully persuasive. So vivid was her description of the cases of cholera in Kireba and the implications for Kuwisha that even experienced journalists began to feel a twinge of sympathy. And when she gave the latest death toll, carefully distinguishing between WorldFeed estimates and government figures, any doubters were won over.

All conceded that it was indeed a decent story. What was

more, it would be cheap and easy to cover. Above all, it was a feel-good story – one that brought together foreign correspondents and aid workers, diplomats and politicians, all happy to focus their energies and talents on an event that gave a purpose in their lives.

While Cecil ferried coffee to his colleagues, Lucy went through the list of resident foreign correspondents, the phone tucked between ear and shoulder to keep her hands free, a pen in the one and a notepad in the other.

She had begun with the news agencies, ringing the bureau chiefs at their homes: Reuters, Associated Press, Agence France Press, followed by the BBC, and CNN. Then came the main British papers: *Guardian*, *Telegraph*, *Times*, *Independent*. Finally she cajoled the UK Sunday papers and the US outlets: the *Sunday Times*, *Observer*, the *New York Times*, *Washington Post*, *Time* and *Newsweek*.

Lucy managed, effortlessly, to make each correspondent feel they had been singled out for special treatment. Each put down the phone with a warm glow of professional pride, for she had hinted that they had been among the first to be told that the cholera outbreak was now official, a tribute to their remarkable track record of objectivity, commitment, and compassion.

It was not an easy day for the correspondents, for there was tough competition for their attention: news of a refugee crisis in Congo had just broken. A chartered flight was due to fly out with the first batch of food parcels mid-afternoon to Kisangani. Renewed fighting between Ugandan and Rwandan soldiers had led to the breakdown of the latest peace pact. If the aid agencies were to be believed, residents were being slaughtered by the score.

The United Nations refugee programme was offering places on a charter flight to the city, which would give the journalists the opportunity to report on the horrors at first hand.

'Bastards,' muttered Lucy, as one call ended. But it was not clear to Pearson whether she was referring to the perpetrators of the killings in Kisangani, the UN agency that was offering the flights, or the journalists who decided to take the charter rather than cover the Kireba cholera story.

She pulled out all the stops.

Everything any hack could desire would be laid on, she promised. The outing would begin at the clinic in Kireba, where with notebooks in hand, the stench of excrement in their nostrils, and photo-opportunities galore, and escorted by the duty members of the Mboya Boys football team, they would blaze a fact-finding trail through the slum.

Those for whom Lucy's original press statement did not provide sufficient grist for their mill could turn for inspiration to three backgrounders: analyses written by the WorldFeed staff, usually distributed on a non-attributable basis. One set out the history of cholera in Kuwisha; another calculated that Kuwisha's external debt repayments was the equivalent of building five new hospitals a year – omitting to point out that this was an entirely notional calculation, as the country had not paid its debt for years; while a third inveighed against the folly of privatising state-owned water companies – although failing to point out that the state service was so bad that people already paid independent suppliers for clean water.

A lazy hack, or a busy hack, or an ignorant but cunning hack, could, with a modicum of judicious subbing, either turn them into a thoughtful three-part series on a health crisis in the region, or use them as the core of an authoritative 800-word profile of Kuwisha.

And like the best of tour representatives, Lucy's tone had an impressive range, sometimes the jovial and jocular, switching easily to the disciplinarian, a firm but patient nurse or a head-mistress demonstrating that she would not tolerate the slackers in the Lower Fourth.

Some of the writers who had early deadlines began tapping

away on their laptops, then and there, as they sat around Lucy's kitchen table. They were preparing their colour pieces, which would be moving accounts of the horrors in Kireba. If they were to make the first editions, they would have to file their stories by lunch at the latest. There was no time to lose. The guts of the story were in the briefing papers after all. And it was no problem to provide vivid well-written accounts of squalor and death, for this was their stock in trade. But they had to put at least a foot in the slum, or stay silent when after-dinner conversation turned to comparisons of Soweto and Kireba. Facts were not necessarily sacred, but woe betide the hack who was caught out faking a dateline.

Hunched over their computer keyboards, the hacks worked their magic.

'A hidden holocaust . . .' said the *Daily Telegraph*, as if to him-self. He had been among the first to arrive and looked like being the last to leave.

Lucy was in mid-phone call, but she was too old a hand to be caught. Out of the corner of her eye, she saw Pearson smirking.

'Hold on a mo . . .'

She cupped her hand over the mouthpiece, and gave the *Telegraph* a cool blue look.

'Who says?'

'Well, not WorldFeed, of course . . .'

The *Telegraph*'s voice trailed off in the hope that Lucy would contradict him, but she remained silent.

'NGOs?' he offered.

'Foreign or local?'

'Come on Lucy . . . it has to be foreign, preferably British.'

Lucy would not budge.

'Nope.'

'So no "Hidden holocaust, say WorldFeed"?'

'Nope.'

'What about potential holocaust? Be a sport.'

'I'll phone you back,' Lucy told her caller, replaced the phone, and gave the *Telegraph* her full attention.

'No. Not according to WorldFeed, not according to British NGOs. Find someone else for your source. We made arses of ourselves in Congo a few years ago by overplaying the refugee story, and you were one of the buggers who encouraged us,' said Lucy.

'It was your fault . . .' he began.

Lucy decided to put him in his place.

'I know you think that aid agencies just shovel up the shit as we follow the elephant. God knows, we don't do a perfect job, or even a good job, and sometimes we do a downright bad job, for all sorts of reasons.

'But just look at the damage done by those bloody hulking elephants, tramping across Africa.

'You can still see where they fought. Moscow and Washington, battling each other during the Cold War; and now it is just one bloody enormous elephant, but doing as much damage as a herd. And the more damage the elephant does, the more cleaning up we have to do. But don't blame us. Blame the elephants! Blame the idiots in charge of the bloody circus.'

Lucy drew breath: 'At least we are not the clowns,' she said contemptuously.

The room fell silent.

The *Daily Mail* stringer broke the ice:

'About the holocaust line, Lucy . . . could we say "scores dead, hundreds in peril"?'

'"Fears mount, scores at risk." Best I can do,' she said briskly.

'. . . "Official death toll climbing, hundreds at risk, warned Lucy Gomball, WF res rep"?'

'Fine,' said Lucy.

'Hadn't finished,' said the *Telegraph*. '"Hundreds at risk, warned Lucy Gomball, WF res rep. Quote: Kireba is a time-bomb . . ."'

'For God's sake,' said Lucy, 'can't you get the bloody World Bank to say that?'

There was no time to lose. The first meeting between the World Bank team and officials from Kuwisha's ministry of finance was later that morning. Just as Hardwicke and Fingers were due to leave their hotel rooms for State House, the phone in the living room of their suite rang.

Fingers listened impatiently as the *Telegraph* ran through a list of questions. They were easy enough to handle – Lucy had already briefed him on the cholera story, and Hardwicke had agreed to put in an appearance at the Kireba clinic.

He covered the mouthpiece of the phone, and called out to Hardwicke.

'Can we live with "Kireba is a timebomb, say World Bank officials"?'

'As long as it is "officials" – but no names, no names . . . we're going to be late. Let's go,' said Hardwicke.

'No names,' echoed Fingers down the phone line.

'The boss does not like that language. Not constructive. And put it in context . . . Hardwick Hardwicke, new World Bank president, his first visit to the region etcetera, will tour Kireba tomorrow, opportunity to inspect progress on new road and the pilot housing scheme. Clean water, roof over head, warm place to sleep, dry place to crap, etc. Otherwise Kireba will become a timebomb. OK . . . Yes . . . it's a quote . . . no, certainly not from me, by a World Bank official.'

Fingers was about to put the phone down, but his professional instincts intervened.

'And if I see any reference to the Bank and "dry places to crap", let me make one thing clear: neither you nor anyone from your paper will be invited on the Mauritius freebie.'

He slammed the phone down.

'What a wanker! God save us. Timebomb. I ask you . . . it went off years ago. He wouldn't know if a bomb exploded under his arse, let alone if it exploded in Kireba.'

Hardly had he replaced the receiver when the phone rang again. This time it was Pearson, fretting about the state of the talks. Since he was the only journalist in town that gave a fig for the outcome, and wrote for the only paper that would report the story, Fingers went to great lengths to reassure him.

'Give me your mobile number, and I'll ring you, Cecil . . . promise.'

He grabbed his jacket and his toothpicks, and followed Hardwicke out of the room.

15

'He who hears the hyena bark will be attacked
by the leopard'

A few hours later Fingers was looking back on what had been a long and trying morning. He sat in his hotel room and attempted to draw up a press statement that would express Hardwicke's strong feelings, while remaining within the bounds of convention.

'Kuwisha's formidable challenges,' he wrote, 'are matched only by its huge potential.'

Every now and then, thought Fingers, you had to tell it like it is. And that sentence, by God, said everything. Fingers lit up a cigarillo, took a deep draw, and studied the words on the screen. No. He wouldn't get away with that. Anyway, it was unprofessional. Fingers took a second draw, and looked gloomily out of the window, with its view of the city's Anglican Cathedral.

The first sign of the trouble that was to come had been the warmth of the president's greeting earlier that day, when Hardwicke and the rest of the World Bank team arrived at State House. It continued to go downhill from there.

Even Hardwicke acknowledged that they had seriously underestimated the man, and there was no comfort in the fact that they were far from the first to do so.

Fingers pulled out from the file on his desk Pearson's profile of the president, written for the *Financial News*' special report on Kuwisha.

Dr Josiah Nduka, the self-proclaimed *Ngwazi* or Conqueror of All Hens, had begun his political career as plain Josiah Nduka, named by his devoutly Christian parents after the biblical character that had provided the name of the mission school at which their son was educated.

The longer he stayed in office, the more frequently Nduka's official portrait appeared; and the longer his title, the harsher his regime became. His face appeared on the bank notes, looking thirty years younger than he was; he never appeared in public without Homburg and dark glasses, flywhisk in one hand, in the other an ornately carved ebony walking stick on which a snake curled from the top to the bottom. According to the profile, he had imposed a mixture of Victorian values with a dash of voodoo, and while it was not a formula which had any success on the economic front, it had left the people of Kuwisha in his thrall.

He never ceased to remind them that he had enjoyed a classical education, having won an open scholarship to Kuwisha's leading school in the days when it was modelled on Eton, and prepared its pupils for an Oxbridge education – although in the president's case, he chose to go to Edinburgh, claiming that he preferred the city's climate.

He was openly dismissive of cabinet colleagues who lacked his education, and he was contemptuous of those who could not exchange epigrams in Latin. The transition from Nduka the democrat to Nduka, authoritarian political dinosaur, was complete by the end of his second five-year term in office, by which time he had started to accumulate the trappings of the international respectability he craved. He was awarded a doctorate by his alma mater, Edinburgh, and a second one by an obscure southern US college.

Nduka never missed a summit of Commonwealth heads of government. Pearson had included a splendid quote in the profile: 'Commonwealth conferences are the only occasion I can debate with my equals,' he once quipped.

'Commonwealth conferences are the only time the president's equals can speak up and not get arrested,' rejoined an editorial in the independent daily, the *Kuwisha Times*. The profile noted that the paper's editor was detained two days later. Allegations that he had been trading on the black market would take 'many months' to investigate, said the chief of police.

Yes, the president was a formidable adversary, Fingers acknowledged as he explored his ears, and sucked his teeth after lengthy probing with a wooden pick. This ritual over, he made a fresh start, preparing the communiqué that would be released when the talks with Kuwisha officials had been concluded.

He pecked out the words on his laptop with a stubby, nicotine-stained forefinger with surprising speed. There was no time to lose. A technical committee of the two sides was due to meet soon, and before that took place, the Bank had to put down a marker. It was after all Hardwicke's first visit. He could not afford to look soft:

'Promise and challenge in Kuwisha . . .' he wrote.

That would show them, thought Fingers, that would really show 'em!

From President Nduka's standpoint the talks had been a great success. A television crew from the state-owned national station was there for the arrival of the Bank team, as was a photographer and journalist from the *Kuwisha Daily News*, the daily paper owned by the ruling party. To anyone familiar with the ways of the president, their presence amounted to a clear warning: something was afoot.

As the television camera rolled, and the photographer snapped away, President Nduka embraced Hardwicke, and grasped his victim's right hand with both of his. He then replaced his expression of warm welcome with one of immense solemnity, and made an announcement to camera.

'I want to welcome Mr Hardwick Hardwicke, president of the World Bank, and his colleague Mr James Adams. Welcome to Kuwisha.

'And Mr Reuttman, who is soon to leave us,' the president added, dismissively.

'We have a lot to talk about this morning. Mr Hardwicke has a busy schedule, which will include a visit to my neighbours, the hard-working people of Kireba. But it is good that we will talk. I will remind our friend from the Bank that we were one of the first governments to welcome greater efforts to ensure transparency, although here in Kuwisha we prefer to speak frankly. No "transparency" nonsense for us! We call it corruption. We must end corruption. We are very concerned about corruption.'

He pronounced it 'corrup-shun', with a pause between the two syllables, and the emphasis on the last, like an old-fashioned sergeant major drilling new recruits.

'And I have some very important things to say. First, I must thank Mr Hardwicke for responding so promptly to my request to come to Kuwisha. We know he is a very busy man. Second, I want him to know what we are doing to tackle this evil, this corruption.'

He beamed at Hardwicke, who had barely been able to contain his irritation. Far from encouraging his visit, the president had resisted until the last minute. As for tackling corruption! Nduka had been stalling for months . . .

The president then proceeded to take the wind out of the World Bank sails, announcing a series of ministerial sackings, cabinet promotions and demotions, beginning with the news that the former leader of the opposition had been appointed chairman of Kuwisha's anti-corruption authority.

The matter of the missing petroleum levy was also dealt with by Nduka. Among the ministers sacked was the secretary of state for feeder roads, who had diverted the levy with the assistance of the minister of works, who had been appointed ambassador to Zambia.

Nduka held back, however, on the alleged involvement of his son-in-law in the unusually costly contract to service the Vosper patrol boats bought from the United Kingdom. It had been on the agenda for the talks, but the matter was postponed at the request of the British high commissioner, who urged caution pending the outcome of an interdepartmental investigation in Whitehall, and – though he didn't say this, the result of an upcoming by-election in the north of England constituency where the boats had been built.

Nor had the high commissioner thought it sensible to ask Hardwicke to raise the maize contract. That, too, was being pursued through what he called 'appropriate channels'. And it was not the time or place to discuss the presidential jet. It was far from clear just how much had gone in commission payments to the maker's own sales staff.

Nduka beamed benignly into the camera.

'Now we must now get down to work. But I know that the president of the World Bank wants to say a few words.'

Hardwicke stumbled through a few platitudes. By sacking three cabinet ministers and promising an immediate inquiry by the newly constituted anti-corruption committee, the president had effectively pre-empted his complaints.

Together they walked in through the main State House entrance, under the arch of elephants' tusks, yellowed with age, and past the stuffed lion, shot by a governor general in the early days of British rule.

The last the television viewers saw of them on their screens that night was the two men walking, still hand in hand, past the courtyard and the water fountain, about to enter the president's study. Fingers, Reuttman and Nduka's private secretary brought up the rear, a deferential five paces behind them.

Once out of camera range, the president had dropped

Hardwicke's hand, his demeanour changing abruptly. The president was usually punctilious in observing the courtesies of these occasions. This time, however, he abruptly excused himself, saying that he had to conclude a previous appointment.

Nduka had then kept Hardwicke waiting in the State House ante-room for a carefully calculated twenty minutes, long enough to put the visitor in his place, yet just short of being blatantly rude – but only by the minute or two before Hardwicke's short temper would blow.

Nduka had ordered further refinements calculated to make the wait uncomfortable. The air-conditioning clanked to a halt five minutes after Hardwicke had been shown into the State House ante-room, with its red velveteen armchairs and heavy drape curtain that ensured that not the faintest flicker of light – or fresh air – could penetrate the room, or enhance the dull glow of the 40-watt bulbs in the ornate chandeliers.

In a final turn of the screw, Nduka had also instructed the duty steward to serve bottles of the sickly-sweet, local orangeade, which had been left in the Kuwisha sun for several minutes. When the meeting finally got under way, Nduka had run rings around the hot, unhappy American. He wasted no time on courtesies, immediately set out in detail the anti-corruption measures he had announced earlier, and continued on the offensive.

'Now tell me, Mr President, what is the new fashion you wish my people to follow? Gender? Environment? Intermediate technology, or is it perhaps appropriate technology? Where is the next boost for Kuwisha's economy going to come from? Let me guess. Micro lending, small business, and stimulation of the informal sector? I doubt that it will be in the form of fair international prices for our tea and coffee.'

Nduka was getting into his stride.

Fingers, invariably the note taker at these meetings, scribbled furiously.

'Improved management capacity, or irrigation schemes? Good governance? Transparency? Multi-party politics? Institution building?'

Next in line for the president's vitriol was Henry Reuttman, who had learnt that morning that his posting to Lagos had been confirmed.

'And you, Mr Resident Representative, I am told you are leaving us. Three years here, and you are leaving us,' he said grimly.

'I was born in Kuwisha, and I studied abroad, and I travelled abroad. I have been in politics for thirty-three years. And I am still learning, each day I am learning. And you are leaving after three years, like nearly every other aid worker and diplomat. It's the three-year cycle. The first year, you people are too optimistic, the second year you start to learn, the third year you decide we're no good, and then you go, for home leave, and then on, somewhere else, to another posting.

'I remember that man Welensky, Sir Roy Welensky, who was Prime Minister of the Federation, the Federation of Northern and Southern Rhodesia and Nyasaland, which I helped destroy,' he said with satisfaction.

'The federation of these three countries we now call Zambia, Zimbabwe and Malawi, was bad for the black man. So I destroyed it. And I was called the Destroyer of Federation – DOF.'

The president grew nostalgic as he remembered these political tales from the past.

'I was no friend, no friend at all, of Welensky, but he said one wise thing. I did not like Welensky, but he said one wise thing,' Nduka repeated.

'Welensky did not like expatriates, people from Britain. They said they loved Africa, loved Aaafricaaa,' said Nduka, simpering. He then gave a contemptuous snort.

'They loved the lifestyle, not Africa; they came to work in

the colonies but left their hearts in England. Welensky, he refused to encourage this. "I want civil servants who go home every night," he said, "not every three years."'

Nduka chuckled.

'I too, want civil servants, technical experts, advisers and consultants, who go home every night, not every year, or leave permanently every two or three years. Kuwisha, poor Kuwisha.'

He took a sip of mineral water, and invited Hardwicke to drink his fizzy orangeade.

'There are more Europeans in Africa today than there were at independence,' said Nduka.

'Excluding South Africa, of course, where the whites seem to be running away. But these new Europeans are second-raters, Mr President of the World Bank. You send us second-raters, and you send your clever, spoilt children, who treat Kuwisha like they treat Africa, as an adventure play-ground.'

Nduka then switched tack, challenging the accuracy of the Bank's figures on inflation with a masterly exposition on the impact of the velocity of money supply on the prices of basic foodstuffs in high density townships. Fingers had to admit that he had a point. However, since the net result was that inflation was running at an annual rate of twenty-seven per cent rather than thirty-one per cent, it was of limited import. But by the time Dr Nduka, whose Edinburgh degree in econometrics had been hailed as one of the best for a generation, had concluded his opening peroration, Hardwicke was a beaten man.

Nduka brushed aside Hardwicke's questions: the new airport in the north, conveniently close to the presidential home but unsuitable for the tourist trade it was supposed to serve, the contract for the new privately owned power station which would provide electricity at an extortionate rate, and the unpaid tax on sugar imported by his brother-in-law. All were being investigated by various commissions of inquiry.

The president kept back what was probably his best card until last.

'I have acted against what you call the political banks,' said Nduka, 'those banks that are owned by the state, and which have made some loans, big loans, to civil servants, and army officers, and supporters of my party – but without proper security. I investigated this matter. And I am sorry to say that it is not only supporters of my party who have received these loans.

'I investigated very carefully, and to my great unhappiness, I have learnt that a certain Newman Kibwana, a young lawyer with big ideas, who has been invited to London, as a guest of the British Government, received a very, very large loan from one of our banks, with no security. I am unhappy,' said the president slyly, 'because when he received the loan he was an MP for my party. I will not tolerate this.'

The news would be a dreadful blow to all who supported democracy in Kuwisha. The papers would have a field day with the information. Newman Kibwana, 'darling of the donors' as the *Kuwisha Standard* called him. The disclosure could hardly have come at a more embarrassing time for Hardwick Hardwicke, the British high commissioner, the German ambassador, and others who had feted him as the new generation of Kuwisha politicians. Even papers that were sympathetic to the opposition would agree: Kibwana's career looked over.

And there was yet another card that Nduka pulled out of his sleeve. All in all, another nineteen politicians were being investigated. Disclosure of the names would be dynamite, particularly if, as the gossip had it, one of them was Anna Nugilu, on whom hopes for democracy were now pinned.

The president still had not finished.

'My brother-in-law has been suspended,' said Dr Nduka. 'I

refuse to tolerate corruption, and it is especially shameful that he is involved' – he corrected himself – 'allegedly involved in a scandal involving maize imports. I just wish that you had raised this matter with me earlier, Mr Hardwicke, whenever it was that you knew about it.'

Hardwicke had been outmatched, outclassed, and outmanoeuvred. Dr Nduka had not bothered to even glance at the dossier, laboriously assembled over the past seven months, and given to Nduka by Hardwicke at the start of their meeting.

Less than an hour later, he stumbled out of State House, blinking in the blinding afternoon sunlight. On the short drive from State House to the Intercontinental Hotel, he spoke only once. When he did it was with the quiet compassion, the heartfelt sincerity, and the near-missionary zeal with which he had approached Africa's problems:

'Fuck 'em . . .'

Fingers grimaced at the recollection. The draft was all but complete. He looked again at what he had written under the headline 'Promises and Challenges in Kuwisha', and struck off the 's':

'World Bank President Hardwick Hardwicke concluded his meeting today with President Nduka with a profound appreciation of both the commitment of the country's leaders to the economic reform agenda and the acute challenge they face in this, one of the world's poorest countries.'

This language was blunt enough, and Fingers was confident that the message would get through. The rest was plain sailing. Thirty minutes later it was done.

'Kuwisha symbolises both the challenges and the hopes of Africa,' it concluded: 'A country that has its own sense of economic direction and is actively engaged in continuously refining its thinking on where it wants to go and how to get there.'

Not bad at all, thought Fingers. True, it bore a close simi-
larity to a Bank statement he had issued at the end of a mission
visit to Ethiopia, but that was in the late 90s. Who would
check? And why waste a good communiqué?

16

'Only the faithless wife hears the hippo's cough'

Through gummy, bloodshot eyes, Titus Ntoto took in a bleak vision. He was half buried in a muddy, oozing, stinking waste-land, the lair of glossy black crows, foraging dogs, ferreting rats and an occasional dead cat. It was all suffused with a stench that entered his very soul. The probing snout of a pig, trailing its uprooted tether, and a tentative tug at his bare foot by one of the dogs, jerked Ntoto into semi-consciousness. For a few moments he believed he had died and was waking up in Hell.

'Could be worse,' thought Ntoto. 'If I could only catch that pig . . .'

Between bouts of vomiting foul liquid, he saw what in his befuddled state he thought could only be the Devil's police-men, advancing on him. Perhaps together they could trap the pig. He started to salivate at the prospect of roast pork. And then, as the men loomed closer, he realised the grim reality: he had fallen into the clutches of the man whom he feared and hated above all others – Mayor Willifred Guchu, close friend of the president, and sworn enemy of the Mboya Boys in general and Titus Ntoto in particular.

It was rotten luck for Ntoto. Usually Mayor Guchu avoided Kireba like the plague, and left his lieutenants to collect rents from the occupants of the many properties he owned in the slum. But with a visitor of the importance of Hardwick

Hardwicke due, Guchu had felt it was necessary to inspect the arrangements for himself, in advance.

Ntoto made a brave attempt to escape. Alas, he had reckoned without Sergeant Sikono, head of the mayor's corps of fixers, gofers and bodyguards. Sikono, who had the physique of an Idi Amin but, in the judgment of his friends, lacked the late Ugandan dictator's sensitivity, was quick to intervene. He gripped the boy by the ankle as he slithered towards the water pipe from which he had been disgorged, for all the world like a snake desperately seeking refuge under a stone.

Sikono had several scores to settle. Ntoto had been the bane of his life, jeering him and his police colleagues as they went about their business of extracting bribes from market vendors in Kireba, demanding protection money from Asian shopkeepers, and imposing arbitrary taxes on resentful motorists.

He scooped up Ntoto effortlessly, and dangled him at the end of an outstretched arm, taking care not to let the rest of the boy's body touch him:

'I've got you at last, you little tick who lives on a hyena's arse.'

Ntoto whimpered again with fear and apprehension, for he had no illusions about the fate that awaited him. Mayor Guchu quickly intervened. It was too public a place for the thrashing he planned to unleash. Like Sergeant Sikono, he had good reason to loathe Ntoto. More than once the tyres of the mayoral Rolls Royce had mysteriously developed punctures when Ntoto and his colleagues had been seen in the vicinity. He motioned to the sergeant:

'Put him down.'

The mayor spoke to Ntoto in a warm, avuncular tone that left the urchin even more terrified.

'Well, well, well,' he said. 'You disgusting reptile who eats dog shit.'

Ntoto began sobbing. Soon the boy's wails were interspersed with the sounds of fist on flesh.

A few hours later, limping after a succession of thrashings at the hands of the mayor, Ntoto dragged himself away from where the flood water had dumped him, and sought sanctuary under a broken-down refuse truck. He gathered scraps of cardboard and old newspapers, made a temporary resting place for himself, collapsed, and dreamed about the family he would never see again . . .

Titus was far more resilient than his skinny frame would suggest. He had emerged from one of Africa's toughest schools of life, hardened by neglect, toughened by abuse, and emotionally calloused by cruelty. But he did not blame his parents, even though he had been left to fend for himself by his mother when he was seven, in a city where street life was based on a hierarchy as complex as a medieval court. At the bottom of the pile were the street urchins, almost invariably orphaned by Aids, or war or poverty, and described as 'abandoned' – though this was a cruel and thoughtless use of the word.

The parents of Ntoto and countless other urchins had not so much abandoned their children as surrendered them, in an act that marked their own defeat in the daily battle for survival. Although thousands of children wandered the streets of the city, eking out their wretched existence by sifting the rubbish dumps or engaging in petty thievery, it was a wonder that there were not more of them.

This was a tribute to the tenacity of their parents, who were driven not simply by paternal and maternal imperatives of love and selflessness, but by an awareness that their children were their only stake in life's lottery. Lose one of your children to disease and deprivation, and you lost a pair of young, able-bodied hands that could help in the family struggle for survival, or provide the labour for the *shamba* that might be your diminishing

144

dream; and you lost one of the slim chances that one of your children could achieve the nigh impossible – a paid job, perhaps as a house steward; and with the loss of a child went any chance of care when you were old and frail.

For years, Titus' parents had struggled to keep a growing family on less than a hectare of land, a four-hour bus journey from the capital. Within two generations rural life in Kuwisha was transformed, as the population doubled and jobs became scarce. In a hazardous attempt to start again, Titus' father sold his share in the family *shamba* to his four brothers, and took his wife and children to the capital, where they had paid an extortionate rent for a home that was no more than a plastic sheet stretched over a wooden frame.

They might have managed but for the brutal politics of Kireba. Encouraged by the city politicians, pursuing an agenda based on the ethnic arithmetic of power in which tribal allegiance came first, neighbour was encouraged to turn on neighbour. The methods were simple and effective. Landlords threatened to terminate leases, longstanding financial debts were called in overnight, or temporary allegiances were bought for a few ngwee.

People from the west of Kuwisha turned on people from the east of the country, people from the south set alight the homes of people from the north. And above all, decent people did unspeakable things to other decent people: not necessarily because of tribe, or religion, or region – although these differences did play a part – but because homes and jobs were at stake. Titus' family, comparative newcomers to the slum, were amongst the most vulnerable. Within days, much of Kireba was in flames, and the Ntotos – but without Titus – were part of a stream of refugees that sought sanctuary back in the countryside.

So Ntoto's parents did not 'abandon' him. Rather they surrendered the unplanned child to fate, to the spirits, in the hope

145

that without a seventh mouth to feed, his six brothers and sisters would have a better chance in life.

Every now and then, encouraged by the euphoria induced by sniffing glue, and curled up somewhere safe and private, he allowed himself to think back to the days when he was part of a family, unfolding his recollections like a scrapbook. But as he grew older, he did it less and less. The past had become hazy as time passed by; and recollection of that past left him feeling disorientated and vulnerable. Instead he felt he had to prepare for the next phase, and be ready to grasp any opportunity to pull himself up the ladder of life.

Before long hunger made him rise. He forced his skinny legs to carry his battered, aching body on a journey that would take him to Cambridge House. It was opposite the central market, where with luck he might find some rotting fruit. Perhaps Pearson would be there. He dropped in to collect mail on most days, and he could offer to wash the journalist's car for a few ngwee. And it was possible that Rutere might be heading there for the same reason – assuming that Cyrus had not drowned in the flood.

He stumbled the mile or so from the scene of his beating in Kireba to the city centre, taking regular sniffs from the glue bottle still dangling from his wrist. Sustained by the fumes, he continued the walk into the city.

To his huge relief, halfway to his destination he encountered another bedraggled figure, driven by the same instinct for survival. It turned out to be the missing Cyrus, whose response to Ntoto's greeting was immediate, warm and unambiguous:

'Phauw, Ntoto! You stink! Have you been sleeping with dead dogs?'

Given that all street boys smell, Ntoto realised that he must smell really badly. But without soap and clean water there was little he could do.

Ntoto ignored his friend's jibe, and gave Rutere a brief

account of his ordeal at the hands of Mayor Guchu. Cyrus shuddered. Like Ntoto, he had been swept away by the wall of water, but had ended up further downstream. Otherwise he would have shared the same fate. But he discouraged Ntoto's talk of revenge. The power of the establishment – defined as just about anyone who was not a street boy – was too enormous to contemplate.

Anyway, he warned, any immediate response would surely lead to even worse disaster. They could get away with defecating in the Mayor's official Rolls Royce when the finger of suspicion might point at several gangs of urchins. But anything that went amiss over the next few weeks would certainly be blamed on the Mboya Boys. And did Ntoto want another round-up of street children? This time the police would not be caught napping. All they needed was to have a fire hose handy, and they would deal harshly with children who covered themselves in their own shit for a second time.

Cyrus' bloodshot eyes contained the wisdom of years of survival in the tough city, and the stunted boy urged his leader and his friend to be careful.

'Do not poison the *ugali* [Kuwisha's staple food] until your belly is full,' he said, the Kuwisha equivalent of 'revenge is a dish best eaten cold'.

Ntoto scowled. As usual, Rutere spoke sense.

'But one day,' Titus vowed, 'one day I will make that Guchu squeal.'

They walked on together in silence.

Cyrus, sensitive to his friend's mood, changed the subject.

'What are you going to do when you are a man?' he asked.

It was not a question that had to be taken literally. Adulthood was not a concept they could readily grasp – rather the question marked the start of a game, in which the two boys explored careers that with hard work and good luck, could be within their grasp.

There was no shortage of options. Ntoto entered into the spirit of the exchange.

'I have decided not to sell newspapers,' he said, and Cyrus nodded.

'Not enough money,' he agreed. 'There is not enough future, no promotion. What about a *matatu* boy?'

Ntoto paused. It was glamorous work, hanging out of mini-vans, those unofficial taxis on which public transport in Kuwisha depended, eyeing the girls, taunting the opposition, yelling out the destinations while soliciting passengers and taking the fares. But it was a job for youths; no one ever saw an old *matatu* boy.

'No.'

'A pickpocket?'

Ntoto snorted in disgust, and gave Rutere a hard look.

'If I thought that you, Cyrus Rutere, would ever become a pickpocket . . .'

Cyrus hastily intervened.

'It is just a question,' he said defensively.

It could be a lucrative business, Cyrus knew, especially if one worked the tourists on Uhuru Avenue. But pickpockets were despised, for they preyed on rich and poor alike, whether the widow who was struggling to bring up her family or a beer-drinking blusterer whose money hung out of his pockets.

Ntoto and Rutere both knew that if a pickpocket was caught, whether dipping a tourist or a local, rough street justice was inevitable. The outcome was not simply a sound thrashing from the victim and members of the public, but often a public lynching.

'What about a burglar, a proper thief who steals money from the banks?'

This time Ntoto was tempted, but not for long.

'No.'

'An *askari*, then,' said Cyrus.

There was a time when Ntoto would have considered that job. In the old days, it was an honourable occupation, and the *askari*, or watchman, was respected. Over the past few years, however, their status had fallen. Many *askaris* were suspected as being little more than a burglar's stooge, who gave information about the house he was supposed to be protecting in exchange for a share of the goods that had been stolen.

He shook his head.

'What about a money changer?'

There were opportunities on Kuwisha's flourishing black market, but realistically Titus could only expect to be the last in a chain of command that in all probability ended with a businessman whose parents had originally come from Asia.

'An area boy?'

Rutere was getting warmer. Ntoto was ambitious. He had set his heart on a job for which the competition was even tougher: he was determined to make it as an area boy, in charge of territory which could extend for several blocks. It was not chance or accident that determined whether you were fortunate enough to be one of those lads who guide the motorist's car to a vacant parking slot on the busy streets. You inherited a patch, or bought it, or fought for it; and having won it by all or any of these ways, you would have to defend it, to wage a constant battle against usurpers, who might have forged an allegiance with the newspaper vendor, or the night-time security guards, not to mention the police themselves.

The complexity of the capital's underclass did not end there. Alliances forged by the area boys controlled the city, block by block, suburb by suburb, slum by slum. Empires rose and fell, and ethnic loyalties began to take precedence over personal loyalties, even loyalties as deep rooted as those of Ntoto and Rutere. And an area boy's life was becoming much more complicated and dangerous. Prospects were clouded by ever-changing challenges, some from unexpected quarters.

Traditional Christian churches were being taken on by a breed of fundamentalist street preachers, silver-tongued critics of a manifestly unfair world, who offered the stark choice of salvation or damnation, as dangerous as their fundamentalist Moslem counterparts. Associated with this clash of values there was the rise of the dreaded *mungiki,* with their simplistic vision, rough justice, and – if newspaper reports were to be believed – obscene ceremonies in which they took oaths of loyalty.

All were players in a world not guessed at by the outsider, seen dimly by even the most curious and perceptive of commentators, a world of temporary loyalties and transient allegiances, rough, tough, and hard to survive.

Yes, there were risks. But to be an area boy! That was a reasonable target. And after that, who knows? Stay on the ladder, and climb the rungs, and before you knew it, you would be in the running to become a member of parliament:

'Titus Ntoto, MP,' he said aloud. It sounded so good, he said it again.

They were still quarrelling, albeit amicably, about which would smell the worse – a dead dog or a dead hyena – when they spotted Cecil Pearson passing Cambridge House in his Land Rover.

The boys went into action.

Cyrus trotted to the nearest vacant parking lot, and stood with his arms raised, defying other motorists to occupy it. Ntoto waved frantically, attracted Pearson's attention, and redirected him to the vacant space. Pearson stepped out of the car, and just as Cyrus had done, recoiled as Ntoto approached.

'What's up?' But before Ntoto could respond, Cecil gave a moan of disgust: 'What on earth have you been rolling in?'

Ntoto retained his dignity.

'It is waste matter, sir,' he said gravely.

'Waste matter? What do you mean, waste matter? It's shit,' said Cecil.

Ntoto nodded.

'Phauw!' said Cecil. 'It may be shit, Ntoto, but goodness knows what you've done to it.'

The comment took a while to sink in. Cyrus could not help but giggle, although immediately felt ashamed of himself. It dawned on Ntoto that Pearson's response was unkind and disparaging. It was the last straw. His final reserves of courage gave out. Exhausted, hungry, demoralised, and aching in every joint, Ntoto collapsed onto the pavement, and started to weep. What began as occasional snuffles, degenerated into prolonged sobs. It was a spectacle that would move the hardest and coldest of hearts. Pearson was no exception.

'You really are disgusting, Ntoto,' he said, recoiling.

'Wipe your nose, for God's sake. And stop wailing. What on earth is the matter?'

He turned irritably to the second boy.

'And you smell almost as bad, Rutere.'

Pearson took a 50 ngwee note from his wallet:

'I want ten mangoes, wrapped, not too ripe. Bring them to my office.'

Rutere could not believe his luck. He was confident that he could get at least a dozen mangoes for that amount. That left him with two mangoes for himself. Two fresh mangoes! He could sell them to the tourists at the nearby Intercontinental Hotel for at least 20 ngwee. Twenty ngwee would be more than enough for a serving of pig's feet and *ugali* at *Harrods*! Things were looking up, and he sped off.

Pearson turned his attention to the snivelling boy at his feet, who poured out his tale and his inchoate thoughts of revenge. He searched in his wallet for another 100 ngwee note. He gave it to Ntoto, who had brought himself under control, apart from an occasional shuddering sob, which he quickly stifled.

151

'Buy some food, Ntoto, have a wash. Use the tap at the market. Then come up to my office.'

He looked at the pathetic figure in front of him, and changed his mind.

'On second thoughts, wait in the corridor, outside the canteen. I'll call you when I'm ready.'

The smell that hung around Ntoto like a cloak was really dreadful, and there was no guarantee that there would be water in the market taps.

As Pearson listened to Ntoto's tale, their row over the timing of the warning call of 'ack-ack-ack' and his outstretched foot was forgotten. If he was handled properly, Cecil realised, the boy could become the tool he needed to put his plan to wreck Nduka's election campaign into effect.

The young victim of the president's henchmen personified all that was wrong in the society over which Nduka presided, and which he had fashioned. And the cholera outbreak was the last straw.

There was no point in tackling the symptom, if one failed to root out the cause. So while he admired Lucy's energy, he doubted whether her clean water scheme would succeed.

Clean water would only flow as long as the reservoir from which it was pumped was properly maintained by the state-owned water authority. And the job of chairman of that authority was in Nduka's gift, part of the president's network of patronage.

Now coming to the end of his posting to Kuwisha, Pearson had concluded that behaving decently and discharging what he saw as the responsibilities of a white man in Africa was not enough. Necessary but not sufficient, was the phrase that came to mind. Even though on balance, he reckoned that he did more good than harm, and that the lives of a dozen or so Kuwisha were measurably better as a result of his actively benign role.

He was, for example, paying for the school fees of one of the daughters of his steward. He had paid the medical fees when the gardener's wife became pregnant. He willingly, even happily, paid what he called the white man's tax, the informal levy imposed by the citizens of Kuwisha on any foreigner from Europe who came to their country, and usually exacted in the form of inflated bills for services rendered.

Indeed, he paid over the odds. He tipped generously. He seldom bargained with curio sellers, tending to pay the asking price. He only occasionally disputed the taxi fare; and he paid Ntoto and Rutere 100 ngwee a month to run errands and find him a parking place outside Cambridge House.

These acts of decency however were no longer enough to satisfy his conscience. Pearson had reached a dangerous stage in a journalist's career: he wanted to do good, to make a change for the better in an unfair world. And he had become impatient with the tortoise-like pace at which the continent was changing.

'Why Africa?' he had asked the foreign editor when the job in Kuwisha went up on the board at the *FN* offices. He knew he had a fair chance of becoming the *FN*'s accountancy correspondent if he was patient. The reply had seemed convincing at the time:

'There are about 650 million people on the continent, and about 65 people who shape the debate about Africa's prospects. Nowhere is the fate of so many influenced by so few,' he said, with the complacent air of someone who had come up with a good line.

It had certainly been enough to convince Pearson, and it sustained him during times of doubt about the continent's capacity to recover from its trials and tribulations. But the longer he stayed in Kuwisha, the more frustrated he became with the slow pace of change – if change it was.

The network of corruption that embraced Kuwisha was

153

killing its economy and enfeebling its people as effectively as the web of a spider traps its victims. Pearson knew that Nduka was no lone predator. He sat atop a system that permeated the society. But the journalist believed passionately that if President Nduka were to lose the coming election, Kuwisha would have a fighting chance to become a better place.

Lucy's disparaging comments when they were sitting together at *Harrods* had also left their mark. In his heart of hearts, he agreed with her: all his news stories, features and leaders had made no difference whatsoever to Kuwisha's problems. Here was an opportunity to have a real impact for the better – and who knows, impress Lucy.

Pearson watched from his office window, lost in these thoughts, as Titus hobbled across the road to the market. Cecil began desultory attempts to clear his desk for his successor, and do his expenses. Thirty minutes later Titus, smelling less and with a clean but badly bruised face, and still a pitiful sight, knocked on the door of the *Financial News*. It was the boy's first time inside Cambridge House, let alone in Pearson's office, and he was mute with wonder. He made a touching, vulnerable sight, but Cecil was nothing if not a journalist. He looked at the boy with a calculating eye.

To say that Pearson was driven by compassion for the wretched boy in front of him would be incorrect. True, he felt sorry for Ntoto. But it was a detached and a calculated sympathy, which saw the boy as little more than a possible lever that could move a far, far bigger cause.

Kibwana's claims at the press conference, his allegations of an imminent meeting between President Nduka and the opposition leader Anna Nugilu, had given him the idea that was now taking shape. But if he were to try what he had in mind, he would have to move fast. Uhuru Day, when the president made his televised address to the nation, was imminent. The deal – if there was indeed a deal – between the president and Mrs Nugilu had to be struck by then.

Cecil gestured towards an empty chair. Titus, still overawed by the fact that Pearson had allowed him into his office, took a back copy of the *Kuwisha Standard*, from the pile in the corner, and carefully placed it on the seat of the chair Pearson had indicated. He then lowered his skinny body, encased in a pair of old hockey shorts and a threadbare grey jersey Pearson had given him. The cast-offs had been washed under the market tap since their exposure to the flood, and were still damp. The rinse had had little impact on the variety of stains that covered the patched and torn garments, and Ntoto felt deeply embarrassed. Nevertheless, for the first time since being washed away, he was able to think beyond his own immediate survival.

He looked round the room. Newspapers sat in ordered piles, the bookshelves had been wiped clean, and Pearson's desk was clear, apart from a pile of used travel tickets, restaurant and taxi receipts, and various grubby slips of paper. It was a strange place to leave your rubbish, thought Ntoto. He longed to stretch out on a rope-and-wood bed, standing in one corner of the office. It was rather like a hammock. Ntoto suspected that it was used by Pearson to sleep off Tuskers. But to lie on it was unthinkable. Instead he allowed his aching frame to rest against the back of the chair, and waited for the first question.

'Tell me, Ntoto, can you use a tape recorder?'

'No, sir,' he replied.

This was not entirely true. Ntoto had watched Edward Furniver operate an identical machine.

'Doesn't matter,' said Pearson, stretching out his feet onto his desk. He continued to look thoughtful.

'That fat boy who plays in your football team, doesn't he work at State House?'

'Yes, sir,' he replied.

Pearson lifted an interrogative eyebrow.

'His name?'

'Ferdinand Mlambo. A kitchen *toto*, sir.'

Ntoto corrected himself.

'Senior kitchen *toto*. He is my friend.'

'And he is an Mboya boy?'

'Yes, sir.'

'Tell me more about him,' said Pearson, and Ntoto complied.

Mlambo was, in Ntoto's considered opinion, easily the most successful of his contemporaries. He was a contender, a potential heavyweight: being a kitchen *toto* anywhere was a remarkable success; to be a kitchen *toto* at State House was a great achievement; but to be the senior kitchen *toto* in State House, at the age of fourteen! It was little short of miraculous, and Ntoto felt proud to call Mlambo his friend.

'Can he get into the president's study?' asked Pearson.

So impressed was Ntoto by the extent of Mlambo's achievements that he answered spontaneously, dropping the caution that was usually second nature to him. He snorted, an action which alarmed Pearson, who feared that Ntoto was so carried away that he was going to blow his nose in finger-to-nostril fashion.

'Mlambo takes the president his tea and scones, every day, in his study,' Ntoto said proudly, and wiped his nose on the sleeve of his jersey, leaving a snail's trail that ran from wrist to elbow.

'He even . . .'

Something about Pearson's look made Ntoto cut himself short. He was a shrewd and perceptive boy, and he would have sworn that the distaste on Pearson's face when he had wiped his nose had been preceded by an expression that had an unpleasant combination of satisfaction and ill-suppressed excitement.

But it was too late. Whatever the damage done by his

impetuous reply, there was no undoing it. The disclosure had been made, and Ntoto cursed his thoughtless response. He sat waiting, tucked his left leg under his bottom, and investigated his toenails. Pearson continued to look thoughtful. It would be a long shot, but with little to lose and much to gain.

Kibwana's claims were not new, and they were common currency at *Harrods*. Few doubted that the president and Anna Nugilu, the opposition leader, were meeting regularly. But how to prove it? They also said that Nduka was far from confident of victory – though there were two schools of thought about the significance of this. The one, led by the Germans, argued that Nduka had not changed his spots; the other, led by the Brits, believed that the president wanted to leave behind a legacy of democracy, or at least a platform of economic and political reforms on which the new Kuwisha could be build.

In Pearson's view, neither theory mattered if Newman Kibwana was right. If Mrs Nugilu could be persuaded by the president to stay in the contest, and then withdraw her candidacy after nominations had closed, in return for a clear run when Nduka stood down, the president's election victory would be guaranteed. At the press conference attended by Pearson, Newman had claimed the two were meeting at least once a week to discuss tactics for the general election. The next meeting between the two, he had claimed, was scheduled within twenty-four hours.

Still looking at Ntoto, who having dealt with his toenails was now paying close attention to a suppurating scab on his left ankle, Pearson rang one if his diplomatic sources to get the latest view on such a meeting. It was very likely, he was told, but it could not be confirmed.

Pearson pondered and plotted. If the gossip could be proved accurate, and Mrs Nugilu was indeed planning to step down and leave politics after presidential nominations closed, the election would become a one horse race. The other candidates were a mixed bunch, their support limited to their home region or their tribe. Nduka's re-election would be all but certain. But should it be shown that the president himself had doubts about his re-election, the opposition could well unite, and Nduka's defeat would be a real possibility. But the evidence had to be cast iron. Speculation would not do. Pearson made up his mind. It was worth a go.

'Sit still, Ntoto. I have something to show you.'

Ntoto, who had been thinking furiously, wondering how he could backtrack on his admission about Mlambo, looked up.

Pearson pulled open his right-hand drawer, and took out a tape recorder, so small it fitted comfortably into the palm of his hand. He placed it near Ntoto, and pressed a button, and continued to quiz the boy.

Pearson then replayed the exchange.

As it happened, Ntoto had heard his own voice before. Edward Furniver's tape recorder was the very same model, and Ntoto had sat at the foot of the wicker chair, at *Harrods*, entranced by the stories about a cat called Stripey that the white man dictated for his grandchild.

But for Pearson's sake, and out of an innate caution, Ntoto pretended astonishment. As their voices filled the room, he covered his eyes with both hands and peeked through a crack between his fingers, and gave fake piteous little cries, part fear, part fascination. Only after the third re-run, when Ntoto had allowed his spurious emotions to be replaced by curiosity and enthusiasm, did Pearson feel that the boy was ready.

He told him he could take revenge on Mayor Guchu and the president, provided he would take part in what was an audacious but feasible scheme.

As Pearson explained what he had in mind, Ntoto recoiled in horror. His worst fears had been realised, and for a few moments he was tempted to run for the door. Instead he assembled the obvious objections: how could a tape recorder, carried by a boy from Kireba, be smuggled past the security checks at State House? Even if that was possible, how could it be placed in the correct position, in the president's study of all places?

'What if we are caught,' he asked. 'What if we are searched?'

'It would be a brave man, or a foolish man, who searched you, Titus.'

Ntoto sniggered. It was a good point. He could strap the tape recorder below his waist, concealed beneath his stained shorts. What went on under those trousers did not bear thinking about.

Pearson was patience personified, betraying none of his own doubts and concerns about the scheme. Once again he reminded Ntoto of the pain and humiliation the boy had endured over the past twenty-four hours. Pain that had been inflicted, Pearson hardly needed to point out, by thugs loyal to Mayor Guchu. And was not Guchu the man who, all agreed, was President Nduka's closest adviser . . .?

Pearson managed to conceal the fact that at heart he felt that his plan had only a slight chance of coming off. Were he not due to leave for London shortly, he probably would not have even have contemplated it. What if Ntoto and his friends were caught? Pearson acknowledged there was a risk of this happening. But who would the security police believe: Kireba urchins and their implausible story? Or a respected journalist who accused the boys of stealing his tape recorder? And anyway, by the time questions were asked, he would be on the plane home.

And if the plan worked . . . Pearson would write the story in London, based on a transcript of the conversation between Nduka and Nugilu. Provided it bore out Newman Kibwana's allegations, the president would be thoroughly discredited. Pearson would return to Kuwisha to cover the elections that would see Nduka fighting for his political life. And his defeat would usher in a new era for Kuwisha . . .

But all that was to come.

Pearson once again explained how the tape recorder worked. Ntoto now looked at it as if it were a snake, ready to bite him. All that was required was for two buttons to be pressed, Pearson told Ntoto: the recorder was loaded, and it would automatically turn itself on, for it was triggered by sound.

Ntoto was not convinced. Getting through the security checks that surrounded State House would be difficult enough. Getting the recorder hidden in President Nduka's study, and getting it out again would be even more dangerous.

'Listen carefully, Titus Ntoto. Listen very carefully. I am going to tell you two stories. Listen carefully, because they will prove that you and Cyrus and Mlambo can be invisible.'

Ntoto sighed. At least he would have a chance to think. He leant forward, anxious not to miss a word. As the stories unfolded, he found himself being pulled in. Every now and then he nodded his understanding, and when Pearson reached the denouement of the first tale, he let out a little murmur of recognition and a squeal of sheer delight, for it was a story about Tom Odhiambo Mboya, the man after whom they named their club. It was well told.

Ntoto clapped his hands enthusiastically, like the fourteen-year-old Cecil too easily forgot he was. For a moment, only for a few seconds, Pearson was concerned for the boy's welfare, and contemplated calling off what could prove a dangerous mission. He paused, and the break was long enough to be noticed by Ntoto.

'Next story, next story,' he demanded. Ten minutes later, Pearson thought he had convinced Ntoto that the plan was feasible.

'Remember, Ntoto. You are invisible to people who think they are better than you, more important than you. As long as you look like a street boy, or a kitchen *toto*, doing the things street boys and *totos* do, behaving like they do, no one will see you. But – and this is very important – you must behave just like yourself, like a street boy, and Cyrus must also behave like a street boy.'

Ntoto still looked doubtful.

'But they will see us, sir.'

'Yes, of course they will see you. But they will see only two small boys, two pieces of nothing,' replied Pearson.

'They will see two small boys, who they think are rubbish. But they will not see that underneath the two boys are two angry young men.'

Pearson looked at his watch. Time was running out. Ntoto still looked undecided and distinctly nervous.

Pearson changed tactics. He stood up, putting the recorder back into the desk drawer.

'Right, Ntoto. It will not work if you are afraid.'

Ntoto gnawed his lower lip, unsure and alarmed, and Pearson played his last card.

'Do you think I would risk my new tape recorder if I thought you would be caught? Do you know that it is worth more than £200 – nearly one hundred thousand ngwee?'

The fact was that whatever happened to the recorder, Pearson was not going to be out of pocket. He was confident that he could claim it on his insurance. But Ntoto was not to know this.

The enormity of the value of the tape recorder left the boy stunned. He still had his doubts about a hare-brained scheme that had little chance of working. But it immediately occurred to Ntoto that he could sell a tape recorder worth 100,000 ngwee on the city streets without difficulty. Even if he got 10,000 ngwee, it was a small fortune. And was not Pearson leaving for London very soon?

'We are not afraid,' he said firmly. 'We will do it.'

'Good man,' said Pearson. 'What about Rutere?'

'Rutere is my deputy,' said Ntoto firmly and confidently. 'He will do as I say.'

'And Mlambo?'

'He is an Mboya Boy. And he is not circumcised.'

'Pardon,' said Cecil, baffled by the relevance of this information.

'He is not circumcised,' said Ntoto again. Surely he did not need to explain further to Pearson?

'Good man,' replied Cecil, still at a loss.

'Good man. Now we must hurry. We will collect Rutere from the market, and I will drop both of you at the State House roundabout.

The two boys achieved another personal first as Rutere joined Ntoto in the back of Cecil's Land Rover and the three of them drove off from Cambridge House. Neither Ntoto nor Rutere had travelled in a white man's car before, although they had acquired a remarkable knowledge of an automobile's features when they learnt the skills of petty thieves – such as how to jump-start an engine, or ways to remove a car radio. They chattered excitedly in Swahili as they sat on the back seat, looking out at the city from this elevated perspective.

'One day,' said Ntoto, 'I will have a white man whose job will be to drive me whenever I want.'

Rutere nodded enthusiastically.

'All drivers will be white men, and if they are lazy or if they are loafers, they will, they will . . .'

Rutere paused, thinking of the worst punishment a frequently hungry Kireba urchin could imagine.

'They will not be allowed to eat at *Harrods*,' he said sternly, 'but they will have to serve the food.'

Ntoto laughed, and clapped his hands.

'What's the joke?' asked Pearson, briefly taking his eyes off the road to check on his passengers.

'What's so funny?'

'We are just happy, suh,' said Cyrus obsequiously, digging a giggling Ntoto in the ribs.

Pearson concentrated on avoiding the city's aggressive drivers, while the boys continued chatting in Swahili.

'He said the tape recorder was worth nearly one hundred thousand ngwee,' said Ntoto. Rutere was awe-struck, and almost lost for words.

'One hundred thousand ngwee,' he repeated. 'Surely we must steal it.'

Ntoto looked at him scornfully.

'Of course we will steal it. Of course. But first we must use it to do our job. We are not stupid. I want to hurt the president. If I hurt him, that Guchu will squeal. This is the start of my revenge on Guchu.'

Rutere was about to comment, and urge caution and restraint, but something in Ntoto's voice made him think again.

Pearson stopped outside the local supermarket, and came back to the car with a small packet. A few minutes later he stopped again, this time alongside a street vendor selling fresh maize cobs that had been roasted on the makeshift brazier. He bought the man's stock – about two dozen cobs – dumped them in a large locally-made raffia bag, and handed it over to the boys.

They had decided against hiding the tape recorder under Ntoto's shorts as too obvious. He watched carefully as Ntoto instead placed it, protected from dust by a black plastic packet, in the bottom of the bag, and covered it with the roasted cobs. There was just one thing left. He looked critically at Ntoto and Rutere on the back seat, and the former defensively wiped his ever-running nose on the back of his hand.

'Probably not necessary, but better to be on the safe side. When the time comes, sniff this.'

Cecil handed over the packet of pepper he had bought at the local supermarket.

'And make sure that you smell like a dead dog. Remember Mboya.'

He wasn't sure why he said that. Nevertheless, he said it again:

'Remember Mboya.'

It sounded like a slogan, some sort of rallying call. Cecil's knowledge of the Kenyan trade unionist was limited. The story he had told to Ntoto had come from a biography that had been part of his background reading when preparing for his posting to Kuwisha, and it had stuck in his memory. But as far as he could recall, Mboya was not associated with a form of political militancy that might appeal to Ntoto and Rutere. The mention of the name nevertheless had a galvanising effect. The two boys, who had got out of the car while Pearson spoke, snapped to attention:

'Remember Mboya,' they echoed with a ferocious gravity: 'Remember Mboya.'

'Good luck, Titus. Good luck, Cyrus.'

Ntoto gave him a mock salute.

He returned the salute. Cecil felt that an appropriate gesture was necessary, and had been about to shake their hands, but thought the better of it.

One never knew where their fingers had been.

17

'Only the lion may piss in the watering hole'

President Josiah Nduka stood in the bay window of his State House study, looking out over Kireba.

Much had changed since that first time he had stood in that study, so many years ago. Then he had looked at a dam, where people swam, and where a handful of sailing craft had been tied up to a wooden jetty.

Today his view was interrupted by a series of obstacles, natural as well as man made. First there was a thicket of mature eucalyptus trees, home to hundreds of crows. Then came rows and clumps of shrubs and bushes, followed by what looked like barracks, but which were in fact the living quarters of middle-ranking staff. Next was a strip of vacant land with the carcass of the occasional rusting car, and which was rumoured to have a few land mines buried below the surface. Then came an electric fence. And finally there was the three-metre-high white wall topped with a roll of razor-wire that surrounded the grounds of State House. And on the other side of that was the now stagnant, weed-encrusted dam that long ago used to be the base for the city yacht club.

Ever since he became president he had wanted to clear the blight that was Kireba. And every few years he sought pledges from aid donors to rehabilitate the slum, and to provide tarred roads, clean water, and electricity, and a primary school and additional clinics.

But the residents did not trust him – they were convinced that were they to move out of their plastic-and-tin shanties to allow the renovation to get under way, they would never again be allowed back. Their land would be sold to supporters of Nduka and his party, and Kuwisha's middle class would welcome the opportunity to buy residential plots in a location so close to the city centre.

They were right, of course.

And so he had changed tactics. The road that was to run through Kireba would in itself be of little benefit to residents, for there would be no pedestrian access. But if the road were to become accessible, the land alongside the highway would rocket in value. Market forces, that creature the World Bank urged him to set free and let roam across Kuwisha, would come out to play. The gentrification of Kireba would become unstoppable. Housing would indeed become available, but unaffordable for any resident of the slum.

Nduka sighed. Perhaps it was no more than an old man's dream . . .

Had the city developed according to any plan, Kireba would never have been allowed in the first place. The very existence of the slum was an accident, going back to a decision to provide cheap land to former soldiers who had served in World War Two. It had been approved by the colonial authority, which had then failed to provide the basic services that the site needed. But planning, whether for white or black residents, had never been the city fathers' strongest suit.

Just as Kuwisha was an accidental country, its boundaries the result of colonial whim, the capital itself was an accidental city. Without the railway from the coast, which thrust its way into the interior some one hundred years ago, it is doubtful whether it would have existed. The city had not been strategically positioned. It was not located, for example, at the point where a huge river could be forded, or where residents could be defended. The men who built the railway had simply stopped for the night at what was to become the country's main administrative centre. It became convenient to make it a staging post for supplies, as the railway pushed westward, carved out of what was called virgin bush, until it ended up in Uganda.

The city's main street, the original Uhuru Avenue, as opposed to the track that ran through Kireba, was lined by palm trees, once stately but now looking threadbare. The banks were built like fortresses, alongside trading houses that could trace their origins to the slave trade. Today, dozens of potholes turned Uhuru Avenue and other city highways into an obstacle course. Formerly an East African landmark, a symbol of modern, postcolonial independent Africa, Uhuru Avenue had become a barometer of Kuwisha's decay.

In Kireba, however, there were no potholes, for there were no roads at all, whether tarred or paved, gravel or scraped. None at all. The only reliable thoroughfare was the walkway formed by the railway line that began hundreds of miles away. It served two purposes: cut into the side of the hill, it demarcated one boundary, while the track of the rails provided the only route through a shanty town of ramshackle shacks and shelters.

On the one side of the track, the formal city began, with brick-built shops, albeit tatty and run down; on the other side was the dam, marking Kireba's western boundary, which used to be the home of the long defunct sailing club. The heavily protected grounds of State House formed the third border, completing the triangle. As many as half a million people were squeezed into this space, the size of a couple of dozen football stadiums. Every now and then the residents rioted and looted, egged on by old rivalries excited by local politicians, exploiting the daily battles for space, jobs, and survival.

Many outsiders believed, indeed hoped, that Kireba could perhaps become the place where a revolution might begin. The more pessimistic analysts of Kuwisha, driven by wishful thinking rather than cold logic, had an apocalyptic vision of the people of Kireba rising as one, joining in with the citizens of the other slums around the city. Together they would march on the so-called 'low density' green suburbs, bearing the loot from the Asian businesses that dominated the city centre, chanting the Swahili equivalent of: 'We cannot take it anymore.'

Back at the British High Commission, a drab grey building near State House that unsuccessfully attempted to combine aesthetics and security, David Podmore was pacing his office and taking stock, sucking on an unlit cigarette, and preparing for his forthcoming meeting with Mayor Guchu.

'You need to know these people if you're going to do business with them,' he would tell his visitors, and Podmore felt that he knew Kuwisha and its people pretty well. In fact, he considered himself something of an Africa expert – a label he modestly denied, but in a way that made clear he had earned the description.

He had become adept at letting his expression grow sombre, with a faraway look in his eyes, as if contemplating distant horrors still keenly felt. Yet Podmore's direct encounters with Africa's bad news were rare, even if the look on his face implied that he was a veteran witness to slaughter, from Rwanda to Somalia, from Liberia to Congo. The truth was that the nearest Podmore had got to the action during his time in Kuwisha was to accompany the British aid minister on a day trip to the Congo town of Kisangani. He seldom missed an opportunity to refer to it, usually in the form of saying 'Kisangani', followed by a doleful shake of the head, as if the city that sat on a bend in the great

Congo river symbolised all the ills and travails of a troubled continent.

Podmore had fallen into a joshing, patronising relationship with what he called the 'ordinary people' of Kuwisha. Waiters or petrol station attendants would be addressed as *bwana*. But if they offended him, he made clear his anger by calling them 'my friend'.

Apart from 'ordinary people', the citizens of Kuwisha were referred to as 'these people', or 'friendly people' and sometimes 'lovely people', who had won his heart. And he told his colleagues that when the time came to leave Kuwisha, he would say his farewells with genuine sadness. But as he approached the last stage of his three-year tour of duty, he readily acknowledged that he was burdened by dark and pessimistic thoughts. It was the sheer cussedness of Kuwisha's citizens that made them partly responsible for their wretched plight, Podmore believed. The stubbornness he found in most of the people he encountered was an obstacle to the good work he and his colleagues attempted to do.

He accepted that corruption was endemic, that the government was venal and incompetent, and that much of the international aid was wasted, or 'inefficiently used'. But one matter worried Podmore more than any other: the failure of the citizens of Kuwisha to put their regional and ethnic differences aside, rally behind a single leader, and take the opportunity to get rid of President Nduka at the ballot box. It had left him perplexed and sometimes despairing.

The phone on his desk trilled.

It was his colleague from the Dutch embassy, proposing a meeting that afternoon of the European Union development counsellors regional economic committee. Podmore reluctantly agreed. If there was any doubt about the validity of national stereotypes, let the sceptics attend one of the meetings of the EU economic and aid committee, he thought. The Germans would be belligerent, the French would be devious, the Scandinavians would be censorious, the Italians wouldn't turn up, and the Brits would do all the work, and take the flack if things went wrong.

The phone rang again. It was that self-righteous prig Pearson.

'What's the line on cholera? Well, by and large, all things considered, on the one hand and on the other, we think it's a bad thing. But that's off the record.'

Podmore guffawed, knowing how irritating Pearson would find this heavy-handed humour.

The diplomat made rude faces at the picture of the president he had hung in his office, and read the selection of droll headlines which he had cut from the local papers, and which he had pinned to the notice board.

'Why not drop round later,' he found himself saying.

'Splendid . . . see you then. Look forward to it, Cecil.'

'Tit,' he thought to himself, as he struggled to light an illegal cigarette with the local matches. 'Devious little prick.'

On the fourth time of trying, the match-head detached itself from the brittle wooden shaft as he struck it, fizzed over his desk, and landed on the carpet. It took two more matches, held dangerously close to the volatile sulphur-coated heads and struck simultaneously, before the cigarette was lit.

Podmore took grim comfort that one of his rules of Africa had been tried and tested, and found good. There was a direct relationship, he believed, between the number of locally made matches it took to light a cigarette, and the state of an African country's political and economic decline. If only one or two did the trick, one was either in South Africa or Botswana, models of stability. If four matches were needed, the country was in trouble. If it took six matches, the country's decline was irreversible.

It was not the only such rule though the others could be more pithily expressed.

'*The more a country needs foreign exchange, the longer it takes to change a travellers cheque.*'

'*The more run-down the country's capital the more expensive the hotels.*'

'*The more incentives offered by investment centres, the more corrupt the country and the greater the problems of the private sector.*'

'*The more prominent the president's wife, the more her husband is on the take.*'

'*The bigger the capital's traffic jam, the worse the economy.*'

Podmore sighed, and called to his secretary:

'Get out Mrs P's shortbread, please Leslie. I'm expecting friend Pearson.'

Before Pearson arrived, however, he needed to read the files in preparation for a meeting with the mayor. He rubbed the palms of his hands together, vigorously, as if he was trying to warm them.

Look out, Guchu, Podmore of the FO was on his way . . .

18

'When maidens dance, hide the corn cobs'

It was time to confront the *jipu*.

Furniver finished drying himself, and crossed the passage into his bedroom. He had given the manoeuvre that lay ahead some thought while lying in the bath: an old rugby injury had left him with a dodgy back, and he was far from confident that his right hamstring was up to it. But there was no alternative. He had to go ahead.

Still naked, he positioned himself with his back pressed against the full-length mirror that was attached to the built-in cupboard in the room. Legs akimbo, he cautiously leant forward, slowly bending from the waist. In his left hand, he held a pot of Vaseline petroleum jelly. The forefinger of his right hand was poised, ready to scoop out a substantial dollop to apply to the itch.

Once in position, he placed the pot of Vaseline on the floor, leaving it within easy reach should he require a further application. Until this point his eyes had been closed, the better to concentrate.

Now came the bit he had been dreading. His back began to feel the strain as he bent closer to the floor. With his head now well between his legs, his left hand propped himself against the cupboard, he forced himself to look.

'Good Lord!' he exclaimed in hushed tones as he looked upon an expanse of pink and hairy flesh. Revealed was a part of his anatomy which Furniver had never imagined he would get to see, the equivalent of gazing at the dark side of the moon.

A lesser man might have given up at this point, and surrendered to the indignity of submitting himself to a doctor's scrutiny, but Furniver was made of sterner stuff.

'Get a grip,' he murmured, and concentrated on the task at hand. Biting his lower lip, he guided his Vaseline-coated finger towards what looked like a mosquito bite with a small off-white head. It now itched acutely.

There were several false starts, due to the confusion created by the mirror image, not to mention the distraction of the distressing spectacle itself. He had to learn that when his finger needed to go right, it moved left in the reflection in the mirror, and vice versa. Finally his lubricated digit was within striking distance of the target. Furniver, brow furrowed in concentration, sweating heavily, muttered to himself – or rather to the maggot:

'Die you bugger, die!'

The imprecation, the knock on the bedroom door, the rattle of the handle as it opened, and the cheery greeting from Didymus Kigali, carrying Furniver's dinner tray, came almost simultaneously.

'Good evening, suh!'

Kigali broke off, his jaw on his chest. It was hard to say which of the two men got the greater shock.

It was the pent up sigh of achievement and satisfaction that Furniver let out as his finger finally hit home that so distressed Mr Kigali.

'Not even a baboon would do such a thing,' Didymus told his wife Mildred when she came home later that evening to find him sitting in the doorway of their plastic-sheeted shelter, looking out into space. It had been, he said, his most trying day in forty years of working for the white man.

Not that Didymus Kigali was a prude. He had observed at close quarters the weaknesses and frailties of white men and their women. He had noted the various sexual proclivities of mankind in general during his time in domestic service, and soon came to realise that neither race, colour nor creed was a barrier to aberrant behaviour. Usually he turned a blind eye to the peccadilloes of his employers. This time it was impossible to ignore such a gross display.

'Even baboons, they do not do such a strange thing with their finger,' he repeated. Given that baboons are notorious for their unabashed and uninhibited sexual behaviour, Mildred Kigali had been sceptical. But when her husband had finished his account, she realised he was not exaggerating.

'How,' he asked Mildred, 'can we tell this to Charity Mupanga?'

Kigali crossed himself, a legacy of his upbringing by Catholic missionaries, and shook his grey peppercorn-curled head.

'Forty years. Forty years I have been doing my job, but never, never have I seen or heard of this business with a finger and Vaseline. And watching, in a mirror.' He shuddered.

His voice trailed off, but his distress and distaste was evident. The ways of the European were very odd, very odd indeed.

Mildred did her best to comfort him. She had seen a thing or two in her sixty-odd years, and kept in touch with the world through that excellent local weekly, *Christian Family*, and *Hi!* magazine, kindly sent to her by a relative in London. She also was a regular attendant at the Kireba Christian Ladies' Sewing Circle, which met once a week at *Harrods*. She had listened, horrified and fascinated, to accounts of the extraordinary things that herd boys did with goats, and the unnatural relationship that some parking boys had with donkeys.

It was her duty to inform Charity Mupanga of this bizarre matter. She pursed her lips, and drew on all the compassion and wisdom of a woman who had seen life, and who was on the committee of the Kireba branch of Kuwisha's Society for the Prevention of Cruelty to Animals. The frustrations of bachelorhood took many forms, but this white man must really be desperate. There could only be one truly Christian response to Furniver's compelling need for physical relief.

Mildred Kigali pronounced.

'Poor man,' she said.

'Poor man. I will speak with Charity Mupanga. It is time she decided. Otherwise we will find that Furniver doing donkeys, or going with goats, even.'

Jonathan Punabantu was insistent, and Pearson gave in: without accreditation, said Puna, there would be no meeting with President Nduka.

He had applied for an interview months ago, more in hope than expectation, and when he did not hear from the president's office, had assumed the request had been turned down. Then came the message from Punabantu, the president's press secretary, telling him to be at the international airport, where Nduka would be on hand to greet the visiting head of state who would be his guest on Uhuru Day, the anniversary of independence.

'Can't promise,' said Punabantu when Pearson had phoned in response to the message passed on by Shadrack, 'but the president will try and fit you in for an audience.'

'And you must have your accreditation card,' added Punabantu, knowing full well that Pearson had never bothered to apply for one.

'Don't forget you'll need three passport photographs,' he said.

And just in case Pearson was inclined to ignore the request, he warned:

'You won't get past the security checks on the way to the airport without it.'

As it turned out, the process was reasonably quick and pain-less.

He presented himself at the information ministry, housed in a prefab – a building constructed from a kit of frame and panels, designed to be erected quickly, with a comparatively short life.

Pearson reckoned the office he was in had been put up in the 1950s, the period when settler rule had not quite realised that its days were numbered, and African nationalism was only just becoming aware of its strength. It had that colonial works' department look about and feel to it, with its cement veranda and vestiges of shrubbery. Inside the style was very different. Offices built of wood panels with a glossy dark veneer had been added, seemingly at random, carving out space by divid-ing and subdividing the original rooms. The passages were now dark and narrow, and partly blocked by the rubbish of decades – chairs with missing legs, rickety tables, dusty files, broken fans, old blinds – which no-one had the authority or the initiative to repair, sell, or simply throw out.

The receptionist's desk was deserted. But a soft brushing noise came from down the passage, and Pearson went in search of it.

'Where is the permanent secretary?'

'She not come,' said an old woman with a home-made broom of grass and twigs, pausing in her work. She went back to her task, and Pearson was tempted to call the whole thing off. Instead he settled down to wait, and as he waited he watched.

Brush, brush, brush, steadily brushing carpets so ingrained with dust that the pattern was barely discernible, and the pile was almost worn smooth. Brush, brush, brush. Pearson won-dered whether the old woman brushed when no-one was present, or was she going through the motions for his benefit. Then he remembered that when he first entered the office, he had heard the rasp of her brush from behind one of the office doors.

Brush, brush, brush. The woman looked in her seventies. Pearson reckoned she was probably in her early fifties. She worked her way steadily down the passage. At first he thought her work was pointless. Whatever was brushed was not collected. There was no dustpan in sight. She also carried a bundle of rags. Every now and then she paused, and took the bundle, and passed it over the surface of a desk, the arms of a chair, the top of the filing cabinet.

Pearson's interest flagged, and he looked around the office in which he was sitting. A gap in the ceiling, where a panel had dropped out, revealed the timber frame. The curtains of both the external window and an internal window into the passage were drawn, and yellowing netting was pulled across the curtains. An air-conditioner laboured and wheezed, but he could still hear the brush, brush, brush as the old woman went about her business.

Pearson counted the calendars. There were three on the wall, and two on the filing cabinet. He read the exhortations above the dates. 'The Lord will Perfect that Which Concerneth Me,' and the single word 'Perfect' was outlined in a rectangular box. 'The Lord will satisfy me with long life and prosperity.'

'God is my provider.'

A yellowing fridge, rubber seal dangling, was marked with the letters and figures: EPD/DIST/04/01, and a picture of President Josiah Nduka hung on the wall, above the desk. Dust was still being moved around the carpet, but Pearson looked again, and now he saw the purpose. He looked first at where the cleaner had been, and then at the stretch of carpet she had yet to reach. It dawned on him. You can tell it has been swept, he realised. It was like raking a bunker, eliminating the crater made in the sand by the golf ball, or removing the traces of the stroke that propels the ball onto the green, and the tread of the golfer. The sand remains, but the contours have been restored.

The permanent secretary arrived and to Pearson's surprise, the official greeted him cordially, but offered no explanation for the delay. Somewhat unusually, there was a photographer on hand to take the mug shots. Within a few minutes he had his accreditation.

Pearson decided to walk from the information ministry to the Outspan, where he had left his car, a journey of less than five minutes. The city centre was quiet. Office workers had left early to start their Uhuru holiday weekend, leaving behind a few *askaris*, handfuls of curious tourists, and prowling packs of feral street children. He set off confidently. Small deft hands brushed against his pockets, as soft and subtle in their grubby touch as the wings of a butterfly.

'Give me ngwee, boss.'

Pearson walked faster, resisting the temptation to run the last stretch.

'Just five ngwee, boss.'

He felt a tug at the case that held his computer, and he struck out:

'Little bastards.'

One of the boys laughed derisively.

'You are shit,' said the urchin, and giggled.

He was a child, no more than ten.

There were now a dozen boys surrounding him, and he flailed out. Tiny fingers dipped into his pockets. Hateful grubby midgets, with stick legs and sunken chests and pot bellies, made him feel like a Gulliver surrounded by Lilliputians, and the image pushed him closer to panic. Fear and anger battled against compassion for Pearson's soul. Less than halfway, with the Outspan almost in sight, he turned back. By that stage, there must have been twenty jeering boys, all with glue tubes, all with glazed eyes and snot-encrusted noses, following a few yards behind him. He heard them mocking as he got into an ancient black taxi.

'Bastards,' he muttered again, and immediately felt ashamed.

'Outspan.'

The driver nodded, and commiserated.

'Thieves. Dangerous.'

The journey took barely two minutes, but Pearson paid double the fare. It did not make him feel any better, and he realised that he was trembling. It called for a gin and tonic. He took the drink to the sanctuary of the hotel's residents' lounge. Pearson had stayed only a few nights, at the start of his posting to Kuwisha, but the experience had left an indelible impression on him. As he sat among the ghosts of the country's colonial past he felt soothed and at ease, his shaking stopped . . . and he let his mind drift into comfortable nostalgia, secure in a hotel that was at the peak of its decline.

The click and clack of balls and cues still seemed to drift from the hotel's musty billiard room, where a stencilled instruction mounted above the scoreboard requested the last person using the table to turn out the lights.

The lounge where he was sitting had deep chintz-covered armchairs, and long forgotten novels sat on the shelves of the glass-fronted bookcase, where another notice said: 'Key obtainable from reception', but the key had long gone missing. You were expected to write your name and room number in the notebook, with a pencil attached by a piece of string. But things had got slack, and no-one bothered any more.

It was a hotel where Pearson had woken to the clink of thick crockery rattling on the trays carrying early morning tea, with the sugar in bowls and not in sealed paper packets, and where a jug of hot water came with a pot of strong tea. He knew if he dozed off, there was no danger of missing breakfast (served

179

between 7 a.m. and 8.30 a.m., except on Sundays, when it is from 7.30 a.m. to 9 a.m.), for he would wake again when the verandas got their daily red-wax polish.

The dining room floor creaked, wooden beams crossed the ceiling, and the food was British colonial. The menu for each table was typed on the receptionist's Remington, which also tapped out the bill at the end of your stay.

He recalled the breakfast menu which had 'Good Morning' without an exclamation mark, and there was no sign saying, 'Please wait to be shown to your table.'

The waiters were not servants but retainers, in bow tie and black jackets and starched white shirts, and expected you to be at your table between 7.30 p.m. and 8 p.m. because they liked to leave for their rooms in Kireba by 10 p.m.

The ceilings in the rooms were high, and geckoes came out in the evening. Guests slept beneath a mosquito net, and watched the flames from the fireplace flicker on the ceiling, and when they awoke the embers still glowed.

At night, even in the city, the sky was clear and the stars lay low, and the sounds of the city drifted in, and cigar smoke hung in the air. No key-cards at the Outspan, just mortice locks and long-shanked keys, attached to blocks of wood, polished by handling over the years. It was a hotel at its decrepit but genteel best. No doubt someone would decide to improve it. When that happened, Pearson decided, it would not be worth staying there any more . . . not that he expected to return to Kuwisha, at least not in the foreseeable future.

It was time to go. He drained his glass, bade farewell to the ghosts, and paid the bar bill. And as he drove to the airport, his spirits slumped, his dislike of President Nduka got stronger, became corrosive. It eroded his judgement and heightened his fears. He should never have discussed his scheme in his office. What a fool! It was almost certainly bugged. And his mobile phone, which a friend in an intelligence service had warned him could serve as a listening device, whether switched on or off . . . he should have locked it in his car. But Lucy's jibes were still ringing in his ears.

Suddenly a *matatu* swerved in front of him, horn blaring, and Pearson found himself sweating profusely.

He pulled into the verge, mopped his face, and took a deep breath.

'Pull yourself together, man, get a grip.'

19

'When young men dance, hide the cooking pots'

Grubby flags hung listlessly from the streetlights that lined the route from the airport to the national stadium, venue for the celebration of Uhuru Day, the anniversary of Kuwisha's independence. Once an occasion of national rejoicing, Uhuru Day had become just another public holiday, distinguished only by the national broadcast which President Nduka insisted on giving, and the presence of the African leader invited as the State guest.

Every lamp post on the route was decorated with red, green and yellow bunting, and a crossed hoe and Kalashnikov rifle, the national colours and symbol of the country whose president was this year's official visitor.

Platoons of smartly clad schoolchildren, clutching miniature flags, lined the route. At the airport itself, the *mbumba* were warming up, the formidable vanguard of the ruling party, and whose patron was President Nduka himself. The guest of honour's plane was running three hours late, and to pass the time the women were going through their repertoire. Every now and then the president joined in, entering the ranks of the dancing ladies, their buttocks and breasts shaking and wobbling in time to the rhythmic stamping that characterised these gatherings.

Their loyalty to the president was not in doubt, and these praise singers and dancers appeared on all state occasions.

Clad in cloth in the colours of Kuwisha, broad stripes of blue, green and black, and prominently featuring the stern but benevolent face of President Nduka, they performed across the length and breadth of the country.

Pearson watched as the buxom ululating *mbumba* were joined yet again by Nduka, unexpectedly nimble for a man thought to be anywhere between his mid-seventies and mid-eighties. Their ranks opened, and the president disappeared, his progress indicated only by the spasmodic emergence of the tip of his presidential flywhisk. Security around the president was invariably tight, but this was one of the few occasions when his bodyguards relaxed, knowing he was safe in the bosom of the nation.

Pearson sat fretful, nervous and apprehensive. Did he really want a face-to-face exchange with a man whose election prospects he was trying to sabotage? What if he had been rumbled, and the interview had become a trap? It might explain the insistence on photos for the accreditation . . .

He had caught Punabantu's eye on arrival, and searched his face for any clue, but the harassed press secretary only nodded amiably and motioned towards the VIP waiting room.

Pearson had spent a good part of his years in Africa simply waiting. 'Somebody, or something, will always turn up,' said an old hand. 'Just wait, read a book, and never lose your temper.'

Often the waiting took place in tacky rooms, furnished with a lack of taste that seemed deliberate. This one was no exception. On the tables was the usual assortment of magazines. Not for the first time, Pearson wondered how it was that, whether in Lusaka or Lagos, Luanda or Lilongwe, the magazines were the same: the glossy products of Taiwan and North Korea, together with the house journals of UN organisations.

Pearson spotted the latest offering from the United Nations Centre for Human Development, which had its headquarters in Kuwisha. He leafed through its forty-page magazine, *Habitat*

Debate. One article in particular caught his attention: 'Shifting Paradigms', by a writer who was unfamiliar to him. 'An equable and holistic view of the city,' read Pearson, 'is what should drive local governments, while all other partners will naturally be driven by their own, narrower, interests.'

True, how very true, he thought.

On the opposite page was an equally engrossing article on redefining international co-operation, which extolled the benefits of a 'common humanity that will allow us to progress together'. It was illustrated by a cartoon that showed a beaming young woman casting off her jacket marked 'capitalism', and shaking the hand of a smiling worker who was discarding a shirt marked 'communism' with equal enthusiasm.

Cecil groaned so loudly that he awoke the occupant of an adjacent armchair. The man graciously accepted the journalist's apologies and went back to sleep.

The *mbumba* were still at it. Pearson felt terminally bored. An hour later, he had come to the end of the available reading material, but something in one of the articles had jogged his memory. He jotted down a proverb:

'Beware the tick bird that eats the seed of the marula tree.'

It was sufficiently obscure, he felt, to give even Shadrack pause for thought. Still no word on the presidential audience. He looked round the room.

There must have been a dozen other supplicants for the favour of great men, patiently waiting, and taking the chance to catch up on sleep. Like the anteroom at State House, natural light was kept out. Air-conditioners whirred and wheezed, coughed or spluttered, but at least they worked. This was, after all, the VIP lounge. Two listless ladies ferried tepid colas and orange drinks to those who were awake, and needed something to wash down the salted groundnuts, set out in white saucers around the dim room.

There was no sign of impatience, no trace of frustration. All

184

present had reached the annex to the rich, the famous and the influential, who had gathered at the airport to welcome the official visitor. Those in the waiting room could do no more than wait. Most of them surrendered to the deep, capacious armchairs and sofas, topped by a crescent of hair oil, closed their eyes, and dozed.

Pearson rebuked himself for his own fidgeting impatience, and decided to pass the time by playing his favourite ministerial waiting room game. The idea was to take four or five words or phrases from a United Nations document, and rearrange them so that the new sentence made as much sense as the original.

He chose a page from a United Nations Habitat press release, and selected the words that irritated him most: capacity building, ownership, partnership, and integral, and set about putting them in a different order. He had made it too easy for himself, however, and the words slotted effortlessly into place:

'Capacity building partnership is integral to ownership.'
'Partnership and ownership are integral to capacity building.'
'Integral to partnership is capacity building and ownership.'
'Ownership of capacity building is integral to partnership.'

Much to the nervous disapproval of the security staff who guarded the entrance to the lounge, Pearson decided to stretch his legs. He stepped through the door and strolled ten yards down the passage, where it was possible to look out at the roped-off reception area on the airport apron.

Pearson was watching the *mbumba*, trying to spot the president, when a hand tapped his shoulder. It was Punabantu:

'Your request for an audience with His Excellency has been granted.'

'Very kind,' said Pearson obsequiously. Punabantu ignored him.

'Follow me.'

Pearson dutifully followed.

To Pearson's surprise, he was still nervous. Although he had attended press conferences addressed by the president, this would be his first one-on-one, his first personal encounter with the man who had dominated the nation for so long.

Punabantu had tried to put him at his ease, but instead of sitting in on the interview, as Pearson had expected, the press officer excused himself, and backed out of the room, closing the doors as he left. The president's personal secretary sat at the other end of a long oak table, notebook open, pencil poised, and looked curiously at Pearson. The president entered, dressed in his usual pinstriped suit, fresh-picked rose in its lapel:

'So, Mr Pearson,' he said jovially.

Pearson, expecting this introduction to be followed up, remained silent, awaiting the next sentence. Nduka looked at him quizzically.

'Is this an example of dumb insolence, or are you just dumb?'

Pearson was certainly not dumb, and had no intention of being insolent. It was simply that despite himself, he was over-awed, seated in front of one of African nationalism's founding fathers.

He had often thought about what he would do in this situation, how he would conduct an interview. Would he leave the tough questions until the end, and spend the first part of the session simply taking stock of the man, and gathering colour? Or should he go straight for the jugular, and raise the issue of corruption that was destroying the country?

As he sat there he felt his resolve falling away, for he was coming under the spell of the old man. To his dismay, he felt uneasy, even fearful. This, after all, was living history in front of him. Nduka was the man who had galvanised his country into rejecting British rule, whose political challengers had all died in road accidents that were never fully explained, and who had presided over an increasingly authoritarian regime in which allegations of torture of political dissidents had become commonplace.

Pearson stammered an apology, and looking down at his notebook to refresh his memory, tried to open the interview with the anodyne question he used at most presidential interviews, along the lines of: 'What are your greatest achievements since independence?'

But the president seemed not to have heard, and Pearson began to wonder if the stories about the old man going slightly bonkers were true. Nduka's eyes were concealed behind his dark glasses, and he seemed preoccupied. Pearson looked desperately at the secretary for help. The man returned his gaze, impassively. Pearson came up with his second question, this time on agriculture. The combination of drought and flood was undoubtedly the main factor in the food shortage, but this happened every year – why should the international donors bail him out?

There was still no response. Perhaps the question had offended the president? Pearson was about to come up with a third and last attempt to engage the man when Nduka broke his silence, and embarked on an anecdote apropos of nothing, yet one he seemed determined to tell.

'When I was a young man, indeed, a boy, before Kuwisha became independent,' President Nduka began, 'I worked as a kitchen *toto*.'

He paused: 'You know what a *toto* is, Pearson? A *toto* is a little boy who usually works in the house, like an apprentice house steward.'

Cecil nodded.

'I worked for a white man called Smiler May, who lived in a

187

small town in the middle of Zimbabwe called Gwelo, now known as Gweru. Other white men had much admiration for Smiler. They said he knew how to manage natives. He knew how to manage natives. I saw it for myself, many times. Whenever his boy, Joseph – they called men "boys" in those days,' he chuckled, 'whenever his boy got drunk, which I must acknowledge was many times, he gave him a sound thrashing, behind the *kia*.'

He broke off, took a sip of water, and continued.

'The *kia*, as I assume you know, Pearson, is the small room in which servants live, at the end of the garden.'

Cecil nodded.

'I expect you have a steward?'

Cecil nodded again.

'And no doubt a pension scheme for him, and for your other local staff?'

Cecil shook his head. The president feigned surprise.

'I assume you and your colleagues pay Kuwisha income tax?'

Cecil started to get an inkling of what it must be like to be a cabinet minister exposed to one of Nduka's public grillings.

The president did not wait for an answer, which Pearson was confident he knew anyway. Neither he, nor any members of the foreign press corps, paid income tax, not in Kuwisha, and not in the UK. The government of Kuwisha had turned a blind eye to this omission, which made a posting to Kuwisha especially attractive; in return, the foreign correspondents were inclined to turn a blind eye to many of the country's failings.

'I digress. I was telling you about the sound thrashings, behind the *kia*. Yes, it was behind the *kia*, and the boys who were cheeky were given a sound hiding.'

The president stopped.

'Do you understand, Pearson?'

The question was rhetorical, and Cecil nodded, and listened, while his questions about corruption and mismanagement became less and less pressing.

'No one was more appreciative of these thrashings than Joseph,' continued Nduka. 'No one was more appreciative of these hidings than Joseph, his boy. That is what Smiler May told his friends. I myself, I heard him say that.'

'But one thing bothered my boss, Mr Smiler May.' The president paused between each of the last words, their subtle venom enhanced.

'Mr – pause – Smiler – pause – May,' Nduka repeated.

'One thing disturbed him. There was something in Joseph's expression. At the end of each thrashing, complained Mr May, the boy was still cheeky.'

'Do I have to explain what this word means, Pearson?'

He didn't wait for Cecil to answer.

'It was the early 1950s, a time when the African nationalist movement throughout the continent was starting to flex its muscles. Cheeky meant dissent, potential rebellion. Today, Pearson, today Africa is again cheeky.'

'You, your people, your institutions, the international community, the donors, you like to take us Africans behind the *kia*. The World Bank, the IMF, the Smiler Mays of today, take us behind the *kia*, and give us a sound thrashing. They think they know how to handle the natives, Pearson.'

The president laughed.

'They give us a sound hiding. But we African boys, we are still cheeky!'

'You thrash us, Pearson. Particularly your paper, the *Financial News*. Oh yes. You and your World Bank friends, and your IMF friends, you cuff us about the ears. Cuff! And we devalue our currencies. Slap! We privatise our state-owned companies. Then comes a punch, and we cut subsidies. Another punch, and we are ordered to become a multi-party democracy! Five years it goes on, ten years, fifteen years of thrashing! Each time, after

IMF agreements and World Bank loans, each time we come out from behind the *kia*, saying, just like Joseph, "thank you my baas, thank you my baas". Just like Joseph, and Mr Smiler May. Thank you, *baasie*, thank you, master.'

The president mimicked the singsong, whining intonation of a South African black man in the days of apartheid.

'But we are still cheeky! We are not stupid, Pearson, we are still very, very . . . cheeky.'

Nduka repeated: 'Very – (pause) – very – (pause) – cheeky.'

Silence fell. In a curious way, the story broke the ice.

Cecil started to relax, and began to encourage the president to reminisce about the past.

He did not need much encouragement.

'Your people, Pearson, remember your history with Africa only when it suits you. But the past is not another country. Your mistakes live on. Just about wherever your people have been involved, there have been mistakes.'

Pearson wondered if it had been unwise to steer the conversation in this direction, but it was too late now.

'Your people sold Diego Garcia to the Americans, and it is now a military base. You sympathised with the white regime in Rhodesia, oh yes. You stopped Zambia getting money from the World Bank to build a railway line to Dar es Salaam, and Kaunda had to trade through white Rhodesia. You were, I remember, against the marriage of my friend, President Seretse Khama of Botswana, because his bride was white. Your rule in Northern Rhodesia lasted sixty years – yet when Kaunda won independence he had a dozen university graduates. You forget that Margaret Thatcher said that the ANC of South Africa was a "terrorist organisation".'

Nduka delivered his last salvo:

'Your people give us lectures about human rights. We may deserve lectures, but I don't like lectures from men who carry big sticks, but who are moral pygmies.'

The two men had been chatting amiably for a good thirty minutes when Punabantu slipped back into the room and whispered in the president's ear. The session was coming to an end, and to his shame, Pearson had failed to ask his tough questions.

'I understand you are leaving us soon, Pearson?'

'Yes, Mr President.'

'Another three-year man – I had hoped for more, Pearson, I had hoped for more. Perhaps we can persuade you to stay . . .'

He chuckled.

'But if we do decide to let you go, I also hope that you will leave having done less harm than good, but I doubt it.'

Pearson's blood ran cold. Could he have been rumbled? Was the president toying with him?

Nduka stood up.

'Have you seen much of our country? There is much to learn. Much to learn, Mr Pearson.'

If he had learnt anything, Cecil had obtained an insight into the old man's curious power over his people. Seldom if ever had he met a politician with such presence.

'Victorian values and a dash of voodoo' – for the first time since he had tossed off the phrase in the *FN* profile, Pearson started to understand what it meant.

He too rose to his feet.

'When I return to Kuwisha,' he found himself saying, 'I would like to come with a few books, relax, and write my own book.'

It was an odd thing to say. Pearson had no plans to return, and had told no-one else about his desire to write a book.

Nduka responded graciously.

'You will be welcome. You can take your books, read and write, on the Nyali plateau,' he said.

'You must feel at home. And look at the animals, the animals will entertain you.'

'I look forward to that, sir,' and once again Pearson surprised himself.

Nduka wasn't finished.

'But be careful not to go too near the lion. And even worse, look out for the leopard. The lion is less dangerous than the leopard. I fear the leopard much more than the lion.'

Punabantu, who had slipped in a few minutes earlier, was getting nervous. Looking at Pearson, he tapped his watch. The interview – or audience – was over. Pearson was gathering his notebook and tape recorder when he looked up. Nduka was leaving the room, but stopped, turned round, and waved. The wave was accompanied by a knowing smile, a smile of complicity and insight, and Pearson felt the hairs on the back of his neck stand up.

The president then nodded at him, and moved slowly out of the room, followed by his private secretary, who had not taken a note throughout the entire session. As Pearson left the room, ahead of Punabantu, a thought struck him.

'As far as I know, there are no lions on the Nyali plateau,' he said to Punabantu.

The press secretary looked at him tolerantly.

'So?'

'So the president was talking about domestic politics?'

'Of course,' said Punabantu, 'of course he was.'

'What did he mean?'

The press secretary smiled.

'You'll have to ask him that next time you see him. You'll just have to come back to Kuwisha. Or perhaps we will not let you go.' Puna chortled, and patted Cecil on the back:

'Only joking.'

Pearson laughed with relief, and then, as Punabantu gave him an odd look, began to worry again.

20

'Only brave men eat the flesh of the old goat'

The road back from the airport into the city was clear, and twenty minutes later Pearson was parking his car outside the high wall that surrounded the British High Commission. He was relieved to be on time for his meeting with David Podmore. The relationship between the two men was strained, and Pearson knew in his heart that he, rather than Podmore, was to blame.

The diplomat, prompted by the high commissioner, had offered to host Pearson's farewell drinks evening. Although grudgingly appreciative, Pearson was nonetheless somewhat miffed, and turned the offer down – prompting Lucy to call him 'a pompous arse'. She was not swayed by his argument that after nearly three years in Kuwisha, during which time he had not caused the High Commission any serious embarrassment, and had never had need of its services, he deserved better than that. A farewell dinner hosted by the High Commissioner himself would have been about right, he felt.

'Cecil!'

Podmore had come down the stairs to collect his guest in a gesture that suggested respect and friendship, but in truth indicated the opposite. He took Pearson up the flight of stairs to his office, where tea and shortbread was waiting. The exchange then followed a long established pattern: mutual expressions of esteem, and insincere regret that they had not seen more of each other. But the conversation soon moved on to more contentious matters, while maintaining a veneer of pleasantries.

The bread-and-butter matters were soon settled: how much emergency aid to Kuwisha would the UK provide? Why so little, given that scores of thousands had been made homeless by the floods? Why so much, given that corruption was endemic? Back and forth the exchanges went, neither side scoring off the other, and neither side caring very much anyway.

The conversation then changed, both in tone and substance. Podmore reminded Pearson that everything had to be 'off the record', a vague term that was frequently misunderstood. Essentially it meant that the diplomat who was being questioned could prevaricate and deceive, knowing that he or she could deny what had been said with a clear conscience.

Podmore had much to get off his chest.

He began by expressing his concerns and doubts about the future of what after all was a delightful country with marvellous people, living in an troubled region. The 'bloody Congo peace initiative,' as he termed it, seemed to have stalled again. Podmore pursed his lips, and put on his Africa expert look. He seemed to take the matter personally, as irritated as a sports-loving headmaster confronted by a stubborn boy who refuses to play rugby.

He fiddled with an unlit cigarette.

'When will these people start to respect their own kind?' Podmore asked, in a tone that made clear that he did not expect an answer to the question. He certainly gave Pearson no time to respond.

'As you know, I have no brief one way or the other for the colonial period. Not my job,' he said firmly, 'not my business. And anyway, it ended more than forty years ago. The past is past, for Christ's sake, it's bloody well over.'

Podmore thumped the armrest of his chair in emphasis, a

gesture that carried the implication that he had made a contentious or controversial statement. By way of confirming that he felt he had overstepped the diplomatic mark, he apologised.

'Sorry,' he said, 'got carried away. It's just that it all gets me down sometimes. But it's true – it's bloody well over.'

Pearson was tempted to argue, but opted for more shortbread.

'Tuck in, old boy, Mrs P's best.'

Podmore took a sip of tea, and Pearson braced himself for what was to come.

'At least they knew what was what,' said Podmore, with a touch of defiance.

'What what?' asked Pearson

Podmore looked at him suspiciously.

'What do you mean, what?'

'Well, just what what was what? I mean, what what were you referring to, exactly . . .'

He allowed his voice to trail away, deferentially.

Podmore seemed mollified.

'You can say what you like about the colonial days, and quite frankly, to be perfectly honest, I would probably go along with much of it. But the *wananchi*, the common people, the ordinary blokes, they could sleep safe in their beds, respected the police and vice versa, the civil service was honest, the rule of law was respected, schools had books, clinics had basic medicines, and so on.'

Pearson was about to break his silence, but thought the better of it.

'I know what you're going to say,' said Podmore. 'And I agree with you.'

He pushed his chair nearer to Pearson, close enough for Cecil to smell that he had been smoking on the sly, and lowered his voice, as if concerned about eavesdroppers.

'To be honest, there should have been more schools, there

should have been more locals in the civil service, and so on. It's unforgivable, a bloody disgrace.'

He assumed the air of a man who was tough but fair.

'Whatever else you can say, and I would be the first to say it, you cannot deny that. A bloody disgrace. But on balance, life was a damn sight better for the average indigenous.'

Podmore sat back with an 'I-may-be-a-British-diplomat-but-I-believe-in-plain-words-and-plain-speaking' expression on his face. It was a touch redder than usual, due to the passion with which he was expressing his views.

Pearson nodded his head in apparent agreement, encouraging Podmore to continue.

It came out in a rush. Strung together with familiarity and a fluency that stemmed from belief and conviction, were all the familiar code words and weasel phrases: *inexperience, impressive, potential, couldn't be friendlier, let down by their leaders, splendid people.* They all emerged in Podmore's lecture, in a tone of baffled frustration, underlaid with irritation, in which he set out what was wrong with Kuwisha in particular, and Africa in general.

Pearson was undecided. Should he break his silence, and tell the diplomat that he was talking balls, or keep quiet, finish his tea and eat the rest of the shortbread? He decided to compromise.

'Ermaagh' he mumbled.

'Help yourself to another biscuit,' said Podmore.

By God, I'm earning every bloody crumb, thought Pearson, and tucked in.

Podmore was in full swing.

'Just take Rwanda,' he said, his face now shrouded in an expression of pain, which hinted that he had seen, at first hand, unspeakable brutality. 'Strictly off the record,' he continued, and Pearson prepared himself for a disclosure of stunning banality.

'Strictly off the record, what I cannot understand is this black on black violence, killing their own kind.'

He looked at Pearson with dislike, despite the professional bonhomie. The sub-text was clear:

'You might think me a narrow-minded reactionary, but I have a point. You damn liberals won't admit the evidence before your eyes. You know that it is all bloody hopeless, and all hopelessly bloody, but you just cannot bring yourselves to admit it.'

'I see what you mean,' said Pearson through gritted teeth and a mouth full of shortbread.

Podmore shot him a look of contempt, and did not reply.

Pearson helped himself to yet another piece of home-made shortbread, drained his cup, and took refuge in the British diplomats' time-honoured way of disagreeing fundamentally with what the speaker had said while remaining polite.

'I hear what you say, I hear what you say.'

That at least was how he meant to end the exchange, but to his shame, Pearson heard himself throw in the towel:

'You have got a point, David, you have got a point.'

Furniver was never at his best in the morning, but today he felt especially awful.

It had been a terrible, ghastly evening. What on earth did Mr Kigali think of his employer? Would he leave his service? And if the steward did leave, how would he explain it to Charity? Jobs were scarce in Kuwisha, and while it was not uncommon for stewards to be sacked, it was almost unheard of that one should resign.

He had got halfway to *Harrods* before he realised that he had forgotten to check the fax machine, which had gone off the night before, when he was in his bath. He turned on his tracks, and let himself in to the office, and went upstairs, puffing slightly with the exertion. Not for the first time, he vowed to cut down on 'bitings'. As he expected, a fax awaited him.

'Bloody hell!'

He read it a second time.

It had come from London, sent in the name of Rupert Fanshawe, a senior partner in the firm of Fanshawe and Fanshawe.

Furniver's heart sank.

He was no lawyer, as he was discovering. And he was beginning to realise the price of the folly into which he had led his dear friend. Charity was sure to lose, and lose heavily. Costs would certainly be awarded against her, and they would be punitive. It stuck in his gullet, but he and Charity would have to throw themselves on Fanshawe's mercy, and the sooner the better.

He read the fax yet again, but there was no mistaking the message.

There was no time to lose. He stuffed the sheet of paper in his briefcase, and set off for *Harrods*.

On the way he rehearsed what he would say:

'It is all very unfair,' he would tell her, 'but it is the law. The lawyers acting on behalf of the London duka are right. You can't blame them. *Harrods* in London was the first to use the name, and that gave it the undeniable rights to use it. Could the bar not be called *Charity's International Bar (and Nightspot)*, for example? Surely this made sense?'

Furniver was sitting in his favourite chair, moving his itching bottom from side to side – rather like Lucy's dog Shango sliding along the living room carpet, attempting to dislodge the worms with which the creature was frequently afflicted – when Charity came round the corner.

The morning rush was over, and she could take a breather before getting ready for lunch.

'Have you seen my rats?' she asked. 'They have missed breakfast.'

But she did not press the matter. While it was unusual for the boys to miss breakfast, it was not unprecedented.

'I have been watching you, Furniver. Why are you talking to yourself? And you seem to be very uncomfortable in that chair . . .'

He opened his briefcase, and pulled out the file on *Harrods*, gave an apologetic cough, and handed over the fax that had arrived the night before. He decided to hold back on his carefully rehearsed case for capitulation. The fax would surely speak for itself.

But as Charity read the single sheet of paper, her eyes narrowed and she sucked in her breath, danger signals that he had come to recognise.

'*Am flying out on the next available BA flight. I will phone on arrival to arrange a meeting in your chambers. Rupert Fanshawe.*'

Any thoughts that Charity may have had of compromise were knocked on the head.

'Furniver!' she barked. 'I have decided. I have been reading and reading that registered letter. Now this fax. It is beastly rude! They have no right to do this. I will not change the name. I will not. Why should these London people care? Everyone in Kireba knows it is the name of my father. And not even white man's law can change that. It is a fact. I am just tired, tired and sick of all this trouble.'

Charity paused for breath.

'Let this man come. Tell his cheeky London people that they must stop bothering me with these stupid letters. Tell them that . . .'

Charity slapped a fly that had dared to settle on one of her scrubbed wooden tables.

'We will tell him that Charity Tangwenya Mupanga, who runs Harrods International Bar (and Nightspot), says they must stop this nonsense. Or else . . .'

She looked thoughtfully across the vista of corrugated iron

and plastic sheeting that stretched before her, and considered the worst she could wish on them.

Furniver waited, apprehensive and fascinated, his own firm intention melting.

'Or else when we go to court, here, in Kuwisha, we ourselves will ask for that thing called damages. We will ask for damage money because my father's name and my name has been damaged.'

She chuckled fiercely.

'And you tell them that the widow of Bishop David Mupanga, bishop of the battered and shepherd of the shattered, a man whom your people in England respected so highly they made him a member of the Leeds Working Club, tell them that I, Charity Mupanga, the first daughter of Mwai Tangwenya, I am prepared to pay the dogs who in this country call themselves judges, to be sure of justice. Tell them in your special language, but tell them, Furniver, tell them.'

Charity wasn't finished.

'These stupid threats by this lawyer are duck's water off my back. We will fight them, and my dear father will be with us.'

Charity took Furniver's stunned silence for assent and support.

She spotted a customer trying to slip away without paying, and shouted after him.

'One more time and you don't come again!'

Charity popped into the kitchen, poured herself a mug of tea, and sipped as she looked over Furniver's shoulder while he unhappily drafted their reply. It would be faxed to Kuwisha's Intercontinental Hotel, where Rupert Fanshawe said he would be staying.

'My client still hopes that the matter can be settled amicably,' it ended. *'As evidence of her goodwill, she has asked me to invite your representative to join us on his arrival in a meal of roast chicken necks and Tusker, a*

*locally made beer of exceptional quality, at Harrods International Bar
(and Nightspot), Uhuru Avenue.*

I await confirmation of your acceptance.

Yours faithfully,

Edward Furniver . . .

'Good, very good,' she said, taking him by the elbow. 'I
knew you would agree. We will explain everything to the man
from London when he comes. Meanwhile, we are correct to
invite him to eat with us, even though he is a lawyer. That is a
proper thing to do. We will eat here, at *Harrods*. He will be
ashamed when he sees that we are decent Christian people,
who work hard.'

A thought occurred to her.

'Can you get roast chicken necks in London?'

Damn and double damn! Furniver was about to explode,
but held himself in check. Chicken necks! How could Charity
bother about chicken necks at a time like this? Nevertheless, he
gave her question careful consideration. Washington DC probably, New York possibly, but London? He shook his head.

'Unlikely.'

Charity's low opinion of the great metropolis was confirmed. It was clear that the prospect of offering hospitality
had cheered her somewhat, and Furniver did not have the
heart to keep to his plan.

'I will make a special dish of chicken necks for this man
from London,' said Charity, determined that whatever faults
Kuwisha might have, its reputation for generous treatment of
strangers would be sustained.

'Then we will talk business.'

Titus Ntoto and Cyrus Rutere, two stick figures in the lush central Kuwisha landscape of purple bougainvillea, red-flowered
flame trees and green lawns, made their way along the winding road that climbed the hill on which State House stood.

Built by the British administrator in 1923 and converted into the country's centre of government at independence in 1971, from afar it gleamed like a wedding cake. The nearer one got to it, however, the less impressive it was. The ornate iron entrance gates were rusting, the drive to State House was potholed, and the sentry boxes needed coats of fresh paint. Scraggy peacocks stalked the overgrown lawns, their screeching the bane of the lives of radio reporters trying to record President Nduka's answers to questions at the many press conferences held in the State House gardens.

His colonial predecessor had overseen the construction of a nine-hole golf course, and the president, who shared his love of the game, had ensured that in contrast to the unkempt lawns, the fairways and the greens were impeccable. The seventh hole was a few feet from the road, and the boys made a brief diversion, so they could experience the pleasure of feeling their bare feet on the soft, recently watered grass. A greenkeeper working on the fairway of the adjoining hole soon spotted them, and waved his fist, and they returned to the road.

Security was tight, and consisted of a series of barriers, the first manned at the main entrance by shabbily turned out soldiers. But they seemed less than vigilant, for much of their time was taken up in negotiations with vendors, mainly ladies, whose wares included chickens, bowls of groundnuts, plastic packets of tomatoes and plump mangoes, and bottles of cooking oil, carried on their broad and long-suffering backs, along with their babies.

Cyrus was getting nervous.

'Are you sure it will work, Ntoto?' he asked, resisting the temptation to nibble one of the roasted corncobs. Privately, Ntoto was far from certain.

'You are invisible, Ntoto,' Cecil had said. 'No-one will notice you, or inspect your bag – provided you behave as you are expected to behave.'

'What *muti* [medicine] did Mr Cecil give you?' Cyrus demanded.

'He didn't give me anything. I have said to you already – he just told me two stories. One about Mboya, the other about a wedding in Johannesburg,' Ntoto replied.

Cyrus looked sceptical.

'Surely, he must have given you some *muti*?'

Ntoto looked at him scornfully.

'We don't need special *muti*,' he said.

'We have our own *muti* – our brains. Let me tell you the stories, Rutere . . . But first I will tell you everything that happened in Pearson's office . . .'

Cyrus listened, asking the occasional question. When Ntoto had reached the end of his account of the time in Pearson's office, he looked sceptical. It seemed he was about to comment, but decided against it.

He tugged at Ntoto's sleeve.

'Now tell me the stories,' he demanded.

'First,' said Ntoto, 'I will tell you the story about Mr Tom Mboya. Pearson says it is a true story, and Mr Mboya tells it himself, in his book about his life,' said Ntoto, as they strode on to State House, which like most strategic installations was located close to the barracks of the presidential guard.

'This is what Pearson told me, exact: One day in 1951, before he became a member of parliament, long before he was killed, at a time when his country was run by the British, Mr Mboya was working by himself, in the government Health Department. He was testing milk.'

Rutere nodded.

'The Europeans who worked with him were away,' Ntoto continued: 'So Mr Mboya was in the office, by himself, in charge . . .'

He paused to give the point emphasis.

'Mr Mboya was in charge, and a European lady came in with some milk to test. She looked around, but did not greet him.'

Rutere looked shocked.

'Mr Mboya said to her: "Good morning, madam." She said nothing. So he said again: "Good morning, madam." Still she did not greet him.'

'Phauw!'

Rutere was astonished. How could she have been so rude?

'Instead she looked around, looking, looking, everywhere,' Ntoto continued, putting his hand to his forehead, and making peering gestures.

'And then she asked: "Is there anybody here?"'

They walked on for a few more paces.

Cyrus looked thoughtful.

'So although Mr Mboya was there, and she spoke to him, she did not see him?'

'Not properly. She saw him, but not as a full person,' said Ntoto.

'That is the end of the first story. Let me tell you the second story, and then you will understand even better,' he said, kicking a round pebble that lay in his path.

'Here is Pearson's second story,' said Ntoto.

'There was a big wedding, a very big wedding in Jo'burg, between two famous people.'

'What were their names?' asked Rutere.

'I do not know,' replied Ntoto, 'but they were white people.'

'The newspapers wanted pictures, but all the photographers were European, and they were stopped by the security guards. Then one editor had an idea, a very good idea. He called in his kitchen *toto* and taught him how to use a camera. The *toto* was then sent to the wedding with a bunch of flowers, in which the camera was hidden. The guards let the *toto* through, without bother. They did not treat *toto*s as real people. They did not search him. The next day, Rutere, photographs of the wedding were in the newspaper,' said Titus.

'And that is a true story. And it is the story that gave Pearson the idea. We can go to places that adults cannot go. We are not seen as proper people even, we are just seen as useless Kireba boys who smell like dogs, and who are treated no better than dogs,' he said bitterly.

There was silence as Cyrus digested the two stories.

'Phauw!' he said, 'Phauw!'

He could not resist adding: 'I still think it would be better if we had *muti*.' But that was all he said – and Titus Ntoto knew the lesson of the stories had got through . . .

As the two boys approached the first security check after the main entrance to State House, a car hooted at them, and Ntoto and Cyrus leapt onto the verge with cries of alarm.

Although they didn't recognise the car's occupants, it was the World Bank mission, on the way back to the hotel after their meeting with the president. The black Mercedes was forced to slow down by the bumps in the road, known to local taxi drivers as sleeping policemen, and as the car drew level, the Kuwisha driver lowered his window and smiled benevolently at the boys.

'Out of my way, dog turds.'

Ntoto hissed with anger, but contained himself.

'Do you know why your wife eats so well?'

The chauffeur could not resist. He slowed down, almost stopping alongside the boys.

'Why, you little snot-bag?'

'Because your brother gives her a bowl of *ugali* every time she sleeps with a soldier.'

Cyrus rocked with laughter.

The driver scowled, wound up the car window, and drove on.

'What's so funny?' asked Hardwick Hardwicke, looking up from his files.

'They are making a joke about the president,' said the driver.

Hardwicke nodded, and looked meaningfully at Fingers, who was in the middle of deciding whether he would use a three or a two iron off the fifth tee.

'You see? The old bugger is on the run,' he said: 'He's losing the confidence of the people.'

The car accelerated, leaving the two boys in its wake.

At the security barrier, Ntoto and Rutere were cursorily searched. As Pearson had confidently predicted, there was much greater interest in the bag of maize cobs. One cob per roadblock was the rate, and once they had paid this levy after some tough bargaining, they were nodded through. There were still two checkpoints to go, but the procedure was much the same, although at each subsequent check there were fewer soldiers, and more men wearing suits and dark glasses.

By the time they reached the last one, there were only three soldiers, but half a dozen civilians, all wearing dark glasses and all carrying mobile phones. It was at this point that Ntoto and Cyrus for the first time felt afraid, and with good reason. These men were thugs, and Cecil's theory was about to be tested.

'Right,' said Ntoto.

He took a pinch of pepper from the packet Pearson had given him, sprinkled the grains in the palm of his hand, raised it to his nostrils, and sniffed deeply. Rutere was caught napping by the explosive series of sneezes that followed, and took the brunt of the blast.

With a shudder of distaste, he did his best to wipe off the bits of recently chewed corncob and saliva with which he had been sprayed from head to toe.

'Good, that is very good, Ntoto,' said Rutere, and taking great care to avoid the yellow stream that dangled from his friend's nose, shoved Titus in the chest.

It looked like a typical adolescent quarrel which was degenerating into a scrap, with each boy taking it in turn to push the other, chins jutting forward and bodies braced for the anticipated punch that would turn a scrap into a fight. Suddenly, without warning, Cyrus slapped Ntoto across the face, and uncharacteristically Ntoto burst out crying. First quietly, then huge, racking sobs as Cyrus slapped him again. Ntoto ran up to one of the plain-clothed security officers, and clung to his leg like a tick on a cow, and appealed for protection. By this time the snot gathering at his nose was spectacular.

'He has taken my corn,' squealed Ntoto. 'He has taken my corn.'

The security officer tried to shake the diminutive figure loose, with no success. But what made him increasingly alarmed was the viscous thread of mucus that was now dangling precariously from Ntoto's nostrils. Before the irate man could wrench himself free, Ntoto delicately used the forefinger of his left hand, blocking first one nostril, then the next, like a professional football player expressing his anger over the referee's decision, and cleared his nose with two powerful snorts.

The snot flew unerringly to its targets. One load attached itself to the cuff of the security officer's jacket. The other clung to his red silk tie, providing a striking contrast in colours.

With a moan of disgust and fury, the officer shook Ntoto off, flinging him several feet, his mood not helped as his colleagues chortled.

'Get going, you loathsome toad,' said one, in between guffaws, as the victim used a leaf to scrape off the snot, almost whimpering in his disgust.

'Go! Go! Go, before he kills you.'

Titus and Cyrus scuttled through the last roadblock, still clutching their sacks of the remaining maize, and exchanging blows until they had rounded the corner of the bougainvillea, within sight of Mlambo's hut.

They collapsed with laughter.

'It worked, it worked.'

Pearson had been right. They had been treated as what he had called 'pieces of nothing', and the anger in their hearts was truly invisible, but surely it would grow.

21

'Beware the tick bird that cleans
the crocodile's teeth'

At about the time the president had been looking out over Kireba and contemplating its fate, Lucy Gomball and other NGO aid workers were at the World Bank's city office, listening to a briefing from Reuttman's deputy on the proposed upgrading of the slum. It was high on the agenda for the Bank talks with Nduka and his officials. Should the negotiations prove successful, the pilot scheme under way would be followed up by a $250m Bank loan.

The new trunk road would go ahead. Provided the Bank was satisfied that the people of Kireba would be the beneficiaries, access roads would follow, opening up the slum to redevelopment.

If all went to plan, Kireba would be upgraded in three phases, over five years. When complete – according to the blueprint drawn up with the help of experts from the UN Development Programme – about one third of the slum's 600,000 residents would have access to electricity, clean water, and decent toilets; they would be served by tarmac roads; two new primary schools, and six clinics would be built, as well as a post office; and the hawkers would have covered stands from which to sell their goods.

There was, however, a seemingly intractable problem: was the scheme a device to turn part of the slum into highly desirable properties for presidential cronies and party loyalists, in a long-term strategy to eliminate Kireba altogether?

In short, could the president be trusted? Residents had been encouraged to give a resounding 'No' to the plan by various opposition figures, including Newman Kibwana – though most believed that if Kibwana were in office, he too would have used the prospect of middle-class homes in 'new Kireba' as a source of patronage.

But as Lucy pointed out, there was a further problem:

'Let's assume it isn't a scheme to provide homes for Nduka's cronies. And let us assume that it will be carried out to the letter. We're still in a pickle, aren't we?'

She had to explain.

'Imagine that – the Bank – and Nduka make the announcement about the $250m at the end of Hardwicke's visit. Nduka agrees that it can be ring-fenced. Contracts transparent, and so on. Well, even the sceptics in Kireba will have to think about it, and a lot of don't-knows will back Nduka. This could be enough to tip the balance and win Kireba for his party. And if he gets Kireba on his side, he can win the capital, and his chances of winning the election will be a jolly sight better than they are now.'

She paused, letting her analysis sink in.

'A clean contract to redevelop Kireba would be a small price for Nduka to pay for another five years in power. Heads he wins, tails we lose.'

All that could be done, Lucy argued, was between them to do their best to make sure that the project was closely monitored. WorldFeed and other non-government organisations would be the first to blow the whistle, she warned, if the Bank or its partners started fudging on transparency.

And then she began to press the buttons that had seemingly baffled Charity: community, self-help, environment, health. Above all, one word cropped up time and again, repeated like a mantra: ownership. If the project was to succeed, whether in the provision of low cost housing, or measures to speed up the delivery of clean water to Kireba, it had to be inspired, driven, monitored, and sustained by the residents.

By the time the meeting broke up, Lucy had won the day. Kuwisha's NGOs would support the scheme. She left the Bank's office with a sense of purpose that she had not felt since the heady first months of her posting to the country. It would be a long and hard struggle, and it would be some time before the results could be seen. But she would know that under her leadership, WorldFeed would have contributed to a lasting improvement in the dreadful conditions that made life hell for the residents of Kireba.

'Ownership,' she muttered as she drove off in her Land Rover, 'ownership.'

With such a busy life, Ferdinand Mlambo had little leisure time. Most of his spare hours – every Sunday afternoon, unless there was a presidential function – were spent playing football with the Mboya Boys. But the weight of expectation, his own and that of his family, hung heavy on him and put a burden on his shoulders. And it was to ease this burden that, every now and then, he indulged in what some would say was a vice. There was nothing Mlambo enjoyed more than to have a quiet smoke in a makeshift tool shed, near the State House kitchen. It was a habit well known to his good friends, Titus Ntoto and Cyrus Rutere, and it was there in the shed that they caught up with him.

Although surprised to see his pals, Mlambo was not alarmed. His senses were pleasantly dulled by the euphoria induced by several long drags of Mtoko Gold, which was the best *bhang* money could buy. But after the initial greetings, and when Ntoto began setting out the plan, and Mlambo's role in it, the kitchen *toto* was shocked out of his happy stupor.

He stubbed out his smoke, and stored it behind his ear.

'You are mad, Ntoto. You expect me to hide this tape recorder you have shown me in the president's study, before Mrs Nugilu comes for her meeting?'

'So you know when Mrs Nugilu is coming?'

Mlambo was affronted.

'Am I not the senior kitchen *toto*? Of course I know. She has been many times.'

He could not help showing off: 'And she is coming today, this afternoon even.'

Ntoto's eyes lit up.

'So what is your problem, Mlambo?'

The *toto* shook his head incredulously.

'And when the meeting is finished, I must go back to the study, get the machine, and come straight away to meet you at *Harrods*, and give it back to you?'

Ntoto nodded.

The effect of the *bhang* on Mlambo seemed to disappear, and his head cleared.

'You must have been sniffing very bad glue, Ntoto my friend. As we say in my country, the bird who picks the meat from the teeth of the crocodile takes care not to shit in its mouth.'

Ntoto smiled.

'Listen to me, fat boy, fat boy from Zimbabwe. As we say in this country, when the elephant farts, even the mighty baobab tree bends.'

Mlambo smiled back, for he had still not taken on board the gravity of his situation.

'You must stop sniffing glue, Ntoto. It is making you crazy.'

Ntoto tried a different tack. Patiently he went through the plan again. He produced the tape recorder. He showed Mlambo how easy it was to operate. Finally, he told Mlambo how much the machine was worth, and hinted that he and Rutere planned to sell it once it had served its purpose.

'It will buy us food for a year at *Harrods*,' Rutere chipped in, forgetting that Mlambo ate very well in the State House kitchen.

Their pleas made no impression on the boy. He was adamant.

'I won't do it.'

He folded his arms, and sat solidly on his substantial bottom, as if daring Ntoto to move him. He then recovered his smoke from behind his ear, lit it, took a deep pull, and blew smoke rings towards the corrugated iron roof of the hut.

Ntoto had expected no less from Mlambo. He changed tack.

'What,' he asked menacingly, 'if I kick your fat *butumba* until you cry?'

Mlambo shrugged. He stood up, turned round and pointed his substantial *butumba* in Ntoto's direction, and invited Titus to do his worst.

'Kick. Go on, kick,' he said, and blew another smoke ring as he bent over.

Ntoto was uneasy about his next move, but there was no alternative. It was now a matter of face. The *toto*'s rebellion could not be tolerated.

'You have read, Mlambo, that *bhang* rots your head? Bishop also said so.'

Ntoto, a great admirer of Bishop David Mupanga, did not know this for certain. In fact, Titus had never met the Bishop, and had never been to church. He was guessing, and as it happened, had guessed incorrectly. Bishop Mupanga had not gone public on the subject of *bhang* before he died, but the papers he left behind had included a draft sermon calling for its legalisation.

Ntoto was right in one respect. Mlambo would not be able to say he was wrong.

It seemed to have little effect, however. Mlambo just shrugged, and continued to present a derisory bottom, while

213

Ntoto put forward as good a case for blackmailing the Zimbabwean as he could manage. Now came the crunch.

'Also,' he said, 'also, the president has praised the *mungiki* who destroyed a *bhang* crop near the city.'

Mlambo nodded, still unmoved and still unconvinced, but wondering what was coming next. He wanted to point out that the *bhang* crop was being grown on land that was to be developed for private housing, and plots had already been allocated to President Nduka's cronies. The *mungiki*, on this occasion at least, were little more than the tools of rich men's ambitions. He decided to hold his tongue.

'Well, Mlambo,' Ntoto continued, 'it would be a great shame if the president was told that you sell his staff *bhang*. Here, at State House. And although you are a young boy, you yourself smoke it a lot.'

Ntoto paused. So far the Zimbabwean had appeared unmoved. What was to come was literally a blow below the belt, and he had to steel himself before delivering it.

'And you are not circumcised, Mlambo, and you know what the *mungiki* do if they find a boy who is not circumcised.'

The enormity of the implied threat sank in. Mlambo could hardly believe his ears. A sound kicking was a price he was prepared to pay for his refusal to co-operate. But to threaten to betray him in this way, with the clear suggestion that he – and in particular, his *shlonga* – would be exposed to the rusty knives of the *mungiki*! This went against the unwritten code of the Mboya Boys club.

He was about to say as much to Ntoto, and then took a second look at the face of the boy in front of him. Ntoto's eyes were hard and unyielding, his jaw set, his lips tight, and Mlambo realised he would be wasting his breath.

He took a final puff from his joint, and listened carefully to Ntoto's instructions.

*

Not even Mtoko Gold had been able to steady Mlambo's nerves when, soon after the meeting with Ntoto and Rutere, tape recorder in hand, he crept into the president's inner sanctum. He was so nervous that for a few moments he thought he would lose his lunch. He was not sure which prospect alarmed him most – the consequences of vomiting on the presidential carpet, or the loss of the tasty dish of *kapenta* [fish] and rice that lined his stomach.

President Nduka was at the weekly cabinet meeting, and the door to his study was ajar. Heart beating furiously, Mlambo pushed on it gently, and slipped in, looking around as he did so. He had lost count of the number of times he had brought the president his mid-afternoon glass of hot water, with a quarter of a fresh lemon and a bottle of honey, or the midday meal, or the morning tray of Earl Grey tea and scones which the president almost invariably failed to touch.

Mlambo never failed to experience a sense of awe at being in the presence of such a powerful man, but the sheer terror he endured now came close to paralysing his limbs.

The study smelt faintly of cigar smoke, even though a cigar had not been smoked there for years, overlaid with the aroma of beeswax furniture polish and the scent of fresh picked roses.

The trembling Mlambo peered about him. He had been mad to have succumbed to Ntoto's threats, crazy to agree to take part in a harebrained plot. But those *mungiki* . . .

Ntoto had refused to tell him what would be done with the tape, although Mlambo could guess. The boy had been very specific: the machine had to be in place, under one of the armchairs, or the desk, in time to record any meeting between the president and Anna Nugilu.

What else could he have done, other than comply, he asked himself? To have lost his job would have been bad enough. But to be held down by those *mungiki*, as they went to work with a

215

rusty razorblade, or a sharpened nail! His testicles shrank at the thought, and his cock seemed to shrivel with fear.

For a few minutes Mlambo stood and snivelled, and then with a low wail, he began confessing to his Zimbabwean ancestors, asking forgiveness, and seeking advice. He imagined his great grandfather, one of the heroes of Zimbabwe's first *chimurenga*, or liberation war, in the 1890s, listening patiently. But advice came there none.

He made a huge effort, pulled himself together, followed Ntoto's instructions, and placed the tape recorder under the president's desk. And not before time. The sound of voices came closer. The cabinet meeting had ended early, and the president was returning.

While Mlambo was a coward, he was not a fool, and had taken the precaution of coming into the study with a tray of tea. The *toto* blew his nose, wiped his fingers on the underside of one of the armchairs, adjusted his uniform of white shorts and white vest, retied the laces of his white plimsolls, took a deep breath, and stood to attention at the entrance to the study.

Nduka entered the room, small by the standards of the rest of State House, comfortably – but not extravagantly – furnished, in a style that seem heavily influenced by Britain of the 1950s.

The president vividly remembered his first visit to State House in the days when it was the seat of the colonial government. He was still a young man, just entering his thirties, but a political veteran who had been hardened by a spell in detention for various offences. The Governor of the day had done something that would have horrified the settlers had they ever learnt about it: he had invited a black man to take tea in what was then the inner sanctum of white rule.

A file was brought out, and some tough words exchanged, and both parties had stuck to the terms of the deal that was struck. And although it was a deal that paved his path to power, what he most vividly recalled was the ambience in that small room: cool on the hottest day, fresh-cut roses on the desk, the smell of polish and a lingering aroma of cigar, and armchairs too comfortable ever to go out of fashion.

When State House was being refitted, shortly before Kuwisha won independence, and Nduka was about to be installed as the country's founding president, he ordered that the contents of the Governor's study was to be saved, including the chintz armchairs and the leather sofa.

None of the furniture would have looked out of place in a conservative London club. Forty or so years later, the armchairs were still there. True, they had been re-upholstered at substantial expense. Every few years they were air freighted to London, transferred to a small family firm in Worcestershire which retained details of the original order, together with bolts of the original cloth, and flown back to Kuwisha, as good as old.

The walls were oak-panelled. On either side of a life-size portrait of the president, which hung over a vast fireplace, were the heads of two lions, shot and mounted by the colony's last governor, Sir James Kennedy. After independence, he kept up his ties, taking tea with the president regularly, escaping the foul British winters each year to soak up the Kuwisha sun.

Both men made much of the fact that as governor during British colonial days, he had ordered Nduka's detention.

'The best thing I ever did,' Sir James would joke.

The president agreed.

'I got my education in detention, at the British government's expense,' he used to beam in response to Sir James' comment. He always called his mentor Sir Kennedy. Whenever they met, the two men would slap each other on

217

the back, hug, and discuss the follies of the world in the presidential study, over Earl Grey tea and scones.

Sir James referred to Nduka as 'young man', and the president would smile with adolescent pleasure. When Kennedy died in a polo accident at the coast he was in his late eighties. Nduka ordered a state service, at which he delivered an eloquent and moving address, and was hurt by the daughter's insistence that the body should be buried on the family estate in Northumberland, rather than in Kuwisha.

Some commentators traced the decline of Kuwisha and the increase in presidential despotism to the former governor's demise, and the loss of his moderating voice. Others claimed that the death of Nduka's first wife, Sally, at about the same time was to blame for a change in the president's personality. Whoever was right, Earl Grey tea and scones were served in the study, every day, at mid-morning, when the president was in residence.

The president was in a mellow mood.

He looked across his desk at the fat boy, still standing to attention at the doorway.

'So, Mlambo, how is the football?' – or 'footyball', as Nduka pronounced it.

If it was true that the tape recorder began automatically, when someone started to speak, it should now be recording.

Mlambo, petrified, stayed silent. This was not the first time Nduka had raised the subject, and invariably he used it as an excuse to wander down the byways of his fading memory – most of which the kitchen *toto* had no desire whatsoever to discover or explore.

'The Mboya Boys United Football Club,' the president continued, rolling the words around his mouth. A distant look came into his eyes.

'Mboya, Mboya ... we met when we were both new members of parliament. Kenya was already independent, and

Kuwisha soon followed. He was a good man, very clever, and a good man. But he was ambitious.'

After a minute's pause, Nduka recited the pantheon of Africa's might-have-beens:

'Chisiza of Malawi, Lumumba of Congo, Mboya and Ouko of Kenya . . . Mupanga of Kuwisha – we all had those ambitious young men. All clever, some too clever. All ambitious.'

The president's voice trailed off. Mlambo stood rigid with fear. He had heard the rumours about Bishop David Mupanga's accident. The last thing he wanted was to know more.

'Would Africa be different if they had lived? What do you think, Mlambo? Your Zimbabwe, it has lost its clever men too . . . Chitepo, Tongogara, Edson Sithole . . .'

The meeting with Anna Nugilu was soon to start, and Mlambo got increasingly nervous.

President Nduka had a grudging respect for Anna Nugilu.

He no longer bothered to conceal their regular weekly meetings, same place, same time. Let the mischief makers and the dissidents spread their rumours. As the elections drew closer, so did the speculation that Mrs Nugilu was prepared to do a deal with him become more widespread. Few voters now believed that he had either the energy or the ideas to lead the country out of the mess into which it had sunk during his tenure.

He poured himself a glass of water, and washed down a handful of pills: one for his heart, a couple of vitamin capsules, and another for blood pressure. With every day that passed, his enemies claimed, the president's energy seemed diminished, and the country's problems became more acute.

Well, he would show them. The old lion was still cunning. He had read the columnists in the local papers. If Nugilu

219

ran, there was no guarantee that she would win, said the analysts; but the outcome would be a close thing. 'The president will know that he has a fight on his hands' concluded one writer.

'Let them try,' he growled. True, he was well past his physical prime. Nduka was the first to acknowledge this, and he made unsavoury jokes about it, inviting opponents to leave their wives with him for a night: 'Then let them judge!'

He would draw on his battle-forged guile. The bar room gossip, which the Central Intelligence Organisation monitored, and passed on to him in their daily state of the nation report, was correct – but only up to a point. Certainly he was tired, and his memory was not what it was. He was, after all, in his seventies . . . or was it his eighties?

'I am tired, very tired, Mlambo. Do you know when I was born? No? I was born in the year of the Great Floods. But was this the floods of 1927, or the floods of 1933? The elders are not sure. Not sure . . .'

But he was not losing his touch.

True, he was far from confident that he would win a clean fight – not that Kuwisha politics were ever clean. It would be a costly business to ensure that the ruling party won the election, even with the advantage of decades of patronage.

Nduka looked at the portrait of Sir James Kennedy hanging on the fireplace wall. What was that advice that his old friend used to give him, about enduring the consequences of difficult decisions?

'Make up your mind, and then lie back, old chap, lie back and think of England – or in your case, think of Kuwisha.'

He owed a stable presidential succession to the party, to the country, to the people of Kuwisha. But what if he couldn't manage it? It was a prospect too ghastly to contemplate.

Mrs Nugilu was due any minute now. She would be a worthy successor. She had chosen her campaign ground shrewdly, choosing not to focus directly on corruption. That was clever.

'All voters know politicians are corrupt,' Nduka was fond of saying: 'All are corrupt. But some are less corrupt than others.'

'They are more efficient, more efficient in putting their policies into practice than others.'

Mrs Nugilu had chosen to campaign on three issues – the environment, health and literacy.

Nduka had had many talks with Nugilu about this.

Kuwisha, she said, was a male-dominated society. 'Like the farmyard, the hens have no rights. We only lay eggs,' she said, to Nduka's croak of amusement.

And the male members of the electorate would surely be resentful of a campaign that smacked of women's issues, or which could be seen as an attack on vested interests. The men of the ruling establishment might be political dinosaurs, doomed to become extinct, but they were wealthy enough to buy votes by the ballot box. Any direct assault on them, however much they deserved it, Anna Nugilu had decided, must be avoided.

Nduka agreed with her, and he watched closely as she took her campaign the length and breadth of Kuwisha. She raised concerns that transcended the hidebound male elite, and went to the heart of the country's prospects. Her concerns about the environment – water, fuel, land erosion, and the effect of the declining stock of wild animals – were uppermost. After all, she pointed out, it was the environment that was the main attraction for the million visitors a year, who made tourism so important to Kuwisha. A healthy nation needed potable water, a right enjoyed by less than half of Kuwisha's people. If clean drinking water was available to all, the fatality rate for the children under five could be halved.

Anna Nugilu had also decided that it was not worth promising huge changes to the country's decrepit educational

221

system. Who would pay for it, after all? The country could not afford to maintain its existing schools, let alone find the money for new ones. Instead she committed her party to a ten-year literacy programme, using newspapers and radio stations, and supported with donor aid funds, at the end of which all adults would be able to read. That at least was the target.

This was also the best way to tackle Aids, she argued. There was nothing in her programme that the ruling class could object to, and there was every reason for the country's women to support her. It was, acknowledged President Nduka, a skilful strategy. He had said as much in the private exchanges with her. And the more he discussed the points she raised, the more he came to admire Anna Nugilu.

Mlambo was getting close to panicking. The tape was running, and eating up the sixty minutes it was designed to last. The president meandered on, having one of his mental walkabouts, those occasions which were starting to trouble his doctor and to alarm his advisers. No-one knew what triggered them, but they could last up to fifteen minutes, during which he would drift off into his own, silent world, or reminisce about events long over and days long past.

It was Mlambo's diffident but insistent cough that finally cut through to the president. Nduka refocused on the boy nervously watching him.

The private secretary announced the arrival of Anna Nugilu. The president dismissed Mlambo, and told him to wait in the gloomy ante-room, adjoining the study. He adjusted his dark glasses. Nduka's optician had advised him that little could be done to save his sight, but the glasses would delay the deterioration. He tugged at the jacket of his pinstripe suit, and moved behind his desk, placing his ornate ivory-handled flywhisk, made from the tail of a Colobus monkey, on the blotter in front of him. First, however, there was something to do, and it would not take more than a minute. He buzzed his secretary.

'Tell Lutuli' – the general manager of the State Bank of Kuwisha – 'that I will make sure that Newman Kibwana repays his loan, but not until after the elections. The bank will get its money by the end of next month. I want a story about this in the papers tomorrow. I have work for Kibwana.'

Nduka took a final look at himself in the mirror, pulled back his shoulders, and went to the doorway to greet his visitor. Twenty minutes later, the meeting was over. Mlambo watched from the ante-room as Mrs Nugilu shook hands with the president, adjusted the carnation in his lapel, gave him a kiss on his cheek, and then left State House.

Slowly and stiffly, the president left the study, and Mlambo thought he heard the sound of President Nduka's knees creaking. Nduka would be back soon to prepare his Uhuru Day message, and the sooner Mlambo got out of the study the better.

'Boy!'

Mlambo stiffened to attention.

'Take the tray back to the kitchen.'

The senior State House steward, Lovemore Mboga, who had brought in the president's afternoon medicine, stayed by Nduka's side. Thankful for the excuse to go back into the study, Mlambo collected the tray, grabbed the tape recorder from under the president's desk, stuffed it down his shorts, and scuttled out.

As Githongo turned out of the ante-room, bringing up the end of the presidential procession, the senior State House steward turned and gave Mlambo the evil eye, a look of venom and malice, enhanced by the fact that his right pupil had a white crescent encroaching on the pupil.

So preoccupied was Mlambo, so upset by Githongo's malign glare, that when he left State House for the rendezvous with Titus Ntoto and Cyrus Rutere, the *toto* failed to take the most elementary of precautions. Not once did he look round to see if he was being followed. Had he done so, he would have seen that a nondescript youth was never less than fifty yards from him . . .

Mlambo had trudged the journey from State House to *Harrods* burning with resentment. If it had been up to the *toto*, he would have washed his hands of the whole business. Ntoto and Rutere, they could go to hell, as far as he was concerned. But the papers that day carried some blood curdling accounts of the *mungiki*'s latest outrages, and the boy from Zimbabwe, unhappy though he was, felt that his decision to cooperate had been vindicated.

It was a cool and awkward meeting.

Mlambo refused Ntoto's conciliatory offer of a dough ball and Coke. And without a word, he handed over the tape recorder, and with it, the tape.

Ntoto fired off questions.

No, said Mlambo, he had not replayed the tape.

No, he insisted, he had no idea what was on it.

Nor, he added, did he want to see Ntoto again.

Ntoto shrugged.

'I was going to give you a share of what we get when we sell this tape recorder, Mlambo, one thousand ngwee, even, but if you don't want it . . .'

Mlambo hesitated. Perhaps he was being too hard on himself.

'Two thousand,' he said, at the same time changing his mind about the proffered dough ball. It was then that Ntoto knew that the State House *toto*, notwithstanding his achievements, was at heart a weak boy.

But he had served his purpose, and served it well, albeit reluctantly. Mlambo waddled off, back to State House. He would go, he decided, via the market, and buy more *bhang*. The lad who had followed Mlambo from State House kept his distance all this time, watching the exchange between the three boys, as they huddled together behind a refuse dump next to *Harrods*. He also noted that Ntoto and Rutere were at pains not to be seen by a young white man who turned up just as Mlambo left. If he was not expecting the two boys, he certainly seemed to be waiting for somebody.

It was all very odd, thought the lad, very odd indeed. Before setting off to follow Mlambo back to wherever the *toto* was going, he jotted down the number of the Land Rover in which the white man eventually drove away. Just in case . . .

Ntoto was in a predicament.

He was determined to keep – or rather, to sell – the tape recorder, but nevertheless he wanted to get the tape inside it to Pearson. There would be time to work something out. Meanwhile the full enormity of what they had done was slowly making its impact on the boys.

Rutere's eyes took on a glazed look, which was not entirely to be blamed on the glue he had been sniffing:

'We could eat at *Harrods* for ever with that money.'

Between them they had worked it out: if each day they were to buy one serving of maize meal with relish, a couple of chicken necks, a dough ball and a Coke to wash it all down, the money would last a year. A whole twelve months! One year, knowing where the next meal was coming from, and a solid meal at that. From their perspective, next week was about as far into the future as they ever looked. Next month was just about conceivable. But a year from today . . . that was to live in a dream. They did their arithmetic again, using a calculator they had stolen a few weeks earlier from a German tourist. They were correct. It was one whole year. And Rutere was right. It was as good as forever.

Ntoto giggled. They had tricked the white man, and the recorder was now as good as theirs. But what had been recorded? Just what had the president said to Anna Nugilu?

The boys retired to *Harrods*, sat on their haunches on the red-polished frontage, and crouched over the tape recorder. Ntoto was fairly confident that it was the same model as he had seen Furniver use, but was taking no chances.

He turned it over in his hands, and examined it from every direction. Only when he was satisfied that he knew how it worked did Ntoto allow his curiosity full rein. Titus was about to press the play button when he heard voices approaching.

It was Furniver, deep in conversation with Charity.

The two adults emerged from the kitchen, and sat down, still talking. Had they not been so engrossed, Ntoto would have been caught red-handed. In the nick of time he pushed the machine away from him, a combination of slide and shove, sending it slithering over the polished cement surface in the direction of the large wicker armchair which Furniver usually occupied. Had Ntoto accurately calculated the effort required, the machine would have slipped under the chair, out of sight, and he could have recovered it when the coast was clear.

As it happened, disaster struck. To Ntoto's dismay, the tape recorder didn't quite make it, and came to a halt within inches of Furniver's briefcase. Charity noticed it as she got up from her seat next to the banker to get him another glass of mango juice. She broke off their intense exchange and bent down.

'One of these days, Furniver, you will lose this machine. You are too careless.'

Furniver, still absorbed in the conversation about the letter, hardly seemed to notice when Charity, without further ado, dropped the tape recorder into his briefcase, and resumed their discussion about the London lawyers and the danger they posed to *Harrods*.

At the end of the melancholy exchange she looked round the bar, decided that she could leave it for half an hour, and turned to Furniver. There was an important and pressing matter to deal with.

'Now come with me, Furniver. We are going to the clinic. My cousin Mercy is expecting you. You are walking like a donkey that has been serving street boys all night. I have seen you, scratching your *batumba*. Perhaps you have worms? Or do you have a *jipu*? I myself think it is a *jipu*, and needs to be lanced. Or squeezed.'

She gave him what is called an old-fashioned look:

'And tell me, Furniver: just what were you going to do with your finger? Your steward, Didymus Kigali, is a very worried man, and I, Charity Mupanga, am a very worried woman and so is Mildred.'

'Bugger Mildred,' he was about to say, when to Furniver's great relief, he saw that Charity was smiling.

It had been with much reluctance that Furniver agreed that after his visit to the clinic he would be escorted back to his office by a group of Boys. There were far too many strangers around, said Charity, and she did not like the look of them. Even Nellson Githongo, she pointed out, had sniffed tension, and had left his bike in safe custody.

Flanked by half a dozen boys, and with Ntoto carrying his briefcase, Furniver got back without incident – though he could have sworn he had caught a glimpse of the boy thrusting his hand into the case. He waited for Ntoto, who lagged behind the group.

Furniver waited, and let the boy catch up.

'What's the matter, Ntoto?'

'Nothing, suh.'

Claiming that he needed to check the papers he needed, Furniver took a quick look inside the case, feeling slightly ashamed that he did not altogether trust Ntoto. But the tape recorder was there, and so were the *Harrods* documents . . .

They had just reached his office when one of the older Mboya Boys beckoned him. The others formed a protective circle around the two of them, and facing out, providing privacy while at the same time ensuring security.

The boy looked around, lifted his shirt, and undid the clasp of his belt. After a final check, he reached down between the belt and his waist, and to Furniver's horror and astonishment, pulled out a small handgun.

While Furniver watched, frozen to the spot, the boy took the briefcase and thrust the weapon, which he had wrapped in an oily rag, into one of the pockets.

It was the first time Furniver had seen a handgun in Kireba, and he tried to explain that he had not the slightest intention of using one. He seemed to be listening to someone else as he heard himself going through the standard objections to weapons, for it all seemed so feeble, so half-hearted.

What perturbed him most was the evidence that a gun culture had taken root in Kireba, and neither he nor Charity had been aware of it. Never before had a weapon been displayed in front of him, and though it looked old, it had the sheen of a gun that was regularly maintained.

He stood at his door to his office, feeling old and silly.

'I will not take it.'

The older lad stayed silent, looked at his feet, but made no move to recover the gun. Furniver was about to dig into the briefcase and retrieve the weapon himself, when to his surprise, Titus Ntoto intervened.

The fourteen-year-old, whom Furniver had thought was little more than the gang mascot, appeared to be the gang leader.

'There are boys, Mr Edward, young men even, in the movement called *mungiki* who are paid by government to do political things. You must be careful, Mr Edward,' said Ntoto gravely. 'If *mungiki* people harmed you, we who are your friends, the Mboya Boys, we would be blamed.'

'For God's sake, Ntoto, don't be ridiculous. Take back this . . . this, er, this thing.'

Ntoto did not budge.

'Why? Why would you be blamed?'

'Because government wants to stop Mboya Boys from organising erections.'

Furniver looked baffled.

'For elections,' said Ntoto, 'organising for elections, against the president.'

The gang took no chances, and left the office only after Furniver had let himself in, and locked the door. Even then, a pair of Mboya Boys hung around, just in case . . .

What to do with the gun? He could hardly leave it in the briefcase. He took it out, and examined it more closely. As far as he could tell it was loaded. Furniver pulled open the drawer on his desk, and pushed it to the back . . .

He sat at his desk, and remembered that he had to finish recording the story he had written for his granddaughter. He reached into his briefcase, and pulled out the machine, pushed the rewind button to bring the tape to its beginning, and then pressed play.

Much to his surprise, the voice that came back was not his. In fact it sounded rather like the president, followed by the voice of a woman, who seemed vaguely familiar. The language was not Swahili, so Furniver could not follow the exchange. Perhaps Charity, or someone else, must have inadvertently pressed the record button when picking it up from the floor at *Harrods*. It did not matter. The easiest course would be to start the whole thing again. After all, it would take only half an hour to complete, and he had time on his hands.

Furniver cleared his throat, checked that the record button

was working, and began to read from the children's short story that was still on his desk:

'*Stripey! Stripeee! The lean striped cat in the garden pricked up his ears, twitched his long tail, and decided to pretend that he hadn't heard. Hole-watching was a serious business . . .*'

Forty minutes later, it was finished. But the lift it had given to his spirits was short-lived, and they subsided as he left the world of Stripey the cat.

The phone rang in the room next door, and kept ringing. Furniver decided not to answer it. He dreaded a call from that aggressive London lawyer, Rupert Fanshawe, due to fly in that day – or was it the next? He was stuck in the office until a Mboya Boy gave the all-clear.

He had no intention of deserting the Kireba People's Cooperative Bank, and far more important, he would never leave Charity.

He wondered whether he had said the right thing to her. He had no doubt about the law. Charity would indeed lose. But should he not have stood alongside her and defied the edict from London? Common sense might be on their side, but the law was an ass . . .

All in all, he decided, they were both in a hole and the letter he was about to type would make that hole deeper. Sitting at his office computer, tapping out the hand written draft of Charity's broadside against the London lawyers, Edward Furniver experienced a dark night of the soul. He was not a man inclined to melancholy or depression, but for an hour or two he succumbed to despair, and in doing so committed what Bishop David Mupanga regarded as a cardinal sin. Furniver was close to throwing in the towel: not because of the correspondence with the London lawyers, painful a process as that was proving; not because Kireba was an especially sad place that day, mired in filth and seemingly without hope; not because the latest BBC World Service bulletins

230

brought grim news from around the continent; and not because he had embarrassed his steward, whom he had come to respect and admire as an honest and decent man. It was none of these things and all of them. A bleak mood of utter despair engulfed him, and for a while, threatened to overcome him.

He knew it was irrational to feel so gloomy, what with Charity's invitation to stay overnight at the *shamba*. But try as he may, he could not shake free of a growing conviction that the future of *Harrods* was in the balance. Indeed, the more he studied the correspondence, the more likely it seemed that the bar would have to close. If the case ever reached the courts, Charity was certain to lose; and should costs be awarded against her the bill would be crippling.

And the more he thought about it, the more he blamed himself for their predicament. The temptation to end his sorrows became well-nigh overwhelming.

Titus Ntoto, back from escort duty, and Cyrus Rutere sat under a table at *Harrods*, which they had turned into a den, by draping four tablecloths down each side. They looked at the huge pile of ngwee in awe. The tape recorder had been sold barely a hundred yards from the bar in a matter of minutes, and Ntoto, who had first extracted the tape and concealed it in his trousers, was boasting about how he had managed to recover the machine from Furniver's briefcase.

Rutere, however, was not as impressed as the situation warranted. Ntoto finished explaining how he had ended up with the recorder:

'When Mrs Charity saw the one I was trying to hide,' he continued patiently, 'she thought it was Furniver's, and put it in his case. You saw that. So when I got the briefcase, I just took it back.'

Rutere persisted.

'Yes, but I have a question, Ntoto. Does not Furniver keep his own machine in his briefcase?'

Ntoto nodded.

'And Pearson's machine and Furniver's machine are the same, exact, yes?'

Again Ntoto nodded.

Rutere paused: 'So there must have been two exact same machines in the briefcase. Then how do you know you have the right one?'

It was a good question, and Ntoto did not have an answer to hand. It did not really matter, and nor did either boy really care, as they gazed in wonder at the pile of ngwee which seemed to transform itself into an enormous mound of sugared dough balls.

22

'Never boil the batongo beans before
the pots are ready'

The World Bank visit to Kireba had been in danger of being
cancelled, but the rain held off, and Podmore parked near the
clinic. Hardwicke and the rest of his team were already there,
and the World Bank president was talking about the importance of 'ownership' to a group of dignitaries.

Stepping delicately through the debris left by the flood,
Podmore joined the band of VIPs. He spotted Guchu, positioned himself within a few yards of the mayor, and waited for
an opportunity to broach the delicate subject of the maize contract. Alas for Podmore. He had underestimated the calibre of
the mayor, a tough veteran of city hall politics. Not for nothing
did he enjoy the confidence of President Nduka. Far from
looking uncomfortable, or trying to avoid the anxious British
diplomat, he pre-empted Podmore and put on a thoroughly
professional performance.

'Podsman!' cried Willifred Guchu.

'Podsman! Here, Podsman!'

The mayor extended his arm with the palm of his hand
facing down, and fluttered his fingers.

'Come, come.'

Hopes of a discreet unofficial exchange were rapidly being
replaced by fears of a diplomatic incident.

'Podmore, British High Commission,' said Podmore, trying

to be cool, while staying courteous. 'I'm glad we have met at last. I've been trying . . .'

That was as far as he got. To his dismay, Guchu embraced him with enthusiasm. Then he shook hands, and to Podmore's intense discomfort, did not let go. Instead he hauled the unhappy diplomat in front of a local cameraman. To Podmore's further discomfort, the mayor, whom Podmore had not met before, called him 'my brother' several times.

'This is my good friend, my brother,' the mayor announced to no-one in particular.

'Podsman, a great friend of the president, and a great friend of Kuwisha,' he announced to the twenty or so diplomats looking on. A round of modest clapping, led by Guchu's entourage, followed.

'A loyal friend, and a generous friend.'

He beamed.

Podmore tried to wriggle free, but the mayor's grip on his hand tightened, and he had little choice but to stand shoulder to shoulder with the man who had become synonymous with sleaze in Kuwisha. Guchu seemed to be enjoying himself.

'Britain has been our friend for many, many years. I know that Podson, a very senior British diplomat who I respect and love, like a brother . . .' He embraced the sweating diplomat.

'I am sure he will help Kuwisha at this time of great need. I know that the president is very grateful that old friends like Britain will be the first to help us.'

The cameras flashed.

'Oh God,' thought Podmore, 'I'll be in the papers tomorrow.'

He suddenly felt faint, and slightly nauseous.

For the first time in their encounter, Mayor Guchu looked directly into Podmore's eyes, put his hands on the diplomat's shoulders, and pulled him into a bear hug as the cameras clicked once again.

'Thank you, Mr David Podmore,' he said quietly.

And Mayor Willifred Guchu winked, patted the unhappy diplomat on the back, and turned his attention to Hardwicke.

'Mr President,' he beamed, 'the people of Kireba welcome you to their homes.'

Hardwicke's tight programme allowed a brief photo call at Cousin Mercy's clinic and twenty-five minutes for a visit to the model housing unit, under construction on a fenced half-acre site in the northern section of Kireba. Lucy was rather pleased with the press turnout, brief though their appearance would be. About half of the resident foreign corps had opted to fly to Kisangani, and the rest had accepted Lucy's invitation to combine an investigation into the outbreak of cholera with coverage of Hardwicke's visit to the pilot housing project.

After assembling at the Outspan, where they wisely left their cars, they went by taxis to *Harrods* in high spirits, dressed in the conventional outfit of a foreign correspondent in Africa. Dark glasses were either pushed back over hair that was unfashionably long, or sat atop shaven skulls that hinted at a military background; a long-sleeved shirt, either washed-out khaki or faded blue, the top three buttons undone, revealing a white T-shirt; cuffs were turned up a fold, and an elephant-hair bracelet adorned the wrist; and for the photographers a safari waistcoat, with at least four pockets and a stitched-on bandoleer for film cartridges, completed the uniform.

Trousers were almost invariably khaki and capacious, with zippered pockets at knee level and just below the waist, and more at the back. All the journalists carried what seemed to be bulky, over-sized briefcases, heavily padded, to which their eyes frequently returned, as nervous as a mother keeping watch on a young child. Well they might be, for the computer and trappings that the bags contained were not simply a means of filing their stories. It was their lifeline, their link to Reuters and

Associated Press and Agence France Presse, the news agencies whose staff are anonymous contributors to every newspaper, and whose information underpins the stories that their newspaper colleagues will compile.

As long as they had the computer, the world was their oyster. It was a magic carpet on which they swooped down on Africa's trouble spots, and landed at the blurred front lines of conflicts across the continent, from Sierra Leone to Angola, from urban rioting to slum violence. Truly life was wonderful, for they were the world's first generation of virtual reality journalists.

Some of the writers who had early deadlines had already filed their stories, but nevertheless turned up for a few minutes, if only to pop into the clinic, and to check that Hardwick Hardwicke had actually made it to the housing scheme. But none of the hacks stayed through the entire event. Had they done so, they would have witnessed an extraordinary confrontation . . .

Tension in Kireba had been building up for some days. Unfamiliar faces were appearing, following up demands for rent, payment of trading licences, or collecting council tax – demands that were waived if the occupier made clear that their political allegiance was the same as that of the burly intruders, who invariably supported the ruling party.

Hardwicke's visit had triggered an unusual demonstration outside the housing project. On one side stood a group of protestors, bearing aloft neatly lettered placards condemning globalisation, and attacking agriculture subsidies in Europe, and calling for fair prices for Kuwisha's tea and coffee.

On the other side stood a group supporting much the same causes, bearing placards with similar slogans, but with a particularly rough-and-ready look to their banners and posters.

The two lots of protestors, each about fifty strong, eyed each other balefully as Hardwicke and his entourage entered the show house. As the minutes passed, the residents of Kireba, gathered at a respectful distance from the fenced-off plot, began to get restless.

'*Skellums!*' cried an old man, waving his walking stick angrily in the direction of the neatly dressed demonstrators, and the rest of the crowd muttered in agreement. They had not been fooled. It was the carefully stencilled placards that gave the *skellums* away, not to mention the lack of spontaneity and their smart-dressed appearance.

No-one had any doubt that the unusually well turned out bunch was sponsored by State House, in an attempt to leave Hardwicke with the impression that the government's poor record in implementing trade reforms was the result of domestic opposition. But the demonstrators Nduka's agents had assembled were no rent-a-crowd mob, recruited from the streets. They were members of the para-military General Service Unit, earning a few extra ngwee in bonuses before the Uhuru Day holiday.

The other group of demonstrators had begun gathering outside *Harrods*, where they had scribbled their slogans on scraps of cardboard using a black felt-tipped pen that was passed around.

They were driven by several motives. They felt passionately that it could not be right that their coffee, which was sold to international buyers for so little, cost so much in its final liquid form in the coffee shops of Europe and North America. Someone was making money, and it was not the farmers of Kuwisha. But the chance to demonstrate was also an excuse to let off accumulated frustrations, including their resentment at the government's cover-up of the current cholera outbreak.

Hardwicke and his team were ignorant of these tensions. Instead they were preoccupied by a claim that plans for the model house they were about to visit included, of all things, a swimming pool.

The World Bank president was introduced by Mayor Guchu to a team of officials lined up inside the half-built house. The session then began, kicked off by Guchu with an appeal for more money.

Hardwicke's opening question was brief. He pointed to a curious kidney-shaped hole in the ground.

'Tell me, Mayor, what is that?' he asked.

'A swimming pool,' said Mayor Guchu, and guffawed.

Guchu patted his guest on the back with one hand, and with the other the mayor wiped his forehead with a large white handkerchief. Alerted by this prearranged signal, one of the project staff approached the two men, unrolled a section of the blueprint which he laid out on a table in front of them, and said to Guchu in Swahili:

'Is it time?'

'Go ahead,' said the mayor, smiling at Hardwicke.

'Thank you, suh,' said the official, bowing and scraping.

His briefing began, competent and unremarkable until he reached a point prearranged with Mayor Guchu. He placed his finger on the blueprint, next to a kidney shaped outline marked in large capitals: 'SEPTIC TANK'.

'The diameter of the waste pipes may be too narrow, Mr Mayor. Should we delay for checking, or go ahead?'

Guchu looked perplexed, as if lost in the calculations of sewerage flow and outlet pipes.

'We will have to have a site meeting. But later,' he said.

'I wish it was a swimming pool,' he added, wiping the sweat from his brow. A thought seemed to strike him:

'Perhaps the scheme should have a swimming pool for the youth of Kireba. As it is, they play in the dam, and get bilharzia.'

He looked impudently at Hardwicke.

'Would the World Bank help?'

Hardwicke, already running late, stalked off to his next

appointment, his angry reply lost in the cry of pain that suddenly rang out . . .

Were it not for a small, bored boy, the tensions between the two groups of demonstrators might have been contained. As it happened, a pebble whistled through the air, propelled from the boy's catapult, in the direction of the demonstrators. The boy ducked behind *Harrods* and reloaded.

'Eweh!' shouted Charity, furious that the bar's traditional impartiality had been abused. She dropped the bucket of peas she had been shelling, pounced on the urchin, and hauled him behind the fridge. With a salvo of Swahili she chastised him, declaring him banned from *Harrods* for four weeks – but not before he had managed to let off another round with his catapult. It was this pebble that thwacked the rump of the plain-clothed officer in charge of the thirty-strong state security unit that was at the core of the phoney demo.

The target had just been using his mobile phone to ring his wife. Live chickens were cheaper in Kireba than anywhere else. Such were the bargain prices he had bought two, and was ringing home to boast of his purchase.

His call was answered by his teenage daughter.

'Tell your mama that it's quiet in Kireba, and I'm coming back.'

'Wait,' said the girl, and handed the phone to her mother.

'It's quiet in Kireba, and I'm on my way back,' her father repeated.

It was a crackly line, and he had decided that the good news about the chickens would have to wait until he got home.

'What?'

'It's quiet in Kireba,' he bellowed, 'I'm on my way back.'

It was at this point that the pebble hit home, triggering what would go down in Kuwisha's history as the World Bank coup.

All that could be heard down the phone was a shriek of

pain, and then ominous silence, for the phone cut off as it was dropped.

After grilling her daughter, who was now howling her head off, the alarmed mother managed to piece together a message that warranted use of the emergency number of the officer commanding the general services unit. There could, they agreed, be no doubt about the plea for help that had come from the heart of the slum:

'There's a riot in Kireba, I'm coming under attack.'

In fact the damage to the officer was more to his dignity than his person. But in a fit of rage, the officer responded in the only way he knew – he ordered his men to use maximum force.

'Globalisation Hurts the Poor' took a swing at 'Fair Trade not Aid', and 'End European Subsidies' lashed out at 'Down with IMF'. Heavily outnumbered as other residents joined in, the State House force beat a reasonably orderly retreat in the face of what seemed the collective outrage of Kireba. Fortunately for the State House protestors, the anger of their opponents was not channelled against a single target.

First there were scores to settle in Kireba itself.

Rent payers turned on landlords, the people from the west of Kuwisha fought the people of the east, and the people of the south got stuck into the people of the north. Only when these local disputes were settled did they close ranks against the common, hated enemy: the army, the para-military units and the police, who by then had deployed in a protective perimeter around the city's central business district.

It was as if the riots complemented the storms that had been rolling over Kuwisha, the man-made equivalent of the huge purple-black clouds that burst open over the land, to the accompaniment of rolls of thunder and bolts of lightning. The violence that ensued, like the rain, did not discriminate. Round-eyed children scampered for cover, and dogs disappeared, both driven by an instinct for survival.

And when the mob drew closer, the sound of its anger grew. It was like the noise of an old steam locomotive, as it pulled out of the station, gathering momentum with long drawn-out huffs and puffs, giving newcomers the chance to catch up and clamber aboard. They joined a cross-section of humanity, some there by choice, others who discovered too late that they had caught the wrong train, and were being carried away to an unknown destination.

Born of the day-to-day frustrations of life on the breadline, of competition for menial jobs and places to sleep, the train of humanity gathered pace. Loafers and idlers, vagabonds and wastrels, and time wasters and chancers, the talented and the unfulfilled, the capable and the hapless, all thrown together, were embarking on a journey that was driven by despair, fuelled by greed.

The rioters stomped through Kireba on their way into town, knees raised high, imitating the South African dance of protest known as the *toyi toyi*. The office of the Kireba People's Cooperative Bank, where Furniver listened apprehensively to the hubbub outside, secure under the protection of vigilant Mboya Boys, was directly in their path. But as the mob, its numbers growing with every step, drew closer, its ranks parted and reformed and the building was left untouched.

By the time the howling, baying cavalcade was within reach of the city centre, the Asian community's early warning system had gone into action. The steel shutters went up on the windows of their shops, and units from the Presidential Guard, based in the grounds of State House, began rolling out of the barracks in their armoured personnel carriers to take up positions along Uhuru Avenue.

With a roar, now more like the sound of a huge wave crashing on the sand than a train gathering steam, the rioters fell on the city. The calculating and sensible ones grabbed what they could, whether television sets which they balanced on their

241

heads, or fridges, radios, or a bunch of dresses, and made good their escape. But they were in a minority. The rest of the rioters were gripped by a frenzy of rage in which an urge to destroy dominated . . .

As for the University's students, usually good for a riot, the timing was bad. They were scattered around the country, most of them at their homes for the holiday weekend. But those who remained could hardly believe their good fortune. Within thirty minutes, they had left their seedy halls of residence, and converged on the road that ran past the campus and led to State House. As far as they were concerned, any motorist was fair game. Rocks in their hands, grievances in their heads, they set about ambushing any and every car that passed.

Like his colleagues, Cecil had left Kireba before the demonstrations turned violent, but with a better excuse than most. He was desperate to see Lucy Gomball before he left. Bags packed and ready for the flight to London, he had all but resigned himself to the loss of his tape recorder – though he was not sure whether to be alarmed or angered by the failure of Ntoto and Rutere to meet him at the appointed time outside *Harrods*.

His mobile rang. Lucy's car had broken down, and she was stuck at home. Could he pick her up, and they could go on to the Outspan for a gin and tonic. After the drink they could go out to the airport together. And almost as an afterthought, she added that WorldFeed were getting reports of a riot in Kireba that was spreading; some claimed it was a coup.

'Hold tight, I'm on my way,' said Pearson.

'Don't make a thing of it, for God's sake. Just come and pick me up. Silly boy!'

Cecil's heart pounded. Seldom had Lucy spoken to him in such intimate tones. His mouth went dry, and his imagination went wild. Perhaps he and Lucy had a future together after all, and the more he thought about this prospect, the more it pleased him.

He began to sing:

Tea for two,
And two for tea . . .

The journey from Lucy's Borrowdale home to the Outspan became increasingly hazardous. Twice gangs of looters emerged out of the dark as Pearson was forced to slow down by makeshift roadblocks. Twice Shango, who had to be restrained by Lucy, barked furiously, forcing the youths into a brief retreat and giving Pearson precious extra seconds.

'Good boy,' said Pearson. He wanted to pat the dog, but decided against it. The brute would probably bite him.

Normally the greatest threat to life and limb on the roads of Kuwisha was the other drivers. This evening, however, there were palpable signs of the tension that suddenly and briefly seemed to be threatening to destroy Kuwisha's capital. At one intersection, rocks and small boulders the size of footballs covered the ground where the students had rioted. Suddenly a rock came out of the evening gloom and smashed into the rear window.

Pearson pressed the accelerator down to the floor. Another stone skidded off the windscreen, and Shango began barking furiously. A third rock crashed through the front window, catching Shango a passing blow on his shanks. Faces loomed out of the night, shouting and screaming, and the wheels skidded as Pearson stamped down on the accelerator.

Lucy cried out: 'Keep going! Keep going!' and the tension in her voice made it shrill. It was then that Pearson realised it was going to be touch and go.

The room was bleak and cheerless, although the chairs were comfortable enough. It was Pearson's turn to speak, and the dozen or so in the group looked at him expectantly. For a moment he felt lost and unsure, and then the reason for his presence came flooding back to him: it was the weekly session of Afroholics Anonymous.

He stood up, but the words he wanted to say, and which he was expected to say, wouldn't come. Encouragement flowed from all sides, reminding Pearson of his high school rugby days. He felt worse than incompetent. He hated the game, and feared the physical contact but dared not admit it to the teachers who ran the practice sessions, and who urged him on: 'Tackle low, Pearson, tackle low. Pass the ball, laddie, pass the ball, get stuck in, for God's sake, Pearson, get stuck in.'

Far from enthusing him, their exhortations had paralysed him. Once again, he seemed back on the rugby field, frozen by fear.

'GooddaymynameisCecilandIamanAfroholic,' he blurted out.

He could have cried with relief. He had done it, he had said it, said it aloud, and now he would say it again.

'Good day, my name is Cecil, and I am an Afroholic.'

Less than a dozen words, yet so hard . . .

The audience, who had sensed his difficulty, now applauded his courage. Cecil had broken the ice. He plunged on, rumbles of support from the other members of Afroholics Anonymous giving him strength. For the first time, the faces started to come into focus, and many of them seemed familiar.

'I would like to tell you my story.'

He began hesitantly, but gathered strength and conviction as he pressed ahead:

'I am an Afroholic,' he repeated, with even more confidence this time.

'For years I have been compulsively and obsessively writing about Africa. But a couple of months ago, I discovered

Afroholics Anonymous. I was staying in a run-down hotel where room service stopped at midnight, where phone lines were poor, and where the laundry promised back on the same day was delivered the next day – and there was too much starch in my shirts.'

There were sympathetic murmurs, and from someone in the back row came a snort:

'Typical, bloody typical,' and there were murmurs of agreement from around the room.

Cecil warmed to his task:

'The business centre ran out of paper, and shut at 8 p.m. The minibar stocked only the local beer, and' – he paused for effect – 'my room did not face the sea.'

More cries of sympathy or shock, fellow feeling or dismay came from his audience.

'While searching in the drawers for the in-house movie programme, which I later found under the laundry list, I discovered a pamphlet that was to change my life. I would like to share it with you,' said Pearson.

'Afroholism, the pamphlet told me, is a progressive illness, which can never be cured, but which like some other diseases can be halted. Many Afroholics feel that the illness represents the combination of physical sensitivity to Africa and a mental obsession with living there, or visiting it, or writing about it, which regardless of the consequences, cannot be broken by willpower alone.'

Again, there were murmurs of agreement, and one member seemed to be weeping.

'Afroholics Anonymous is a fellowship of men and women who share their experience, strength and hope with each other so that they may solve their common problem and help others to recover from Africa.'

Pearson was disconcerted to spot Hardwick Hardwicke, in the audience, nodding sympathetically. And surely that was

Fingers, sitting next to him? Odd, how very odd, he thought to himself, but continued nonetheless.

'The only requirement for membership is a desire to stop talking and writing about Africa. The men and women who consider themselves members of AA are, and always will be, Afroholics, even though they may have other addictions.'

Pearson felt that he was starting to run out of steam, and was in danger of losing the thread:

'I write compulsively about a dying continent. I relish news of death, I get my kicks from disease and disaster. I am the journalistic equivalent of a necrophiliac . . .'

He did a double take. Was that Lucy, coming towards him, getting closer and closer? Surely she, of all people, wasn't a member of AA?

Pearson suddenly felt nauseous and dizzy. As his stomach began to heave, he decided to close his eyes, and let nature take its course. How strange that the insistent voice of Lucy Gomball seemed to be murmuring to him, while her tongue was doing something delicious to his ear.

Despite his nausea, it made his spine tingle with pleasure.

He began to wretch and heave, and he decided to open his eyes. As he did so, the room seemed to spin around him, and then disappear, and Fingers and Hardwicke slid down holes in the floor, which had opened up under them.

He retched again as he realised that the Afroholics Anonymous meeting had been a figment of his imagination, the product of an hallucination. His last rational recollection was Lucy screaming 'Drive! Drive!' and Shango barking.

Cecil lifted his hand to his head, and it came away red and sticky. He winced.

He must have been hit by a stone, flung by one of the rioters. His surroundings came into focus, and he looked into the blue eyes of Lucy Gomball.

'Tosser,' said Lucy, in a matter-of-fact tone that melted

Pearson's heart. She dodged the jet of vomit that spurted from him in a convulsive heave, and restrained the slobbering Shango, who in an unprecedented display of affection had been anxiously nuzzling the journalist's ear.

'Move over,' she said, brushing away the nuggets of glass from the shattered windscreen that lay like a coating of frost over the front seat.

'I'm driving the rest of the way,' said Lucy angrily.

'I told you not to go past the students' hall of residence. Those buggers throw stones for the same reason that Shango pisses on lamp posts,' she said, grinding the gear as the wheels spun on the gravel verge. 'They can't help it, they're just marking their territory.'

The rest of the journey to the Outspan, where Pearson would spend his last few hours in Kuwisha, went without incident.

Word of the riots soon reached the dingy conference room at the Ministry of Finance, where Fingers and his Kuwishan counterpart, the permanent secretary in the ministry, were drawing up the final communiqué. The unrest, as it was called, became a factor from which both sides could and would seek to take advantage.

For the Kuwisha government negotiators, it was evidence that the pain of structural adjustment measures imposed by the World Bank and the IMF was becoming intolerable, that the economic performance targets were too tough. For the Bank, the riots were evidence of frustration over the government's incompetence, over the corruption that was slowly strangling the country.

But behind the largely good humoured exchanges between the team from the Bank and the officials of the ministries of finance and of planning, was a cold-hearted analysis of the country's prospects. Much was at stake for Kuwisha: on the outcome of these talks rested hundreds of millions of aid dollars.

The men in the room – there was not a single woman – knew each other well, and for the most part respected each other. Yet each joke came with a barb, and there was a story behind each witticism or verbal sally. For the insiders of the aid business, every line of the communiqué that would emerge from the talks, drafted paragraph by paragraph, was a battleground. To the uninformed eye the official statement would emerge as a bland resume of discussions; but to anyone with an insight into 'donorspeak' the result spoke volumes.

The statement eventually emerged in the form of a communiqué, issued on behalf of the government of Kuwisha. Fingers rang Cecil on the journalist's mobile, and ensured that a copy would be faxed to Outspan, where the representative of the only foreign newspaper that was interested in the outcome of the talks was waiting agog with excitement.

Lucy ran her fingers lightly over Pearson's freshly bandaged head and peered over his shoulder as he sat on the Outspan veranda reading the two-page statement.

Cecil's response was hard to gauge. Sometimes he broke out into chuckles, sometimes he cursed, other times he nodded with enthusiasm, and highlighted particular passages. Finally Lucy could take no more, and demanded a translation.

'Can't see what you're so fussed about. Says nothing, really.'

Pearson attempted to explain.

'In fact, it's pretty tough. Not as tough as I would like, but still, pretty tough.'

Lucy looked sceptical.

'Explain something. You think it's tough. But I get the impression that the meeting went rather well. Listen to this.' Lucy took the statement from Pearson and read aloud:

'"Mr Hardwicke complimented the government on the

sustained implementation of efforts to stabilise the economy."
That seems pretty positive . . . Yet you say that the Brits and
everyone else will be cutting aid to Kuwisha.'

Pearson laughed.

'What you've read is pure donorspeak, sweetheart. Look for
the weasel words. For "efforts", read "should have tried
harder."'

'What about the next sentence?' Lucy asked, and again proceeded to read it aloud:

'"Donors noted in particular the sharp reduction in the
budget deficit, the reduction of inflation to single digits, and
the recovery of economic growth to 3 per cent in 1994."'

Pearson tried to avoid sounding patronising.

'The weasel word here, Lucy, is "noted". In this context it is
the equivalent of a heavy sigh of exasperation. Let me show you.'

He recovered the statement from Lucy:

'"Donors also noted"' – another heavy sigh – '"government's success in strengthening the financial sector, initial
implementation of civil service reform, and recent progress in
implementing privatisation."'

Cecil handed the World Bank statement back to her with
two words underlined – 'initial' and 'recent'.

'Two more weasel words, used very cleverly. "Initial" shows
that the donors doubt that what has been started will be continued. And "recent" is the way donors show their frustration
that it has taken the government of Kuwisha so long to get
round to putting promises into practice.'

Lucy was now starting to get the hang of it.

'So when the statement goes on about "the need to acceler-
ate efforts to clarify the operating environment and targets for
strategic state owned companies", they are really very unhappy
with the government?'

'Indeed,' Cecil replied. '"Clarify the operating environment" can mean only one thing: "Stop corruption."'

'And "misappropriation of public resources and the need to reinforce the independent role of the Auditor General" is another go at graft,' Lucy chipped in.

'Precisely,' replied Cecil. 'Then they really cut up rough: "Donors expressed the strong hope that there would be positive developments that would allow them to provide a volume of external support commensurate with Kuwisha's development.""

The lights on the veranda seemed to grow in strength as in a matter of minutes, dusk became night.

'Good God!' exclaimed Lucy. 'So that's why you think that the donors are cutting aid?'

'Absolutely,' Cecil said, looking smug.

'And there's more. Fingers has done a good job: "Donors hoped that the outstanding issues would be resolved quickly to facilitate rapid agreements with the Breton Woods institutions on further balance of payments support.""

'Presumably that means: get a move on and reach an agreement with the IMF,' said Lucy. 'But why do they not just say so?'

The sound of the rioters receded as they made their way out of Kireba and towards the city centre, and Edward Furniver was left alone with his thoughts.

The rattle of a key in the front door broke into his reverie. A clatter of cups from the kitchen followed, and Charity Mupanga appeared with a tray of tea and a plate of chocolate biscuits.

The visit should have raised his spirits, but the effect was mixed. He was delighted to see her, but despondent that she could not stay for long. There was much to get off his chest. For a few minutes, the two of them sat quietly, talking of this and that.

He pushed the letter he had typed across the table and listened with half an ear to what she had to say, for he had already come to a decision. He sipped his tea, and took a deep breath.

'My dear,' he said. 'I have something to tell you. I am very sorry . . .'

Charity reached across the table, took his hand in hers, and squeezed it gently.

'I know, Furniver, I know.'

'You do not know, Charity,' he said firmly. 'I should have warned you about these lawyers. Instead I played a game . . .'

'We have both played foolish games. We forgot David's warning.'

For a moment, Furniver was nonplussed.

'Sorry, Charity, don't quite get you? What do you mean?'

'Remember the prayer David wrote for the children?

> *"Don't overtake on corners blind,*
> *Keep sharp lookout for who's behind" '*

Furniver's confusion deepened. The thought occurred to him that the strain was proving all too much for Charity. She repeated the lines, and added:

'The verse is not only for children, Furniver. Adults should read it as well. We did not keep sharp lookout,' said Charity.

'Well, erm, yes, absolutely,' he said. The worst of his confessions had yet to come. He was distracted by the next thing he had to say, something that would leave Charity's dreams shattered.

'About costs, Charity . . . I think these London lawyers will demand a lot of money . . .'

Again Charity interrupted. This time there was a sharp edge to her voice.

'Sometimes, Furniver, sometimes I think that you think that I am stupid. I know this thing called costs. If we have to pay, we have to pay.'

'I could lend you . . .'

Charity put a finger to his lips.

'Never,' she said.

Furniver could barely look her in the eyes. He was tempted to put off what he had to say, but then gathered his resolve.

'Then I think you may have to sell *Harrods*,' he said, and waited for an explosion of grief, or anger, or both.

It did not come.

Charity merely acknowledged that grim prospect with a brave nod, although Furniver noticed a tear or two rolling down her cheeks.

She gave his hand another squeeze.

'It is just a pothole,' she said.

Once again Furniver appeared baffled.

Charity took pity on him:

'On the potholed road of life . . .' she recited, and paused.

'Respect the um, vows of er, man and um, wife,' continued Furniver, and blushed.

'We must together keep our thumbs up, Furniver.'

She kissed him gently on the cheek as she set off back to *Harrods*. Edward Furniver knew he had lost his heart to a very remarkable woman.

Among the first to realise the marvellous opportunity that chaos and confusion provided were the Mboya Boys, at their fighting best. Solidarity and discipline, forged on the football field, were their watchwords. Like a coach urging on his players, Ntoto yelled instructions as the Mboya Boys made for the city centre. The cheap tat and cloth shops were ignored. Or almost ignored. As a diversionary tactic, one which sowed alarm and confusion in the ranks of the city's security guards, a handful of shopfronts were smashed and the contents set alight.

But the most lucrative targets – the shops with televisions

and computers and stereo sets that lined the official Uhuru Avenue – were better guarded, and reaching them would be more difficult. A second diversion got under way, and Cyrus Rutere led a unit of some twenty boys towards the university halls of residence, where they would enlist the students' support, or plunder their rooms. Ntoto himself took charge of the main body of street boys who headed straight for the shops in the centre, and for a hugely satisfying twenty minutes, smashed windows and looted to their hearts content.

Only one terrifying moment spoiled the evening for Cyrus.

He was about to leave a ransacked shop when he looked up, cried out in alarm, and recoiled in horror before the apparition that taunted him.

A black face, surmounted by a coarse blond wig, with rouged cheeks and badly applied red lipstick, leered at him, from a few feet away. A brassiere was strapped, lopsided, outside a greasy green jersey, and the bizarre creature had frozen in its tracks, perilously balanced atop high-heeled shoes. It held the terrified Rutere in a weird drug-induced stare, the product of glue sniffing, *bhang* and raw home-brewed liquor.

'*Mungiki!*' Cyrus shrieked, summoning help.

'*Mungiki* are here!'

He swung out at the grim, crazed beast, just a few feet in front of him.

The mirror shattered.

Fortunately no-one had heard him call, such was the hubbub, but Rutere had lost his appetite for the fray. Just then there was a loud bang, and he got a whiff of tear gas. His eyes had begun to water when Ntoto burst into the room, giggling maniacally. He grabbed Rutere by the arm, and shoved him through a small window that opened into a back yard. The two boys made good their escape.

Within a couple of hours order had been restored. Kuwisha's

security forces had acted with a speed and brutality that was impressive, a deterrent to anyone who may have got the idea that Nduka was getting soft in his old age.

In fact, the riots were over so quickly that the foreign correspondents who had responded to Lucy's invitation missed out on any first-hand experience. None of them, with the exception of Pearson, were interested in the outcome of Hardwicke's visit to Kireba. Most of them had filed stories that drew heavily on Lucy's briefing papers, used the rival demonstrators for a few paragraphs of entertaining colour, and then returned home to enjoy the holiday weekend.

And when they were called later that night by their foreign desks, and asked to match the news agency stories about rioting and a possible coup attempt, they did their best. Pickings were thin, however. Many of the Western diplomats they relied on for quotes had left for the coast, taking advantage of the holiday weekend. Aid officials were baffled by the riots, and other sources had nothing or little to offer, while it was assumed that it was not worth even trying to find a government spokesman.

But as they rang each other to compare notes, they were increasingly confident that they had the broad structure of the story in place: all agreed that a coup attempt was under way. That much seemed certain; they also agreed that 'scores' had either been 'killed', had 'gone missing' or had been 'rounded up'.

The next day the world's press would reveal that a coup attempt in which scores had died had been put down in Kuwisha, and that the situation was 'tense and confused'. Thereafter, however, readers could pay their money and take their choice. Some reports claimed that WorldFeed and other aid workers had been singled out for attack. Others suggested that the terrified expatriate community were taking refuge in the city's leading hotel.

The situation varied from 'tense' to 'tense but calm', although some journalists reported that 'sporadic rioting continued into the early hours'. It was unclear whether the reporters had been on the front line of the riots, or talking their way through roadblocks in the city manned by either 'drug-crazed rebels' or 'surly government troops', but no-one was asking.

There were herograms all round, those laconic messages of congratulations from foreign desks to reporters – except for Cecil Pearson. He had of course filed, but had failed to overcome the disadvantage of being on the spot, and knowing something of what he was writing about.

Had he been more experienced, he would have led on a coup, even if he knocked it down later in the story. But Pearson still had a lot to learn.

An account of a coup that was not a coup, or even an attempt at a coup, but an accidental riot that had been put down in hours took, in his view, second place to the outcome of the World Bank talks. In Pearson's judgment, it needed 600 words to convey the significance of the World Bank's seemingly bland, though in fact hard-hitting, communiqué. And while Reuters had led on what it cautiously called 'an apparent coup attempt', Pearson had not even used the word 'coup'. True, he mentioned the rioting, but seemed to dismiss its significance, for the event only made the sixth paragraph. What is more, he made no mention of his nasty encounter with the rioters.

Not surprisingly, what to the foreign news editor earlier in the day had seemed a decent story, had fizzled out. That was bad enough – but Pearson had not warned the desk, and the news editor had to scramble to replace a promising story.

Only when his mobile rang did he appreciate the extent of his disgrace.

'Hang on,' said the *Financial News* switchboard, 'here's Steph . . .'

'Where's my bloody coup then?' demanded the news editor. 'I've got a hole on my page!'

Pearson reached into the bowl of roasted cashew nuts, and flicked one at Shango, draped as usual around Lucy's feet. They were sitting on the wide veranda of the Outspan. He had won back editorial goodwill after his lapse by offering a leader on Kuwisha. Since it was a slow news day and not much was happening in the world, there was a chance that the paper would want one. If so, the desk would ring back.

They could hear the occasional sound of a gunshot. Or was it a car backfiring? It was impossible to tell whether it was the police knocking off another looter, or settling an old score, or the normal quota of gunfire in the city at night. The bus was expected shortly, and would take hotel guests who were passengers on that night's flights to the airport.

Pearson decided to indulge himself, and lit a cigar, and as he blew the smoke towards the ceiling, he happily ruminated about other African hotels in countries in crisis . . . the Mount Nelson in Cape Town in the mid 80s, Meikles, in what is now Harare, in the last days of Ian Smith, the Intercontinental in Kinshasa when Mobutu still ruled, the Polana in Maputo after the collapse of Portuguese rule.

He was wondering whether the Oyster Bay Hotel in Dar es Salaam should be added to the list when his mobile trilled.

The *Financial News* did want an editorial. Pearson could say what he liked, as long as he drew some lessons for the rest of Africa from Kuwisha's example.

'I'll write it in the residents' lounge,' Cecil told Lucy, and pretended not to hear her irritable sigh.

It was to be the last editorial that Cecil Pearson would write from Kuwisha, for his departure for London was a matter of hours away. Sitting at the desk in the lounge, he put his heart and soul into the leader, seeking a balanced combination of optimism and realism.

He decided to give it a working headline:

KUWISHA'S LESSON.
Recent developments in Kuwisha, a country that has had more than its share of misfortune since independence, are but a symptom of a deeper malaise. A mixed colonial legacy, erratic commodity prices, crippling external debt, corruption and government mismanagement, all lie behind the country's tragic failure to realise its potential.

Half an hour later he was through. He was quietly pleased with what he had written. Even Lucy would concede that it was a tough but fair appraisal of Kuwisha's prospects. Tough but fair: those were the watchwords.

He dictated the leader over the phone to the London office, and was about to join Lucy on the hotel veranda. Pearson looked at his watch. There was one final thing he had to do, something he had to find out. What on earth had happened to Ntoto and Rutere? Why hadn't they turned up at *Harrods*, as arranged? God forbid that they had been arrested. There was time before the bus came to take a taxi for the five-minute journey to Kireba, and the headquarters of the Mboya Boys. If Ntoto and Rutere weren't there, their friends might be able to help.

He could be out and back in half an hour. No need to trouble Lucy. The taxi driver demanded three times the normal fare. Pearson had no choice but to agree. He set off on the short journey from the Outspan to the edge of Kireba.

23

'The baboon never barks at the rhino's horn'

Exhausted but exhilarated, tired but triumphant, the Mboya Boys returned to their Kireba headquarters without mishap and laden with the spoils of looting. They prepared to celebrate late into the night. The bus that served as their clubhouse had survived the floods, as had the rusting carcasses of the nearby cars, one of which looked newer than the other, with some of the original paintwork yet to be erased by weather and rust.

Stolen by Ntoto and the gang nearly three years earlier, it had been stripped of anything that had any value. From wheels to windows, every moving part and every part that could be moved had been detached by nimble and knowledgeable young fingers, who had learnt their trade at the city break-down yards, where they sold their spoils.

Pearson asked the taxi driver to wait. Ten, perhaps fifteen minutes, should be enough to get the answers to his questions. His head started to ache and his joints throbbed. He spotted Titus and Cyrus, gathered with twenty or thirty Mboya Boys around a sooty fire of discarded car tyres. He looked more closely at the wrecked car. There was something familiar about it. Battered though it was, the outlines of a Subaru were unmistakable. He couldn't help himself:

'Bugger me, Ntoto, you little thief. That's my car. Or at least it was my car, and then it disappeared two weeks after I got here.'

Pearson tried to ignore the bizarre appearance of several of the Mboya Boys. Like Rutere, most had rouge on their cheeks, and swathes of lipstick, looted earlier in the evening; and several boys sported brassieres, or wore petticoats, trophies from the fashion shops.

Ntoto shrugged, expressionless behind the huge dark glasses, acquired during the looting, and which perched precariously on his nose, while his lips gleamed a glossy red.

'Yes, we stole it. But that was before we became your friends.'

'And what happened? You were supposed to meet me at *Harrods*! Where the hell is my tape recorder?'

Ntoto burrowed in the recesses of his baggy trousers, took out the cassette tape he had retrieved from the tape recorder in Furniver's briefcase, and handed it to Pearson, who accepted it gingerly, with thumb and forefinger.

'And the tape recorder,' he asked, holding out his hand. Ntoto seemed uncomfortable but defiant. He thought of confessing the whole story: of how he and Rutere had planned to steal it; how they hid when Pearson came to *Harrods* to meet them. And how he could only watch as Charity put the machine in Furniver's briefcase . . .

But it all seemed so complicated. And would Pearson believe him, Ntoto, an Mboya Boy who smelt like a dead dog?

He looked coolly at Pearson, and shrugged again, with narrow expressive shoulders.

'Rooted. It was rooted.'

For a moment or two Pearson was baffled, taken aback by the boy's demeanour.

'It was stolen. We were mugged.'

Pearson was about to remonstrate, but decided against it.

'You can get insurance money,' said Ntoto.

Was that an insolent note he detected? Was the little brute taking the piss? Pearson gave him a sharp glance.

'So what happened? What the hell happened?'

Anger gathered, like bile in his throat, as the boy shrugged again.

This time Ntoto did not bother to say anything.

He knew that he lied badly, and did not care about it. The other boys, sensing that something was amiss, gathered protectively around their leader.

'What the hell,' thought Pearson, 'what the hell.'

The ache in his head had returned. The acrid-sweet smell of *bhang* hung in the air, mixing with the nose-tickling aroma of glue. One of the boys thrust a joint into his hand. It had already been lit, and Pearson pulled the smoke deep into his lungs.

Another tape, one of a handful stored on the site, was put into the club's cassette player. The boy in charge turned the volume up to its peak. As the music blared across the wasteland, with the flickering shapes and shadows from the fire rising and falling, the boys began to dance to the music of Prince Buster, the acknowledged 'King of Blue Beat'.

His heyday was over long before the boys had been born. Prince Buster had blazed his music trail in Jamaica in the 1960s. His music, predecessor to reggae, was known simply as ska, and the rhythm was infectious, persistent. The boys' favourite track, 'Enjoy Yourself', had been recorded in 1963, but the beat was irresistible and the message seemed timeless.

> *It's good to be wise when you're young,*
> *'Cos you can only be young but for once.*
> *Enjoy yourself, an' 'ave lots of fun,*
> *Serve God and live my friend and it will never done.*

Shikkah boom, shikkah boom, shikkah boom went the beat.

Until this point, the boys were silent, seemingly engrossed in their complex, conga-like shuffle around the blazing fire. But when the chorus came, they joined in, singing as if their lives depended on it:

> *Enjoy yourself, it's later than you think,*
> *Enjoy yourself, while you're still in the pink,*
> *The years go by, as quickly as you wink,*
> *Enjoy yourself, enjoy yourself, it's later than you think.*

A sweet, soaring trumpet took over, and a handclap had replaced the oompah-oompah. The shikkah boom shikkah boom of ska gave way to a touch of jazz. At the last note, the boys again fell silent, but continued to dance and stomp:

> *Get wisdom, get knowledge and understanding,*
> *Those three were given free by the Maker.*
> *Go to school, learn the rule*
> *Don't be no faker,*
> *It's not wise for you to be a footstool.*

But as the final chorus got under way, they once again raised their voices, with a fervour that would have done justice to a national anthem, skinny supplicants before an altar on which their grim fate had been laid out from the moment of their birth. Glue tubes bouncing, elbows pumping and pelvises thrusting, knees raised high, bare feet stomping, they sang in enthusiastic unison:

> *So enjoy yourself, it's later than you think,*
> *Enjoy yourself, while you're still in the pink,*
> *For years go by as quickly as you wink,*
> *So enjoy yourself, enjoy yourself, it's later than you think.*

In the far distance there was a rumble of thunder, but the rains were retreating, and so were the floods that had washed

261

over Kuwisha. Above them, the bright-starred African sky spread like a warm, dark blanket, which let in pinpricks of light.

Ntoto approached Pearson, and with a little bow, handed him a bottle of Tusker beer, unopened. Pearson inspected it, and handed it back to the boy, who without a word, adroitly flicked the cap off with his teeth.

It was time for Pearson to bid farewell.

'Well, Ntoto,' he said. It didn't seem quite right, and he started again.

'Well, Titus,' striking a more familiar note.

'I will write to you.' Even as he said it, he knew he was not going to keep the promise, one which he had made to just about every recipient of his business cards. Ntoto looked uncomfortable, and said nothing.

'What is it?'

Ntoto took a sniff of glue, and removed the dark glasses.

'I do not want to be called Titus any more.

Pearson was puzzled.

'What do you want to be called then?'

Ntoto looked Cecil in the eye.

'I want to be called by my proper name.

Pearson was nonplussed.

'What on earth do you mean, Titus. What's wrong with Titus Ntoto?'

The small boy was both nervous and determined.

'I want to be known by my African names. My real name is Odhiambo Mboya Ntoto. I am an African.'

He looked at Pearson, and said it again, like an incantation: 'Odhiambo Mboya Ntoto.'

Elbows protruding through the worn fibre of one of Pearson's cast-off jerseys, and still wearing the old hockey shorts the journalist had given him months earlier, the boy did not look back as he rejoined the sinuous, shadowy circle.

Shikkah boom, shikkah boom, shikkah boom.

Pearson felt his stiff, inhibited limbs slowly start to relax as the *bhang* took effect, and twitch to the music. What began as a cramped shuffle became something close to a dance. Before he knew it, he had joined in the jigging and jiving procession around the fire, heedless of the acrid smoke and its effect on his linen jacket.

Shikkah boom, shikkah boom, shikkah boom.

For the first time since coming to Kuwisha, Pearson dropped his English reserve, and gyrated and cavorted around the blaze. The sense of despair, as bleak as any experienced by Conrad's legendary Mr Kurtz on his African journey, began to lift. The fear that his plot would somehow be exposed melted away, and his anxieties seemed irrational. Titus and Cyrus had been the vulnerable players, and both were safe. Safe! Pearson took a long, deep pull of his reefer and put his heart and soul into the dance, joining in the conga around the fire. He was now singing along with the boys, and he found it oddly comforting:

'Enjoy yourself – enjoy yourself, while you're still in the pink – enjoy yourself, enjoy yourself, it's later than you think.'

The *bhang*-induced euphoria still held him in its grip as the taxi took him back to the Outspan, where he would collect Lucy and go on to the airport. Otherwise he might have noticed the two cars that followed him.

24

'When you hear the ghoghla drums,
guard the maize harvest'

By Africa's grim standards, the death toll at the end of the rioting was not high, and the conditions that caused the fatalities
were not unusual. The official count was thirty-seven, although
the real figure was probably closer to double that.

President Nduka was well satisfied with the outcome, and in
a good mood, which was just as well for Ntoto and Rutere. But
there were a few loose ends to be tied before he could drive to
his farm, with its irrigated green paddocks, and talk to his
cattle.

One matter in particular continued to niggle the president.
He wondered whether he was right to reconsider his plan to
send *mungiki* thugs to kill Ntoto and Rutere.

It had not taken long for Lovemore Mboga, the intelligence
boss who doubled as State House steward, to piece together
the childish plot. The lad who had trailed Mlambo had
reported back, and the fat kitchen *toto* had confessed all. And
Pearson had been traced through his car registration . . . it was
all too easy.

But it seemed that Ntoto and Rutere, the two young rats,
worked for this woman, Charity Mupanga, who ran Harrods
International Bar (and Nightspot), that popular Kireba watering hole. She was a strong woman, widow of the bishop. She
could well cause trouble. Nduka was not happy. The old lion

sniffed danger from this unlikely source, two glue-sniffing street urchins, two cunning leopard cubs. His instinct said kill them, but not yet, not yet . . . Nduka picked up the phone, and Ntoto and Rutere were reprieved. No car crash for them. Ferdinand Mlambo would not be so lucky.

Putting down the riot had proved a useful exercise. The General Service Unit had been getting restless, 'out of match practice' as the president had put it, and its officers had relished the opportunity to put their men through their paces. The looters had, in the words of the Unit's commander, 'been given a sound thrashing'. In short, there had been no reason for Nduka to delay the recording of his traditional Uhuru Day message to the nation as scheduled, although its actual transmission was delayed by an hour or two.

The broadcast showed him at his best: his authoritarian streak combined with a near-avuncular presence: 'On this day, Uhuru Day, my first and foremost duty is to you, my people. As usual, there have been many rumours, many of them promoted, I am sorry to say, by men and women who call themselves journalists. In fact they are no better than rumour peddlers, dangerous rumour peddlers, all too often misled by their foreign colleagues . . .'

He rejected the stories that the grain market had been manipulated. These were the imaginings of his political enemies, who had 'insects in their head', as were claims that the upcoming election would be rigged.

It was true that there was a danger that some citizens could go hungry: 'Not even the government can control the weather.' So as father of the nation, it was only proper, he said, that he make the opening contribution of maize. And Mayor Guchu had been instructed to launch an international appeal for food and clothing on behalf of the people of Kireba.

Guchu had calculated that the company he and the president controlled would make an extra million dollars, as grain prices on the local market had risen. In the course of the rioting it emerged that a UN food warehouse had been burned down. Rumours that it had been set alight by the ruling party's thugs were dismissed by the president.

Then he got down to business:

'My first announcement is this: Mrs Anna Nugilu, leader of the opposition, came to see me yesterday for a final session of talks about our two parties.

'As you know, I have great respect for Mrs Anna Nugilu. We discussed the benefits of co-operation. I am happy to announce that Mrs Nugilu has agreed not to contest the presidential elections due shortly.

'I am even happier to announce that, with immediate effect, Mrs Anna Nugilu will serve as my first vice president. Her main duty will be liaison with the World Bank, whose president, my friend Hardwick Hardwicke, has completed his first visit to this country. I am pleased to say that he has recognised the great reforms we have introduced in Kuwisha.

'And I am happiest to tell you that I believe the search for my successor is over. The candidate for the presidential nomination of the party when I retire now will be . . .'

At this point the camera panned from the president's desk in State House, and across his study to where Anna Nugilu was sitting on one of the sofas.

'Mrs Anna Nugilu. Subject, of course, to the approval of the party. After all, we are a democracy!'

There was still more to come. President Nduka had saved the most dramatic part of his announcement for last.

'Finally, people of Kuwisha, I must tell you that twelve months from today, on the next Uhuru Day, I intend to step down, having used my prerogative to call a presidential and parliamentary poll three years earlier than the constitution provides for.'

The wits of Kuwisha had a field day.

Anyone who acted with the slightest degree of impropriety or opportunism was called a 'Nugilu'.

Uhuru Day, the day on which Kuwisha experienced one of its worst riots since independence, would henceforth become known as 'World Bank day'.

And the phrase 'World Bank' passed into the everyday language of the people of Kuwisha, as a synonym for something that did not work. Cars with flat batteries were 'World Bank', fridges that failed to chill the beer were 'World Bank', and traffic lights that did not operate were 'World Bank'.

Indeed, some cynics went so far as to suggest that Kuwisha itself was 'World Bank' . . .

When the British high commissioner requested an urgent meeting, the president responded with alacrity. He positively relished the prospect.

'Tell him to come, right away,' he said to the cabinet secretary, who had relayed the request. 'Tell him that old friends are always welcome.'

The high commissioner began by congratulating the president on what he called a 'statesmanlike' Uhuru Day address.

Nduka cut him short.

'With the greatest respect, I doubt that you sought this audience in order to convey your government's appreciation of my political talent.

'I gather you are here to express your concern about abuses of civil rights over the last few hours. I can confirm that at least twenty-seven looters have been shot. You say that your government is anxious that the rule of law is respected.

'The police tell me the looters were ransacking the shops of the Asian community. At least three of their women have been raped but Asian leaders have asked me to keep that confidential.

'Some of the ringleaders of the unrest have been detained under the state of emergency I briefly imposed.'

He smiled. 'Of course I don't need to explain its provisions to you. Emergency powers were first used by the British when Kuwisha was a colony and you were a young district officer here.

'I have acted properly under the powers invested in me. I hope the ringleaders will be executed. They were abusing the civil rights of the people of Kuwisha. Is this the abuse you were referring to?'

The high commissioner was determined to give as good as he got. He looked at the man in front of him, with so many faces, so many personalities, who could be so charming, and could be so ruthless. What did he have to lose by speaking frankly he asked himself? He heard a small voice in his head saying: 'Quite a lot actually – there's the military agreement which allows us to use Kuwisha's military facilities, five billion dollars' worth of British investment, and 30,000 Asians who are British passport holders who we'd have to find a home for if Kuwisha were to collapse.'

Nevertheless, the high commissioner decided to let rip.

'I have it on good authority, Mr President, that most of the bodies in the central morgue have gunshot wounds which suggest they were shot in the back. I don't challenge the right of the state to discipline those suspected of attempting to overthrow legitimate authority, but was it necessary to arrest their wives, sons and daughters, Mr President? And before leaving for this meeting I was told that several of the bodies of the looters bore marks that suggested they had been tortured. I suggest that an independent examination would bear out my concerns. But with respect, Mr President, I doubt that your judges, whatever their intellectual qualifications, are morally equipped for such a task.'

For a moment he thought he had gone too far. But it seemed that Nduka was enjoying the exchange.

'You British, always you claim the moral high ground. Yes,

it is possible that some of my judges are corrupt. Let us not mince words. But who are among the worst offenders? The chaps you sent out, whose salary you help pay, the chaps sent to help us natives maintain standards.

'Now let us talk about morality, High Commissioner.'

He took a sip from the glass of water beside him.

'I assume that the Vosper patrol boats you sold us a few years ago were to assist Kuwisha in the defence of civil liberties? Nothing to do with the jobs the order saved in that marginal constituency in the north of England?

'Kuwisha has always been a friend of the West. I do not think that you people are a friend of Kuwisha.'

President Nduka took the notes he had been making, and deliberately and slowly tore them in half.

'With the greatest respect, as you people say, I am telling your government to take a running leap.'

Later that night the high commissioner re-read his telegram to London, signed it, and passed it on to the communications officer. After a resume of the developments of the last twenty-four hours it went on:

'The president, who responded promptly to my request for a meeting, clearly shares our anxiety about civil rights and law and order. He expressed his own deep concerns in characteristically forceful terms, and emphasised the importance to Kuwisha of long-standing ties with the UK and the value of military treaties with HMG and Washington.

'The forty-minute meeting also provided the opportunity to raise questions about the maize contract set out in my earlier note. We agreed that much of the British press coverage has been unhelpful. The president acknowledged that the privatisation of the maize board had allowed some unscrupulous traders to take unfair advantage of Kuwisha's widening food deficit, and he informed me that Mayor Willifred Guchu will head a commission of enquiry. Fortunately Podmore has already established a close and cordial working relationship with this controversial but able figure. (See my earlier telegram.)

'I recommend that we interpret the president's passionate response to HMG's concerns as an emotional and heartfelt demonstration of the significance of UK–Kuwisha links, and of his determination to maintain close ties with Britain.'

Back at the Intercontinental Hotel, Hardwick Hardwicke and Jim 'Fingers' Adams had packed their bags.

Hardwick Hardwicke had no doubts that the riots had been a seminal lesson for the government. Nothing could dent or penetrate the carapace of his tireless optimism. President Nduka, Hardwicke believed, had undergone a painful lesson.

'He got his ass kicked,' he had told Fingers.

Hardwicke was nevertheless relieved that Dr Nduka was still in charge at what was generally seen as a critical and delicate stage of Kuwisha's transition to good governance and a sound economy, a view shared by Britain's foreign office.

'It is a painful business, implementing reform,' he said to Kuwisha's finance minister as they made their farewells. 'You just need to watch for inappropriate allocation of state resources,' he said, amidst convivial laughter.

Like the press, Western diplomats were divided in their analysis. David Podmore had little doubt that there had been an attempt to overthrow Nduka by the middle ranks of the military. Officers no longer enjoyed a subsidy of cooking oil, his military sources revealed, and tribal tensions within the presidential guard had come to a head in advance of the coming elections.

The French suspected the British of fomenting dissent, and then tipping off the president, thus ingratiating themselves with the man. The British suspected the French of doing much the same thing – but with the objective of overthrowing Nduka, and persuading his successor to buy the out-of-date

270

French-built Mirage fighter jets rather than the out-of-date British-built Hawks that were on offer.

Yet another explanation about the riots came from the aid workers in WorldFeed and the other non-government aid organisations. They claimed that the rioting was what they called 'a spontaneous expression of anger'. The people, they said, could no longer tolerate the brutal cuts in subsidies of basic foods, carried out at the insistence of the World Bank and the International Monetary Fund.

25

'The bird that picks the meat from the crocodile's
teeth leaves no droppings'

Lucy's parting with Cecil at the airport the night before had
been unexpectedly difficult. She had not expected him to be
nervous, but he seemed insistent that they agree to meet in
London.

'Soon?' Pearson asked.

'Soonest,' she had replied: 'Promise.'

There was good news when she got home. A message from
the head office of WorldFeed expressed enthusiasm about her
proposal for a partnership with the Bank and the UN
Development Programme. Before going to bed, Lucy switched
off her mobile phone; tomorrow would be a busy day. Within
seconds of her head hitting the pillow, she was asleep.

The next morning she set off for Cambridge House.
Somewhat to her surprise, Mayor Guchu's Range Rover was
parked outside the building, under the watchful eye of half a
dozen of his security people. She walked down the corridor to
the *Financial News'* office, humming to herself, her spirits
buoyed by the prospect of throwing WorldFeed's support
behind the Kireba water project.

She was early for the meeting with Newman Kibwana, but
there were one or two things to collect from Pearson's office. In
his rush to leave, he had forgotten a large brown envelope
packed with assorted slips of paper and blank invoices. The

nondescript collection of unclaimed expenses was probably worth several hundred pounds.

Her humming ceased and her nose wrinkled as she encountered a waft of carbolic soap and urine from the men's toilet. She passed the offices of the Japan Television News Agency, where the agency's correspondent was talking animatedly to a colleague.

She was approaching the canteen when she heard familiar voices. To her astonishment, Newman Kibwana and Mayor Willifred Guchu were sharing the podium, and Guchu was winding up some sort of appeal. Lucy stopped. It must be really important if it could bring two such sworn enemies to share a podium.

'Never again,' Guchu was saying.

'Never again,' Kibwana repeated solemnly.

Lucy looked into the room:

'Never again will the citizens of Kireba be subject to these horrors. Today we stand together, Newman Kibwana and Guchu, putting aside our political differences, for the sake of the people of Kireba. Clean water will change their lives.'

A young woman scribbled assiduously, and messengers and office workers listened, and looked bored.

'Tomorrow night,' Guchu continued, 'we fly to London to prepare for the fanfare overseas launch of the project that will change their lives, for ever . . .'

'Already the two of us, Kibwana and Guchu, have discussed the Kireba Water-Aid Project. As you know, it has the support of the World Bank and the United Nations Development Programme. If we mobilise together, with their help, the first tap carrying clean water will be ready in three months.'

Guchu spotted Lucy, caught her eye, and smiled. Newman Kibwana, now clinging to the lifeline thrown to him by President Nduka, nodded a welcome at Lucy.

'Ownership,' Guchu was saying. 'Ownership is what counts.'

Lucy unlocked the door to Pearson's office, stuffed the envelope in her bag, and was about to leave when her mobile phone rang.

It was Jonathan Punabantu. Could she call in to see him at State House? No, it could not wait. Cecil was in trouble . . . serious trouble.

As she locked the office door behind her, Lucy felt her arm being tugged. It was the bureau chief of the Japan Television News Agency, as polite as ever.

'Rucy, could you please tell me: where are the riots?'

26

'Women who pick the ripe dongo berries
make lazy wives'

The Uhuru Day holiday was about to end, and Kuwisha was returning to its routine. The prostitutes were on the prowl again, stalking the city hotels. The four-wheel-drive vehicles would soon carry their owners back from the country and coastal resorts, back to their homes in Borrowdale and other suburbs. They were needed in their offices, pursuing their good causes. More had died in Kireba, where the cholera outbreak was now in full spate. But the scourge had now been officially acknowledged, and for the international press corps the story had lost its appeal. What is more, there were reports of a massacre of civilians near Kisangani, and a charter flight to the scene was to leave early the next day.

At the city's international airport, the tide was changing.

The outgoing travellers who arrived as pink visitors were returning to Europe. They now sported tans, and wore safari chic: multi-pocketed trousers, and khaki waistcoats with epaulettes. Some flaunted their newly acquired words of Swahili. They ordered a last Tusker at the airport bar, '*baridi sana*', very cold, and demonstrated their egalitarian principles by calling the bar steward bwana. Bored passengers looking for a final bargain wandered into the airport's many souvenir shops, and wondered whether they should spend their last ngwee on a wooden giraffe, or a malachite rhino.

Meanwhile, Kireba licked its wounds.

Parts of the slum had been destroyed by rioting residents, by the police and by the army, although which of the three had done most damage was a moot point. At first glance, *Harrods* seemed to be one of the casualties. Yet although the bar's appearance suggested the opposite, it was untouched by the rioters. Well before the mob advanced on the city, the steel doors of the two giant containers had been swung shut by a group of Mboya Boys, with the fridge, chairs and tables, and the stock of beers and soft drinks, all safely secured within.

But to the casual observer, *Harrods* looked as if it had been attacked by an arsonist. Someone had piled several old car tyres against one of the containers, and set them alight. The thick oily smoke had left a film of soot on the container walls, and had made the *Harrods* sign all but illegible.

The scene seemed utterly without hope. But to the sharp-eyed, and the indigent, there were pickings to be had.

Titus Ntoto and Cyrus Rutere scoured the ruins of burnt-out stalls along either side of the main track, the so-called 'Uhuru Avenue', where the food vendors, the watch repairers, the cobblers, the coffin makers, the tinkers, the tailors, and the traders were slowly putting their lives back together.

The two youths were lounging near the Kireba clinic. They watched as a taxi approached, and parked at the point where the road ends and Kireba starts. A figure in a pinstriped suit emerged, peering at a scrap of paper. He spotted the boys. Taking care to ensure that his taxi driver stayed close behind him, the man in his mid-forties approached them, talking slowly and loudly.

'I'm looking for' – he paused, and checked the paper, even though the address was now painfully well known to him – 'Harrods International Bar (and Nightspot), on Uhuru Avenue.'

*

276

The journey to Kuwisha had been without incident for Rupert Fanshawe, partner in the well known London law firm of Fanshawe and Fanshawe. After delays in getting a reply to their letters, and provoked by Furniver's impertinent response when it eventually arrived, they had been driven to this last resort. Fanshawe and Fanshawe were determined to make an example of Charity Mupanga and Harrods International Bar (and Nightspot).

Fanshawe and his partners had agreed: the only way of settling the dispute was for someone to fly to Kuwisha and have it out with that woman, Mupanga, and her incompetent lawyer.

Some degree of third world experience for whoever made the journey was advisable, the partners felt. On the basis of Fanshawe's recent fortnight in Mauritius, he was the obvious candidate. And he was due a spot of leave. Once the matter had been settled, said the senior partner, why not take a few days off at the coast?

It turned out to be a tough assignment. Checking in at the city's Intercontinental Hotel had been straightforward, but thereafter it had been 'hell, sheer bloody hell', as Fanshawe would tell his admiring colleagues on his return.

'Africa,' he would say, rather like David Podmore, shaking his head sadly, and looking preoccupied by an impenetrable private grief brought about by horrors he had seen at first hand: 'Africa.'

It had all seemed clear enough when he studied the map of the city on the plane. It was a short walk from the Intercontinental Hotel to Uhuru Avenue, but there was a problem. Two problems, in fact, Fanshawe told the office.

After covering the length of the potholed, palm-tree-lined route, and asking passers-by, Fanshawe had been unable to locate Harrods International Bar (and Nightspot).

And as for the street children: 'A bloody menace,' said

Fanshawe. 'Blighters should be in school.' Only when he asked one of the gang that was trailing him did he ascertain that the city had two Uhuru Avenues – one official, the other in Kireba. With much irritation and some unease, he hailed a taxi and gave fresh directions to the driver.

'Leave the taxi at the clinic,' the boy had instructed him.

'The place where the bar should usually be is very close. But there has been much rooting, much rooting.'

Rooting? Rooting? Where the bar should 'usually' be? What on earth did the boy mean, 'usually'?

Fanshawe had become increasingly unhappy. But the taxi driver seemed confident that he knew where *Harrods* was, although he seemed puzzled that the lawyer should want to go there. A bit of discipline, thought Fanshawe, that's what is needed. Firmly, he repeated the address. He had flown 8,000 miles to find this bloody place, and he was not going to give up now.

The two urchins who were watching the stranger as he looked around, his fear and bemusement almost palpable, conferred in Swahili:

'You take the briefcase, I'll snatch his watch,' said Cyrus Rutere.

Ntoto was about to agree, then thought again.

'Just a minute,' he said to Cyrus, and approached the stranger.

'Where are you from, sir?'

'London,' snapped Rupert Fanshawe, and held his briefcase tighter. He looked around.

'London,' he said again, more emphatically this time.

His tone suggested that if he said it often enough and loudly enough, he would either be able to make sense of the squalor that surrounded him, or be magically transported back to his chambers in London, EC4.

Ntoto looked at Fanshawe speculatively and turned to his companion.

'I think this is the man who is giving Mrs Charity all the trouble,' he said in Swahili.

Cyrus looked around.

'Where will we put him?' he asked.

'Don't be so stupid,' said Ntoto. 'If we harm him, police will come from London to look for us. He is a European! No, we will pretend to help him, but we will make sure he does not find Mrs Charity.'

He turned back to Fanshawe.

'Please, sir, tell me again the name of the place you are looking for. What is the street?'

'Harrods International Bar (and Nightspot),' Fanshawe replied, with a touch of impatience. 'Uhuru bloody Avenue.'

Ntoto repeated the address, and made sympathetic clucking noises.

'I am very sorry, sir. I have news that is very bad. *Harrods* is World Bank.'

'World Bank? World Bank! I don't want the bloody World Bank,' said Fanshawe. 'I want this bar . . .'

Ntoto turned to Cyrus.

'You tell him.'

'Sir,' Cyrus began diffidently. '*Harrods* bar is World Bank. It is not working. It is finished.'

'Finished? What the hell do you mean, finished?'

He looked around desperately.

'Is anyone here? Is there nobody I can talk to?'

Just like the Mboya story, thought Ntoto, and suppressed the urge to giggle.

'It is finished, sir. It was rooted.'

'Rooted? Rooted? What do you mean, boy, rooted?' said Fanshawe, exasperated, starting to sweat in his pinstripe suit.

Ntoto and Cyrus had a whispered exchange.

'Is he stupid?' asked Cyrus.

Ntoto tried again.

'Sir, it was rooted. It was attacked and burnt by the rooters.'

The penny dropped.

'And where was it?'

'We are standing near where it was, sir. It was run by my sister's aunt, Mrs Charity Mupanga.'

'That's the woman,' said Fanshawe excitedly, 'that's her.'

Ntoto gestured towards *Harrods*, and began to wail.

'She was killed by the rooters, sir. She was like a mother to us.'

Fanshawe looked around him, incredulity, relief and horror following each other across his face.

'My God,' he exclaimed, 'the bloody bunch of savages.'

What a story he would have to tell back in London.

'A-bunch-of-bloody-savages,' he said again, giving each word an angry emphasis. Killing their own kind! So this was black on black violence! Too bloody much! No wonder Africa was in such bad shape. Fanshawe fished in his pocket, and extracted two 100 ngwee notes. His job was nearly done.

'Thank you, sir,' said Ntoto.

Fanshawe took the first few steps towards *Harrods*. Something unpleasant had attached itself to his left shoe, and the blood of a recently slaughtered goat dribbled into a nearby ditch. He studied his surroundings with distaste. 'Like the Somme on a bad day,' he thought, and looked dubiously across the forty-odd metres that lay between him and *Harrods*. Fanshawe took a deep breath, and was about to make the journey, but Ntoto intervened.

The boy tugged at his jacket.

'It is still very dangerous,' he said, looking around with mock unease. 'There are looters nearby, I am sure. We will escort you back to the hotel you are staying. It is very, very dangerous. More trouble is coming, for sure.'

The pinstriped lawyer looked around. The awful smell of the place would cling to his suit for ages, and his stomach churned. Slivers of smoke were still rising from around the blackened containers that used to be *Harrods*. Why take the risk? He already had an extraordinary tale to tell when he got back to London. Fanshawe brushed aside Ntoto's guiding hand.

'For God's sake,' he exclaimed irritably as Ntoto persisted. 'Take your filthy fingers off me, boy!'

The lawyer walked briskly to the waiting cab, parked near the clinic, followed by his driver. He hopped in. 'I may look like a London gent,' he thought to himself, 'but I'm not stupid.' The hotel staff had warned him about the hazards of city life. High on the list was the risk of being mugged by the marauding gangs of street kids.

'I can manage,' he said confidently, winding up the window until it was an inch from the top, and locking the door.

'Back to the hotel,' he ordered the driver.

Ntoto moved round to the driver's side. The man looked at him fearfully and contemplated a quick get-away. But the track was muddy, and the car could easily get stuck in the attempt. What was more, he recognised Ntoto, who could, should he choose, make life very unpleasant for him.

Ntoto told him: 'The white man is very frightened, and very stupid. He believes more trouble is coming. Tell him he is right. Take him to his hotel, and tell him he should collect his bags, quickly, and then drive him to the airport.'

'Why should I do this?'

Ntoto chuckled.

'Because if you don't, me and my friends, we will shit in your car. Every day.'

He pulled out the notes Fanshawe had given him, gave the driver half, and stepped back as the taxi pulled away.

*

Safely back in his room at the Intercontinental, Rupert Fanshawe was on the phone to London.

'Absolutely ghastly. Bloody unspeakable. Didn't get to meet that bugger Furniver. Rang his office, no reply. Either his phone doesn't work. Or holidays, local holidays, gone native . . . what's that? *Harrods*? Burnt to the bloody ground, destroyed, by the rioters. That Mupanga woman was killed. Yes – killed their own kind . . . Just before I arrived . . . Dangerous? A bit . . . but I kept my head down. Mauritius taught me a thing or two, when my hotel was caught up in that waiters' strike. Damn nearly turned nasty. Yes, yes, I'm OK, really. Met these two local lads, gave me the full story. We can close the file on this one.'

Fanshawe packed as he spoke, and took a stiffening gulp of the gin and tonic he had poured himself from the room's minibar.

'*Entre-nous*, I've been tipped off. Local sources. And dips here say more trouble likely tonight. I'll catch the next plane home, go to the coast another time . . . Can't help feeling sorry for the two boys. Thick as short planks, but couldn't have been more helpful. Related to her, apparently. Suggest we make a donation to what's-her-name's estate.'

He rustled through the file.

'Mupanga, that's it, Charity Mupanga. Send it to her lawyer, that prick Furniver. Perhaps it can pay school fees for the lads. Whatever. We don't want the story to get into the hands of the press, tho'. We can make the payment conditional on silence, just in case . . . How much?'

How much indeed?

Fanshawe was feeling hugely relieved. The taxi driver was waiting outside, keen to get to the airport as soon as possible.

'The taxi chappie's wetting his pants,' Fanshawe chuckled. 'Just as well I know how to look after myself . . . Bloody lucky to be getting out of this alive.'

Fanshawe accepted the congratulations of the senior partner.

'Couple of hundred pounds will do, but with a pretty stiff letter along with it,' said Fanshawe, and his colleague at the end of the line agreed.

'Make it clear we're peeved. Clear breach of trademark, and so on. Not much point in trying to recover costs. Place was a wreck, absolute shambles. As for the state of that poor woman . . . hacked to death, I gather.'

The partner kept a respectful silence, and hoped that Fanshawe would not go into the details. His colleague had seen horrors that no decent man should ever see.

'But we don't want to give these people the wrong idea. We're not a soft touch. Don't want them coming back for more. Yes, a couple of hundred pounds will do.'

It was only when checking out that Fanshawe realised that his wallet was missing.

Edward Furniver had lost track of time.

Judging by the noise, his office had been on the front line, though every ten minutes or so a Mboya Boy had shouted through the letterbox, assuring him that there was never any danger that the rioters would damage it. Not that Furniver cared – he had taken refuge in his computer, checking the loan accounts that he feared no longer mattered.

At least his embarrassing itch had been efficiently dealt with, during his visit with Charity to the clinic. He had undressed behind a screen, re-emerged wearing an old dressing gown which Mercy had asked him to put on back to front, stretched out face down on the clinic's rudimentary examination table, and apprehensively awaited the first probe.

It was over in a minute.

He felt no more than a slight squeeze, and had closed his eyes when Mercy tried to show him the result.

Charity admonished him.

'You men! You get embarrassed about foolish things, always. Just like David.'

'I must tell you, Furniver,' she continued, as he re-emerged from behind the screen, hitching up his trousers, 'always make very sure that your underpants are properly ironed. Didn't your friends at the Thumaiga Club tell you that? What do you men talk about?'

Mercy looked at him sternly as she washed her hands, and joined in.

'She is right, Furniver. Everyone knows this. Even those people at the club. They know it. You are lucky. If it had burst . . .'

On the way back from the clinic, he and Charity had bumped into Mildred Kigali.

'Furniver had a *jipu* in his *butumba*. Mercy removed it without bursting it,' Charity said proudly, while Furniver, embarrassed, looked at his feet.

Mildred gave a whoop of delight and relief.

'I will tell Mr Kigali. He will be very pleased,' and she hurried to break the news to Didymus, who had gone into a deep depression since his traumatic experience.

'Did Kigali not iron your underpants?' Charity asked.

Wasn't this where I came in, Furniver asked himself? *Jipus* and underpants . . .

Perhaps he should have defied the Mboya Boys, who had continued to provide a protective presence around the building, well after the rioters had passed on. He should have returned to *Harrods*, and stayed at the side of the woman he loved. But even the short journey to the bar could be dangerous, and his presence might well imperil Charity. At times like this, a white face could attract unwanted attention. So with heavy heart, he had stayed put.

The knock on the door broke into Furniver's downcast mood.

It would not be Charity – she had a key. It could not be a looter, nor – an even worse prospect – a government soldier. Neither would have bothered to knock. The air-conditioner suddenly cut out, and within minutes Furniver had started to sweat.

Not for him the genteel, tiny-beaded perspiration of Europe. Rather it was like the African storm that was now passing. Huge drops of sweat rolled off his forehead, spattered on to his desk, drenching his cotton shirt.

Another knock. This time Furniver pulled himself out of his office chair, his trousers sticking to his thighs. He went downstairs, through the accounts room, past the table with three legs and the filing cabinet with a drawer missing. He reached the door just as the knock came for a third time, deferential, yet insistent.

'Who is there?' Furniver called out.

'It is me, sir.' There was a pause, as the caller realised that this in itself might not be sufficient identification.

'It is Nellson Githongo, sir.'

Furniver unlocked the steel-frame door, followed by the grill that had been installed at the insistence of the insurance company. About time he shopped around for another company, thought Furniver, for the premiums were huge, and most of the conditions unnecessary.

Nellson Githongo stood on the threshold, a battered brown trilby in one hand, the other clutching 100 ngwee, plus 20 ngwee penalty. Although he had surrendered his bike just a day earlier, it seemed to Furniver as if it had been long ago, in another era.

The sound of what seemed to be a gunshot made them both jump, although it could have been a car backfiring.

'I would like my bicycle, sir. It is safe now. Otherwise I cannot travel.'

Furniver was about to question him, and then thought the better of it. He went into the stock room, where the bicycle

285

was stored, along with an old radio, a black and white television set, a couple of sewing machines, and a steam iron. He wheeled the bike out and handed it over.

'I will repay the rest of the loan.'

'I don't think it matters, Nellson.'

Nellson cocked his head, unable to conceal his dismay. He looked speculatively at the sweating white man in front of him.

'But it is not all finished, sir . . .'

Suddenly Furniver felt himself surrendering to his low spirits, trapped in an Africa crippled by debt, disease and disaster. Nellson Githongo was looking at him with concern.

'Do not worry, Mr Edward.'

Here it comes, thought Furniver, here it comes. Another bloody incomprehensible Kuwisha proverb.

'Your people in England say, sir, that the darkest time is just before the dawn.'

And with that Githongo tipped his hat, attached the two sacks of oranges he was carrying to the handlebars, adjusted the aerial of the mock radio that adorned the bicycle, and tweaked the bell.

'Thank you for looking after it, sir.'

Sacks swaying, he wheeled it carefully through the doorway, across the muddy surrounds and towards the track that would take him past the clinic and on to paved roads.

Furniver watched as Nellson wobbled on his way. The defaulter did not look round. Yet just as he was turning the bend that would take him out of sight, he raised his right hand in farewell.

Furniver waved back, and returned wearily to his office, and sat at his desk. Earlier he had finished recording the story for his granddaughter, but it was too late and too dangerous to go to the central post office.

The stand-by generator had cut in automatically. He marginally adjusted the framed photos of Dorian and Dorcas –

'my ex-children', he called them. He then propped up a photograph of Charity taken during one of the visits to her *shamba*.

Nothing that had happened over the past twenty-four hours had surprised him, least of all the rebellion, or insurrection, or coup – whatever it was called.

For a while he managed to resist the temptation of succumbing to the panacea that lay in his desk drawer. Then his resolution broke. Furniver opened the drawer, and reached for oblivion . . .

27

'If the goat roars and the lion bleats,
bring out your spears'

Titus Ntoto and Cyrus Rutere lay in the sun outside *Harrods*,
having undertaken the messy task of clearing up around the
bar, which had yet to be reopened for business.

They had told Charity the story of how they had met and
deceived the lawyer from London, and had considered themselves fortunate to have been let off with a lecture about the
obligation to be helpful and hospitable to strangers.

'It could have been no dough balls for a week,' said Rutere.

Ntoto agreed:

'We were lucky.'

The skies were clear for the first time in weeks, their stomachs were replete, their glue bottles were full, and *Harrods* was
safe. The world was as good for them as it was ever likely to
get.

Rutere, however, still needed one or two questions
answered before he could relax.

'Who but *mungiki* would do this thing?' gesturing at the
smoke-blackened containers that made up the bar. 'Why make
a fire?'

Ntoto nodded. 'You are right. *Mungiki* are here!'

Rutere looked up, startled. If *mungiki* had the cheek to
intrude into the heartland of the Mboya Boys, things had
come to a pretty pass.

'Perhaps they helped Mrs Charity,' Ntoto added.

Rutere could hardly believe his ears. Surely Ntoto was not suggesting that Mrs Charity had any sympathy for *mungiki*.

Ntoto, if you think that Mrs Charity would help these *mungiki* in any way, then you must be, you must be . . .'

He paused as he searched for the word that would do justice to Ntoto's fantastical allegation.

'You must be stupid.'

So cross was Rutere he could hardly contain himself, and Ntoto realised he had gone too far in teasing his friend.

'You are stupid yourself, Rutere. I was joking about *mungiki* – but telling the truth about Mrs Charity,' and Ntoto went on to explain that Charity had indeed lit the fire herself:

'Just to fool any *tstotsis*. When they saw smoke, they would think that *Harrods* had already been looted.'

Rutere was lost in admiration for the sheer cunning, the deviousness, of this ploy, and once again had to search for a word that would do its perpetrator justice.

It did not take him long:

'Clever! Mrs Charity is very clever.'

Rutere belched, but cupped his hand over his mouth, as he had been taught by Charity:

'Excuse,' he said, and winked at Ntoto.

'I excuse,' said Ntoto languidly, doing his best to imitate Fanshawe's plummy English voice.

'I say, have you seen my wallet?'

Ntoto reached into his trouser pocket and pulled out a leather wallet with the initials R and F embossed on it.

'For God's sake!' Titus drawled, 'Take your filthy fingers off me, boy!'

Rutere clapped his hands, and a beatific smile slowly spread over his face. Then he frowned.

'I thought it was wrong to pickpocket, Ntoto. You yourself said so. How can you take this lawyer's wallet?'

Ntoto shrugged. 'He is a rich man . . .'

His voice trailed off.

Rutere did not argue.

'I have one last question, Ntoto. Why are you sure that the traffic lights are not being broken by *mungiki*?'

'You have *mungiki* on your brain, Rutere. Always it is *mungiki*, and always you are looking for *muti*.'

Rutere ignored the provocation. He was too comfortable to quarrel.

'Tell me,' demanded Rutere. 'Who is breaking the traffic lights?'

'The cripples. With catapults.'

Rutere was astonished.

'How is that?'

'You cannot beg from cars when they are passing you very fast. So cripples break the lights, using their catapult to make a traffic jam. But only green lights. They use the pieces of glass from broken lights to make emeralds to sell to tourists.'

Rutere saw the logic, but wasn't convinced.

'I still think it is *mungiki*.'

Ntoto's chin dropped on to his chest as he began to doze, and Rutere soon joined him, snoring gently.

Charity emerged from the interior of *Harrods* where she had been taking stock, and looked on tenderly.

Her two little rats. They looked as dangerous as dormice. And yet her dream told her otherwise. There were many, many mice in Kuwisha's store of corn, eating, eating, always eating.

A time of reckoning was surely coming. She felt sure of that. For Titus Ntoto and Cyrus Rutere and the other members of the Mboya Boys United Football Club, the events of the past couple of days had been no more than a brief respite from their daily grind. The same ancient hunger that so distracted the pilot of the ageing Dakoto was stirring in the skinny loins of the two boys and all their friends. It would not be denied.

290

They were about to enter life's great gamble, and the prospects of them surviving the draw were as slim as their chances of winning Kuwisha's weekly lottery.

But these were thoughts that smacked of despair, and she tried to put them out of her head. Kireba was recovering rapidly. It was time to decide. Mildred Kigali was right. It was indeed time to decide.

First, there was a legal matter to attend to . . .

Thanks to Ntoto and Rutere, she had survived the first round in the battle over *Harrods*, but Charity had little doubt that more fighting would surely come. If she continued to trade as *Harrods*, it was surely just a matter of time before the London lawyers found out that they had been tricked. They would be back.

What would her dear father, Mwai Gichuru Tangwenya, have wanted? What would he have advised?

There was only one thing to do. Charity summoned Philimon Limuru, the sign-writer, who lived nearby.

The negotiations were less complicated than she had feared. The man had a sweet tooth, and they soon settled on a price of two dough balls a letter, and two Tuskers as a bonus if he did a really good job. He started right away, and as she watched the man and his brush go to work, any doubts she may have had soon disappeared.

Half an hour later it was done, the letters alternating in brilliant blue, the colour of Kuwisha's sky, a rich ochre, the colour of the soil, and the green of the country's tea and coffee bushes:

Tangwenya's International Bar (and Nightspot)

Charity felt nothing but pride. It would be a while, she suspected, before people got used to calling it *Tangwenya's*. For some of the older folk, it would always be *Harrods*. That was as it should be. She would neither encourage nor discourage the use of one name or the other.

She had made the right decision. The bar was now ready to be reopened, and it deserved to be celebrated.

Charity chalked a piece of good news on the menu blackboard.

'*Today Only: Tusker 20% off*'

'Last orders,' Charity announced to the small crowd that had been patiently awaiting the reopening of the bar.

'Last orders at *Harrods*.'

A loud cheer went up from the excited customers, led by Ntoto and Rutere.

'New orders tomorrow, at *Tangwenya's International Bar (and Nightspot)*', and the cheers were even louder.

Charity gazed around for the umpteenth time. One could not be too careful. The strangers who had been hanging around Kireba had left, and the slum was quiet. It seemed safe enough – certainly safe enough for Furniver to emerge from his confinement.

Now for a truly momentous decision, as momentous as any she had taken since the day she had accepted David's proposal of marriage. It seemed only right to her that she should in some way consult him. Perhaps there was a message to be found in the words of his last sermon, reprinted in a leading Kuwisha newspaper on the day of his funeral. Charity had cut it out, and kept it in her purse. As she read it, David came alive . . .

Bishop Mupanga seldom delivered a conventional sermon. Rather he conducted a benign exchange with the congregation, this time packed into the cathedral behind the city's Intercontinental Hotel. Both arms resting on the pulpit, like a man assuming a raconteur's position in his favourite bar, the Bishop had begun on a typically informal note:

'They say there are no atheists in the trenches of war.

'Perhaps that is why we so often thank God in Africa. Whether we live here, or whether we are regular visitors, we thank God, or Allah, for our many deliverances, with fervour and humility.'

The congregation murmured its understanding and muttered their agreement. The sound was like the first breeze of the day, as it drifted through the clump of tall eucalyptus trees near her bar . . . Charity shut her eyes, and imagined herself back among the cathedral congregation, listening to the rest of the sermon, delivered in David's confident, deep voice:

We thank God when we arrive safely at our destination, whether by car or train, or ferry or aircraft. We thank God that the car's brakes did not fail during long journeys on Africa's potholed roads; we are grateful that the driver spotted the lorry ahead travelling without taillights; and give thanks that the overloaded ferry did not sink.'

As the congregation picked up the rhythm and cadence, they echoed his opening phrase, producing a growing rumble of assent and endorsement.

'Thank God!'

This time, however, it was not so much a gentle morning breeze as a powerful wind that precedes an African storm.

If David Mupanga had been receiving death threats, as was widely rumoured, he gave no sign of stress or tension as he delivered his sermon that Sunday, just three days before his fatal crash on the road from the capital to the small town of Nongo.

'We give especially heartfelt thanks when we arrive safely at our destination after travelling at night, unmolested by the armed robbers that make their living along the highway, who so often seem to be dressed in uniforms stolen from the army or the police force.'

'Thank God,' answered the congregation with especial enthusiasm.

A baby started crying, but was soon hushed back to sleep by its young mother. Nearby worshippers looked on sympathetically and indulgently.

'We live with risk,' said David Mupanga, 'some more than others. But we all live with it, whether the risk of Aids, or the risk of a car accident because we lack spare parts, or the risk of malaria or even worse, catching malaria that has learnt to defy pills.'

'We thank God' – 'Thank God,' came the echo from the congregation – 'when we have the energy to face the day, that we do not have bilharzia, or other intestinal worms and parasites that suck the vitality of their victims.

'We thank God when a child enjoys a birthday, and we thank God if he or she survives the hazards of being young in Africa. We thank God if our children are lucky in Africa's lottery. We thank God if they are not one of the three million children who die of preventable diseases before they reach five.

'We thank God if they emerge numerate and literate. We are particularly thankful if it is a girl who survives, because for her the hazards of life are much greater.

'We do not despair, because that is a cardinal sin, and we try not to succumb to fatalism. But instead, if one is a Christian, one soon learns from the wisdom of another faith and utters the precautionary word that reminds one of human frailty: *Inshallah* – God willing.

'We thank God for a decent meal, because most of the 600 million souls who live on our continent go without adequate nourishment.

'We thank God if we live in peace, because millions of us have lives made hell by war. We thank God if we have clean water to drink, because most of us do not, and we consider ourselves especially fortunate if we do not have to walk miles to fetch it.

'We thank God if we are not a refugee, on a continent

where so many millions have been forced to flee their homes, seeking sanctuary within or without the country that is home. So in Africa we thank God, or Allah, with unusual frequency. And we are especially thankful if we end the day alive and well, with a meal in our stomachs, with a bed to sleep in, and our loved ones safe.

'No doubt this is because there are so few of us who are so fortunate. Above all, we thank God for our friends.'

And as David Mupanga stepped down from the pulpit he embraced the ever-present plain-clothed security detail, one by one.

'Amen,' said Charity.

She had been deliberating for long enough.

'Odhiambo!'

Ntoto's head jerked up, and he looked around. Suddenly he remembered. He was no longer Titus. He had chosen what he called his African name. He was now Odhiambo Ntoto.

He trotted to her side. Charity cocked her head. Kireba was coming alive.

'Listen, Odhiambo, listen. It is the sound of bees.'

Ntoto shrugged. If there were bees, he could not hear them. A thirsty customer called out for another Tusker, and Charity summoned Rutere to lend a hand behind the bar.

'Now go, Ntoto, and bring back Furniver,' said Charity. 'First, give him this message.'

She noticed that her customers were following the exchange with great interest, and lowered her voice. This is personal, she thought, not something for Kireba gossip.

Charity whispered into the boy's ear, and sent him off with a slap on the rump.

'Now hurry, or the chicken necks will get cold.'

28

'The words of a fool sound loud when spoken
through a trumpet'

Ntoto hammered at the door, but there was no response. He let
himself in with Charity's key, and tiptoed upstairs, his heart in
his mouth. The power supply was still off, but the stand-by
generator was still chugging away. In the gloom, across the
room, was an inert Furniver, slumped over the desk, head cra-
dled in his arms.

For a few seconds that seemed like hours, Ntoto feared that
Furniver was dead. It would not have been the first corpse he had
seen. But it was the first one he had cared about. He sat in the far
corner, across from the body, knees pulled up to his chin, and for
the third time that week, was about to howl in despair and misery.

He dreaded breaking the news to Charity. Nor could he
handle the tragedy on his own, and was about to leave the
building in search of help, when he heard a groan from the
recumbent figure, followed by a few slurred words.

So overwhelming was his relief that he forgot himself.

'What? What?'

Then he remembered Charity's stricture about politeness:

'Beg pardon?'

Emboldened by another incoherent rumble from the man
he thought dead, Ntoto tiptoed across, and removed the empty
gin bottle from Furniver's limp hand. He then checked the
half-open drawer.

Thank goodness, the gun was there. Ntoto tucked it into his waistband, and pulled his jersey down.

Furniver stirred, and mumbled something about Tuskers and mango juice and chicken necks and Charity.

The boy tried to rouse Furniver.

'Come on, *mzee*, get up, get up, old man.'

He spoke directly into Furniver's ear.

'Tuskers . . . and bitings . . . chicken necks.'

Furniver rose unsteadily to his feet, one hand on the thin bony shoulders of Ntoto, the other gripping the top of his chair.

'Come on, Mr Edward . . . Mrs Charity sent me to find you.'

Charity had told him to say two things to Furniver, one of which the boy had no difficulty remembering. Indeed, if he needed a reminder, he had only to lick his lips.

'Mrs Charity says she has cooked your favourite dish. There are chicken necks on the menu tonight.'

A slight tremor went through Furniver's frame. His eyes, which until then had the soft vague look of a baby benevolently looking out at the world from its pram, narrowed and began to focus.

There was something else Charity had asked him to say. Ntoto was having difficulty remembering it, no doubt because he did not entirely understand the message. He was, after all, preoccupied by chicken necks and dough balls, food that never could be taken for granted, even with the money from the tape recorder. He searched his memory.

It was important, Charity had said to him, very important that he got the words right. He felt an unexpected burden of responsibility. Instinctively he knew that the outcome of his excursion would shape the future of the only two people who cared for him. He was determined to be word perfect. For a few ghastly seconds his head seemed empty, and dominated by a single image of roasted chicken necks on a white plate, piled high with maize meal, swimming in peanut relish, and topped by a dough ball.

Then, to his huge relief, he suddenly remembered the final and most important part of the message. He rattled it off so fast that Furniver had to ask him to repeat it. Drawing himself up, Ntoto spoke slowly and loudly, as if Furniver was deaf or stupid.

'Mrs Charity Mupanga, she also says: "Come home, *mzungu* [white man], it is time to come home."'

EPILOGUE

'When the Great She-Elephant breaks wind, even
the mighty baobab tree bends'

'No bloody good at all.'

*The rebuke broke into the baffling words that Pearson was listening to
on the cassette player he had bought at the airport's duty free shop. It certainly was not the voice of the president:*

'My government has watched with growing concern the
increase in cat-chasing incidents at post boxes. The cats of
Britain are safe in this government's hands.'

*Surely it was Furniver . . . yes, it was Furniver, dictating his children's
story . . . how on earth?*

A hand gripped his shoulder.

'No damn good at all.'

*He sat up with a start. The security officer, accompanied by the cabin
steward who a few minutes earlier had served him the glass of fresh orange
juice, looked down.*

*'You haven't filled out your departure card correctly,' said the officer,
smiling broadly. Pearson's guts churned as he realised that it was the same
man who had been checking his holdall and mocking his novel.*

'Call yourself a journalist?' he asked jovially.

He was still smiling.

'No damn good, no good at all, suh.'

The cabin steward sized things up, and decided that it was no more than a slight hitch. It could be resolved before their departure. He joined in.

'We're told that it will just take a few minutes,' he said reassuringly. 'It's just a formality, Mr Pearson, but it has got to be done. You have to return to the departure lounge. Need to check you off on their computer.'

He went off to guide another passenger to his seat. For a split second Pearson saw his reflection in the security man's dark glasses. He looked as he felt: like the fabled bemused rabbit, frozen in the middle of the highway, dazzled by the lights of the oncoming car. His head had started to throb again. He slowly stood up, and looked for his holdall. The officer had got there before him, and had already removed it from the overhead locker.

The man had also taken the tape player from Pearson's limp grip, and with a hand on the journalist's shoulder that seemed avuncular rather than custodial, he guided him through the cabin door, back onto the soil of Kuwisha.

As they crossed the threshold of the plane's exit, the man's grip tightened. His hand shifted from Pearson's shoulder to the back of his neck. With forefinger and thumb, he gripped it tightly, the pressure increasing as they left the plane. And, his voice lowered to a level of sibilant menace that only Pearson could hear, and which made his gorge rise in sheer terror, the officer hissed:

'No bloody good, Mr Pearson, no bloody good at all . . .'

APPENDIX:

THE PROVERBS OF KUWISHA

The proverbs were gathered by the author during years of travelling around Kuwisha, and further afield. Wisdom is no respecter of boundaries, and most of the proverbs are, with minor variations, found across the East African countries and beyond. Although rooted in the past, many are now used in a contemporary context, such as describing the impact of economic structural adjustment programmes advocated by the International Monetary Fund and World Bank. Some are more readily understandable when accompanied by appropriate gestures or movements.

Of the many works consulted by the author, one seminal study stands out: *The Wise One Never Needs the Umfazi: The Ancient Wisdom of Kuwisha*, originally published by the Nordic Foundation for African Studies, Oslo in 1973. It was not long after publication that the Institute became a victim of spending cuts by the Norwegian government. I am indebted to the Nigerian Institute for the Study of Democracy, which now holds the copyright, for permission to draw on many of the paper's insights, and to the Institute's acting director, Dr Ekim Namloh, for the generous allocation of his time.

'*The long grass is safe only for short men*'
Don't get out of your depth.

'*He who follows the warthog's trail risks meeting the lion*'
Do not be distracted from your main purpose.

'*Do not trust the jackal that fails to howl at the moon*'
Do not trust those who act out of character.

'*Beware the leopard that limps when the lion roars*'
Appearances can be deceptive.

'*Rotten bananas make the strongest beer*'
Kuwisha equivalent of 'It's an ill wind . . .'

'*The baringa nuts are always green when hunger strikes*'
Self-explanatory: 'It's sod's law'.

'*When the buffalo move south, wise men check their trouser buttons*'
Origin disputed, meaning obscure. Contributed by Mr M.
'Flogger' Morland, former district commissioner, Nyali
province.

'*Beware the wildebeest that sleeps with the hare*'
Judge people by the company they keep.

'*If you eat the ugali [maize meal] you must stoke the fire*'
If you sleep with the girl, you have to marry her. Commonly
used in discussions about the wisdom of accepting foreign
loans.

'*Marula fruit always taste sweet to the elephant*'
If you have an insatiable appetite, you are not likely to be dis-
criminating in your choice of food. Elephants will search far

and wide for the berry, travelling as much as 15 miles to reach a single tree.

'*If the snake hisses, the elephant coughs*'
Obsolete, meaning disputed. Nevertheless, the proverb is enjoying a revival in western Kuwisha, where the introduction of schools fees, supposedly at the insistence of the World Bank, had created much resentment. Thus a common rejoinder from parents to primary school headmasters when the latter threaten to expel students for non-payment of fees: 'If the snake hisses, the elephant coughs,' usually accompanied by a defiant shrug of the shoulders.

'*Fortunate is the bird that nests while it sings*'
Most often used by the pastoralists of central Tanzania, and not in common use in Kuwisha, presumably spread by the lorry drivers who work the main route between the two countries. Ironic: you cannot have your cake and eat it.

'*When the elephant spits out its phlegm, don't try to measure its tusks*'
Incomprehensible. Efforts by the author to find a meaning have been unsuccessful. One theory is that the obscurity is deliberate, and the proverb is used as a polite way of bringing a conversation to an end, or signalling a change of topic. Slow, thoughtful nods on the part of the listener indicates consent.

'*Only dogs can tell the difference between hyenas and jackals*'
Obscure since the source is Shadrack Gachara – Pearson's steward – its authenticity is debatable.

'*Foolish is the mujiba [herdboy] who eats the marula berries*'
Don't get ambitions above your station – elephants are especially fond of the berry (see above) and protect the trees in which it grows. Only *warangu* – warriors – dare challenge them for the fruit.

'*He who hears the hyena bark will be attacked by the leopard*'
Get your priorities right: don't be distracted by the inconsequential.

'*Only the faithless wife hears the hippo's cough*'
Hippos are at their most active, and at their noisiest, in the hours before dawn – when a loyal wife should be sharing her husband's bed.

'*Only the lion may piss in the watering hole*'
Obey the pecking order; abide by the conventions of the community. Professor Ian Phimister, head of economic history at the University of Kuwisha, has produced cogent arguments in support of his view that the proverb is of comparatively recent origin, and refers to the failure of the European Union to tackle agricultural subsidies. Readers should be aware that most if not all of Dr Phimister's conclusions involve his work on the adverse impact of EU subsidies on African producers. See for example: *Breaking the Mould: Subsidies and the Wankie Strike of 1923*.

'*When the maidens dance, hide the corn cobs*'
There are several interpretations of this popular proverb, most of which are self-evident. The most common use is in the course of criticism of exchange rate policy. Unique to the Bulonga people. Usually accompanied by graphic gestures performed by recently circumcised adolescents. The use of hand gestures to accompany this proverb gives it a very different interpretation. Dr Phimister (see above), argues that it is of much older origin than generally recognised (he puts it circa 1920, the time of the strike at the Wankie coal mine). He suggests that the current use is an example of indigenous opposition to the World Bank's decision to lift fertiliser subsidies.

'*When the young men dance, hide the cooking pots*'
A bowdlerised version of the common proverb: an obscene reference to maidens has been replaced by cooking pots.

'*Only brave men eat the flesh of the old goat*'
Originally meaning: you have to be very hungry to eat tough meat. Now commonly used to refer to renegotiated IMF programmes.

'*Beware the tick bird that seeks to clean the crocodile's teeth*'
The Kuwisha equivalent of watch out for a wolf in sheep's clothing. Tick birds live on the backs of cattle.

'*Never boil the batongo beans before the pots are ready*'
Batongo beans have a high sugar content, and the liquid that is produced after several hours of boiling is left in clay pots overnight, when it sets as sweet jelly, much enjoyed by the Kuwisha. The clay pots, however, need to be specially prepared; for Kuwisha with a sweet tooth, there is always the temptation to shortcut the process and use plastic bowls. The proverb carries much the same message as the old Nagombo saying: 'The wise hunter avoids the elephant's phlegm,' the meaning of which is obvious.

'*The baboon never barks at the rhino's horn*'
Interpretation is disputed, but usually understood to mean one should treat people with respect and courtesy.

'*When you hear the ghloghla drums, guard the maize harvest*'
Ghloghla drums (once common in northern Kuwisha) were beaten at times of war: when peril approaches, lock up your valuables.

'*The bird that picks the meat from the crocodile's teeth leaves no droppings*'
Do not foul one's own nest.

'*Women who pick the ripe dongo berries make lazy wives*'
Green dongo berries make the best traditional beer, but peeling them and then soaking the berries for several hours make for a time consuming and demanding process; although ripe berries are easier to peel and do not need to be soaked. Aficionados of the beer insist that the green berries produce the better brew. The closest English equivalent is probably 'The devil finds work for idle hands.'

'*If the goat roars and the lion bleats, bring out your spears*'
When someone behaves out of character, be prepared for trouble.

'*The words of a fool sound loud when spoken through a trumpet*'
A dismissive reference to journalists and their newspapers, particularly newspaper editorials.

'*When the Great She-Elephant breaks wind, even the mighty baobab tree bends*'
Bow to the inevitable.